continued . . .

Kill Me

"A thinking person's thriller." —Jeffery Deaver

"Big, provocative, and downright gripping."
—Michael Connelly

"Thriller aficionados should pick this up on a Friday evening when they have no other plans for the weekend."
—*The Denver Post*

Missing Persons

"A psychological thriller that will capture readers' interest until the very end." —*Rocky Mountain News*

"One doozy of a whodunit." —*Booklist*

Remote Control

"Dark and fascinating. . . . Stephen White writes thrillers of the first order." —Nelson DeMille

"Psychological suspense at its best." —Jeffery Deaver

Private Practices

"A near-flawless web of evil . . . fast as a downhill slalom."
—*Publishers Weekly*

"Intriguing . . . and believable . . . will keep you guessing to the end." —Phillip Margolin

Privileged Information

"The action zooms along." —*Rocky Mountain News*

"A dazzling new talent." —Tony Hillerman

Cold Case

"Entertaining, insightful, and enlightening."
—The Denver Post

"Elegantly plotted, with brilliant characterizations."
—The Cleveland Plain Dealer

Manner of Death

"Pulls readers along like a steam train. . . . Don't crack this thing unless there's nothing else to do, because once you get started nothing else is going to get done."
—The Denver Post

"Chilling. . . . The invigorating twists and turns . . . [will leave readers] gasping."
—Publishers Weekly (starred review)

Critical Conditions

"A superior psychological thriller."   *—Chicago Tribune*

"Spine-tingling . . . another compulsive read."
—Library Journal

Harm's Way

"Gripping."   *—The New York Times Book Review*

"Taut, tightly spooled storytelling . . . difficult to put down."   *—Rocky Mountain News*

Higher Authority

"Sinister and scary." *—The New York Times Book Review*

"A dazzler."   *—The Cleveland Plain Dealer*

DRY ICE

STEPHEN WHITE

A SIGNET BOOK

SIGNET
Published by New American Library, a division of
Penguin Group (USA) Inc., 375 Hudson Street,
New York, New York 10014, USA
Penguin Group (Canada), 90 Eglinton Avenue East, Suite 700, Toronto,
Ontario M4P 2Y3, Canada (a division of Pearson Penguin Canada Inc.)
Penguin Books Ltd., 80 Strand, London WC2R 0RL, England
Penguin Ireland, 25 St. Stephen's Green, Dublin 2,
Ireland (a division of Penguin Books Ltd.)
Penguin Group (Australia), 250 Camberwell Road, Camberwell, Victoria 3124,
Australia (a division of Pearson Australia Group Pty. Ltd.)
Penguin Books India Pvt. Ltd., 11 Community Centre, Panchsheel Park,
New Delhi - 110 017, India
Penguin Group (NZ), 67 Apollo Drive, Rosedale, North Shore 0632,
New Zealand (a division of Pearson New Zealand Ltd.)
Penguin Books (South Africa) (Pty.) Ltd., 24 Sturdee Avenue,
Rosebank, Johannesburg 2196, South Africa

Penguin Books Ltd., Registered Offices:
80 Strand, London WC2R 0RL, England

Published by Signet, an imprint of New American Library, a division of Penguin
Group (USA) Inc. Previously published in a Dutton edition.

First Signet Printing, March 2008
10 9 8 7 6 5 4 3 2 1

To Jane Davis

It is always easier to fight for one's principles
than to live up to them.

ALFRED ADLER

Three may keep a secret,
if two of them are dead.

BENJAMIN FRANKLIN

PROLOGUE

THE SKY above the mountains was stained with the last pastels of a mediocre sunset.

Headlights approached from the east.

Cruz climbed from the raw dirt to the bucket, jumped from the bucket up to the ground, killed the diesel, and prepared to meet the maintenance supervisor halfway between the fresh grave and the truck.

The work was running late.

The Ford rolled to a stop on the crushed granite with its brights aimed directly at the grave. Ramirez stepped down from the pickup's cab and marched toward the hole. Crazy shadows bent every which way as the beams from the truck and the wash from the floods above the excavator competed to obliterate the creeping darkness.

One at a time, Ramirez rubbed the tops of his cowboy boots on the calves of his jeans. Not content with the results, he polished the leather on one boot a second time before he tucked his right hand into the pocket of his down vest, turned his head, and spit. Ramirez kept his boots shinier than a new quarter. If he was outside he almost always spit before he spoke a word.

"Should've been done an hour ago. Two things," he said to Cruz, holding up his left hand like a peace sign. "Don't like one-man crews." He folded down his index finger, leaving his middle finger pointing skyward in unintended profanity. "Don't like digging in the dark. Alonso knows that. People get hurt. I'm two-hundred-twelve straight days nobody hurt. Tomorrow's two-thirteen. Understand?"

Cruz's eyes were focused on the ground in front of Ramirez. "All done diggin', Mr. R.—had to pull a couple big rocks. That slowed us, but I'm just about to get the casket placer set and the drapes hung. Alonso said it's an early interment, wants everything ready before I go. I know that's the way you like it too."

Ramirez was oblivious to being played. Alonso joked that the man wouldn't spot an ass-kiss unless the suck-up's lips ended up Krazy Glued to his butt.

The boss looked around—the trailer with the folding chairs wasn't near the grave. "What about chairs?"

"Alonso'll bring 'em out in the morning—said nobody wants to sit on a chair covered with dew."

"Doo?" Ramirez asked. "Why the heck would there be any doo on the chairs?"

Cruz coughed to disguise a laugh. "Sitting out at night? That kind of dew?"

Ramirez spit again. He pulled a sheet of paper from his pocket and angled it so that it was illuminated by the

Ford's headlights. "I want forty-eight. I want a center aisle, and I want 'em in place by eight-fifteen. Not eight-twenty." He stuffed the paper back into his jeans and gestured toward the fresh rectangular scar in the sweep of bluegrass. The lawn was just beginning to green up for spring. "Right there. Between there and the path. Sun at their backs."

"No problem, Mr. R."

The shiny chrome components of the equipment that would manage the weight of the casket as it was lowered into the grave were already lined up square beside the hole. Ramirez knew his gravedigger's job was almost done. He spit again, shooting saliva four feet to his left through the fat gap in his front teeth.

"Eight-fifteen. I mean it. Gonna be cold. Some wind maybe. Where the heck is Alonso anyway?" he asked.

Alonso had worked maintenance at the cemetery for eighteen years. He operated the compact excavator at grave sites. His most important job, though, was keeping the short-timers in the corral, which saved Ramirez a lot of work and even more aggravation. Alonso used up most of the accumulated goodwill trying to keep an eye on his adopted teenage daughter. He used what was left to create some cover for the younger members of the crew, kids like Cruz who tended to be less diligent than their mentor.

Cruz said, "Toothache. Dentist."

Getting Alonso to take off early had promised to be the trickiest part of what Cruz was doing. The plan had been to fake an emergency call from Alonso's daughter's school. It seemed that happened at least once a week, anyway. The abscess was a gift.

"No moving that equipment," Ramirez said. "We both know you're not ready for that." He laughed at the thought of Cruz driving the little excavator.

"Soon as I'm done squaring it off I'll lift the bucket and set the frame. We have that other plot to dig—the double by the lake? I promised Alonso I'd get the installer on this one and get the drapes done tonight. He'll move the digger over there early and we'll start on that double as soon as the mourners are gone."

Ramirez didn't reply.

The boss's silence caused Cruz's anxiety to rustle. "Alonso wasn't sure you wanted a canopy up for the family. Sun'll be low when the service starts. No weather coming, but we've had that wind the past couple of mornings." Cruz thought Ramirez was leaning forward, examining the grave. "If you want a canopy, Mr. R., just say the word. I'll throw it on the trailer and bring it out with the chairs."

Ramirez took his hands from his pockets. He spit. "Almost done?"

"Five minutes. Clean up the hole a little. Line up the placer, check the rollers, tighten the straps. Drape it just the way you like."

Ramirez spit again. "Want a hand?"

Ramirez didn't much like labor. He viewed himself as a supervisor, even if the only one he supervised was

Alonso, who didn't need any watching. Alonso did all the real herding of the crew of kids who cut the grass, plowed the snow, placed the headstones, and did the shovel work on the deep caverns in the bluegrass. Had Cruz asked for actual help, Ramirez would have pretended that his pager had gone off and he had someplace important to be.

Like his "office" in the equipment shed.

"No, Mr. R. I'm cool. Square corners, level base, perfect depth."

Ramirez took two steps toward the grave. Two more and he'd be able to see the bottom of the hole without any trouble, and he'd be able to make his own judgment about how level that base was and how square those corners were. "You like the Hepburn?"

Ramirez was asking about the new casket placer they'd been using since the beginning of the month. The contraption cost a fortune. He liked to show it off whenever he could like he was displaying a new car on his driveway to make his neighbor envious.

Cruz nodded. "Sets up much faster than the old one, Mr. R. Much smoother, too. The bearings on the rollers on that old one were—"

The boss didn't like the word "shit," so he completed the sentence himself. "I know. Shouldn't be no squealing around funerals. Finish up then."

The lights danced again as Ramirez walked back toward the truck. He stopped for a moment in a position that left his shadow covering the black rectangle of the grave. "I get wind you moved that digger, I'll fire your ass. Understand?"

"Mark it right where it's at. That's where it'll be in the morning. All I'm going to do is lift the bucket."

Ramirez pulled himself into his truck. Behind him the profile of the Front Range marked a jagged break between the darkening sky and the frantic lights of Boulder at rush hour.

Cruz knelt down and tested the rollers, just for show. The new equipment was working fine.

The taillights of Ramirez's Ford disappeared down the access road.

Only one more thing to finish before installing the Hepburn and hanging the drapes. Cruz hopped onto the bucket, dropped back down into the grave, and said, "Bingo."

ONE

I THOUGHT I spotted a rosy glimmer in the water sluicing through the fountain.

My next patient was sitting calmly ten feet away, covered in blood.

I thought, *I don't need this.*

Diane Estevez, my longtime partner and friend, had recently decided to renovate the waiting room of the old house that held our clinical psychology offices. She thought the time had come for the parlor's evolution into a transitional space, like the quiet stone and bamboo anterooms she loved to visit prior to being welcomed into a favorite spa.

The focus of Diane's designing enthusiasm had a simple purpose—it was the spot where our patients hung out before their psychotherapy appointments. To me, a simple purpose called for a simple room.

Diane once shared that naïve vision. But no longer—the changes she envisioned were far from mundane.

When she began to conceptualize her project, the room was furnished with the pedestrian crap we'd bought from office-supply catalogs when we'd first hung our practice shingles. Her case for transformation was simple: "We're not dentists and we shouldn't have a dentist's waiting room."

I'd replied that I thought the room was fine, but my argument was pro forma. In the best of times I lacked the will to stand up to a determined Diane.

Diane was determined. It wasn't the best of times. Not even close.

Is that . . . blood? I thought. *I just don't need this.*

Diane and I had co-owned the little Victorian house for a long time. The building was on the edge of the once-sleepy, once–light industrial side of downtown Boulder, the few blocks closest to the foothills, a neighborhood that after a couple of decades of determined gentrification had earned the moniker the "West End."

The natural light in the waiting room came from a pair of north-facing double-hung windows. The dusty mini-blinds came down and bronze curtain rods as thick as my wrist replaced them. Soon the indirect sunlight was being filtered through silk panels that were the color of the worms that had spun the threads. Diane had a name for the hue that I forgot within seconds of hearing it. New lamps—two table, one floor—provided just enough illumination to allow reading. The shades on the lamps were made from nubby linen in a color that was a second cousin to the one she'd chosen for the drapes.

"Organicity," Diane had explained for my benefit. "It's crucial."

No, I hadn't asked.

As resolute as Diane was to transform, that's how committed I was to stay out of her way.

Paint? Of course. Not one color, but four—two for the walls, one each for the trim and ceiling. The new furniture—four chairs, two tables—reflected Diane's interpretation of "serene." Two chairs were upholstered and contemporary. Two were black leather/black wood slingy things, and contemporary. The rug was woven from wool from special sheep somewhere—I thought she'd said South America but I hadn't really been paying attention and the sheep may have been shorn of their coats in Wales or Russia or one of the nearby 'stans, maybe Kazakhstan. The rug—indifferent stripes of muted purples in piles of various heights—was placed so that it cut diagonally across the ebony stain Diane had chosen for the old fir floor. She'd put the rug in place one morning while I was in a session with a patient; I came out to greet my next appointment to all its angularity and hushed purpleness.

"Need to break the symmetry, Alan. We can't have too much balance," Diane explained to me over our lunch break.

Neither symmetry nor its absence had ever caused me angst. But I said, "Of course." The alternative would have been to ask "Why not?" Diane's answer likely would have troubled me. I feared that I would have had to set my feet and steel myself for the words "feng shui."

I didn't want to have to do that. I really didn't.

As a lure to join her for the waiting room picnic she'd picked up takeout from Global Chili-Chilly on Broadway. The bait had worked. My role, I suspected, was to applaud as she admired the purple and the stripes. My mouth was on fire but the curry was good so I didn't mind the heat. Truth was, I didn't really mind the rug either.

Diane didn't specify a fountain as the design of the room evolved, but when she announced that the room lacked a focal point I knew that running water was a coming attraction. I could feel it the way I can taste a thunderstorm a quarter hour before the first lightning bolt fractures the clarity of a July afternoon.

The water feature was the final piece to arrive. Diane had it custom-made by a water artist who had a studio on a llama ranch a couple of miles east of Niwot. I could tell that all of the details—the ranch, Niwot, the llamas— were important to her. I didn't ask for particulars. Again, I didn't really want to know.

The fountain had been installed the previous weekend.

The red tint in the water? I couldn't make sense of it. *I really don't need this,* I thought again.

*   *   *

The sculpture was a clever thing of black soapstone and patinated copper that sent water coursing through a series of six- and eight-inch bamboo rods in a manner that I found phallic. Diane was blind to any prurient facet of her gem so I kept the critique to myself. Since the fountain's presence was a fait accompli I comforted myself that the scale was right, even if the volume of all the gushing water was a little too class-five-rapidish for the size of the room.

I told her the fountain was "nice." I could tell that she'd been hoping for something more effusive.

My share of the renovation was absurd. I wrote a check.

Why had I acquiesced when Diane had suggested that our waiting room was overdue for transformation? Why had I agreed to let her do whatever she wanted? Diane had suffered through a brutal couple of years—the waiting-room project was important to her. I knew its purpose had much more to do with her emotional health than with any design imperatives. For her the room represented a new beginning.

And basically I didn't give a shit.

Less than half a year before, I'd watched a patient of mine killed on the six o'clock news. That event had shaken me to my core.

I knew that my reaction to his death—emotional withdrawal mostly, my downhill slide lubricated with too much ETOH—was upsetting the equilibrium in my marriage. Controlling my decline felt beyond me. The timing wasn't ideal. My wife's MS, always a worry, was in a precarious phase. She and I each needed caretaking. Neither of us was in great shape to give it.

That's why I was way too weary to quarrel about remodeling with a friend I adored. The design of the waiting room wasn't likely to climb high on my ladder-of-life concerns. Dental? Psychological? Didn't matter.

I drew a solitary line in the sand at Diane's request for piped-in yoga music. She didn't call it yoga music; she'd said something about needing the sound of humility in the space. I knew what kinds of tunes she wanted. She was talking Enya.

Uh-uh.

She didn't argue when I vetoed the background drones. Her silence didn't indicate abdication. She planned to wait me out. If I was serious about wanting to keep Enya at bay I would need to be vigilant.

I doubted that I had the energy to keep my flanks defended.

Diane knew me well. Well enough to know that about me.

TWO

I WAS slow, but I got there.

Holy shit, he's covered in blood.

The pink hue and the slimy red worms of coagulating plasma that were streaking through the water in the fountain had befuddled me at first—naïvely, I didn't immediately consider either sign to be alarming. My initial, fleeting impression was that Diane had introduced yet another new design concept into our waiting-room ambience and I was too far out of the current consciousness loop to recognize it for what it was.

Only seconds before I opened the door and spotted the fouled fountain I'd been walking down the hall from my office to retrieve my next appointment, a young man named Kol Cruz, whom I'd seen only twice before. As I turned my attention from the perplexing fountain and its pink water I spotted Kol sitting on one of Diane's new chairs opposite the water feature. Despite the profusion of blood—the glimmering mess covered his hands, arms, and face as well as the front of his shirt, his fleece vest, and his trousers from the knees up—he seemed reasonably serene.

The waiting room was having the effect that Diane so cherished—for Kol her design intervention seemed to be having an anxiolytic impact equivalent to high-dose beta-blockers or IV Valium.

"I tried to wash up," Kol said without looking at me. Although he sometimes glanced toward my face, his gaze never settled higher than my mouth.

On closer examination, the rosy mess on his delicate hands and arms did appear to be diluted. I was still thinking *I don't need this,* but I was also reflexively preparing to try to do something useful, even—well—therapeutic.

I reminded myself of a lesson from my distant internship training in a psychiatric ER: The single most important thing to do during an emergency is to take one's own pulse. After that? In the current circumstances I had no idea. I didn't know whether Kol needed a seventy-two-hour hold, an ambulance, stitches, or a big roll of Brawny.

"Are you still bleeding?"

"No," he said.

Okay. "Is that . . . your blood?" The alternative was worrisome.

"Yes."

I was somewhat mollified. I put on a serious, concerned expression and said, "Kol? Are you all right? Don't you think you need to . . . maybe see a doctor? That's a lot of blood."

He said, "You are a doctor, Dr. Gregory."

Kol had me there.

THREE

I HAD misread the early clues.

Over the first couple of days of the previous week the musical soundtrack that accompanied the bustling early-evening family time in our house had traveled from the familiar territory of the White Stripes, Oasis, and Neko Case to a surprising but far from disquieting pause at the second and third U2 albums. After Bono's extended cameo the musical selections moved back in time to Joni Mitchell, the young Van Morrison, Dusty Springfield, the Doors, Don McLean, and then on a particularly wacky turn, to Leonard Cohen—*Leonard Cohen?*—before settling for a couple of evenings on a repetitive set of Erik Satie interspersed with some alluring tracks from Tord Gustavsen.

Other artists made brief appearances. Patsy Cline and Johnny Cash each got two-song auditions in advance of dinner one day, and a Keith Jarrett piano improvisation lasted all of five minutes late the next afternoon while Lauren was deveining shrimp for stir-fry. John Coltrane didn't even get to finish introducing a haunting little melody before he was banished into the digital ether as I was loading the dishwasher after supper.

Although I recognized that changes were occurring in the score that accompanied our lives' pulse—Leonard Cohen's laments as counterpoint to the delight of my daughter's bath time was a contrast that was hard to ignore—I was too intent on trying to force the data into the confines of my experience to see it for what it really was.

Since her previous birthday my wife, Lauren, had become the family DJ. Why? She had a new iPod. Although I was the gift-giver, I didn't share her enthusiasm for the device; I had only recently started feeling comfortable with CDs.

Lauren moved into the digital world without me. Her wireless network humming, she'd curl up with her laptop in our bed in the evening and download songs and develop playlists in the quiet hours after Grace was in bed. All that was left for her to do was to stick the iPod into a slot in front of a pair of speakers and we would have music coursing through the house.

The tracks she plucked from her iPod's inventory hinted at her moods. The better she was feeling—pick a category: about life, about her health, about work, about her husband—the more contemporary and upbeat was the music she chose. The more troubled or reflective she was feeling—increasingly common moods those days—the more oldies and ballads and jazz and classical reflections tended to accompany our family routines.

I used the music as a barometer—if I knew the aural pressure variants, I liked to delude myself into believing I could forecast which way the winds were blowing.

Maritally, it had been an inclement winter. It was looking like an inclement spring.

When the tunes were downers those days I considered myself to blame.

I tried to decipher the meaning of Lauren's recent playlists and their melancholic homage to whatever part of the past they represented. Even if I ignored Patsy Cline, Johnny Cash, Keith Jarrett, and John Coltrane, I remained mystified by the Morrisons—Jim and Van—and Leonard Cohen. I was completely confounded trying to fit the loop of Satie and Gustavsen into any category. Upbeat they were not.

I feared something was up, maybe something more than her growing intolerance for an increasingly distant husband who stayed up nights alone drinking vodka.

"How are things at work?" I'd asked. "You feeling okay?"

Her answers told me nothing. I waited with trepidation. I was coveting routine those days, holding on to it with the kind of denial that a nine-year-old uses to keep bedtime at bay as he grips the last light of a summer evening.

That night in bed Lauren mumbled something into the still air. Her breathing had been regular and shallow, her body so tranquil below the thick comforter that I suspected she was vocalizing unintentional color commentary on the progression of a dream. But I hadn't understood her words, if words they were, and I decided not to risk waking her by intruding with a vocalized "What?"

Then she sighed. I opened my eyes. People don't often sigh in their dreams.

"Music hurts," she said ten seconds later as part of a rushed exhale.

The was-my-wife-awake-or-was-she-asleep conundrum wasn't totally resolved. "Music hurts" was a vague enough pronouncement that I couldn't fit it into either level of consciousness. The earlier sigh remained unexplained.

I was beat up. I was tired physically and in just about every other way. I flirted with pretending she hadn't spoken. I wanted to close my eyes and pray for sleep that wouldn't come. But when she sighed a second time I asked, "You awake?"

My question was reluctant. My words weren't generous. A rote performance of concern was the best I could do.

I don't need this. My mantra those days. *Om.*

"Yes," she said. Although her reply was whispered, it shouted "defeat" as clearly as a white flag on a stick and a throaty yell of "I surrender, sir."

I considered waiting for her to go on, but I said, " 'Music hurts'? Did I hear that right?" My impulse was to add, "If that's the case, Leonard Cohen must be excruciating." Instead I rolled closer to her onto the chilled cotton that marked the middle-of-the-night no-man's land in our bed. My hand found her warm, smooth abdomen, the tip of my pinky sinking into the shallows of her navel.

"Remember the brain mud? When we left Diane's party?"

"Sure." I thwarted a deep sigh of my own. *No, no. Please, no.*

For at least a year Lauren and I had been discussing having a second child. Despite her looming biological finish line I was more eager than she to get on with it. Her health was the stated reason for her reticence. She wanted to be sure she was stable for the stresses of pregnancy and infancy. Brain mud meant that she wasn't stable enough.

A fortnight or so before, Lauren and I had been at a birthday party at Diane and her husband Raoul's foothills home up Lee Hill Road above North Boulder. Raoul was a handsome, rich, charming Catalan-born tech entrepreneur. The celebration was for his *anys*. Long before the party started to ebb Lauren searched me out on the deck where I was sitting in front of a roaring fire pit trapped in a protracted discussion with a business associate of Raoul's who was inexplicably fascinated with the delivery of the Internet over the electrical grid. Lauren put her lips close to my ear and asked if I would mind leaving the festivities early.

"What's up?" I said. Still whispering, she admitted

she was beginning to feel foggy and that her thinking was sluggish—a condition she'd long ago labeled "brain mud." We had come to consider the onset of brain mud a warning sign of an imminent multiple sclerosis event, either a fresh exacerbation of her disease, or, if we were lucky, merely an irritation of an existing lesion. A fresh exacerbation meant a new symptom, which could be a crisis. An irritation would usually mean a temporary re-run of an old, unpleasant episode.

I excused myself at the precise moment my companion was getting into the meat of his argument about the money that could be made by people with vision. I didn't exit the conversation reluctantly—those days I counted myself among the blind masses.

On the way home I checked with Lauren about a chronic problem that had only recently waned—deep pain that crept up her legs from the soles of her feet, sometimes reaching all the way to her hips. The pain had been worsening gradually over a period of years. During the previous eighteen months it had become insistent enough that it was one of her major daily challenges.

The agony had caused her to go on and off narcotic painkillers, but Vicodin and Percocet had proven less than effective palliatives. Even when they helped she despised the sedation that came along for the ride. Any discussions we'd been having about having a second child became a casualty of her chronic pain and her reliance on narcotics. We hadn't talked about conception in months.

Cannabis provided her with some relief, but she had

reached a decision that she didn't want our daughter to associate her mother with the telltale aroma of weed, and she had given up using it. I remained ambivalent about her decision.

When coupled together, U.S. law and Colorado law regarding cannabis form legal quicksand. For registered users with a prescription, marijuana is legal in the state of Colorado. Federal statutes allow no such exception; marijuana is an illegal drug under U.S. law. Lauren had chosen not to sign up for a state authorization card as a registered marijuana user—she feared the professional consequences if the system's anonymity failed and the news leaked out.

Although I respected Lauren's concerns about Grace, I was also aware that by choosing to forgo cannabis Lauren was shunning something efficacious. And where MS symptom-abatement was concerned not too many things were efficacious.

More selfishly I found that the time we spent together on the high deck of our house in the evenings after Grace was in bed—Lauren toking on her bong, the gurgling water floating with fresh-cut lemon flutes—were nice moments. As the cannabis did its thing and her symptoms abated we often had our softest interlude of the day.

On the way home from the party Lauren assured me that the pain wasn't worse. We stayed vigilant over the next few days, steeling ourselves for the inevitable caustic punch line to the brain mud—for her vision to deteriorate, for her equilibrium to evaporate, for some muscle to lose its tone or its strength or to begin to spasm, or for her bladder to stop emptying on command, or . . .

The list of possible consequences was endless. With MS, wherever there was a CNS pathway there was a potential symptom. But nothing emerged. No new symptoms. No reruns of old symptoms.

Or so I thought. I'd never considered that the new symptom would be the infiltration of some nefarious music-killing poison into her ears.

"Music hurts," she repeated. "It irritates. It's like . . . rubbing a burn. Or touching a blister. Or having an eyelash in my eye. It's just so . . . unpleasant."

Oh. The recent cornucopia that she'd selected from the iPod suddenly made more sense. "All week long you've been looking for songs that—"

"Don't hurt," she said.

"Find any?"

"*Ground* isn't too bad." *Ground* was the Tord Gustavsen Trio album. "And Satie's not awful. But it all hurts. Loud, soft. Jazz, rock. Vocal, instrumental, country. Everything. Even the Wiggles," she said, laughing a laugh that made me want to cry. The Wiggles had caused us pain for more months than either of us could count, but the pain of the Wiggles in the hands of a child was merely the pain of endless repetition.

"Anything harder to listen to than the others?"

I heard her swallow. "Dusty Springfield. And Don McLean."

Ballads? I thought. *Odd.* I lost a moment trying to imagine what it felt like—for music to hurt, especially music as comfortable as Dusty Springfield and Don McLean. I couldn't get there. I also realized what I had missed as Lauren had left unconscious clues during the week. The most sobering hint?

The melancholy lyrics of Don McLean's "American Pie."

Bad news on the doorstep, indeed.

"Any other new symptoms? Fatigue? Dizziness?" The conversation was easier in the dark. For both of us. Talking about her illness was something we had never done well. Since the previous autumn we'd done even worse. I kept telling myself that history and love would guide us through it.

"Same as always."

"The pain in your legs?"

"It's okay. Whatever I'm doing . . . is working."

"What are you doing?"

"Nothing. Some stretching."

She wasn't convincing. Lauren was one of the few adult females I knew in Boulder who—despite a brief flirtation—didn't at least dabble in yoga. I would have bet good money she couldn't tell Iyengar from Bikram from Ashtanga.

"Really?" I asked. "You haven't gone back to Percocet?"

"No."

I wanted it to be true. Some good news would be welcome. "It's just whatever's going on with your ears? Did you talk to your neurologist?"

After a poignant pause she said, "No. And it's not my ears; it's my brain."

I knew that. I did wonder about the edge in her tone, but gave her the benefit of the doubt and risked another question. "Will you talk to him?"

I felt her abdominal muscles stiffen below my hand. She said, "Maybe."

There was a time in our marriage when I would have chosen that instant to press her. I might even have gone through the motions of trying to insist. Maybe I was older and wiser. I was definitely more weary. Fighting would have required energy I didn't have.

"I'm so sorry," I said. A better spouse would have known better words. I once knew better words. But those days I wasn't a better spouse. The path of least resistance was to provide compassion. Comfort if I could. "Is there anything I can do?"

She didn't even bother to tell me no. She asked, "Can this disease really take away music?" Her voice was hollow, disbelieving. But not disbelieving at all. "Can it?"

She wasn't waiting for me to answer. Hers was the most rhetorical of questions. We both knew that her disease could take away anything.

"Maybe it will pass. Most of these things do."

My words were the literal truth. But the phrase also served as a palliative to the uncertainty of MS. "Maybe it will pass" was the artificial levitation of hope we inflated to counterbalance the gravity of looming sclerotic despair.

Much of the time the illusion worked.

I heard that sigh from her again. For the second time she said, "Yes." To my ears, the word still shouted "defeat." If the room hadn't been so dark, I probably could've spotted that flapping white flag.

I surrender, sir.

Me, too. I thought. *Me, too.*

FOUR

I WAS ruminating when Lauren mumbled into the dark that music hurt.

I was in the midst of an extended phase where I didn't often see sleep before the bars emptied in the city below our home. I knew what was going on—if I had the courage to look in the mirror, I would have seen a cloud racing to catch me from behind. I'd lived for over two decades believing that I could outrun it before it consumed me.

My refusal to look had long been evidence of hubris and of fear. The hours I spent after midnight longing for sleep meant that my hubris was in hospice care. It was dying.

My fear wasn't.

I'm a clinical psychologist. As part of my job I learn other people's secrets. I know secrets about drugs, and sex, and crime, and infidelity. I know secrets about money—who spends it, who hoards it, who steals it, who borrows it, and where it's stashed. I know work secrets, big-business secrets, old family secrets, boring secrets, and the occasional fascinating secret. I even know secrets about secrets. Most of the secrets are much less interesting than the person guarding the information suspects.

I've learned by listening to the nuances of many confidences that the power of a secret is generated not only by the nature of what's hidden, but also by the potential charge that is kept at bay by the act of segregating its existence.

When someone moves information from the category of "private" to the category of "secret" the knowledge takes on the kind of potential energy that is locked inside atoms and contained within huge concrete and steel domes. Infinite energy. Destructive energy. Because of that potential force the truth that is locked away takes on a connotation greater than simply "hidden."

Revelation of something private might mean embarrassment. Revelation of something secret would mean blame. Or guilt. Or worse, shame.

But my own lifetime living with secrets had taught me that many of us had greater fears about our secrets, fears that did not diminish, but grew exponentially over time.

The first oversized fear was that revelation would mean loss of control.

The second big fear was that the act of having chosen to keep a secret from a loved one would become more potent than whatever knowledge was hidden. We choose secrecy at one point in our lives—presumably it makes sense to us at the time—and we protect the secrecy through the phases that follow. Do the facts truly remain dangerous later on? Worthy of all the subterfuge? Or does the existence of the secrecy become the real danger requiring protection?

Often my job as therapist was simply to help my patients move the explosive information back to where it belonged—to shuffle it from the radioactive territory of secret to the safer land of private, or to the supposedly inert land of disclosed.

Sometimes that work is as simple as it sounds. More often it is not. Secrets feel more powerful than they are. Once we create them we become the wizard in our personal Oz, and we guard the secrets with all the resources and all the artifice of our mythical kingdom. We willfully slaughter Toto before he gets anywhere near the curtain.

I don't treasure the secrets I learn from patients, and can't remember a time that I felt an advantage from knowing one. Often quite the opposite. My professional career is littered with bruises I endured and bruises I caused by safeguarding patients' trusts. But the work mandates that I keep secrets. Most of them get relegated to the kind of mental storage where I stash more mundane information I might need to pull out on a moment's notice—patients' grandchildren's names, or the states or towns where a client lived as a toddler or a teenager.

Rarely did the facts of a patient's life stay in my conscious mind in the hours and days after a therapy session, circulating through my brain like oxygen-deprived blood being pumped back to my lungs. Almost never did a patient's secrets resonate later in a way that interfered with my sleep, or cause me to ruminate on my own rotting truths.

But that night as I lay awake—the night that Lauren admitted that the music hurt—I was reviewing one particular patient's secrets. I was thinking about the patient whom I had watched die on the evening news. The patient whose death remained available on video feed only a click or two away on the Web.

In none of the news reports was my name, Alan Gregory, mentioned. Even if it had been, I could never admit that the man had been my patient; I could never tell anyone his many secrets. Although he'd shared them with me, they were not mine to reveal. He was important to me because his death and the existence of his secrets never failed to remind me that I had my own secrets, and that mine remained very much alive.

When I was feeling especially drained my secrets were not just a looming cloud, but they chased me like a pack of wolves that smelled fatiguing prey.

I was feeling weary a lot. I often smelled the stink of wolf.

Lauren knew none of it. And she wouldn't. Nor would she know that my patient's death had upset my equilibrium so much that the echoes of the shot that killed him continued to infiltrate my thoughts and distill into my dreams. I was convinced that Lauren wouldn't understand my secrecy about the man. Wouldn't understand that I couldn't even hint to her that he, briefly infamous, had been my patient.

She had no way to understand that if I was too vulnerable, that if I opened that first door, it might allow her to peek through the other door, the one that I absolutely couldn't permit her inside.

It wasn't fair of me. I wouldn't give her the chance to understand because I had convinced myself that even her understanding would change everything. Over time the presence of my secret had become as imposing an obstacle as any fact that I was hiding.

And I was hiding a whale.

There had been a day—I mean that literally, *a day*—when I could have told her and she might have understood. The solitary window of opportunity had come years before I'd ever met the patient whose death had been chronicled on the evening news. I still don't believe that Lauren would have understood my secret had I shared it that day, but at dispassionate moments I believed it was possible that she *could* have. But . . . even had she understood, nothing would have been the same between us from that moment on. My confidence in that was unwavering.

Sometime after Cabo San Lucas ceased being a sleepy fishing village but before it became a resort, Lauren and I had traveled from Boulder to the tip of Baja for a weekend away. It was early in our dating relationship, and all the fuel that makes fresh love so combustible was present in abundance. Passion and reticence were colliding like the masses of warm and cool air that spawn the most enormous of thunderstorms.

It was a time between us that was dangerous and alluring. Dangerous because of the allure. Alluring because of the danger.

We were sitting in a restaurant overlooking the bay, thirty yards of sand separating us from the Sea of Cortés. The sky was post-dusk without a moon. Reflections of white stars danced on black water. For young lovers it was a perfect time for romance and for risk.

Our waiter, a weathered, middle-aged man in a sweat- and food-stained *guayabera,* cleared away an unfinished plate of grilled shrimp and the skeletal remains of a *huachinango.* He left glasses with the dregs of our margaritas sweating tropical rings onto the tablecloth.

I remember details of that meal and of that night that I should have forgotten. I remember little things—the shrimp were overcooked, the snapper was prepared with too much garlic—the way that a bride remembers minutiae from her wedding. I remember so much because it had been a night of so much possibility.

It was Lauren, not I, who took the risk. Before the waiter returned with our crappy Nescafé she said, "I have MS."

Until that instant her illness had been secret from me. I recognized at some level that her words were not a simple moment of revelation. They were also a warning. She was cautioning me not to love her. More, she was pleading with me not to invite her to fall in love with me before I ran away.

She was, I think, prepared for me to leave even as she was challenging me not to. Perhaps right then, before I finished my shitty coffee. I complained that she was demonstrating little faith.

"You want faith," she'd replied, "earn it."

I could have chosen that instant to tell her about the darkness that was chasing me. Telling her about the cloud would have been a monumental act of faith. I didn't. I'd decided long before that disclosure wasn't an option. And I had vowed never to decide again. No one would see me—no one could ever see me—against the backdrop of that cloud.

I was the one demonstrating little faith on the edge of that beach in Cabo. I was young and convinced I could forever outmaneuver the cloud. I could run faster, pedal harder, love better. I could earn her faith in other ways.

History isn't destiny, I had told myself. But running from history is. That was the part I didn't fully grasp until I watched my patient die on the evening news.

The irony is that Lauren might have understood the part about history and destiny. But I had no way to know that then.

My history remained secret.

My destiny? The cloud was closing. On weary days, the wolves salivated.

FIVE

LAUREN HAD a more contemporary secret.

She was a deputy DA with the Boulder County District Attorney's office. Her recent assignment involved a case she was either preparing to take, or was actively taking, before a grand jury. Lauren didn't say what the grand jury was considering. Under Colorado law grand jury investigations are, well, secret. Who or what was the focus of the present inquiry? I didn't know. I would not know unless Lauren's boss, the DA, decided there was some advantage to be gained by public disclosure of the fact of the probe, or if there was a leak and details hit the local paper.

Was the investigation my wife was stewarding a big deal or a little deal?

I could only guess. Grand juries aren't an everyday part of Colorado jurisprudence; they are more common in some other jurisdictions than they are here. In Colorado, decisions about most criminal indictments are made by the locally elected District Attorney after consultation with law enforcement. Grand juries of citizens empowered to hand down indictments are typically reserved for cumbersome investigations into controversial or unusual cases.

Why are they used? Grand juries have investigatory powers that cops don't possess. Grand juries can compel testimony that detectives can only cajole through cleverness, persistence, badgering, or quasi-legal—or extra-legal—threats. Sometimes grand jury subpoena powers are necessary to advance an investigation that's bogged down; sometimes they're essential to leverage the cooperation of one player in a criminal enterprise against another. The secrecy of grand juries is sometimes utilized in investigations of public corruption to avoid the appearance of conflicts of interest by the investigators or to shield innocent parties from public scrutiny as they provide testimony.

What was the reason for this grand jury? That was Lauren's secret. The only thing I knew about the grand jury was that my friend Sam Purdy, a Boulder police detective, was somehow involved in its work. I knew that tidbit because Sam had recently started calling our house and asking to speak with Lauren and not with me. "It's a cop thing," he'd say to me in explanation before I asked. "We have some work to discuss."

Although suggestive, that small clue alone wasn't enough to convince me that the work had anything to do with a grand jury. Reaching that conclusion required one more piece of information.

On a recent Saturday while I was on an errand in town

buying Grace some soccer shoes—Lauren and I never discovered what happened to her old pair; they were just gone—Sam and Lauren were meeting at our kitchen table. Halfway to town I realized that I had forgotten my wallet and I backtracked home to retrieve it.

Later, during Grace's first game in her new pink shoes, I asked Lauren about the meeting. "Is Sam investigating something for you?"

She was quiet for almost half a minute before she said, "Yes."

I opened my mouth to press for more information. She held out a hand to stop me. "That's all I can say," she said. She kissed me lightly on the lips to let me know that her parsimony was nothing personal.

That's when I knew about the grand jury. By acknowledging the need for discretion, she had handed me the confirmation. She knew what she had disclosed by telling me she could disclose nothing more, and she knew that I knew what she had disclosed by telling me that she could disclose nothing more. If Sam was investigating something for her but she could reveal no other detail, Lauren was telling me that she was involved with a grand jury case that the powers had stamped "Top Secret" and that Sam was temporarily on leave from his regular duties as a Boulder cop and was functioning as a special grand jury investigator for Lauren and the DA's office.

I had no way to know then that the latest layer on the *torta* of secrets wasn't the second. The *torta* had been under construction for a while.

*   *   *

Lauren found sleep shortly after she told me that music hurt.

I didn't.

Before climbing into bed the first time that night I'd had enough to drink that I wasn't quite sober but I wasn't quite drunk either. I knew only one way to remedy inebriation limbo. I got back out of bed, walked to the kitchen, and poured four fingers of chilled vodka into a glass.

I had expected a dog or two to follow me from the bedroom, but neither of them did. Ten minutes later I was wrapped in a blanket on the deck outside the great room, the mountains looming black-purple to the west, the lights of Boulder at my knees. I had accomplished what I'd hoped to accomplish with the vodka: I was no longer in sober's zip code.

The digital clock on the microwave read 3:11 when I woke up shivering on the deck. I stopped in the bathroom before I climbed back into our bed.

Lauren hadn't moved.

SIX

BY MORNING she had reached a decision. She wasn't going to tell her neurologist about her acute aversion to music. "For things like this all he has is a hammer. If he wants to treat this at all, he's going to want to treat it like it's a nail."

Translation? If her neurologist took the new symptoms seriously he would want to start her on a course of IV steroids. My wife wasn't willing to go down that, for her, highly inhospitable road. Instead she was choosing a riskier course that promised fewer side effects—she was planning to let the dice continue to roll and hope that the number that came up wouldn't sing craps.

Left unsaid? In my heart, I knew that Lauren wasn't going to imperil whatever prosecuting she was doing with the current grand jury for a fortnight or more of Solumedrol-induced hell that she knew offered no assurance of any salutary effect on her musical antipathy. She reserved the Solumedrol lottery for assaults on symptoms that she judged significant enough to impact her mobility or her vision.

I knew there was another reason that she wasn't eager to endanger her position with the grand jury. Her current assignment was as close to a full-time job as Lauren had tried to manage in a long time. In the many years since her diagnosis, the growing fatigue precipitated by, and the chronic pain of, her illness—not to mention the occasional acute symptoms—had caused her to cut back her office and courtroom time until she was working only half as many hours as she had when she'd been healthy. Whether she could do all the work necessary to command the grand jury investigation—and do it without getting sicker—was a big test for her. Temporarily at least, work would be a priority.

Selfishly I believed that if she were convinced she could endure the demands of the grand jury she might also be convinced she could endure the demands of a second pregnancy.

Over breakfast our compact family—Lauren, me, Grace, and our two dogs—listened to *Morning Edition* instead of Coldplay. Lauren's speaker-dock was empty; the little iPod was nowhere in sight.

Grace noticed that the music was gone but she was notoriously hard to knock off balance. The anti-emotional-vertigo trait wasn't on a gene she had inherited from me. To no one in particular, she said, "This is Daddy's *car* music. Now *that's* a change."

She was in a phase where she was big on selecting a solitary word for emphasis in her sentences. The affectation made me smile. I knew I would miss it when it passed. And I knew it would pass.

If Lauren's symptoms persisted I would soon need to try to explain to Grace about her mother's fresh aversion to song. I wasn't looking forward to that talk.

During late April in Colorado, weather is a crapshoot. Seventy-five and gorgeous? Reasonable odds. Forty-five and rainy? There's a good chance. Twenty-five and snowing? If enough cold air is backing up against the Front Range from the north, and enough moisture is traveling our way from the Pacific or one of the southern gulfs, well, yes, that will happen, too. Two or three of the above in the same day? Coloradans see those combinations every year.

I drove down from Spanish Hills to my office that late-April morning to a day breaking with the clarity of my daughter's laugh. Bright, welcoming, warm, even a little brash. I could tell that the good weather wasn't going to hold. Though the Divide to the west was clear along the Peak to Peak, from my vantage on South Boulder Road I could see a distant wall of gray much higher than the foothills blunting the view to the north toward Wyoming. If winds started huffing our way from the north-northeast, whatever Canadian chill was hidden beyond that gray slate would soon become an important part of Boulder's spring day.

The first gusts, wimpy as they were, confirmed that a system was moving our way. The front arrived during the middle of my third therapy session. The old lilac hedge on the east side of the yard leaned over to placate the wind but held tenaciously to its freshly opened blossoms. After ten minutes of insistent gusts a thin squall blew through with an interlude of aromatic rain. A second round of buffeting winds sent twigs and leaves flying and carried in another squall that caused intermittent raindrops to begin to fall, each one announcing its arrival with an audible plop. Soon the rain was replaced by a steady wet snow that persisted for the rest of the afternoon.

Lauren phoned as I was getting ready to head to the waiting room to collect my last patient of the day. "Can you get Gracie?" she asked, sounding distracted. "Something's come up. She has to be picked up by six."

"Six?" My final therapy session would be over at five-thirty sharp. I knew I would need to spend some time trying to get Kol's blood off the leather slings of Diane's new waiting-room chairs. Boulder's sclerotic east-west rush-hour traffic flow would determine whether or not I could make it across the valley to Gracie's school before six. In this weather the odds were maybe seventy-thirty. Throw in a traffic accident or some road construction and the odds could go ninety-ten in the other direction.

"Yes. What a mess. We lost a witness. I know I said I'd get her, but . . ."

The witness? *Misplaced? Defected? Died?* I was curious but I knew that Lauren wouldn't share details, so I didn't ask. I said, "I'm sorry about your witness. Yes, I'll get Grace. We'll take care of dinner too."

"Thank you."

"You feeling okay?" I asked.

"Later," she said. "I'm fine."

Where Lauren's health was concerned, "fine" covered a lot of ground. The poignant "later" gave me pause.

I was numb as I cleaned up the blood and replaced the water in the fountain. I did the chores only so that Diane wouldn't have to.

She didn't need that.

It had been only a couple of hours earlier that I directed Kol to the small office powder room to clean off the blood before his session. When he emerged five minutes later he no longer looked like a refugee extra from a Wes Craven movie. I could only guess what the bathroom looked like. I followed him into my office.

"This is my parents' idea," he said moments after he sat. "Seeing you. Is that where we left off? Am I right?"

Had he forgotten that he'd told me that therapy was his parents' idea? I waited for a reasonable interval to see if he'd elaborate on his own. Alternately, I thought he might illuminate his decision to remain in the waiting room as some weak vessel in his nose spurted blood like an arterial puncture. He didn't take either route. Gooseflesh dotted the follicles of the fine hair on his forearms.

"Your parents?" I said, going with the flow.

"They're insisting. Well, one of them is. Want to guess?"

He uncrossed his legs and leaned forward, his elbows on his knees, his eyes directed toward my feet. I didn't guess. Didn't plan to.

"Fifty-fifty. Got to like the odds. Bingo."

I waited some more.

"If I don't do this—see somebody—they're going to make me sell my place and move back home. That's the deal."

"They're going to make you sell your place?" Left unsaid: *Didn't you say you were twenty-six years old?*

I was keeping the "one of them is" question on deck. That clarification was significant, but it could wait. He might settle the question on his own. If he didn't, I'd draw him back to it.

"I live there, but it's . . . theirs. May actually be my mom's technically. The money is hers. He's at a bit of a disadvantage. You know what that's like. They don't see eye to eye on . . . ? But they own it, or she owns it, and I don't— I mean I've never—" He grimaced.

"Worked?" I said. It was a guess. Right or wrong, however, it should have been a silent guess. I regretted speaking the word the moment I could no longer retrieve it.

He was unfazed. "With my problems I've never been able to . . ."

Take responsibility? I thought. But what I asked was, "You have trouble . . . what?"

"With all that . . . you get depressed," he said. "It's hard."

You do? He didn't seem depressed.

"Holding a job. Workin' on the railroad. All the live-long day. Bingo."

"Are you feeling depressed now?"

"Now? This minute now? What?"

I backed up. I was floundering. *What am I missing?* "Your parents want you in psychotherapy because they're concerned about . . . ? That you get depressed?"

Kol sighed. "More 'her' than 'they.' My father's not so much in the picture. I mean it's not like what happened with—" He stopped. Looked up—almost at my face—then back down. "Your dad? Is that right? No?"

My dad? What?

"And the making-a-living thing? How hard is that? For sure they don't get that. The driving thing is the other part. Those are the current biggies. This week, *sí.* Next week? Stay tuned."

"Your dad?" Is that what he said? His dad? Was that a question? Or is he . . . Could he mean my *dad? No. No. He couldn't.*

I refocused on the options he'd just presented. Choice points like the ones he placed in front of me can be tricky ground for therapists. I could have asked Kol about either the "making-a-living thing," or "the driving thing." The risk? I would choose the wrong topic, one with little emotional load. As an alternative, I could have waited and let him choose to expound on one of the two parental concerns on his own. The risk there? He might elect to change the subject entirely. If that occurred I would be forced into lassoing him and facing the original clinical dilemma all over again.

There was also the revelation about his depression. And his mama. And whatever he meant about "your dad."

I waited. I do that a lot in therapy.

"So what do you think?" he said. "We're cool?"

I had an epiphany right then. Kol wasn't using the phrase "We're cool?" in the conversational vernacular of the day. He was using it as a plea. Kol needed assurance that I wasn't offended by his act.

Huh. "Hardly," I said to Kol, my voice containing as much padding as I could stuff into it. I didn't want him to think I was going to accept his proffered clinical road map without question. "I have a hint, and only a hint, about what your parents—or at least your mother—want you to achieve. But I'm still not at all sure what you hope to gain from therapy."

He sat back on the chair. "My life. My freedom."

"From?"

"Them. Her."

Them? I assumed he meant his parents, but I cautioned myself that I didn't really know him well and that he might have been talking about iridescent blue men who work for the FBI and have a co-op in his armpit. *Don't assume,* I reminded myself. *Don't assume.* "Them?" I asked.

"My parents," he said. I was relieved. There were so many other "thems"—the iridescent blue men among them—that would have caused me mighty concern. "It's a small price to pay. You know what that's like. God."

What is a small price to pay? And what does he mean that I know what that's like?

I downshifted, reengaged a gear, and slowly let out the clutch. "If I'm hearing you right, Kol, you're saying you want to be in therapy to keep your parents off your back? Mostly your mother?"

"More or less. Don't worry. You'll get paid. They're loaded. My mom's family. Pemex? You know it? Black gold? Tehuacán tea? That's her family. Hey. Bingo."

I sat silently for a moment, noting his apparent lack of discretion, before I asked, "Is the depression a concern to you?"

"What? No. I don't really have any problems," Kol said. "Other than the who-I-am stuff. But that's nothing special. Been going on awhile. Now I have a guide."

Am I the guide? I didn't think so. "A guide?" I asked.

"Yes."

I waited for elucidation. It wasn't forthcoming. "No other problems?" I said. "The depression?"

"No. My guide has shown me the way."

"Your guide is . . . ?" *More evidence of dependence?* I thought.

"Do I look depressed?" Pause. "Cool?"

He was smiling. He had great teeth. White as a new T-shirt. Fine orthodontics or some expensive cosmetic dentistry. Maybe just good genes.

"Looks can be deceiving," I said.

"Got the right guide? Urges disappear. Problems go away. You know what I mean? Mama doesn't know. Bingo."

"About your guide?"

He nodded, arched his eyebrows.

I said, "Your guide is . . . ?"

He shook his head.

Man or woman? Life coach? Mentor? I would have to guess. I took one more stab: "You're avoiding my questions."

He shrugged. I took a long moment to consider his gaminess. I was on the verge of confronting it further when instead I said, "In the whole 'problem' category, I can think of a couple of areas that might be worthy of your consideration." I hoped that I hadn't sounded too sarcastic. I should have confronted him, not been sarcastic with him.

"Shoot," he said.

Shoot? As it sometimes did—often out of the blue— the word caused my mind to go into excavation mode. The excavation made my pulse start flying. I felt a conscious urge to purge my lungs of carbon dioxide and to flood my blood with oxygen.

My patient—the one who died on the evening news— had been shot.

Shoot. I tried to recover my balance. I said, "Your parents—your mother, at least—think you need to be in therapy. You don't agree. From my point of view, that's one problem."

His face was impassive.

"And . . . you seem to be willing to c[...]
parents' intrusion into your life in order [...]
mortgage paid and keep them off your bac[...]
consider that to be another problem."

He seemed to think about it all before he said, [...]
you know all the places Angelina Jolie has traveled to d[...]
humanitarian work?"

What? "No," I admitted, as I allowed myself to be
floated by the tide that was being lifted by Kol's odd
moon. I was wondering whether I was witnessing a conscious diversion on Kol's part, or evidence of tangential
thinking. Tangential thinking wouldn't be a good sign.
The iridescent blue men remained a possibility.

"I do," he said. "Do you want the list before she was
named a Goodwill Ambassador by the U.N. or after? Pre-
Brad, or post?"

I shrugged my shoulders.

"Chronologically? Or by continent?" he asked, but he
didn't wait for an answer. He provided the list chronologically, pre-Brad.

It took almost ten minutes. Kol knew the names of
airports, villages, refugee camps, and even some coastal
resorts where Ms. Jolie had decompressed after her apparently voluminous humanitarian efforts.

I was amazed at the performance. It was like watching
a savant recite pi to four thousand places.

Huh.

*　　*　　*

I handed Kol his first

ession not started with

ing him the bill would

sion, not the last.

vest pocket without

n him, I said, "It's a

...it directly to your insurance

company."

"I don't have an insurance company. I have a *madre rica*. I'll give this to her," he said, tapping at his jacket pocket. "Do good work with me and she'll probably give you a tip. Maybe your very own oil well."

He smiled, his eyes following my lips. I didn't know what to say.

He said, "Bingo."

SEVEN

MANEUVERING ACROSS town through rush hour I thought about all the things I had neglected to ask Kol about the blood. It was a depressingly long list.

I retrieved Grace from day care with minutes to spare and got her strapped into her car seat for our errand. She wanted to talk about the physics—or magic—that caused hard-boiled eggs to be sucked into soda bottles, so we did. I pretended that I remembered something about the relative effects of temperature and air pressure.

Grace pretended I was a genius. I adored her for it.

Lauren called again just as I was steeling myself for the insanity that was the Whole Foods parking lot at rush hour. My unkind thought: *Now what?*

"Where are you?" she asked.

"We're about to try to find a place to park at Whole Foods. If that proves successful we're going to pick up something for dinner."

Grace laughed.

"Get enough for Sam. He and I will be working to-night. Do we have beer?"

"Sure. Yes, we do have beer." In my mind, I doubled the amount of food I would get. Even in his latest, healthy incarnation Sam had an above-average appetite.

When Gracie and I came back out with our takeout supper in tow, the upslope winds had stilled, the snow had stopped, and the cloud cover had migrated south along the Front Range. With the blanket of insulation gone the northern air left in the wake of the departed front was chilly. I wondered if there would be a hard freeze. A night in the mid-twenties would be a tough lesson for those gardeners blessed or burdened with enough denial to have already planted their tomatoes.

Thirty blocks across town the stark faces of the Flatirons were bearded in snow. High above the Divide a few stars glistened in the darkness. Closer to me and Grace, across Pearl from the Whole Foods parking lot near Target, the boughs on the northeastern side of the evergreens were straining under the heavy load of wet snow.

Things had been moving fast, meteorologically speaking.

Had I not still been so distracted by the session with Kol I might have recognized the value of the metaphor.

That I had thought that Kol, covered in blood, needed to see a doctor was ironic. I was not yet convinced that he truly needed to be seeing a different species of doctor—that was me—for psychotherapy. It was surprising that I was intrigued by seeing Kol at all—so much of my recent therapeutic work felt like clinical calisthenics.

Any reticence I had about treating Kol wasn't because he seemed normal. He was definitely peculiar. His name, for example. He'd explained that his given name was actually Cole but that he'd decided that it should be written K-O-L after having gone all the way through high school near San Diego insisting to his teachers that it be spelled C-O-A-L. "That's me. Anthracite, man—I'm the black panther" had been his explanation for the adoption of the juvenile sobriquet.

I had long before developed a bias that "peculiar" didn't qualify as a clinical problem. Maturity and experience had convinced me that trying to eliminate peculiarity in the guise of seeking normalcy was not only outside my therapeutic purview, but also a light-year beyond my skill set. I suspected, too, that trying to eliminate peculiarity was an endeavor of dubious value—although that was a philosophical debate more than a psychological one.

Peculiar or not, I remained unconvinced that Kol met my criteria for psychotherapeutic intervention. Over my years in practice the should-this-person-be-in-treatment checklist had evolved to a point that the decision tree was a relatively simple three-step process. First, a patient must have at least one identifiable problem of the mental-health variety. Second, the problem must have a solution that I had the skills to assist in shaping. And third, the patient must demonstrate an interest, however dim, in

marrying the solution with the problem and engaging
with me in the intervening process.

My assessment with Kol was that numbers two and
three on my list were problematic, and number one was
no slam dunk—I had reached a tentative conclusion that
he might have a workable problem, just not the one he
suspected.

During his intake visit a few weeks before he had been
one of those thoughtful patients who had announced his
DSM-IV diagnosis for my benefit. He'd walked in the
door to my office, plopped his narrow frame down on
the chair across from me, and—before I'd said a word, let
alone asked a single question—spared me the trouble of
having to conjure up a clinical tag for him. Kol reported
that he and his parents thought he was an "adult autistic
with ADHD"—attention-deficit hyperactivity disorder.

"An adult autistic?" I'd asked. The closest I could
come to a recognizable label would have been someone
with "residual autism," a nonspecific diagnostic tag for
an autistic child who had grown into adulthood hobbled
by the echoes of the earlier developmental disorder. As I
listened for Kol's additional diagnostic thoughts I made
a tentative decision to proceed as though that was what
he'd meant.

"I was a mildly autistic kid. Now I'm an adult."
Kol was twenty-six. "Okay, maybe moderately autistic.
Ergo, I'm an adult autistic." He said it with more pride
than ennui. For him it was a badge of honor of some
kind, not a limiting label. I was cool with that, though

residual autism raised a problem with number two on my need-to-be-in-therapy checklist. I had no ready intervention for that disorder in my clinical toolbox.

That first day I wasn't prepared to commit to anything diagnostically but my impression of the man sitting across from me would not have placed residual autism high on the short list of disorders I was ruling out. I cautioned myself that children with a history of autism rarely present as adults as simple grown-up versions of the child who had suffered from the early affliction, and that the aging diagnostic formulations reflected little of the rapidly accumulating wisdom about autism.

"Can you tell me a little bit about the autism? When you were younger?"

"I was an animal, man. An animal." He shot a quick look in my direction, then away. "Skittish. Scared. Didn't like to be touched. Got fascinated by weird things. Motion. I could go off on something moving for, like, ever. A second hand on a clock? Whoa. A merry-go-round? That'd be a day."

I sensed he wasn't done. I waited.

"Did I mention loud noises? They freaked me out. And I was, like, persnickety."

"Persnickety?" I was pretty sure it was the first time I'd spoken that word in my office.

"Everything had to be just so. I don't like stuff out of place." He stuck a slender fingertip into a slit on the edge of the cushion on the chair on which he was sitting. I hadn't previously been aware that the cushion had any damage. "Like this. I don't like stuff like this. It's not right. You should fix it."

I think he was waiting for me to hop up and pull out a needle and thread and do the job right then and there. I waited for him to continue. When he didn't I asked, "And the ADHD?"

"Textbook," he assured me. "I have the attention span of a puppy. I was a little-yellow-bus kid. Only thing was music. Repetitive, techno. You know Moby? Do you?"

He wanted an answer. I said I knew Moby. I didn't say I wasn't particularly fond of Moby.

"Moby's cool," he said. "In school? Music, yeah. Theater, okay. Some. Classes? No way, no . . . way. I lived on Ritalin. Lived on it. Bingo."

It was impossible for me to know it during the initial moments of that first session with him, but punctuating the end of sentences with the word "bingo" was one of Kol's peculiarities.

His description of his early experiences rang reasonably consistent with someone with mild autistic impairment. I was allowing for the possibility that Kol had indeed suffered some degree of childhood autism and that he continued to struggle with the aftermath. While I pondered the range of possible diagnostic sequelae—all the way from residual autism, through Asperger's, past some personality and mood disorders, to the territory most of us called normal—I gave him a full minute to resume the discussion of his symptoms on his own. He wasn't inclined to continue. He had withdrawn into an intense focus on the way the upper joint of the index finger of his left hand worked. It was interesting: he could bend his fingertip while keeping the rest of the joints aligned.

Clinically I was more than a little lost. I retraced my steps and decided to go all the way back to start.

"So how can I be of help?" It was usually my first line as I sat down with a new patient, but Kol's premature diagnostic pronouncement had interrupted the natural rhythm of the beginning of that first session.

At least I recognized that I had some catching up to do.

EIGHT

WHILE I waited for Sam and Lauren to arrive at our house I put some of the takeout in the refrigerator, some of it in the oven, fed the dogs, and set the table for dinner.

I was still thinking about Kol's explanation for all the blood.

I was thinking, too, about what he'd said: *Was it "I mean it's not like what happened with—your dad?" Or had it been "I mean it's not like what happened with . . . your dad."*

My dad? Or a generic "your dad." Which? No. It wasn't possible. How could he?

A sudden nosebleed, Kol had said. "I get them sometimes. It's not a big deal. Weak blood vessel or something. Get 'em when I'm on 737s coming out of the sky. Bingo. Got one on Pirates of the Caribbean at Disneyland. Did I freak the mice-men out? Double bingo."

I didn't believe the nosebleed story, at least not a hundred percent. The rest of the patter? It felt like noise. I wondered why he'd needed it.

Diane and I shared a concern about security in our office. We kept a locked door between the unmonitored waiting room—like many psychotherapists we didn't employ a receptionist—and our clinical offices. Because of the hundred-years-ago architecture of our old building, the locked door had a secondary, unintended impact: it didn't allow our patients access to the first floor's only bathroom.

That simple fact could have explained why Kol hadn't chosen to wash up in our building's restroom. But it didn't explain why Kol hadn't just gone home. He lived only a couple of blocks away in one of the recently built, multiuse condo/loft buildings south of the Pearl Street Mall near Broadway. If he was having such a vicious nosebleed, why didn't he rush home, pack his nostrils until the bleeding stopped, clean himself up, and change his clothes before coming to our session? Wouldn't being a few minutes late for the appointment have been preferable to fouling Diane's prized fountain with his blood and then showing up for therapy looking like he'd just wandered down Elm Street and done ten rounds with Freddie?

I couldn't figure it. I tried to write it off as merely a fresh indication of Kol's peculiarity. But that didn't feel right, either.

"It's not like what happened with . . . your dad." My in-

testines cramped like a clenched fist as I replayed those words in my head. *Does Kol know? Of course not.*

No one knew.

Grace and the dogs all beat me to the front door to greet Sam. He arrived before Lauren; I'd been expecting them to show up together.

"Hey, Alan. Long day. Gracie! How's my favorite little girl?" He threw a heavy shoulder bag on the floor and lifted my daughter into his arms while simultaneously trying to greet both dogs. His comment about the length of the day wasn't an inquiry about how mine had gone. It was a declaration about his.

I probably wouldn't have told him about my patient who had shown up covered in blood. Some things are best not dangled in front of a police detective's eyes.

"Sorry," I said. "Lauren said you guys misplaced a witness. That's true?"

"We didn't lose her, if that's what you're asking. The witness might have misplaced herself. More likely, somebody else might have helped misplace her."

"That would complicate things?"

I didn't really expect him to respond. Finally he mumbled, "Yeah, you could say that."

"She's important?"

"You could say that, too." He looked at me as though he were trying to weigh how much I knew about the grand jury case. I kept my face impassive. "Tonight your wife and I are supposed to come up with a viable plan B."

"Okay then," I said.

He followed me from the entryway to the kitchen, dodging the dancing dogs. Grace was already bored with the adult conversation. She squirmed from his arms, said, "Hi, *Sam*. Bye, *Sam*," and ran back toward the bedrooms where she'd been playing.

Our kitchen is at the back of a great room that has a wall of western windows that frame a stunning view of Boulder, and beyond. The "beyond" was a hundred-mile-plus section of the central Colorado Rocky Mountains from the hogbacks to the fourteeners of the Continental Divide, and from Pikes Peak to Longs Peak and then some. Sam took a seat on a stool at the counter of the kitchen island. He was facing the remnants of a sunset that was dissolving in the distance, which left me with a view of the back of his abnormally large head.

I pulled a couple of beers from the refrigerator and handed Sam a Smithwicks. He popped it open and took a long pull before he glanced at the label on the bottle, which I knew he couldn't read without fumbling to find reading glasses to stick onto his nose. He apparently didn't recognize the color pattern of the label. "So what is this?" he asked. "Should I be impressed?"

"You like it?"

"It's all right. What is it?"

"Irish ale. Smithwicks." I pronounced it "Smith-icks," with no *w*, the way a gracious publican did in Kerry after I'd mispronounced it when I'd asked for one after I began to tire of the Irish diet of stout. How many years before was that? I'd lost count. Before Lauren. All the way back to Merideth. Wife uno.

Sam elevated an eyebrow and said, "I thought they all drank Guinness."

"Misconception," I said. He didn't really care. Although he was a fan of some local Colorado craft beers, he would have been just as content with a Pabst or a Bud. For me, tasting Smithwicks was like eating fresh soda bread, or seeing thirty shades of green in the same vista. It was a little bit of Ireland, bottled.

I changed the subject. "How's Simon?"

He looked back over his shoulder toward me for a second before he returned his attention to the post-sunset colors over the Divide. "Good. Better than good." He paused. "Sherry's started a campaign to convince me that he should be going to private school in Denver. Better fit academically, she says. Better hockey team too. That's for my benefit. She doesn't really give a shit about Simon and hockey. If she had her way he would take up swimming, or ballroom dancing, or something. She thinks he's going to get hurt."

Sherry was Sam's ex. She'd been living in one of Denver's booming northern suburbs since their split. Sam had stayed in their modest house in Boulder after the divorce. He had Simon during the school year and on weekends during the summer. He liked the arrangement just fine, considering. Although he and Sherry had their share of disagreements I'd always gotten the impression that the divorce was civil.

"Sounds expensive," I said, picking the least controversial of what I imagined would be Sam's myriad objections to Sherry's plan.

"Only about a third of my salary. But Sherry's new boyfriend is going to pay the tuition, or so she says." He belched—a short, vibratory thing—after the boyfriend/tuition pronouncement. "The boyfriend's generosity is supposed to make me feel better."

"Does it?"

He belched again. I gave him points for a failed effort at trying to suppress the second eruption. "Let's say we put him in private school. Number one, that means he lives with his mom during the week, not with me. That sucks. The boyfriend pays the tuition for a few months. Then Sherry dumps him like she dumped her last three boyfriends, or he dumps her like he probably dumped his last ten girlfriends. Then what? Eh?" He drank some beer. "The new boyfriend? He's an endodontist. Name's Kevin. Know what that means? Kevin does root canals all day. Then he does them all day the next day. And then he takes a day off. But the one after that? More root canals. Can you imagine? Kevin may have enough extra money to send my kid to private school, and to have a ski condo in Avon, and to buy himself some big old German car, but every one of my bad days is better than his best day. You asked me what works to make me feel better when I've had a crappy day? Well, that's what's working right now. That works just fine. Sherry's Kevin doing root canals."

When I didn't reply Sam looked around. The two dogs were feigning sleep on the kitchen floor, waiting for the imperceptible—to us humans, at least—sound of crumbs falling on hardwood. "Where's Grace? She close? You know, within earshot?" he asked.

"She's probably in her room. Playing or reading. She tends to tune us out this time of day. Decompression. Why?"

He said, "Remember Michael McClelland?"

NINE

IT TOOK me a second to make sense of Sam's question. Maybe even two seconds passed before the syllables registered in my brain and I matched the sounds with a name and the name with an identity. Only then did the fear—no, not just fear, but fear and guilt—burst up inside me like a just-ignited bottle rocket.

I don't need this.

"What did you say?" I managed. It was partially a "What?" asking for repetition, a need to hear Sam say the blasphemous name one more time so I could be certain I hadn't been imagining it, and partially a "*What?*" demanding clarification, a need to hear why the hell he was using that profanity in my house.

Sam spun 180 degrees on his stool and faced me. His beer was half gone. The sunset's pastel halo surrounded his head like he'd arranged for some personal aurora borealis. He inhaled before he said, "McClelland's on the loose."

I dropped the knife I'd been using to cut the takeout pizza *margherita* into appetizer-sized pieces. The big blade ricocheted off the edge of the counter and clattered to the floor, scattering the semi-vigilant dogs. I was so stunned by Sam's revelation that I didn't even feel a reflexive instinct to dance out of the way of the bouncing weapon.

"What do you mean, he's on the loose? They let him out?"

"They didn't release him. He escaped. Actually he just walked away." He looked toward the floor. "You dropped your knife. Might want to take a second and count your toes. Five on each foot is the target."

I had ten questions, one for each toe I'd had before I'd dropped the knife. Since I couldn't ask all ten questions at once, I tried to prioritize. But I failed. The question that had the most energy rushed to the head of the line.

"What the hell do you mean? He tried to kill my wife. He should never get out."

Sam shrugged, the way he does. "He tried to kill you, too. And me, for that matter. But you don't see me throwing cutlery around the room."

McClelland's violent intrusion into our lives—Lauren's first, then mine, and later Sam's—had taken place many years before. The last act had played out in Aspen, where McClelland's appetite for retribution exploded. All of us were there that night. McClelland ended up in the custody of the Aspen police with a bullet in his chest.

None of us—Sam, Lauren, me—had forgotten what McClelland had done to us. None of us thought for a moment that McClelland had forgotten what we had done to him. Sam was reminding me of that.

I said, "How, Sam? How?"

It was not an important question to have answered at that stage of the discussion, but my prioritizing skills were impaired and the dumb questions were the first ones to escape the pen. I gave Sam credit for not even bothering to try to cajole me into calming down. He was a model of restraint, keeping his voice low and his tone matter-of-fact—probably a wiser course than trying to force me to rein in my indignation.

"He's been part of some study at the state hospital. Some neuro-, psycho-, pharmo-ologist from the Health Sciences Center is—oh, hell—I don't know what she's doing. A 'study.' Anyway, some of the hospital staff were taking a group of . . . their freaks—excuse my French— to a clinic in Pueblo for some new brain scan to try to find out why crazy-shit-ass people do the crazy-shit-ass shit crazy-shit-ass people do, and somebody screwed up. They let him slip away. Somebody took off his metal restraints so he could get scanned. Somebody else was supposed to put on some plastic restraints, which apparently didn't happen. At some point one of the guards counts his nutsos and he realizes that he's short exactly one nutso. Michael McClelland was the missing one."

"Just like that?"

He kept a wary eye on me while he lifted the bottle to his lips and downed another quarter of the beer. "Security camera has him going out the door of the clinic and down the sidewalk in front of the building like he's heading to the corner to buy a Coke and some Twinkies at 7-Eleven. Then? Nothing. No sign of him."

"Where's Lauren? Does she know about this?" Those should have been among my first questions.

"The call was routed to me from Aspen. That's where the Pueblo cops called first. We lost some time because of that confusion. I told Lauren myself this afternoon. She took it better than you, if you're curious."

I glared at him.

Sam went on. "A sheriff's deputy is driving her home right now. Or, actually, following her home right now. Your wife refused to let him drive. Sheriff's already decided she's going to have security 24/7 until we find McClelland or at least until we know what the hell he's up to."

"A deputy will be here round the clock? What about when she's at work?"

He made an equivocal face. "That's where things get sticky. The sheriff decided that Lauren is probably at more risk than you, so the security will shadow her. It'll be here when she's here. At work when she's there."

"The sheriff decided?"

"He got elected, so he gets to decide shit like this. It's one of the perks."

Sam liked to use the same argument when we disagreed—which we usually did—about whatever the president or the governor was up to.

"What about Grace?" I asked.

He raised his chin. "Yeah, Grace. You want the argument?"

"Sure." I thought I was showing admirable restraint.

"Good. The argument is that McClelland doesn't even know Grace, maybe doesn't even know she exists, so she's not a likely target. If she's not a target, she doesn't need protection."

"What kind of idiotic f—"

"*Who* doesn't know me, Daddy?" Grace was in her stockinged feet, scooting down the hardwood hallway toward the kitchen from the direction of the bedrooms. Her fluid motion was more like a cross-country skier than an ice-skater.

Next winter, I thought, *we have to get her up on some cross-country skis.*

Sam, laconically, said, "Knife."

Shit! A second before my daughter arrived in the knife's vicinity, I reached down and retrieved the blade from the floor and put it on the counter.

"Somebody your mom and dad knew before you were born, sweetheart, but that you've never met," I said.

"Oh," she said. She reached up and grabbed a square of pizza off the counter and turned to scoot back out of the room. With an adorable wrinkled-up nose she asked, "Is *this* dinner?"

"No. It's an appetizer. A snack."

"Good. Is dinner *soon*?"

"Soon. Take a napkin, Gracie."

She made a cute face. I thought I saw some defiance

coming, but she reached for a napkin. Without a word she'd made it clear that she had no intent to use the napkin. But she was carrying it. From a parenting point of view it was a victory. I waited until she was back out of earshot down the hall. "It's *Doctor* McClelland, Sam. Not 'Mister.'"

He raised an eyebrow. "Your point? You better not be insinuating you want me to start calling you 'Doctor.' I think I've made it clear that I think Ph.D.s are way overrated."

"McClelland may be disturbed, but he's not stupid."

"Disturbed? That's what, your word of the day?" Sam finished his beer, stood up from the counter, and carried the empty over to the pantry. He knew from experience where we kept the Eco-Cycle bin. In the distance, I could hear the sounds of the Wiggles escaping from Grace's room. "You made him sound a lot more than 'disturbed' when that judge sent him away to mental-health camp instead of to the state pen."

Sam hadn't replied to my reminder about Michael McClelland's intelligence, so I pushed on, determined to make him remember. "You know what he did for a living?"

Sam said, "If I recall, he was a weatherman."

"He worked at NOAA. He has a Ph.D. in meteorology and his specialty was severe storms. Severe storms. And you know as well as I do that he didn't just forecast them. He created them."

Sam put both hands on the island counter and leaned

toward me. "I'm working on this. For me, for Boulder, it's only a couple of hours old. I've been talking to my captain, I've been trying to open some lines of communication with the sheriff. Lauren's been talking to the DA. I know the guy's a bad actor. You know he's a bad actor. But most of the people in the department don't remember him. My captain doesn't know him. The new chief doesn't know him. The current sheriff wasn't around when everything came down with McClelland. That all happened . . . years ago. And keep in mind that it ended in Pitkin County. It never even went through the courts here."

Pitkin County was Aspen. It was an Aspen judge who ultimately bought the argument that McClelland's mental illness was so pronounced that he couldn't stand trial. The judge had sent McClelland to the state hospital.

I could tell Sam wanted me to acknowledge something. I said, "So?"

"An open-ended 24/7 security detail to protect a prosecutor and her family for an old crime when there hasn't been a single threat? Even if the sheriff thought it was warranted—which he doesn't—in this budget environment he doesn't even know where to begin to find those kinds of resources."

Budget environment? That didn't sound like Sam. "I don't give a shit about the county's budget problems. He's a dangerous, vindictive . . ."

Sam opened the refrigerator and grabbed two more beers. He handed me one. He either hadn't noticed, or didn't care, that I'd barely touched my first. I watched him unsuccessfully try to twist off the cap before I handed him a bottle opener.

"Yeah," he said. "I remember him too." He sniffed the air. "He almost killed a cop in Aspen. I don't forget that kind of shit. So what are we having tonight besides that skinny pizza?"

"Roast chicken. Red potatoes. Cole slaw."

"At your house? Normal food? Never thought I'd see the day."

I spotted headlights driving up the lane. One pair a hundred yards or so in front of another pair. The second pair would be the sheriff's deputy.

I felt a chill. It had come to this. "When? What time did he get away?"

"This afternoon. Just after lunch."

"In Pueblo?" I asked.

Pueblo is a town about the size of Boulder on the Front Range of the Rocky Mountains 110 or so miles south of Denver along Interstate 25. A legendary mill town, Pueblo had been hit hard by the collapse of the domestic steel industry and for as long as I'd been in Colorado it had had been trying to reinvent itself. Pueblo—many locals pronounced it "Pee-eblo" for some reason that has always escaped me—is also home to the antiquated, sprawling Colorado State Mental Hospital, which is where Michael McClelland had been living since he recovered from the wounds suffered during his arrest and after the judge declared him mentally incompetent to proceed to trial for his numerous felonies in Pitkin County.

My opinion of Pueblo? If I-25 were an artery between major organs—like, say, Denver and Albuquerque— Pueblo would be an aneurysm, a little bulge. That's all. I knew people who might be less forgiving and describe it as a lesion, or a tumor. I also knew some people—fewer—who had family or business there and said nice things about the community and its residents and their determination to revitalize their town. But most people knew Pueblo as a place with a little highway congestion that they drove through, or past, on the way to somewhere else—usually Denver to the north, Albuquerque or Sante Fe to the south.

Drivers stopped briefly in Pueblo if they needed gasoline, good Mexican food, or a bathroom.

They stopped for a long time if they needed an extended stay in a state psychiatric facility.

Sam nodded. "Yeah, in Pueblo." I was thrilled that he didn't pronounce it the way the locals did. "The hospital there has a new PET scanner. That's what the geniuses from the university were doing. PET scanning the nutsos. Whatever the hell that is."

Sam knew what a PET scan was. He kept a fine file handy to manicure his I'm-a-dumb-cop facade. What was curious about his current act was that he didn't often do the fine-tuning with me.

"No sign of him since he walked?"

"Nothing since the security camera lost him."

"Did he have help? A car waiting?"

"Possibly."

"Witnesses?"

He feigned surprise and hit himself in the forehead with an open palm. "Witnesses? Damn, we didn't think of *that*."

I sighed. "Sorry."

"We don't know where he is, Alan. The cops in Pueblo seem to have handled it fine. The way I would've done it? No. But they did okay. There's a BOLO here and in surrounding states. Usual stuff. He hasn't been a troublesome patient, apparently. The hospital says not to worry. No violence while he was there. No threats."

"Well, that's reassuring." I wiped my hands on a towel and started toward the front of the house. Lauren would have parked her car in the garage by then and collected her things to come inside. "You may not know where he is, but you know he's coming back here," I said. "To Boulder."

"I suspect he is. Either here or someplace as far from here as possible. But if I had to guess, I'd guess here. That's why I'm doing what I'm doing with the brass."

Lauren walked in the door and dumped her overflowing briefcase on the floor and her swollen purse on the beat-up table where we tossed our keys and mobile phones.

She tried to smile and bluff away her health concerns but I saw a telltale sign of trouble the moment she blinked.

Her eyes closed one at a time, their natural synchronicity a casualty to the stress of her day. The asymmetric eye-blink told me that at a neurological level she had crossed the threshold that exists between "tired" and "exhausted." I hadn't yet seen her walk, but I surmised that she'd be limping, too, or fighting to disguise her limp. Whether the limp would be from spasticity, weakness, or from pain, I wouldn't know right away. But I knew she would try not to let Sam see it.

She needed to rest. Not sit-in-a-chair-and-have-a-beer rest. She needed a bed. Nothing else would help.

The dogs had raced down the hall to attack her and Grace was running from her room to join the fray. I turned to Sam and whispered, "She shouldn't be working tonight. She needs a bath and a bed."

He whispered back, "How about you tell her, Kimosabe."

TEN

SAM AND Lauren worked in the basement on the absent-witness problem until nine. I let Grace stay up late so that she could spend a few minutes with her mom before they both went to bed.

Sam found me on the narrow deck outside the living room. We stood at the railing above the lights of the Boulder Valley. Emily, the big Bouvier, followed Sam outside. She sniffed the air for a few moments to check for the presence of rascals before she plopped down on the redwood decking. Her inelegant landing shook the house like a moderate earthquake.

"Carmen's good?" I asked. Carmen, a detective in Laguna Beach, California, was Sam's long-distance significant other.

Sam had switched from Irish ale to Eldorado Springs water. I liked the fact that I could see the source of the water from my house. He took a sip. I didn't think it mattered to Sam that he could see the source of the water from my house.

"Her being there, me being here, it gets hard to manage. I've never tried to do one of these things before. A long-distance relationship. I'm not an e-mail type of guy."

"Either of you think about moving?"

"Her daughter's in school out there. She has family. I have Simon here, and . . . Sherry. Orange County is a long way from Minnesota. Carmen doesn't like winter. I'm not that fond of . . ."

He seemed unable to find the right word. "California?" I suggested.

He laughed. "I was going to say 'summer,' but yeah, it's goofy out there. I'm a pretty flexible guy, but . . . Laguna Beach almost makes Boulder look normal."

"Sam?"

"What?"

"You're not," I said. "A pretty flexible guy. Don't kid yourself."

"Better than I used to be."

"Amen," I said. I decided to press him a little more, sensing that something was unsaid. "But you and Carmen are cool?"

"The back and forth is hard. You ever done one? A long-distance thing?"

I thought about an old love. Felt my stomach flip just a little. "Yeah," I said. "It didn't work out."

"See. There you go." The "go" had an extra *o* or two tucked on at the end. It was the Iron Ranger in him talking.

"You have plans to get together soon?"

He glared at me in a one-degree-less-than-friendly kind of way. It was a signal that he was done with this part of our conversation and would appreciate it if I played along. He said, "She wants us to meet up in Mexico before it gets too hot and before the monsoons come. Me and Simon. Someplace on the gulf in Baja. Her little brother runs a cantina and a scuba shop. She thinks we can take lessons, learn how to dive."

He sounded skeptical. "Nice offer," I said.

He sipped some more water. "My Spanish isn't too hot."

Nonexistent, I thought. Sam couldn't pronounce "*gracias*" to save his soul. "Carmen's fluent," I said.

He grunted. "And I'm pale."

Sam was pale. Whale-belly pale. Minnesota-in-January pale. He was the kind of guy who could get sunburned watching the sun rise. In a movie.

"I assume Carmen has seen you naked, Sam. She knows to wear sunglasses."

"She hasn't seen me naked in the sunlight."

It took a moment for that unsettling image to depart my consciousness. Night sounds took over. A breeze whined as it bent the new grasses. A dog barked in the valley. Emily growled. I said, "Think wetsuit."

I'd hoped for a laugh but I didn't get one. "You think Adrienne's up?" he asked. "I should tell her what's going on."

Sam knew Adrienne—our neighbor and friend across

the lane. I said, "She and Jonas are visiting family in Israel. Just left. They'll be gone for a few weeks."

"Just as well. We should have him back in custody by then."

After an interlude of silence I said, "This is my fault, Sam."

It would have been a good place for him to disagree with me, were he so inclined. But he didn't. Instead he did what a good conversationalist or a good interviewer would do. He changed directions right along with me and he waited for me to go on without giving a hint of his reaction.

He said, "Yeah? You think it's your fault?"

"After he was arrested? He seemed too . . . crazy. Too paranoid. I should have told the judge that."

"He'd been your patient, Alan. You couldn't tell anybody anything."

"If . . . I had figured out a way to challenge the testimony of those shrinks his defense attorneys found, he would be living the rest of his life in a small concrete room in Cañon City, not in the hospital in Pueblo."

"Cañon City" was Colorado-speak for the maximum security state penitentiary, New Max. "Pueblo," in the same institutional vernacular, meant the indefinite sentencing limbo of the state mental hospital. A criminal who was sent to the penitentiary was shackled with a determinate sentence, usually a lengthy one. Criminals were sent to the forensics side of the state hospital primarily for two reasons. Those who are tried and found not guilty by reason of insanity stay at the hospital until the court approves their release. Those deemed incompetent to proceed are housed, and treated, in Pueblo until a judge determines they have become sufficiently mentally competent to confront the criminal justice system.

"If McClelland had been sentenced to Cañon City—as he should have been and would have been—he wouldn't have been part of some study outside the walls. He wouldn't have had a chance to walk away down some street."

"Yup," Sam said. He hadn't had to think about it at all.

I stated the obvious: "There are hundreds of people in maximum security who are crazier than Michael McClelland."

"Thousands," Sam offered.

"Well, that could be hyperbole."

Sam shifted his weight and scratched at the whiskers on his neck below his chin. I could tell the next words he spoke would be carefully measured. "I always thought you wanted to believe . . . he was crazy."

Was that a question? I wasn't sure. At some level, I recognized that his words were considerate, almost kind. He was offering me some room to maneuver, a chance to rationalize what I'd done a decade before when I'd declined to offer a statement to the court about my patient, Michael McClelland. I could have launched into a self-serving, defensive lecture to Sam about ego-dystonia, character disorder, and psychotic transference, but Sam wasn't really interested. I also recognized the underlying critique inherent in his comment. I asked him, "You can say that now even though you thought what those shrinks testified was pure bullshit?"

"Don't kid yourself. I still do. We looked at the world differently back then. The defense experts overwhelmed that idiot the prosecutors found. She was the one who sealed the deal—the prosecution shrink. Not those defense experts. Remember her? That hair?" Sam shook his head at his memory of the prosecution psychiatrist's unfortunate perm. "She was something else, I swear. She—that frigging psychiatrist—was even wackier than the defense experts were saying McClelland was. The state lost that one. The defense didn't win it. Me? I don't win them all. I move on. It's easier on my heart."

"That works?"

"I've learned a lot from you over the years, Alan, but your need to rationalize away stuff like what McClelland did? I don't get it. Not then, not now. You seemed intent on finding an explanation for him. Not only for what he did to his poor sister and those other women, but also for what he put Lauren through and what he did to that poor cop in Aspen. I'm not even talking about what he eventually tried to do to you and me that last night up there. That was combat. Just a cornered rat trying to survive.

"But you needed to believe everything he did was really out of his control, maybe to find something you thought could be fixed with some of your smart talk. As though if that turned out to be true that it would excuse what he did. I admit how you handled him and how you chose not to even make a victim statement didn't make any sense to me then—and it doesn't make any sense to me now.

"Even if you were right about him and you had some special insight into the guy, I never understood why it should make any frigging difference what happened in his past. But I believed you believed it. At least back then, that's what I believed."

I waited a moment to be certain he was done.

"What I thought was wrong. I should have found a way to make a statement. Staying silent was wrong. I was wrong."

He raised his eyebrows. "Yeah, you were. But don't beat yourself up about it. That judge wasn't about to let you give a clinical opinion on the guy."

"McClelland's evil, Sam. What I was thinking about him back then went way beyond the bounds of what I know about psychopathology. I'm not the same psychologist I was then. He should have been sent to the penitentiary, not the state hospital. I screwed up. I'm embarrassed by it."

"Well," he said. "Bravo, Alan. I didn't think you had it in you, but I commend you for coming around to the sane way of thinking."

"Your way is the sane way?"

"You haven't noticed?" He smiled. "You ready to re-visit the wisdom of the Reagan Revolution?"

I laughed.

"How long have you felt this way?" he asked.

"A while. While he was locked up, I convinced myself that it didn't make any difference whether he was in the state pen or the state hospital. Now it does. He wouldn't have escaped the state pen."

"So why did you cut him all that slack?"

"What you said before about me believing that because of other things he'd been through in his life what he did was out of his control, and that he shouldn't be held responsible—that's not it. Some traumas leave marks, they stain people in, in . . . ways that leave them predisposed to certain behaviors. Most people overcome those predispositions . . . but some don't."

"You're saying McClelland didn't?"

"I'm saying McClelland didn't. I had—or I wanted to have—a belief that the predisposition he was fighting argued for a different judicial path, a different empathy . . . Now, I'm not so sure. I'm thinking that if other people with the same damage could overcome the predisposition, so should he."

"Well, he's out now. One thing I do know? If he's heading this way, or worse, if he's already here, I don't think he's coming to thank you for all your efforts on his behalf."

ELEVEN

I DIDN'T spot the purse that had been discarded in the yard the next morning, but my nine-thirty patient did.

The building that Diane and I owned in downtown Boulder—the one with the newly serene waiting room—was an old house remarkable not for its understated Victorian architecture, but rather for its terrific location two blocks from the Pearl Street Mall. Land within walking distance of the heart of downtown Boulder at Pearl and Broadway was apparently plentiful back in the 1890s when the house was constructed because our lot was big and our backyard, especially, was spacious.

Raoul, Diane's entrepreneur husband, had been encouraging us to sell the land to a developer who was eager to combine our place with a couple of adjacent lots. The developer wanted to construct some building that would have the maximum footprint and fill out the maximum bulk-plane that the city planning board would permit. I imagined something designed more by an engineer than an architect.

After the effort she'd invested in the recent waiting-room makeover, Diane wasn't receptive to Raoul's suggestion to scrap our offices, so I wasn't worrying about the developer's hot breath on my neck. I figured in downtown Boulder there would always be a developer, or six, who coveted our land, and I was in no hurry to sell.

I really didn't want any drastic changes in my life. The thought of selling, packing, and moving gave me a headache. Or made the headache I had worse.

The handbag in the yard was resting on a clump of patchy bluegrass near the six-foot-deep planting bed that hugged the rickety thirty-inch-high wood slat–and-wire barricade that had at one time probably been consistently vertical enough to have been called the back fence. Or at least the backside of the rabbit pen.

The purse wasn't concealed in any way and it wasn't difficult to spot. If I had taken the time to stand at the back window of my office that morning to enjoy the southern view toward Chautauqua, or if had I taken even a single step out the French door that led to the yard from my office, I would have seen the purse on the grass. But I hadn't. I'd walked into work without even a glance at our superfluous yard.

My nine-thirty patient eyed the bag as she glanced out the window on the way to her chair.

"There's a purse out back," she'd said, pausing and

pointing. "In your yard. By the fence. See it? I think it's a Coach."

My nine-thirty was one of those patients who had secrets. Hers had a few parts. She was the wife of a cross-dressing man—that was one secret—who owned a wildly successful student bar in town. Together they had two children. The second child, a seven-year-old boy, wasn't her husband's biological son. Her husband didn't know that.

That was the second secret.

Small-town secrets. Let them loose and all the usual consequences were possible: shame, guilt, loss of control, recrimination.

More germane to the discovery in the yard, however, was the fact that my patient was a fashion maven who could reliably recognize a handbag's pedigree from twenty paces. I didn't doubt her assessment of its heritage. After she pointed it out—and after I accepted that it had more of her attention than I did—I excused myself, stepped outside, retrieved the purse, returned to my office, and set it on my desk.

"Aren't you curious?" she asked. "Don't you want to know whose it is?"

"That can wait. This is your time," I said. It was a therapeutic thing to say. This patient's favorite form of resistance was diversion. Since she knew most of the town's movers and shakers, she always had some compelling gossip to use as bait with me. It was my job not to be seduced by the tangents. The purse was definitely tangent bait.

"It's last season's, or the one before that," she said, casting her fly into the stream one more time. She'd been unable to resist adding a final editorial assessment to sweeten the lure. I could tell she was hoping to feel a tug on the line. I noted that despite some effort to keep the dismissiveness from her voice she had ultimately failed. I gave her points for trying and allowed myself a moment's conceit that her restraint was an indication of some nascent therapeutic progress. She'd been working on her critical tendencies.

"No one is wearing that shade of green anymore," she added, under her breath.

I mentally removed the gold star from her chart. One of my patient's other issues was the way she used condescension and sarcasm as relationship foils.

I didn't respond to the "shade of green" comment. She and I had many more important things to discuss, although I didn't have much confidence that we would get around to them anytime soon. Instead we would spend the next forty minutes swatting at the impediments that she erected in the path of anything that resembled change.

After my client left my office at the end of the session— her mental health in no better repair than it had been when she arrived—I took a closer look at the purse. The bag was fashionable, but worn; its owner was not a woman who changed purses regularly or treated her handbags gently. And yes, a postage-stamp-size leather tag hanging from a brass chain on the strap identified it as a Coach. I didn't see any indication that the bag had spent much time out in the elements. I guessed that it had been tossed or dropped on the lawn sometime the night before.

Inside the zippered top was a wallet that was much older than the purse, a cheap spiral notebook with most of its pages ripped out, an opened package of tissues, an almost-full tin of cinnamon Altoids, a spare battery for some electronic device, the non-business end of a USB thumb drive, some Apple earbuds, two well-chewed pencils, a deck of playing cards wrapped in a rubber band, a tennis ball, and a few golden foil wrappers that had been spun and pressed into tiny round balls. I guessed the foils were from candies. In an inside pocket of the purse, also zippered, was a cheap pen and a prescription bottle with about a dozen remaining caplets of Valtrex.

I made two safe assumptions: The purse was owned by a woman, and she suffered from genital herpes.

The condition of the tennis ball—the ball was hairless and covered in what appeared to be dried slime—suggested to me that the owner of the purse used it not to play tennis, but rather to play fetch with a dog. As the owner of a dog that was addicted to the chasing and mouthing of tennis balls—but one that had never mastered the retrieving part of the "fetch" activity—I recognized a canine tennis ball when I saw one.

The wallet was missing anything that might be considered valuable. It contained no cash and no credit cards. And no keys. The only pieces of paper that provided any clue to the owner's identity, other than the prescription label on the Valtrex, were an expired health-insurance card from a big managed-care provider and a library card from Jefferson County, Boulder County's neighbor to the south.

After directory assistance failed to help me find an address or phone number, I wasted a few of the precious minutes I had between sessions trying to weasel a contact number from representatives at both the health-insurance provider and from the library, but I made no progress getting anyone to bend any rules for me. With the current HIPAA regulations I didn't even consider the possibility that the pharmacy at Target was going to tell me anything about the identity of the woman taking medicine to control genital herpes.

Secrets.

With only a few minutes remaining before my ten-thirty appointment, I took the easy way out and called the nonemergency number at the Boulder police department. After an interlude on hold I explained the situation to the man who had answered the phone and asked for instructions on what I should do with the purse. He asked for my name and phone number and the name of the purse's apparent owner. He repeated everything, mixing up my first name and my last name. Straightening it out took much longer than it should have.

"Hold, please." A minute later he came back on the line. He said, "Somebody will call you."

I volunteered to drop it by the department on my way home from work.

"Somebody will call you," the man said again.

"I'm not that easy to reach during the day. I don't usually answer my phone."

"Somebody will call you," the man said yet again.

"They'll get my voice mail. We'll end up playing phone tag."

"Somebody will call you," the man said for the fourth time, his tone unaltered. I got the impression that he would repeat the line with the same inflection all morning long if I really wanted him to.

"That's it? Somebody will call me?"

"Somebody will call you."

I hung up, stuffed my hands into my pockets, and strolled down the hall to get my ten-thirty patient. I figured somebody would call me.

Forty-five minutes later I repeated the steps down the hall to get my eleven-fifteen from the waiting room.

At 12:05 I was trying to decide where to hustle for a quick lunch when I noticed a shadow darken the window in the door that led to the backyard.

My first thought? *Michael McClelland.*

My pulse soared. But it wasn't McClelland. It was Sam Purdy. For some reason, I was confronted with an unwelcome image of him lying naked and pink on a beach in Baja.

Damn. I opened the door. "Sam," I said. I was happy to see him but I was instantly wary for two reasons. The first was general: Sam didn't often visit me at work, and on those rare occasions when he did, he usually camped

out in the waiting room and either napped or read magazines until I made my next scheduled appearance. It was
possible that he'd already tried the new waiting room
and decided that all the serenity was too much for him.

The second reason I was wary was more worrisome.
Once I'd gotten over my fear that it was Michael Mc-
Clelland at my back door, I'd immediately started dealing with my fear that Sam was at my door to tell me that
McClelland had somehow managed to get to Lauren or
to Grace. Sam wouldn't bother to come over to my office
to tell me that McClelland had been caught—for that an
e-mail or voice-mail message would have sufficed. But if
the news were bad enough, Sam would come over to my
office to deliver it in person. That's what I feared he was
doing at my door.

"Alan," he said.

I weighed his greeting for nuance. I didn't sense anything. I said, "Is Lauren okay, Sam? Grace?"

He held up both hands, fingers spread, and shook
his head. He said, "Yeah, yeah. Fine. Nothing like that.
That's not why I'm here. Nothing new on McClelland
at all. The trail's still cold. We're looking—don't get me
wrong—but nothing yet."

I felt my body struggle with what to do with all the
useless adrenaline that was surging through my veins.

Sam raised himself on his toes and looked over my
shoulder in the general direction of my desk and said,
"Is that it?"

What? "Is what 'it,' Sam?"

"Is that the purse you found?"

"They sent *you*?" I asked. My tone conveyed my in-credulousness. Sam was a senior detective. He didn't do minor errands for the police department. And anyway, he was currently working for the DA on Lauren's grand jury.

I should have connected the dots right away. I didn't. Because I didn't, his next question ambushed me.

"What did you touch?" he asked me. The swap was subtle, but I realized that Sam had changed over to his cop voice.

I'd never been especially fond of his cop voice.

TWELVE

WITH THAT question, in that tone, I realized what was going on. And among the things that I knew was going on was that by examining the purse earlier that morning I had inadvertently learned the name of the grand jury witness who had gone missing.

I said, "So that's why you're here. It's her purse, isn't it? Your witness? The one who went missing yesterday? I hope this helps."

"What did you touch, Alan? Be specific."

Sam's inflection hardened with repetition. He would not have made a good substitute for the monotonous guy who answered the phones at the department.

I tried to shrug off the attitude attached to his question, but I didn't quite manage to hide my defensiveness. "Lighten up. It never crossed my mind that the purse was important. I figured it had been stolen and that someone had tossed it over the fence. What did I touch? I went through everything; I touched everything. Inside, outside, the zipper, the wallet. The cards with her name on them. I was looking for her ID so I could call her and tell her I had her purse."

Deep inhale. Loud exhale. "Shit."

I added, "Even the tennis ball. She has a dog."

"Where did you find it? Exactly."

I gestured over his shoulder. "Back there, by the fence. I'll show you the spot if you want."

"Not right now," he said as he craned his neck to look toward the rear of the lot. At what? I couldn't tell. Then he turned and faced me. "Hey, can I come in?" he asked.

His tone was friendly again.

It was an odd moment for me. After many years married to a prosecutor and after many years as a friend to a cop, I knew that his question was not as uncomplicated as he was trying to make it appear. I knew there was an outside chance that he wasn't asking to come inside as a friend wanting to get out of the spring midday sun, but instead that he was asking as a cop seeking permission to enter a citizen's private property.

His friendly tone might also have served as a warning to me that he didn't want me to recognize—and certainly not to ponder—the legal implications of his request.

What were the legal consequences of acquiescing and inviting him in? I'm no lawyer and probably didn't know all the ramifications, but I thought I knew one: once I had voluntarily invited Sam inside my office, anything within plain view was vulnerable to his examination as a peace officer.

I had alternatives to inviting Sam inside. I could go over and get the purse and hand it to him, but considering the question he'd just asked me—"What did you touch?"—I assumed that doing so would render him apoplectic. I also had the option of simply saying no—I could be a jerk about the whole thing and tell Sam to leave the property. What would that mean for Sam? If I did deny him entry and he really wanted to come into my office and look around, he would be forced to go to a judge and ask for a search warrant.

Sam didn't like stopping his life to get warrants. He wouldn't be forgiving if I insisted.

Were my attorney wife standing beside me, she would have admonished me to make Sam apply for a warrant. She would have said, "Don't invite a cop inside your property. I don't care if the cop is your friend. Don't invite one in. Ever. Don't do it. If a cop wants inside your property you need to call a lawyer."

But Sam was my friend, probably my best friend. He'd earned my trust a dozen different times over the years. Odds were that he was at my door simply to retrieve his missing witness's purse. I quickly thought through what would happen next and came up with an uncomplicated scenario: I would invite him in, Sam would step into my office, he'd pull on some gloves, collect the purse, and that would be that.

I did what a friend would do; I gave him the benefit of the doubt. "Sure," I said to Sam. "Come in."

With that invitation he literally crossed the oak threshold and figuratively crossed the legal threshold that granted him a valid law enforcement reason to be in my office, and with it, the freedom to look around. As his foot touched down on the fir floor my constitutional protections against illegal search vaporized like a ladle of water on the hot stones in a sauna.

I was so trusting of him that I didn't even hear the sizzle of the water on the rocks.

"You can have it," I said. "It's right there. Everything that was inside is back inside. I can't stay and chat, though—I barely have time to run to Amante and grab a panini before my next appointment. Give me a call later if you want to talk about it."

"When's your next appointment?" I was perplexed that Sam hadn't moved into the room; he was still only half a step inside the door, a dozen feet from the purse.

"Twelve forty-five," I said.

"We won't be done by then. You'll have to cancel."

"I'm not canceling anything. Take the purse. Go. Get out of here. I really need to get something to eat before my next patient."

I did not comprehend the nature of my dilemma.

Sam recognized my ignorance before I did. He waited until I was looking at him before he spoke. "I'll go if you want me to, Alan. If you insist. But if I do leave you will have to come with me. The purse stays where it is. Your office and your yard are now part of a crime scene. The forensics team is going to go over this room and your yard with all of their best toys. I'm sorry. Your day is, well, fucked."

He didn't sound sorry. "You're not serious, right?"

"Do I look like I'm not serious?"

I added up the negatives before I responded. No, he didn't look not serious. Not even a little.

He used his cell phone, not his radio, to call dispatch. He requested two cruisers and a full forensics response. Without removing the phone from his ear, he turned to me and asked, "What's the address here? The number?"

I told him. I didn't feel like telling him, but I told him.

Since the New Year began I'd been working on my pettiness.

My next thoughts? My appointment calendar was sitting open on my desk. My file cabinet was unlocked. Three different clinical case files were in a clumsy pile on the top of the cabinet. I absolutely could not leave any of that information out for casual perusal, let alone detailed examination, by anyone from the Boulder police department. The cross-dressing man who owned the busy nightclub on The Hill would not be happy with me. His wife and her ancient affair? God. I didn't think I had those details in the chart, but I wasn't totally certain.

I gestured in the direction of my desk. "Those are clinical records, Sam. You guys can't examine them. You can't even see them."

"Please don't tell me she's one of your patients."

"Who?"

He thought for a moment about how to answer the question. He finally settled on "The purse lady." Although by then we both knew the grand jury witness's name, he didn't want to say it out loud.

Some sort of bad grand jury karma.

After a moment's reflection, I decided I could ethically answer the simple question about whether the purse lady was one of my patients. That didn't happen a whole lot when Sam, or anyone else, was asking me questions about my clinical practice. The only reason I could answer is because the owner of the purse wasn't a patient. "No," I said, "she's not one of my patients."

"Then don't worry. She's all we care about. We don't want to read your crappy files."

"There are names on the files. Those files, right there." I pointed. "On the outside, you know, on the tabs. You can't see those names. The identity of those patients is privileged, and you know it."

"I said I'm sorry. You're the one who invited me in."

"I invited my friend in so he could pick up a lost purse and get on with his grand jury investigation." I emphasized "grand jury." "I didn't invite a cop in so he could start being an asshole. I was being nice."

"That may prove to be an interesting distinction for your lawyers to argue with the supremes someday at a time very, very far in the future, but it doesn't interest me much right now. If we end up collecting any information that we're not entitled to have, you can ask a judge to suppress it."

"But you'll already know it, Sam. It's my responsibility to keep you from even knowing it. I take that responsibility seriously."

"You invited me in."

"How about this?" I said, bargaining. "What would you do if I, say, walked over and put those files away? Locked the file cabinet, put that appointment calendar in a safe place?"

"You're not going anywhere near your desk, and you're not touching those files until forensics is done working this room. There might be trace on those files from the purse. We need to know exactly how the purse got into your yard, Alan. We need to know how long it's been there and, most importantly, we need to know who put it there."

I said, "You know how the crime-scene people work. It'll take them all day to do this room." He didn't disagree with me. I babbled on. "The files are on the cabinet, Sam. The purse is on the desk. Locard's principle, you know? Remember that? The purse never got anywhere near those files. I guarantee it. Hell, there's much more likely to be trace on me than there is to be trace on those files."

I regretted the argument the moment I made it.

"Thanks for that. I'll keep you here, too, until the forensics guys can examine you for trace."

"I'm not leaving those files out, Sam."

"I'm not offering you a choice. The crime-scene van will be here before long. I'm sure we can work something out."

Over the years, I'd heard Sam pander to a lot of citizens. The "we can work something out" sounded like he was pandering to me. I knew he wasn't planning to work anything out, at least not to my satisfaction.

"Sam, come on."

"Don't beg. It's unbecoming. This is a crime scene."

"I'll call Cozy," I said, feeling like a wimp being terrorized by a bully, threatening to call a big brother to defend me. Cozier Maitlin was my lawyer—a big, tall, smart, arrogant son of a bitch whom even Sam respected. Sam had once enlisted Cozy to defend his partner when a capital charge was looming.

"It won't change anything. Not today. Not about this." He exhaled audibly through his nose. "You shouldn't have invited me in," he said.

"This is bullshit," I said.

Sam shrugged. As always, being his friend turned out to be much easier when he and I were on the same side.

THIRTEEN

THE SILENT standoff stretched from one minute to two. Sam didn't want to get physical with me. He wasn't eager to order me to assume the position, and he didn't want to resort to cuffing me. I didn't want to make a mad dash to my desk to lock up my files. Had I run, Sam probably would have tackled me. Even before he'd lost all the weight he had been quick on his feet. Any physical contest between us would have been no contest. If he could catch me he could subdue me.

Diane saved us from our bad choices and interrupted our standoff by pulling her latest convertible into the driveway. Her tires made a popping racket on the gravel path, drawing Sam's attention outside.

Our long driveway runs down the side of the house to a decrepit single-car garage that I'd always assumed was built originally for either a horse-drawn buggy or one of Henry Ford's first models. Diane and I were convinced that any attempt to actually open the barnlike garage doors would cause the structure to tumble over, so we parked our cars side by side about ten feet away.

For a decade we'd been waiting for a good Chinook to blow the thing over and end our ambivalence about what to do with it, but the predominant tilt of the structure was to the west, allowing it to lean into the Chinooks, which always originate in the mountains. We'd long guessed that when the thing finally fell it would tumble toward the setting sun, and that our cars were safe when they were parked on the north side.

Sam turned and watched Diane shut down her Saab, gather her things, and then climb out of the car. When she started schlepping everything toward the yard and not toward her office door—probably drawn by the unusual lure of Sam's presence in the open back door to my office—he adjusted his position so that he could stand in the doorway and prepare to stop her advance.

"Diane, don't go there," he said. "Stay out of the yard. That's a police order."

She replied with a non sequitur. "Hi, Sam. Did you see the new waiting room? What do you think? Pretty cool? Like that fountain? That's soapstone, by the way. Just in case you were wondering." She thought he was kidding about the "police order" part. Not that it would have made a whole lot of difference to her if he wasn't. She knew Sam well enough to know he wouldn't give the soapstone a moment's reflection.

"Diane, you can't go— Stop right where you are. It's

a crime scene. There's been a— Please don't— Diane, goddamn . . ." He raised his voice and yelled, "Hey!"

The "hey" was Sam's acknowledgment that Diane had kept right on walking as though she hadn't heard any of his admonitions. Diane generally wasn't amenable to authority. If the authority was trying to tell her what she could and couldn't do on her own property, the rebellious streak in her nature would be aggravated.

"Yeah, right," she said to him, confirming my thesis.

Diane was in my line of sight by then, and she was heading straight toward my open door to see what was up. Diane was a fine clinician. She also had an intuitive nose for controversy, conflict, and gossip. She must have detected molecules floating in the air indicating the presence of all three.

Sam stepped outside and jumped down the two steps to get physically between her and his suspected crime scene.

I hopped forward, slammed the french door shut behind him, and turned the lever that locked the deadbolt. "You're officially uninvited," I said to him through the glass.

Petty? God yes.

A second later his eyes told me all I needed to know about his reaction. He was furious. I forced myself to walk in measured steps across the office, where I gathered up the clinical files I'd left in view, put them away where they belonged, locked the filing cabinet, and put the key inside my appointment book. I then packed my calendar into the shoulder bag I carried each day and slung it across my body. I scanned the office to see if anything remained in view that could reveal the identity of any of my patients.

My phone memory. I dialed my home phone from my desk phone so that the last number dialed would be my own. I then cleared the call history from my mobile phone.

Satisfied, I walked back across the office and reopened the French door. Diane hadn't moved. She was arguing with Sam about where she couldn't go, and why.

"Get your warrant," I said to Sam. "You're not coming back in here without one."

"Who's missing?" Diane asked me. "What's he talking about? What purse? Why won't you let him in your office?"

"I'll tell you later."

"No, you won't," Sam said. "You won't tell anyone a damn thing."

"Staying out of my office until you get a warrant is a Fourth Amendment thing. Telling Diane whatever I damn well want to tell her is a First Amendment thing. In case you've forgotten the limits of your police power I don't think you have the authority to suspend random sections of the Bill of Rights at will."

Diane threw in her two cents' worth. "He's right, Sam. I think random suspension of constitutional rights remains the sole purview of the executive branch." Sam and I had wasted a couple of pitchers of beer debating the Patriot Act and whatever the hell the NSA was up to. Diane had no way to know how much he disagreed with the point of view she was espousing.

"Alan," he said with a sigh. He was holding one hand out, beseeching me to be reasonable, while he was holding up the other hand like a traffic cop imploring Diane to wait where she was and, by the way, to shut the fuck up. He'd temporarily lost his advantage and he needed us both to behave.

"Get your warrant," I said. I closed the door again. I locked the deadbolt, again.

I pulled out my mobile phone and called Cozy Maitlin's office.

Sam either heard what I said, or he read my lips. He reacted with a mumbled, "Goddammit. Not him."

Cozy's assistant, Nigel, said he was with a client.

"I'm pretty sure I'm about to be arrested, Nigel. It would be nice to talk to him before that happens. I suspect this will be my last opportunity."

Sam looked at me through the glass like he was about to kick down the door. It wouldn't have surprised me too much if he did. Behind him, Diane's mouth was agape.

"Now what?" my lawyer said. Hand-holding wasn't his thing.

I explained the situation to Cozy.

"What would he do if you tried to leave?" he asked me.

I thought about it for a few seconds. "I think he'd put me in some kind of custody. Handcuffs, backseat of his car. He wasn't in a good mood when he got here. He's in less of a good mood now."

"We don't want you in custody. Can you just . . . stay put?"

"I have patients all afternoon."

"Don't think so, not today. Given what little you've told me, he'll get the warrant. The only question is whether he's going to let you off the hook about the files you put away. He could go by the book and arrest you for obstruction or—"

"I screwed up?"

"Water under the bridge. You made the first mistake by inviting him in. Sam exploited that. But he got sloppy and left an opening. To your credit you bagged one of his pawns. If he's pissed-off enough he may go after one of your bishops or your rooks. Sam is capable of looking a few moves ahead. Will he? Different question."

Criminal defense was a contest for Cozy. The chess metaphors were a fresh touch—I was more accustomed to hearing sports analogies from him. Usually basketball.

"Can you come over and . . . act imperious?" I'd seen Cozy do it before. I'd seen it work before, too.

"I'm touched by your confidence in my abilities, but I have a hearing at one. I'll come over and act imperious after that. I doubt that Sam will manage to get a search warrant before then. Have you talked to Lauren about this?"

"No. What's going on right now would put her in an

awkward position. I'd like you to try to work this out without either of us having to make that call. She's under a lot of stress because of an old case that's resurfaced. A fresh conflict-of-interest between her grand jury investigator and her husband isn't exactly what she needs right now."

"Bailing her husband out of the slammer wouldn't improve her day much either."

"I'm counting on you to keep that from happening, Cozy."

"We'll see," he said, not agreeing to anything. "This one o'clock is a motion to suppress that I absolutely must win, and I can't be late for the hearing. It's Judge Lu. Enough said?"

"Yes." My wife had suffered the wrath of Judge Lu. Trudy Lu's nickname was "Don't-Be-Tardy Trudy."

As Cozy hung up, Diane appeared in my office door. She'd apparently entered the building through her office, and then used our shared hallway to come to my door. I barked, "Stop. For your own good, don't come in here."

To my surprise she stopped. "What's going on?"

"Someone threw a purse over the back fence last night. A patient pointed it out. I brought it in here, which was apparently a grievous sin. It turns out that it may be an important purse in an investigation of Sam's. Given his mood I promise that you don't want to find out what will happen if you set foot in here."

"Sam said I couldn't use the waiting room."

"How many patients do you have today?"

"Three," she said. "They all really like the new waiting room."

I said I was sorry. Diane looked like she was about to cry. *Las Vegas,* I thought. *She hasn't recovered from Las Vegas.*

"Can you put up a note and ask them to wait on the front porch? Then bring them in the side door into your office?"

"Are the police going to screw it up? The waiting room?" she asked.

FOURTEEN

I ENDED up driving home that evening wearing a zip-up paper suit. On my feet were some beat-up flip-flops I found in the cargo section of my wagon.

The Tyvek jumpsuit was a gift from a member of the crime-scene team. A young female tech offered it in exchange for the clothes I had been wearing when I'd had the misfortune to come in contact with the apparently radioactive purse from the backyard. She had me stand on some sheets of clean paper and undress while she retrieved and individually bagged my shirt, my sweater, my trousers, my socks, and my shoes. It was only after some prolonged deliberation with her boss that they concluded that Locard's principle—one of the guiding tenets governing the transfer of evidence from one surface to another at crime scenes—wouldn't apply to my underwear.

I think I was supposed to be grateful.

Sam requested warrants for the office and yard, and for my person.

While we were waiting for the warrants to arrive, he and I maintained a standoff through the glass of the French door. Sam stood a step outside with his arms folded across his chest, silently daring me to go near my desk again. I sat on the floor opposite the door with my back against the wall, silently daring him to come back in without a warrant.

I used my cell phone to cancel my appointments. I thought briefly about calling Lauren and asking her to intervene, but I didn't. She was already juggling enough and didn't need a new conflict of interest added to her stress load. I also knew she wouldn't intervene and I didn't want to know what that would feel like.

Cozier Maitlin and the warrants showed up almost simultaneously just before two o'clock. I heard Cozy's booming voice, and stepped to the door just in time to see Sam hand Cozy the papers. While Cozy flipped pages Sam appeared to be greeting someone I couldn't see. Cozy refolded the warrants, put a hand on Sam's shoulder, and started talking with him in a low voice.

Sam's a big guy, but he was dwarfed by Cozy. My lawyer is six-eight.

Not thrilled at being excluded from the negotiation, I opened the door to join their tête-à-tête.

Each of them raised a hand to stop me. Sam added, "Stay where you are."

Cozy nodded. "Do what he says." His voice filled the atmosphere the way a fart fills an elevator. "And close that door."

Do what he says? I closed the door.

That's when Kirsten Lord walked into the frame. She had apparently been waiting out of my sight down the driveway. She was dressed in modest heels, a skirt that fell just below her knees, and a tailored long-sleeved shirt. She had a slim briefcase slung over her shoulder.

She looked like a lawyer, which shouldn't have surprised me. Kirsten was a lawyer. The last time she and I had talked, though—and it had been a while—she hadn't been practicing law; she had been apprenticing as a restaurant cook at the Boulderado Hotel. But before that she had been an attorney whose allegiances were firmly on the prosecutorial side of the bar. If she was accompanying Cozy, it was clear evidence that she had crossed over to the defense table.

Kirsten had once, briefly, been my patient. The timing was easy to recall; Lauren had been pregnant with Grace during the interlude when Kirsten had been seeing me for treatment. Gracie was almost five.

Sam and Cozy continued to confer for three or four more minutes. While they chatted, the crime-scene team began to congregate near the garage. Kirsten waited a few respectful steps away from them, as if at attention. She didn't look my way. Finally, Cozy walked away from Sam and disappeared from my sight down the driveway. Kirsten spun and followed him.

Sam began talking to one of the forensics guys, pointing at the back of the yard where I'd picked up the purse, and then at my office. Seconds later, my cell rang.

"I'm out in front of your building. Sam's going to let your little indiscretion with the files slide."

It was Cozy. "He is?" I asked, surprised but grateful.

"He could have insisted that the files be collected and be turned over to a judge or special master. Or he could have busted your ass and thrown you in jail for obstruction."

"Why is he being so . . . nice?"

"I don't know. It concerns me a little that I don't know. But my primary goals were to keep you from being arrested and to protect your clinical files. I am two-for-two. I think that means I get paid double. Are you going to need any more help cooperating, or can I go back to my office?"

"The warrants are good?"

"The warrants are stupendous. They cover your yard, your office, the hallway, and the doorway you use to the waiting room. Sam said you maintain you never moved past the doorway. Sam's playing nice—he wrote them quite narrowly. He could have gotten the whole building. There is another warrant for your person. The judge gave them the right to collect exemplars from you. Today, they'll just get a complete set of your prints, but they have the right to sample your hair and blood, too. I assured him we would cooperate." He paused. "We will cooperate if and when they request the blood and the swabs and the hair, won't we, Dr. Gregory?"

"It's just a damn purse, Cozy."

"Not to them. When they ask for your blood, your

reply will be to expose a vein, one of your favorites, click your heels together, and say, 'How much, sir?' "

Through the door's glass I noted that a police photographer was busy taking a series of establishing shots in the backyard. "You have a new associate, Cozy?"

"I didn't tell you? I think you know her. Ms. Lord is a tad green about the nuances of this side of the law, but she's sharp and she provides some needed estrogen at the defense table. Juries like that. Depending on how this evolves she may end up helping me with your . . . situation. I have some travel planned. She knows a little about the people's side of these things. It's a perspective I have a tendency to lose sight of."

Cozy wasn't prone to admitting deficiencies. I didn't know what else to say, so I asked, "My day is history, right? My practice, I mean. My patients?"

"Yes," Cozy said. "The poor souls will have to muddle along without your guidance for another week. I don't know how I manage some days." He hung up.

Empathy, like hand-holding, wasn't his long suit.

I had the right to observe the search. I wanted to make sure that no one tried to breach the locks on my file cabinet, and I wanted to make sure that no one confused Diane's office with mine.

Though the search did include the connecting hallway between our offices, the search warrant did not include Diane's consultation space, nor did it include the cramped upstairs office where our software-entrepreneur tenant labored on occasion. I couldn't even remember the last time I'd climbed those stairs. Certainly months, possibly years.

From my perspective, it did appear that the forensic bloodhounds were doing what Sam had said they would do—looking for trace that might have been transferred from the purse to surfaces in my office or on my clothing. Since I had admitted to Sam that I'd made a couple of round-trips to collect patients, the techs were also looking for trace that I might then have inadvertently transferred to surfaces in the hallway or the interior doorway to the waiting room.

Sam didn't speak to me until late afternoon. By then I was growing fatigued with my paper clown's outfit. He approached me, holding one of the warrants that he'd shown to Cozy. "Don't know what Mr. Maitlin told you about this, but it includes your garage," he said, poking at the paper with his stubby index finger.

I laughed. Not my brightest move, considering the circumstances. And the suit.

Sam didn't see the humor. In a tone intended to remind him that we were friends—good friends—I said, "Don't waste your time, Sam. I haven't been anywhere near the garage. The purse hasn't been anywhere near the garage."

"Since when?"

"Since . . . ever."

"You know where the purse has been?"

"Of course not. I was talking about after I saw it the first time. Jesus."

"Then what—you're telling me you've never been in your own garage? You expect me to believe that?"

"I've never been in there. Look at it, for God's sake. Sneeze and the thing will fall on your head."

"What's in it?"

"I don't know. If you look through the cracks in the walls it's pretty much empty. An old rake, maybe. A shovel. Some jars. Lumber."

"I think we're going to take a look," he said. He was inspecting the exterior as he spoke. I watched him as he paced around the perimeter of the thing as though he were looking for vulnerabilities in an enemy's fortifications. He ended his tour in front of me, examining the two front doors.

I guessed what he was thinking. "I wouldn't open those." The moment I said the words, I knew Sam would take my suggestion as a challenge, not as a caution.

"We'll see about that."

"You should have the photographer take some pictures of what it looks like right now, before you go in. Something I can use to file a damage claim later on."

Sam shook his head dismissively, pulled on a pair of fresh latex gloves, and stepped up to the big hinged doors at the front of the rickety structure.

"I'd suggest a hardhat," I said. "Or body armor. Or maybe one of those cool little bomb-sniffing robots."

He tried his best to ignore me but I could tell he found my protests aggravating, which provided me some small measure of satisfaction.

The handles on the garage doors were rusty, the wooden exterior weathered and cracked. The hinges and the door hardware were powdered with dark orange-brown oxidation. Whatever paint had once been on the surface of the wood had been sandblasted away by a century of Chinooks. The only evidence of the building's original hue was some dark green tint deep in the fissures of the wood.

Sam yanked on the left-side door. The handle came off in his hand. He tightened his fist around it and held it up close to his face. I could tell he wanted to throw it at someone. Someone like me. Instead he tossed it at my feet and moved his attention to the right-side door. Given the way the building leaned, the right door was the structural member that I thought had been propping up the building since sometime shortly after the end of the Coolidge administration.

"I wouldn't. Seriously. I'm not being difficult. The thing is a hundred-year-old house of cards. It's going to collapse if you pull that door out."

"It's been here this long, it'll be here one more day. We have lots of buildings like this in Minnesota."

Sam was from the Iron Range in the northern part of Minnesota. It was probably true that he had seen a lot of crumbling pine buildings. That day his confidence was misplaced, though. I was sure of that.

He set his feet and pulled hard at the handle. The door emitted a loud squeal as though it had been injured. But it didn't move. I stepped back, anticipating catastrophe. Sam lowered his center of gravity, grasped the handle with both hands, and gave it a good yank. The door creaked outward about six inches before that handle, too, came off in his hand. He stumbled backward and fell ignominiously onto his ass in the space between my car and Diane's. By then, I had retreated far enough that I was standing about six feet behind him as he propped himself on his elbows.

I was trying not to laugh. The paper suit helped with my restraint.

Wood began to creak in the garage. The creaks were almost immediately accompanied by pops. The pops were followed by a few measures of the eerie screeching sound that old nails make as they're being yanked at awkward angles from dry wood.

"Get out of the way, Sam," I said. "She's coming down."

Sam scooted back like an insect retreating from a foe. Three loud cracks snapped in quick succession.

For five seconds the building stood silently with dust, like smoke, rising in little puffs from its joints. The structure seemed to be quivering like an athlete at the end of a long workout, and I had almost convinced myself it was going to remain standing when it groaned and creaked and screeched even louder than before.

Then it tumbled over.

The garage fell to the west as I had long suspected it would. But it didn't fall over dramatically like a redwood sawed off in an old-growth forest. It fell like an old man who had suddenly lost purchase with his cane. Slowly. Inelegantly. In a heap.

Once it had finished collapsing onto its side with a final cacophony of pops and cracks, the building sent up a cloud of dust that quickly covered the cars, and Sam, in a fine, likely toxic, film.

"Damn," Sam said, still on his elbows and ass, his head inches from my feet.

If I hadn't been wearing the Tyvek jumpsuit and that pair of sky blue flip-flops, I think I would have said, "I told you so."

FIFTEEN

LAUREN GOT home even later than I did that night. When I greeted her at the door, I spotted a Boulder County sheriff's cruiser parked at the entrance to the lane.

Oh yeah, I thought. *Michael McClelland. Him.* I'd almost forgotten.

She and I had only a few seconds to talk—she'd ordered Chinese delivery for dinner—before she got a call she insisted she had to take. She retreated to the bedroom with her phone. By the time the call was over, her second evening meeting in a row was about to begin. Sam arrived in a convoy with a young female deputy DA named Melissa something. I didn't know Melissa. Lauren announced that they would be working upstairs. Lauren undoubtedly told her colleagues it would be more comfortable than our basement. As true as that might be, I also knew that her decision to work on the main floor was a sign that my wife's legs likely weren't behaving well enough for her to descend stairs in the company of company.

I shook Melissa's hand—it was cold. So was she. I said a quick hello to Sam. He'd showered and changed since his afternoon spent playing destructo-cop with the garage. He was wearing what I thought of as his "Carmen clothes," which meant he was dressed as though he gave a damn how he looked.

Like a good spouse—one who hadn't been strip-searched that afternoon at the order of one of my houseguests—I politely retreated and spent the evening with Grace in the bedrooms.

I stepped out to the kitchen only twice. The first time I put together two plates of lo mein and spicy shrimp with peppers, and I then I went back out once an hour or so later on to get Grace something to drink. Lauren smiled at me, but no one spoke while I was in the room. A whiteboard had been set up on an easel on the far side of the kitchen table and was covered with a bulleted list of possibilities of how the purse had ended up in the backyard of my office. I examined the options casually as I poured and then diluted some juice for Gracie.

• *Thrown from Canyon*

The back fence of my yard was a good thirty yards from the closest westbound lane of Canyon Boulevard. It made no sense to me that someone interested in getting rid of a stolen purse would attempt to make that kind of throw, either from the sidewalk or from a moving vehicle. A person could have stepped across the adjacent empty lot and dumped it over the fence, but I couldn't figure out why someone would do that. Boulder Creek was nearby. The empty lot between the office and Canyon would have been a much better place for disposal. The surrounding downtown area was dotted with Dumpsters and trash cans. There were plenty of available places to stash a stolen purse and run little risk of having it discovered.

• *Wanted it to be found*

Couldn't really argue with that one. The purse had been tossed, or placed, out in the open. If someone had thrown it over the fence into our yard so that someone would find it, the effort had been successful.

• *Some connection to Walnut Street offices*
 —*patient*
 —*doctors*
 —*what?*

They are actually considering the possibility that Diane or I are involved? I picked up Grace's juice and retraced my steps down the hall. The last thing I heard behind me was a whispered question from the young DA. Melissa had one of those unfortunate whispers that carried like the bark of a neighbor's dog. "Did he see the board just then? Could you tell? Was he looking?"

Sam's cynical reply: "He saw it."

*   *   *

Later, after everyone had left and after I'd taken the dogs out for a final stroll, I joined Lauren in bed. She said, "Sam told me about this afternoon. You and I probably shouldn't discuss it. You understand?"

I thought I understood. But I said, "Not really."

She was ready with the rationale. "If it turns out that you're involved in the . . . work . . . we're doing—even inadvertently—it will compromise my ability to lead the investigation. And it might interfere with Sam's ability to participate. In the meantime the DA doesn't want either of us to have any conversations with you about . . . any of it."

"I can't tell you my side?"

"Once the forensics on the purse and your . . . things . . . come back negative and we're confident that it's just a coincidence that it ended up in your yard . . . then we can talk. I'm really sorry you got dragged into it, babe. This investigation is a big deal. That's why Sam's being the way he is." She kissed me slowly. It was almost an invitation.

"How are you feeling?" I asked. "Your legs? You didn't go downstairs tonight."

"My legs are fine. I wanted to use the table—to spread some things out. Thanks for keeping Grace occupied."

She wasn't telling me anything about her health but was tacitly acknowledging that the stress was taking a toll. I said, "Kirsten Lord has started working with Cozy. Did you know that? She showed up when I called him for help with the warrant today."

"I heard something a few weeks ago. I didn't mention it?" she said.

"Don't think you did."

"I haven't seen her that much the past year or two."

"You were pretty close friends for a while."

She crinkled her nose. "One of those things. We really can't talk about this. What happened. Your attorneys."

I nodded.

She said, "I'm sorry."

I had met Kirsten Lord during a brief window when I'd volunteered to be the acting Regional Psychological Consultant to the United States Marshal's Witness Security Program—WITSEC—popularly known as the Witness Protection Program. Kirsten was a newbie enrollee in the program. She was not a typical WITSEC mobster or drug informant—she was a prosecutor from New Orleans whom the government was protecting as a threatened law enforcement officer after her husband had been gunned down in the French Quarter in retaliation for one of her prosecutions.

She and her daughter had been resettled in Boulder for their first stint in government-devised anonymity purgatory. She'd ultimately decided to leave the protection of the program after the threat diminished and their security situation stabilized. She'd also decided to stay in Boulder. She and Lauren had become friends and that's how I knew that Kirsten had spent a few of the intervening years exploring alternative careers. The fact that she'd recently hooked up with Cozier Maitlin, one of Boulder's most prominent criminal defense attorneys, seemed to indicate that her days of career wanderlust had gone full circle.

Our psychotherapy relationship had terminated when she chose to leave WITSEC. Beyond "Hello" and "How are you?" she and I had not spoken since she'd asked me for a referral to a new therapist.

Twenty minutes after we'd climbed into bed I whispered, "You still awake?"

Lauren didn't answer. I listened for a while to the rhythm of her breathing, my ears tuned for the cadence of sleep. I didn't hear it. I climbed out of bed, pulled on some sweats, wrapped a throw over my shoulders, and shuffled out to the narrow deck off the living room.

I was thinking about secrets. Lauren's and Sam's. Mine.

Later, in retrospect, I realized that my focus was probably a few degrees off-target. Secrets usually aren't as important as our motivation for keeping them. I should have been thinking about the motivation for secrets.

Tops on that list? For years I would've argued that the top spot on the list was reserved for shame. That night, though, I should have been thinking that the top spot on the list had to do with control. Specifically, the control we lose when we free secrets from their locked dens. I should have been thinking about control.

About losing it.

When I finally slept that night I dreamed the garage had collapsed again. I was inside it. A man had his hand around my ankle.

I had a gun.

SIXTEEN

KIRSTEN CALLED me later that week, on Friday evening. I took the call in the kitchen. Lauren was reading to Grace. No music was playing in the background, not even the Wiggles.

After a greeting that I thought was too formal by double-digit degrees, Kirsten asked, "Do you still ride your bike?"

"Whenever I can," I said.

It was a lie. Since the previous fall my bikes had been collecting dust. Biking had long been my primary stress-reduction tool, but for four or five months I'd been using the winter—cold, ice, road sand—as my excuse not to ride. With the weather improving I'd been compelled to become more imaginative with my rationalizations. Admitting the reality—I hadn't felt like riding in half a year—wasn't palatable. My denial wasn't impregnable—I was aware it wasn't a good sign that I'd traded in quality cardio for a diet of high-proof clear liquids.

"We need to get reacquainted, Alan. There are some

developments that you and I need to discuss. Are you up for a ride tomorrow? We can talk."

"You ride?" I said. "You have a road bike?"

Kirsten Lord's laugh told me she did, and that she found my incredulous tone amusing.

"Cozy doesn't want to be part of this?"

"The talking part, or the riding part? Sorry," she said. "I have trouble visualizing him on a bicycle. Doesn't matter—he's in La Jolla for a few days looking at a new weekend place. He found a condo with ten-foot ceilings and a partial view of the cove. So you're stuck with me on this for now. I'm assuming enough water has passed under the bridge that you're okay with us working together."

Five years? Was that sufficient ethical insulation between the termination of a doctor-patient relationship and the initiation of an attorney-client one? Probably. There weren't any fixed guidelines in my profession. My personal rule of thumb was that five years was a wide enough moat between the doctor-patient relationship and most of what might come next. Regardless, my ethical reticence wasn't germane—given my unusual circumstances I wasn't in a position to be too picky.

"Sure," I said. "What developments?"

"In person. I have to do this early. Is seven okay? You can choose the route. Just not all mountains, please. I can definitely climb, but I can't climb indefinitely."

Lauren and Grace were still asleep when I got out of bed.

Kirsten arrived right at seven, and we started off down the lane a few minutes later. I waved good-bye to Lauren's sentry—a solitary sheriff's deputy slouched in the driver's seat of her cruiser. The deputy was sipping from a container of coffee that I'd delivered a few minutes before along with a heads-up about Kirsten's imminent arrival.

Kirsten didn't ask about the deputy's presence. I figured she already knew.

We began the ride on safe ground, literally and figuratively. The route north from my house on the eastern rim of the Boulder Valley is mostly rolling hills. Early on Saturday morning we would see little traffic. For the first few miles we rode side by side on quiet lanes and talked about our kids. Kirsten's daughter, Amy, was solidly into the domain of teenage-girl no-parents' land. I told Kirsten about Grace.

The conversation moved to the events that had brought us together the first time. Neither of us had heard from Carl Luppo, the charismatic ex-mob guy who was my other WITSEC patient, since shortly after Kirsten had asked for "the paper"—her ticket out of Witness Protection. She was convinced that Carl was still alive somewhere, kicking ass. I wasn't as optimistic as she was, but I kept those fears to myself.

She pulled ahead of me and wasted no time getting her spin way up, maintaining a determined push that I wasn't prepared to match. I tried to change mental gears and find a little competitive fire. I failed; within minutes of her acceleration I was struggling in her wake. My winter malaise had left me out of shape. We were almost due east of Niwot before Kirsten dropped back and rode side by side with me again.

"You're good," I said, trying to sound unaffected by all the exertion.

"Never knew I liked doing this until I moved here. Same for snowshoeing. And fly-fishing. I guess I owe WITSEC something, right? Who would have pegged me for an outdoorswoman?" She laughed.

She laughs with much more ease than she used to, I thought. "I guess," I said, thinking it prudent to limit myself to short sentences. Kirsten had arrived in the Rocky Mountain West as a young professional woman and mother more inclined to a fine pedicure than a tough training ride.

"You have some problems," she said, without a hitch in her rhythm. I glanced over at her. Although she'd slowed her spin, her helmeted head was down, and her Lycra-molded form was almost perfect.

I mentally checked my own form, tuning in to the vibrations passing through the tires and frame of my bicycle. I didn't see the problem, and I didn't feel the problem.

"Not a riding problem, Alan. You have legal problems."

Shit. "Sam's going to press for access to the files that were on my desk?"

"I wish it was that simple," she said. "Worst possible

outcome of that would be manageable." As she wet her lips with her tongue, I could tell she wasn't even breathing hard. "The shoes they collected during the search? Cozy has a contact somewhere in the department. In the lab maybe. There was blood on the sole of one of your shoes."

I was mystified by the revelation for a couple of revolutions of the pedals. Then I remembered Kol and the bizarre fountain-bathing episode. "I know what that is. I had a patient who had an amazing bloody nose last week—a day or two before the purse thing. I can check my calendar and be more precise. There was blood all over the waiting room. I'm not surprised that some got on my shoes. It's no big thing. Don't sweat it."

We both slowed to see what an ancient hay truck in front of us was planning at the upcoming intersection. The driver had slowed the truck to a crawl and was straddling the center line of the two-lane roadway. One of two brake lights was illuminated, but neither turn signal was flashing.

"Male patient or female patient?" Kirsten asked. Her eyes were locked on the flapping tarp that covered the ass of the truck.

"Male," I said, wondering why it was an important distinction.

She looked at me. "Then it wasn't his blood on your shoes."

She returned her attention to the road and braked hard. Reflexively, I did, too. In front of us the truck started a wide right turn across the road. The driver paused his maneuver just long enough to hold his hand out and flip us off. I'd been riding for too many years to be surprised at the gesture. The truck driver's manners didn't faze Kirsten.

"It wasn't his blood," she repeated as she stopped her bike.

"I cleaned it up—it was everywhere. His clothes, the fountain in the waiting room. The floor. My partner's new furniture."

"Cozy's source says it was a woman's blood."

"What woman?"

"All we know is that the initial DNA shows no y chromosome."

I sat up straight on the saddle. "Maybe it's Diane's. She might have cut herself. Or maybe one of the workers . . . We have this new fountain. Maybe the water artist cut herself." I waved vaguely west. "She's from near here. A llama ranch in Niwot."

"What?"

Kirsten hadn't been in Boulder quite long enough for phrases like "the water artist" or "llama ranch in Niwot" to become vernacular for her. I provided a translation. "A woman was doing some metal work in the waiting room—maybe she cut herself."

She asked, "Any other way that your shoe could have come in contact with a woman's blood?"

"Lauren? Sure, I suppose. Gracie? She's a kid—you know what that's like; she cuts herself all the time. Scrapes and things. But those shoes? I wear them mostly to work. The only blood I remember seeing recently is from this patient and his nosebleed. I bet Cozy's information is wrong."

"There's another office, right? Upstairs."

"A software guy. A man. He's not around much."

"Does he have employees?" I shook my head. "Visitors? Clients?"

"Hardly ever."

"Receptionists? Janitors?"

"Somebody comes in and cleans a couple of nights a week, but that's a man, too. I'm sure the blood on my shoe is from the mess my patient made in the waiting room."

Kirsten released her handlebars and sat up tall on her saddle. She wore half gloves and her exposed fingernails showed the care of a recent manicure. The gaze she used to corral my attention was much more piercing and much more confident than anything I recalled from our earlier relationship when she was patient and I was doctor.

"Okay, let's say you're right and that Cozy's information is wrong. Anything else you want to tell me before this goes further?" she asked.

She didn't quite believe my protests about the blood, but hadn't quite concluded I was lying to her. The consequences of what Kirsten was telling me became clear: A witness, crucial to a grand jury investigation, had gone missing. Her apparently ransacked purse had shown up in the yard of my building. A trace of a woman's blood had been discovered on the sole of one of my shoes. What woman? That was unclear. What was clear was that I was a person of interest in some part of the grand jury investigation. The witness's disappearance? Probably, but I didn't know that for sure.

The cops probably didn't even know that for sure. What did they suspect had happened to the witness? *Witness tampering? Intimidation? Assault? Murder?*

I watched the hay truck disappear over a distant rise on the intersecting county road. I went with the obvious: "I'm in some trouble here."

"Cozy and I are concerned, yes."

She'd adopted her new boss's tendency for understatement. "What happens next?" I asked.

"We don't think they're planning to arrest you yet."

"Jesus."

"Do I need to caution you not to talk with anyone? Certainly not anyone from law enforcement." I hesitated. She repeated, "Do I?"

I felt a sigh coming on, but thwarted it. "My wife is a deputy DA. My best friend is a Boulder detective temporarily assigned to her office."

"We know that it's going to be awkward. We've discussed asking you to move out of your house until this gets resolved."

"Excuse me?"

"You could inadvertently say something incriminating to Lauren. Or to your friend. It's a risk that we can't afford to take." She pulled her sunglasses down to the end of her nose and smiled at me. Her eyes were kind. "You helped me once. I'd like to return the favor. Will you let me do that?"

By asking me to leave my family? I nodded.

"Who is the patient with the nosebleed?" she asked. "I need to talk to him."

"I can't tell you that without his permission."

"Then get his permission."

SEVENTEEN

TWENTY MINUTES later I broke off the climb that we'd started up Lefthand Canyon toward Jamestown. We turned around long before Kirsten seemed fatigued by either the exertion or the altitude gain. I took the lead and chose the most direct route down the length of the Boulder Valley toward Spanish Hills. Her rider's etiquette was refined—she offered to lead for a while and allow me to draft. I declined. I wanted to get home. And I wanted to arrive tired. More than tired. Exhausted.

When we completed the final incline up the lane off South Boulder Road toward my house, the sheriff's cruiser was gone from its location on the dirt shoulder. I tried to remember if Lauren had an early appointment on Saturday or any plans for a morning errand. I didn't think so.

I helped Kirsten get her bike onto the rack on top of her car before I thanked her for the ride and told her I'd call her after I reached my nosebleed patient. She cautioned me again to be discreet with Sam and Lauren.

We shook hands—it was awkward—and said good-bye. My cleats click-clacked on the gravel as I heel-toed toward the house. Almost immediately I noticed a piece of paper had been stuck in the jamb. From a half-dozen steps away I could identify the paper as a common lined index card.

I moved up onto the porch. From five feet away I could read the card. In a simple, neat, almost architectural hand, someone had written, "The second happened here."

I stopped. "Kirsten," I called without turning around.

She was right behind me. I hadn't even heard her approach. She put her hand on my shoulder. "I saw it from my car. What is it?" I shook my head. "What does it mean? The second what happened here?" she asked.

I turned and looked at her just as she remembered. She'd let her blond hair down. Her bicycle helmet was in her hand. She'd also lowered the zipper on her Lycra to allow some air to circulate to her chest. The flesh below her neck was mottled pink from the ride. I watched recognition darken her eyes—she had been at my home when the first happened. Her daughter, Amy, had been there, too.

The answer to her question wasn't a secret. It was old history for us—the night that the men who had been after Kirsten caught up with her. The final scene of the last act played out between me and one of the killers in the rubble of my front porch. I'd driven Adrienne's Land Cruiser through the wall in an effort to destroy the man who was after Kirsten's family and mine.

It had all happened right where we were standing.

"Oh my God," she said. "That's what this is about?"

My breathing was shallow. My pulse was racing. My instinct was to run to find my family.

"There's this guy named Michael McClelland," I said. I struggled to find a way to make the long story short for Kirsten. A way to help her understand what had happened between Lauren and me and Michael McClelland so long before. I said, "Back in New Orleans? Before you came to Boulder, before we ever met? The man who ordered your husband killed, what was his name?"

She swallowed once. "Ernesto Castro," she said. Castro—someone she had prosecuted for rape who had promised to take revenge—was one of Kirsten's secrets. The man's name came out of her mouth in a hoarse whisper. The pink hue drained from the flesh on her chest. What had been mottled was uniformly pale.

The difference that day? She knew Castro was neutralized. I knew McClelland wasn't.

"Michael McClelland is Lauren's Ernesto Castro. A long time ago he tried to rape her—or kill her—as a way of getting even with me. I have no doubt he would try again if he had the chance. He escaped from the Colorado State Hospital a few days ago. We're afraid this is his chance."

"That's why the deputy was here this morning? For Lauren's protection? Cozy told me something about a problem with a case of hers. He didn't make it sound that important."

I looked at the note and nodded. *The second happened here.*

"Get even with you for what?" she asked, unwilling to let go of the question of McClelland's motive.

It was a tough question to answer. I said, "I figured out what was going on between him and Lauren. Learned a little of what he had done before he met her. Guessed what he might do next. Sam helped me. We stopped him just before he . . . hurt her. We ruined his life. Now I think he wants to return the favor." I fought a flush of despair at the simple equation I'd sketched.

"Lauren's not the only possible target," Kirsten said. "He can hurt her in other ways." She was speaking from experience. She'd been steps away from her husband when a small man in chinos shot him in the head on the sidewalk outside Galatoire's in New Orleans's French Quarter as the couple rendezvoused for their wedding anniversary.

Kirsten's husband had been an innocent.

"I know," I said. "Grace is in danger, too. And me. And Sam. He was there at the end."

Watching a patient—or ex-patient—have an acute episode of post-traumatic stress outside the office is not something most therapists get an opportunity to see. Usually, we hear about the awful moments and the insistent symptoms later, after the actual terror has abated, after the palms have dried, and after the pulse has slowed. But right in front of my eyes Kirsten was being flooded with the feelings of panic and terror and horror from the time of her husband's murder, and from the time that her life and that of her daughter were so much at risk. Right on my front porch.

I reminded myself that I was no longer her therapist. I was her client. "Are you okay?" I asked.

She nodded. She wasn't okay, but she didn't know what she wanted from me. "Oh God," she said. Kirsten's personal nightmare was coming into fresh focus. She crossed her arms over her chest. "It's not enough, you know? A deputy to keep an eye on her from across the road? It's not enough. Not if the guy's determined."

"He's determined. He's vengeful. And he's very smart."

She knew the words to that tune. Her eyes went back to the note. "What does he have to do with that night? The night here? With us. Why would he mention that?"

"I don't know," I said. But I had a guess: *Because McClelland knows.* To know there was a second meant he knew there was a first.

"Why 'the second'? What does that mean?"

"I don't know," I said. It was a lie. A lie I hoped to get away with because Kirsten was asking the wrong question. She should have been asking about the first.

I pulled out my cell phone and tried Lauren on her mobile. It rolled over to voice mail. I called Sam Purdy at home. He answered after two rings. I told him about the note. He sounded neither friendly nor sympathetic. He said he'd notify the sheriff and warned me not to go near it.

To Kirsten I said, "Sam is on his way. He's calling the sheriff."

She reached out and touched me on the arm. She managed a rueful little grin, arresting in the circumstances. She said, "What you need is a Carl Luppo, you know? That's what you need."

I smiled just as ruefully. Carl Luppo had turned out to be Kirsten's unlikely guardian angel while she was hiding from Ernesto Castro's bloody minions. Carl, an organized-crime refugee, had been secreted out of Boulder by the U.S. Marshals after he'd put his life on the line to protect Kirsten's family, as well as mine. I knew that finding my own Carl Luppo wasn't going to be easy.

Kirsten knew that, too.

I said, "McClelland could be watching us right this second." By saying it aloud, I convinced myself that it was true—I looked over Kirsten toward the top of a bluff a few hundred yards away. On that bluff, at the spot where the turnpike from Denver dropped down the valley into Boulder, was the edge of the parking area for a scenic overlook. I half expected to see the outline of a familiar man standing on the rim staring right back at me with a pair of good binoculars.

I didn't.

"Alan?" She was holding a business card. I took it. "I have to go get Amy. My cell is on the back. So is my home number. Call me as soon you know something."

I watched her drive away.

McClelland knows, I thought. *He couldn't.*

EIGHTEEN

SAM DIDN'T have to show up along with the sheriff's investigator and county forensics tech who arrived to collect the card from my door. But he did. I was more grateful than suspicious.

I overheard a deputy tell Sam that a car was searching a perimeter around my home. I presumed the search was for McClelland. A helicopter would have been ideal, but Boulder law enforcement didn't own one. I had no hope McClelland would be found.

Sam stepped back and leaned against his old Jeep. He watched from a distance as the tech took pictures of footprints that may or may not have been McClelland's and of tire marks in the dust and gravel that may or may not have been left behind by a vehicle he may or may not have been using. The tech dusted the door for latents that neither Sam nor I thought belonged to McClelland. We watched the meticulous collection of the index card as it was placed into a lint-free envelope. Compared to what the forensics crew had done a few days before at my office, this wasn't a big job, and it didn't take long.

Sam kept his distance until the sheriff's personnel were getting ready to leave. As the tech packed up, Sam sidled up beside me and asked, "You know what the note means?"

"On the card? Some kind of taunt."

"Why 'the second'? What was the first?"

Sam didn't miss the obvious. "I couldn't say," I replied.

Sam probably knew I was lying. If he did, he let it go. The only reason he let it go was because he knew he shouldn't have been talking to me without my attorney present. He said aloud what I'd been thinking: "They're not going to find anything. The index card will be clean. Latents on the door won't be his. Footprints and tire tracks won't be worth shit." He added a sarcastic afterthought: "Just like on TV."

"Yeah," I said.

"It's like me and ice-fishing. I drank a lot of beer and lost a lot of bait. Hardly ever got a pike. I was a legendarily bad ice-fisherman. But if you don't raise the shanty, if you don't drill the ice, if you don't hang the smelt, if you don't drop the line, you know you're never going to get a pike. That's for sure."

I'd never been ice-fishing. Sam grew up in northern Minnesota. He had been ice-fishing. "And the beer?" I asked.

"Made losing the bait more tolerable."

"I was surprised to see forensics at all. This is pretty minor league."

"McClelland almost killed a cop. Doesn't matter how long ago it was—we don't forget. Lauren see any of this?" he asked.

He meant the card. I shook my head. "No." I held up my cell. "I was on a bike ride when she left with Grace for a soccer parents' meeting. I talked with her while you were on the way here."

"They're all right?"

"So far. A deputy is with them."

He pointed across the lane at the big farmhouse that was slightly uphill from my home. Our house had originally been built as a caretaker's cottage for the farmhouse. I'd rented the shack while I was in graduate school and later bought it from the woman who lived in the farmhouse and owned the surrounding acres.

Sam asked about the current owner of the big house. "You said Adrienne's gone. No house sitter? No chance anybody saw anything?"

Sam knew our friend and neighbor Adrienne well. She was a urologist who had once helped him with a plumbing problem of some kind. I shook my head in reply to his question. "They're just off to Israel—she has a second cousin in Tel Aviv. I'm keeping an eye on the house."

The forensic tech finished loading the van. Sam said something to him that I couldn't hear before he turned to me and said, "I'm going." He walked over to his dusty Cherokee and climbed in. He pulled out his cell phone and speed-dialed someone. I guessed he was checking his voice mail. The van pulled away.

Once the forensic vehicle was over the rise on the lane, Sam stepped back out of his Cherokee, put his arm on my shoulder, and said, "Get the dogs. Let's go for a walk."

"Do I need my attorney?"

He glared at me. "You think *you* shouldn't be doing this? I'm the one who shouldn't be doing this."

Since I'd discovered the purse behind my office and unwillingly inserted myself into the grand jury investigation, I knew it was a risk for Sam to be seen talking with me in any nonofficial role. "It was a joke, Sam."

"Oh. I'll call the forensic guys back to search for the funny part."

I switched my bicycle cleats for a pair of beat-up tennis shoes before I used the side door to collect Emily, our big Bouvier, and Anvil, our faux tough-guy foster dog. Anvil, a miniature poodle, had been in our temporary care since Carl Luppo, Kirsten's mob hit-man guardian angel, had been whisked out of town by WITSEC years before.

Carl had been Anvil's second owner. At some point I would have to accept that Lauren and I were his third owners. I had promised to take care of him until Carl got back. So far, Carl hadn't gotten back. Anvil was getting old. Carl was too.

After our odd posse had ambled about a hundred yards from the house we moved from the dirt lane to one of the trails that ventured uphill into the dried grasses on the rolling hillside above Adrienne's house. Anvil stayed close but once I freed Emily from her leash she lunged into the tallest grasses, looking for something willing to be herded. She preferred mammals of the bovine persuasion, but would try to herd just about anything that moved. Fortunately, her familiar hopping lope made it easy to spot her as she progressed through the grasses in the open fields. The fine Front Range spring day was growing lovelier by the hour, the air so clear that I felt I could reach across the valley and finger the rough surface of the vaulting Flatirons.

"I'm sorry about all this," Sam said, breaking the tranquillity.

I didn't know what he meant. "All what? The Michael McClelland thing? The grand jury thing? Or the knocking-over-my-garage thing?"

He laughed. "I can't fucking believe what I did to your garage."

I laughed too. "It's been a hiccup away from catastrophe since Pearl Harbor. Don't worry about it." I paused. "But the stuff you're sorry about? Does that include the my-best-friend-treating-me-like-a-suspect thing? Where's the love?"

He pinched the crease above his nose with his thumb and index finger as though he were trying to ward off a migraine. "I'm trying right now. You want to cut me some slack? If not, let's just turn around. I don't need the aggravation any more than you do."

"You're right. I'm sorry."

"I don't like the position I'm in. I'm sure you don't like the position you're in. But what happened at your office is a problem. It's not going to go away because we want it to. It's serious. And that's all I have to say about that."

"I understand."

"Today? We both know McClelland wrote the card. Will we prove it? We won't."

"Agreed. What's more important to me right now is convincing the sheriff it was McClelland who left it. 'Cause if he's close by—and we know he is—I'm not comfortable with the level of security the county's providing to protect my family."

Sam took a couple of steps before he responded. "Here's the sheriff's dilemma: If he lets himself get convinced that McClelland is lurking around here, and certainly if he convinces himself that McClelland is stalking one of the county's prosecutors, it will end up costing a shitload more money than he's already spending. He has a strong financial incentive to stay skeptical."

"The card? He'll consider that . . . what?"

"Absent some latents or a witness? He'll conclude it's a prank. Something. Kids."

I kicked at the dirt. Not in true frustration, just acknowledgment. I wasn't surprised. "There's no sign of McClelland anywhere near Boulder?"

"Not here. Not in Pueblo. He hasn't been seen since he walked out of the frame on the surveillance tape outside the clinic."

Emily came bounding back through the grasses, literally touched base with us—she put one of her big front paws on each one of my feet before she lowered herself into a canine version of the downward facing dog—and then immediately hopped back out on her determined search for a sheep or a cow or a wildebeest with wanderlust. Anvil stayed with Sam and me, oblivious to the excitement that his buddy was feeling.

Nature wasn't Anvil's thing.

Sam asked, "You thought about taking Grace someplace? You know, for . . . her safety? I try to imagine what it would be like to be in your shoes right now, if I thought someone had his sights on Simon . . ." His hands tightened into fists.

I blinked a couple of times and wished I hadn't left my sunglasses back at the house. "I've thought about it. I'm still thinking about it. Lauren's sister would take Grace. But that's not a good option. Her personal situation isn't . . . ideal."

"What about your family?" he asked. "You're an only child, right? Your parents alive?"

What? My heart started pounding. When I didn't answer right away, Sam said, "How come I don't already know that?"

"I'm an only child," I said. Sam did know that. *Are my parents alive?* Sam may have asked once or twice; I wasn't certain. I was sure that I'd never answered directly. "My mother's alive but she's not . . . available for this. My family's not any better an option than Lauren's."

I wouldn't even know where to begin to try to explain to Sam about the other stresses in Lauren's life, the fact that music hurt her ears, and that she was trying to manage her pain without the nightly companionship of her lemon-scented bong.

"Carmen and I aren't exactly on the same page right now, either," Sam said.

I felt relief at the change of subject, followed by an eruption of surprise that burned out fast. If Sam didn't volunteer something, how would I know how they were doing as a couple? I rarely saw the two of them. "Really?" I said. "I'm sorry."

Is he thinking Lauren and I are having some trouble? How can he tell? Did she say something? "The long-distance thing?" I asked.

"How 'bout we not go there?" Sam had tried to force some levity into his words. He was turned away from me, his eyes following the bouncing dot that was Emily running in the distant fields.

"I know about the blood on my shoe, Sam."

He snapped his attention back to me. "You do? Shit. Who told you?"

It wasn't hard to guess what he wanted to hear. "Not Lauren."

"Sometimes I think that this law enforcement community couldn't keep a secret if . . ." He picked up a rock and threw it halfway to the turnpike.

"I know the blood means trouble. But I didn't have

anything to do with that purse. I found it in the yard. That's it."

"You and I can't talk about that. You need to keep Cozier Maitlin from wringing your neck. I need deniability with my bosses. No matter how this comes down, I need to be prepared to go on the witness stand, raise my right hand, and say you and I didn't discuss any of it. And I need to be able to do that without perjuring myself."

That he was right didn't matter much to me at that moment. I wanted to hear him say that he believed me.

"If things get any worse for you," he said, without looking at me, "things will get awkward for Lauren. Professionally. And indirectly the same is true for me, too."

"I know."

"If the DA decides your involvement in our investigation isn't just piss-poor luck, then Lauren's conflict of interest will be clear as a martini. She'll have to bow out, or she'll get pushed out. Given that you know almost every member of the DA's staff, including the DA herself, she'll have no choice but to bring in a special prosecutor from another district to take over the investigation."

"It won't happen, Sam. I'm not involved."

"God, you're naïve. You can't taste the politics here? You think this is about reality? It's about perception. If it looks funny, it smells bad. If it smells bad . . ."

The trail narrowed as we neared the crest of a ridge. I allowed Sam to go first. To the back of his head I said, "You're on loan to the DA?" He didn't say yes, didn't say no. "The same conflict-of-interest net that catches Lauren will catch you, too."

"Assuming I'm on loan to the DA."

We reached the top of the ridge. I cupped my hands together into the shape of a horn and bellowed out a long, low note that Emily knew meant, "Come on home, girl."

She changed direction in the prairie grasses and started bounding back toward us. Sam had watched me and my cupped hands as though I'd just magically levitated a few inches. "How the hell did you make that noise?"

"As a kid I could never whistle with my fingers. I learned how to do that instead."

"Huh," he said, shaking his head and staring at his own hands.

I greeted Emily with a treat from my pocket. She inhaled it and immediately started nipping playfully at Anvil. "Sam?" I said. "No matter what else happens, no matter what else you learn that makes you have second thoughts, remember I have nothing to do with any of this. That's the truth, as screwy as it sounds."

"The truth?" he said. "Don't be reassured by what you think you know. Be wary—very wary—of what you don't."

"What does that mean?"

He shook his head. "I got a thing I have to do in town."

"Simon?"

My question was about his son. "He's with his mom. I have this other thing I'm doing. An appointment."

"You okay? Like a doctor?" Sam had suffered some serious health problems over the previous few years.

"No, I'm good. I'm seeing a nutritionist. Somebody I met at Rallysport."

"You're seeing a nutritionist?" I wouldn't have been more surprised if Sam had just told me he was planning to spend the weekend purifying himself in a sweat lodge with some local Lakota.

He patted his gut. "I'm putting some weight back on. I thought I'd get some help. Make sure I'm doing the right things with my diet. I don't want to be a fat cop again. I don't want to be a fat dad again. She's been helping me out."

Boulder changes people in ways they never suspect. Sam had to be example number one. I waited for him to tell me more. It didn't happen.

He said, "Since I don't know who might have shown up at your house since we left, I'm going to walk to my car by myself. Give me ten minutes before you follow. I can't afford for anyone to know we talked."

NINETEEN

AFTER A shower I carried a glass of orange juice, the portable phone, and my appointment book out onto the deck.

I had used the brief time in the shower to reach what felt like an inevitable conclusion: I had to get Kol to admit to the police, or at the very least to Kirsten and Cozy, that he had been responsible for the trail of blood in my office. I'd also decided that I couldn't wait for his next appointment to roll around before I approached him.

I hadn't even allowed myself to guess how Kol would react to my entreaty. I could have predicted the reaction of some of my patients. But not Kol. I didn't know him well, and what I knew I didn't quite trust.

The dogs joined me on the deck. I paused to observe the carefully choreographed canine dance—Anvil waited for Emily, the resident alpha female, to plop down somewhere before he edged up close by and settled beside her so that some part of his body was in contact with some part of hers. As he aged, Anvil had chosen to make Emily his security blanket. To his queen Anvil had adopted the role of eunuch. In its own pathetic way it was quite adaptive. In seconds the dogs' waltz was complete.

I punched in the phone number that I had filed under the initials "K.C." in the section of my address book calendar that I reserved for current-patient contact info. Given the unfamiliar prefix of the number I assumed that it identified Kol's mobile phone and not a Boulder landline. I thought I had only ever called the number once—on the day I'd returned his call requesting an initial appointment.

After less than a complete ring I heard a female voice begin the familiar drone of "The number you have reached is no longer in service. If you think you have reached this number in error—" I hung up. Tried again. Same result.

How long had it been since Kol's first call to me? A month? Sounded about right. Apparently, Kol had changed his phone number in the interim. *No big deal,* I thought. *Happens all the time.*

I checked my records for Kol's Canyon Boulevard address and called directory assistance to get a home number. The operator said that they had no listing for that name and address. I asked him to try an alternative spelling for his first name: C-O-L-E and to please check anywhere in Boulder. Ten seconds later, he told me that he had no listing for that name anywhere in Boulder. I then asked him to try just the last name, without any first name, anywhere in Colorado.

He informed me that I was only permitted two searches. If I would like to call back, someone else would be happy to assist me.

I called back and got the additional searches. My luck didn't improve.

I felt the best of my bad options was to drive downtown and ask for Kol's permission face-to-face. After failing to find any street parking on the east side of Broadway near downtown—no surprise on a sparkling Saturday in the spring—I parked my wagon at the office in front of the pile of rubble that had once been the garage. The cops had actually placed a ring of crime-scene tape around the heap of cracked boards and broken shingles. A second ring marked the spot where the purse had landed in the back of the yard.

I walked down Walnut to the building where Kol's mother had purchased him his loft. Depending on the size of the unit, but given the prime downtown location, I had no doubt that Kol's mother had invested a good-size chunk of Pemex change in her son's home. His building, and its neighbors, had been recently erected in the Boulder Creek flood plain between Canyon and Walnut adjacent to the Downtown Mall. They were mixed-use structures with retail and commercial space on the first floor and offices or condos upstairs.

The little residential lobby of Kol's building was sterile. Expensive sterile—stone floors, heavy nickel hardware, two stainless steel benches—but sterile. Diane wouldn't have liked it. She might have appreciated its organicity but would have had trouble with its serenity, or maybe vice versa.

I checked the list of residents' names on the short roster beside the security phone for the correct number to push to connect with Kol's unit—his patient information sheet said he was in unit 307—but beside that number was a single word and an embarrassment of exclamation: "AVAILABLE!!!!!!!!!!!!"

Available? I lifted the receiver and pressed the black button that followed the last of the exclamation points. A phone started ringing. Three rings. Four. I was about to hang up when I heard, "Marty Driver." Pause. "Hello, Marty Driver."

"Hi, um," I stammered, not expecting to be speaking with Marty Driver. "I was trying to reach a resident in this building, um, in unit number three-oh-seven and—"

"You're in the lobby? Three-oh-seven? Three-oh-seven? That contract fell through. Long story. Great unit, though. Calls to all the unsold units get forwarded to me. You interested? Terrific views. Seriously. Flatirons, Chautauqua. The developer is willing to do some upgrades on the last two units. Granite in the kitchen? Motorized shades on those southern windows? Extra hardwood? Tumbled marble? You like bamboo? It's all possible. I'm the exclusive listing agent for the property and I am happy—"

"I apologize, Mr. Driver. I must have hit the button for the wrong unit number. I'm not in the market; I'm looking for someone who already lives in the building."

"I know everybody. I was the second unit to close. Who you looking to find?"

Marty was friendly. Could I ethically answer his simple question? I could. Marty Driver didn't know I was a psychologist. I'd reveal nothing privileged by revealing Kol's name. "Last name is Cruz."

"Like Tom?" he laughed.

"No, Cruz with a *z*."

"No Cruz. Not that building. And not the one next door, either. Same developer. I'm the exclusive listing agent for both—I said that already, didn't I? My girlfriend says I say it in my sleep sometimes. Not as many speculators bought as you'd think. A couple of tenants are renting from owners, but I know them, too. No Cruz. I have to run."

Marty had recognized that I wasn't a prospect. "Thank you. You've been very helpful." I hung up just as someone was walking out the security door into the lobby. He was a trim guy wearing a pin-striped business suit over a gray silk T-shirt. He had flip-flops on his feet. He also had a lovely little Shih Tzu on a purple rhinestone leash. I smiled at the dog as it strutted across the stone floor like a Great Dane on the prowl. Pleased that I seemed to like his pet, the man held the door open for me. I thanked him, stepped inside, and squeezed into the elevator as the door was closing. I found my way down the third-floor hallway to the door with a stainless steel plaque etched with the number 307. The style of the etching made the sign look like graffiti.

I touched the doorbell. I waited. I knocked. I waited some more, hoping for someone's eye to darken the small circle of the peephole in the door. Hoping that Kol would open the door and prove Marty Driver wrong. But that didn't happen.

Before I returned to the elevator I used the interior landmarks around me—the elevators, the fire stairs, and a tall, thin solitary window that faced toward busy Canyon Boulevard—to try to ascertain the exposure that number 307 would have to the street. It appeared that Kol's unit, or his purported unit, would indeed face both Canyon and Broadway and have fine views to the west and to the south.

Back out on the sidewalk I screened my eyes and looked up toward the windows that I thought belonged to 307. I saw nothing but glare. I crossed over to the other side of Canyon and looked up again. From that vantage, it was apparent that there was nothing about the unit that made it appear to have been occupied. No window coverings. No planters on the small balcony.

Shit. Absolutely unbidden, Kol's words from our last session exploded into my head: *"I mean it's not like what happened with . . . your dad."* Those words were immediately followed by a visual image of the note on my door—*The second happened here*—and by Sam's questions from earlier that morning: *"What about your family?"*

Oh my God—Kol does know about my father.

Kol knows. Then, chasing it like a wolf after prey, *Does McClelland?*

TWENTY

I DIDN'T notice the bandanna until I got home from my unsuccessful search for Kol's loft. The kerchief may have been there when I'd driven away from the house, but if it was I had missed it.

Adrienne, our neighbor, owned the small barn that had been part of the original ranch property. The barn backed up to the edge of the ridge at the southern end of the lane. Behind the barn the ridge dropped off into an undulating valley before rising up toward the scenic overlook on Highway 36.

Adrienne's husband, Peter, since deceased, had expanded and renovated the barn into a shop for his carpentry studio. The new garage that Lauren and I built in the intervening years partially obscured our view of the barn from the front of our house. As I drove back in the lane from town the bright blue fabric of the bandanna that was tied in a loose knot around the handles of the sliding barn doors was hard to miss.

My mouth fell open when I saw it. My mind made

most of the connections without any conscious direction. The bandanna was a thunderstorm parked over a canyon, unleashing a flash flood from my past. But the bandanna didn't feel like a mere trigger for my memory. I knew instantly that it was also a warning.

Before his arrest, the bandanna had become McClelland's terrorist calling card. Old feelings of vulnerability washed over me. *Cicero. Oh my God.* After he'd stolen my dog—it was his way of boasting that he could get to me at will—he'd tied a bandanna around her neck before returning her.

I stopped the car near the garage and hit the button on the opener. The big door swung up. Lauren's car was absent from her parking space. She wasn't home. I wasn't aware that I had stopped breathing, but when I spotted the empty stall in the garage, I felt my lungs fill again. I told myself that my family was safe and I tried to believe it.

I killed the engine and ran back toward the house. I fumbled trying to unlock the door, dropping the keys twice in the process. I finally got the key in the lock and the door open and found Emily and Anvil waiting eagerly on the other side.

The dogs were fine. To their great dismay I left them in the house and retraced my steps toward the barn. By then I was convinced that the message of this bandanna was not about the dogs—it was about the barn.

After her husband's death years before, Adrienne had never been able to bring herself to use Peter's studio for anything other than household storage. I knew that Peter's tools and power equipment would be in the same locations they were when he died. Discarded furniture from the house and toys that Jonas had outgrown would be piled haphazardly wherever Adrienne had left them. Most of the mess was just inside the front doors.

I tried to remember the last time I had been in the barn. It had been years.

I stepped up to the rolling doors. As always, they were secured together by a galvanized hook and rasp and a big brass padlock. The lock appeared undisturbed.

The addition Peter had built on the western edge of the structure had a shed roof and a solitary window facing the lane. I cupped my hand over my eyes and peered through the dirty glass. Peter's longest workbench was shrouded in duck cloth, as it had been since his death.

Nothing seemed out of place.

I stepped back and tried to spot any sign of forced entry on the front of the barn. The windows were intact. All that was unusual was the bandanna loosely tying the door handles together.

I began a slow march around the building, starting with Peter's addition. No broken glass. I peeked in each window. Stepped back to check the condition of the skylights. I saw nothing of concern. The two square windows high on the barn's southern gable were intact. I kept walking.

The only other door into the building was on the east side, just around the south corner. When I turned that corner I saw the door was open about an inch, propped in place with a brick.

Michael McClelland. He'd been there. In the barn. Through that door. He wanted me to know that he'd been there. He could have closed the door. He probably could have relocked it. But he didn't. McClelland had left it open so that I would find it. He'd left the bandanna so that I wouldn't miss it.

Why? So that I could find whatever it was that he had left for me inside.

Was he in there? Was this *mano a mano* time? I backtracked to the garage and pulled my favorite old softball bat from the jumble of sports equipment that Lauren and I kept stashed in a plastic bin in the far corner. I thought of calling Sam but I rejected the idea. I knew he'd take over and ultimately he wouldn't let me see whatever was inside the barn. Ditto for the Boulder County sheriff.

My wife had a carry permit for a handgun. I wondered if I'd feel safer with her semiautomatic in my hand.

Three things gave me pause about the gun. One, I'd never fired it. Two, given the fact that McClelland was on the loose, I was relatively certain Lauren had the gun with her. In her purse. Or in her briefcase. Certainly in her car.

The third thing was the most compelling: my history with guns was far from illustrious.

I settled for the bat. And a dog. I went back to the house and got Emily and put her on a lead. Bringing Anvil wasn't an option; despite his tough-guy posing he wasn't built for combat any more than I was. Bouviers with fangs bared are, on the other hand, terrifying.

Although I have significantly more power from the right, I've always been able to make decent contact from the left side of the plate. Given the location of the open door—on the far end of the east wall—I decided to walk inside the barn batting goofy. The danger, if it came, would most likely be on my right as I stepped inside. The instant I sensed any jeopardy I was going to swing at danger as though it were a high fastball.

I was hoping Emily would be a beacon for me, would give me a little warning about what was coming. When she sensed something, she'd pull back onto her haunches as she snarled and showed her teeth. When I felt her warning I'd swing at the letters. Letter-high is where the meat would be. I didn't need a home run. Swinging high—above the level of Emily's head—would keep her safe.

I took Emily off her lead and slipped my fingers beneath her collar. I asked her if she wanted to go see Peter. Her ears perked up at the question. She'd loved her days hanging out in the barn with him while I was at work. Then I mouthed, "Hey, Peter, take my back," as I moved the brick aside and pushed the door open with the toe of my shoe.

The space was flooded with light from the skylights on the shed roof. But the glare was from the west and everything I could see was in shadows. I knew the layout of the space well—Peter and I often drank beer and talked at the end of the day as he cleaned up the shop after he'd shut down his tools.

The barn was mostly one big room. Along part of the east wall was an old animal stall that Peter had finished out and rocked-off for painting and staining his pieces. A large exhaust fan had pulled fumes from the space.

On the southern wall was a counter with a small refrigerator, and Peter's throne. Up two steps, behind a lovely mahogany outhouse door with a curved quarter-moon, Peter had framed-off an area no bigger than a large closet. Inside was a toilet. The stainless steel, composting contraption had been state of the art when Peter installed it. He'd been quite proud of the thing. Environmentally. Design-wise. Craftsmanship. Everything. He'd called it "The Good Head" and happily showed it off to anyone who visited his studio.

The area under the center gable was wide open, divided only by support beams and posts, ventilation ducts, Peter's power equipment, his workbenches, lumber storage racks, a complex system of dust-collection hoses, and the carcasses of a few projects that he'd left unfinished when he died.

I let go of Emily's collar. "Go find Peter. Good girl."

She took off as though she were heading into the brush after a red fox. I choked up a couple of inches and followed her inside.

TWENTY-ONE

MY ONLY other patient suicide had happened years before, early in my career. A knock on my door by a Boulder cop—a detective I'd never met named Sam Purdy—and a simple but loaded question: "You have a patient named Karen Eileen Hart?"

Sam Purdy had found his way to my Spanish Hills door to inform me that my patient, Karen Hart, had ingested a lethal overdose of antidepressants and alcohol in her Maxwell Street apartment near downtown.

He had a few questions for me. She had been depressed, yes. It was why I was treating her. And, yes, I had arranged for the consultation with the psychiatrist who had prescribed the antidepressant she used to overdose. Would I have considered her suicidal? No. Far from it. Had someone asked me the day before she died, I would have listed Karen among my therapeutic success stories. She had been getting better. Sure, every therapist learns early on in his or her training that the most dangerous time for a suicidal patient is the brief transition after they begin to appear clinically brighter.

But it wasn't like that for Karen. She *was* getting better.

She'd recently gotten braces, for God's sake, and had begun to end her extended self-imposed social isolation. *Who gets braces,* I remember wondering, *when she's planning to kill herself?*

The pieces explaining the tragedy fell together in the months following her death as I came to understand what had happened to Karen Hart, and what—or more precisely, who—had precipitated the acute despair and hopelessness that had led her to swallow the antidepressants and the vodka. I'd never gotten over her needless death, though. Nor did I ever expect to.

My personal history had taught me that some stains never bleach.

Some days are never forgotten. They are indelible.

The most eerie part of the second suicide? The one that day in Peter's barn? Kol's body was still swinging when I discovered it.

I looked away, gagging down vomit. It took half a minute to compose myself before I could look a second time.

Kol's body swung in a tiny arc, no more than two or three inches back and forth. My eyes followed the sway involuntarily. This way, that way. A slow-motion tennis match.

The look on his face was more shock than agony. His eyes were open and aghast; his tongue fat and protruding from his lips as though he'd died from gagging on a piece of raw meat.

The look on his face was *Holy shit, I didn't know it would feel like this!*

His neck was clearly broken. The cincture's single harsh tug had snapped his head to the side at an angle that no intact cervical vertebrae would permit. I saw no evidence that he'd used his fingernails to scratch at his throat or at the rope locked around his neck. I couldn't imagine that anyone suffocating, no matter how intent he had been on dying, could refrain from scratching at a ligature strangling off his airway. I concluded that the cruel yank of the initial fall had killed him.

The fall killed him. I hoped that the fall had killed him. I had read somewhere that dying from the fall wasn't the rule with hangings—most victims died a more excruciating death from asphyxiation. That Kol didn't appear to have died in prolonged agony made it easier to be in the room with his body.

His knees were hanging at my eye level; his feet were about four feet from the floor. Much higher up, the rope was attached to a crossbeam that ran east to west near the top of the center gable of the post-and-beam barn. That location would have given him just enough room to sit on the beam while he tied off the thick rope, fashioned a noose, placed the noose around his neck, and . . .

Jumped. The jumping part had to have been hard. *Jesus.*

The swiftness of the jerk as the rope finished playing out its slack? It would be like—what? I wanted to never know.

"Were we here, girl?" I asked Emily. "When he did this?" *How big had the initial arc of the swing been? How long does it take for a pendulum of a certain length, travel-ing a certain initial arc, carrying a certain weight, to stop moving?* I actually tried to remember some physics from high school. I failed.

Michael McClelland wanted me to see this.

My next thought: *Bingo.*

Emily didn't bark when she ran inside the barn ahead of me. She hadn't sensed danger. But she had sensed some-thing.

She ran to the floor below Kol's body and did two familiar things. First, she did a series of patented Bou-vier des Flandres four-footed leaps—levitating, spinning moves that carry the big dogs straight up on all fours. Emily reserves the quad leaps for times when she is eager to be able to fly. She'll use them to close the gap on a squirrel in a tree, or to get closer to a particularly annoy-ing raven perched above her. She uses them to let traffic helicopters know what she thinks of them hovering over the turnpike near her home. She once used one to try to nip at a 757 making a western approach into DIA during an upslope. On a good four-footed leap Emily can get a yard—maybe a little more—off the ground. At that alti-tude she's capable of completing a 540-degree spin while she's in the air. It's an impressive spectacle.

She completed three leaps and then did something else that is peculiar to the breed—she sat and looked up at the man dangling on the rope, and she started talking.

Bouvier talking is difficult to describe. It is not barking. Bouvier barking, especially serious Bouvier barking, is not easily misconstrued as anything other than what it is. Bouviers bark in order to warn, to get attention, to give orders. If a Bouv is barking, it is clear that the Bouv expects someone or something to heed.

The wise listener does just that. But Bouvier talking is something else. It is a throaty, not quite whiny, open-mouthed sound that is modulated by the dog's cheeks. The sounds have multiple inflections and can go on for long enough periods of time that it often seems as though some punctuation is called for.

After many years as a companion to Bouviers I've deluded myself into believing that I can understand some of the conversational nuances when my dog talks to me.

That time, no. I didn't think Emily had a schema for the dead guy hanging from the rafters in Peter's barn. She was as perplexed as I was. Were I to guess, that's what I would have guessed she was talking about. That she didn't quite get the guy on the rope.

As with Karen Hart's death so many years before, I didn't see this suicide coming.

Had there been warning signs? If there had been, I'd missed them.

After the inevitable lawsuit was filed and after Kol

Cruz's rich mother's fancy attorney finally got a chance to depose me, or after some judge granted the lawyer access to my therapy notes, I would need to reveal the embarrassing fact that over the time I'd been seeing Kol I had not scratched out one single concern about suicidal ideology, let alone any specific suicidal threat. Kol, my notes would maintain, hadn't been currently depressed. Hadn't expressed any suicidal ideation.

Suddenly I thought: *history?* Did Kol have a history of suicidal behavior?

Ideation? Gestures? Attempts? I had never asked. I had never done a suicidal history with him. I had never perceived a need for one. In fact, I hadn't done a formal mental-health history with Kol. My failure to take a history—my "professional negligence" is how Kol's mother's attorneys would characterize it—wouldn't look good for me. My malpractice carrier would not be pleased.

"Well, Dr. Gregory," some lawyer would ask at my deposition, *"what did Mr. Cruz say when you asked him about his history of prior suicide attempts?"*

Shit. *How bad at a profession can one person be?* Most therapists had never lost a single patient to suicide. I had now lost two.

Double bingo.

The bat was heavy in my hands. It was as useless as I felt.

I bent my knees a little, raised the wood to a ready position behind my left ear, and took a smooth swing through the middle of an imaginary strike zone. In my mind the pitch was a slow curve that broke as though it had rolled off the edge of a table. A Sandy Koufax curve.

I misjudged the break completely. My errant swing made strike three.

When I looked up from my reverie, Kol was still there.

But Emily was gone. I did what almost any dog owner would do. I said, "Emily, come." It was a command that she obeyed about three times out of ten. I figured she knew what the words meant. I also figured that she knew that as the purported leader of her pack I wasn't much of a disciplinarian. The consequences of ignoring me were quite tolerable. I wrote off the 30 percent compliance rate to chance, or canine generosity.

A few feet away Kol was still swinging on his rope. The arc was growing smaller. The sway that I could initially measure in inches would soon require millimeters. Before long the pendulum keeping time to his death would find neutral.

I cupped my hands into a horn and made the low bass call that I'd demonstrated for Sam earlier in the day. Emily didn't come at the sound. But she talked to me. The particular vocalization was half bark, half Bouv-talk. The last time I'd heard that mix of sounds from her, Emily had been straddling the entrance to an earthen den, convinced she had a prairie dog cornered. She had been wrong. The prairie dog had simply descended into that particular tunnel before he transferred to an alternate line in the great rodent subway system, amused that the big dog was sniffing for clues at the wrong station.

I followed Emily's sounds, stepping over to the longest of Peter's workbenches. With the bat I lifted the hem of one of the shrouds covering the bench. Emily was sitting below the table, her nub of a tail in frantic motion. She looked at me for an instant, her ears straight up, before she returned her gaze to her discovery.

What had she found? An air mattress and a sleeping bag. A cheap foam pillow without a pillowcase. The bag was laid out on the mattress, which was inflated. It appeared that someone had slept in the setup recently. My first thought was that the lair had been Kol's, but I soon recalled the bandanna on the front doors of the barn and I thought, no. I felt a shiver shoot up my spine.

Michael McClelland had been sleeping two dozen steps from my front door.

From my sleeping wife. From my playing daughter.

My left hand tightened on the handle of the bat. "Come on, girl," I said to Emily. To my surprise, she stood up and heeled. I reclipped the lead to her collar.

It took us a few minutes to complete a slow search of the rest of the barn. I used the bat to lift the corners of the various shrouds that covered the planer and the jointer and the sanders and the saws, looking for further evidence that someone had been living in Peter's studio.

Emily and I didn't find much more evidence. The veneer of dust was disturbed on some surfaces. The little refrigerator was plugged in. I used a shop rag to tug it open. Inside I found two sealed containers of yogurt, some cheese, some hard salami, and a half-eaten loaf of organic Rudi's sourdough. All of it was fresh.

The walled-off room that Peter once used to put finishes on his work was empty. After so many years it still stank of shellac and stain. Peter's throne room showed no indication of recent use. The years of dust on the toilet and on the floor around it hadn't been disturbed.

Out loud I said, "You're much too calm, Alan. You know that, don't you?" The truth was that given the circumstances I was much too calm. Kol's death was a complete shock to me. His suicide? Almost unfathomable. So unfathomable, in fact, that I was reluctant to believe it. My eyes kept returning involuntarily to his hanging body while my mind kept returning to the image of the bandanna that was tied on the barn door handles outside.

I was convinced that whatever had happened in the barn wasn't so much about Kol as it was about Michael McClelland. Somewhere in this building was evidence of that connection, but I didn't know where. And I didn't know what it would look like.

Why? I was not even close to why.

In a candid moment I might have admitted that I was also feeling some relief at Kol's death. Cognitive dissonance being what it is, though, I was reluctant to acknowledge the relief, even to myself.

"I mean it's not like what happened with . . . your dad."

Kol wasn't going to be sharing my secret with anyone.

That was for sure.

TWENTY-TWO

EMILY HEARD the sounds of a car approaching on the lane before I did. Her excitement meant she had identified the vehicle as belonging to someone she was eager to greet. She yipped once, then a second time. I could tell she was preparing for a full-fledged chorus of happy welcoming barks.

I said, "Quiet." She quieted. I was amazed. I peeked out one of the barn windows that faced down the lane.

Lauren was home with Grace. Fifty yards behind the car, a sheriff's cruiser was rolling to a stop in position at the end of the lane. I realized that I hadn't decided how to play any of this, and that with the arrival of law enforcement my options were about to be severely limited.

I pulled out my cell and speed-dialed Sam. I had two motivations for making the first call to him. One, he knew the history with Michael McClelland, had a personal emotional investment in what happened to the guy, and because of that investment I wanted Sam to be part of whatever happened next inside Peter's barn. Reason number two? Sam would have throttled me if I'd left him out of the loop on this.

He wasn't home so I tried his cell. It rolled instantly to voice mail. "Sam? Alan. I'm in Peter's barn." Sam knew the building—he needed no further explanation. "Mc-Clelland's been here, in the barn. There's a dead body inside, a hanging victim. It's not him, McClelland, but it's—fresh—still swinging when I got here. I hope you pick this up soon or the sheriff is going to get here before you do."

I might have revealed to Sam my theory about the nature of the connection between McClelland and Kol Cruz, but I didn't have a theory. Nothing made sense.

Next I called Lauren. She was standing at the open door to the backseat of her car, where she had just started leaning over to unbuckle Grace from her booster seat. As the ringing started in my ear, I watched her through the barn window. She stopped what she was doing and grabbed her phone from her purse. A glance at the caller ID told her it was me. Her face grew perplexed as she looked over at my car a few feet away. She had just surmised that I was home, and she was wondering why I was calling.

"Hey," she said. "We just got home. I'm outside. Be there in a second."

"I know," I said. "I see you through the window. Take a couple of steps to the east and then face the barn. Be inconspicuous if you can. You'll see me standing inside Peter's shop, at the window. Don't react. Just look." She followed my directions. I waved when she looked right at me. She didn't wave back.

"What's going on?" she asked.

"I found something in here that I don't want Grace to know anything about. Do you understand?"

She hesitated before she said, "Does this have to do with—"

"It might."

"Oh God," she said.

"Sam's on his way. Can you take Gracie over to Teryl's or—"

"Are you okay?" Lauren asked in a hurried whisper.

"Things are about to get complicated for me, but yes, I'm okay. You need to take Grace to a friend's house, or somewhere, and then get back here as soon as you can."

She said, "What about the deputy?"

"The deputy will follow you. If we tell him what I found he won't leave, and Grace will be exposed to whatever happens next."

She didn't say yes. She didn't say no. She just stared at me through the dirty glass window of the barn. I was pretty sure she could see nothing but my silhouette. What did I see in her eyes? Concern, yes. But some suspicion, too.

Finally she nodded and said, "I'll drop Grace somewhere and be right back."

She said something to Grace, got back in the car, and drove off down the lane. The sheriff's deputy did a U-turn and followed.

Emily and I waited half a minute or so before using the back door of the barn to walk outside. I put Emily in the house with Anvil and sat on the cold concrete step of the front porch. I had the outline of a plan in my head. I reviewed it and couldn't think of anything I should do differently. I pulled out my cell and called 911. In reply to the dispatcher's bored "Nine-one-one. What is the nature of your emergency?" I tried to explain the situation dispassionately. Her reaction was a little incredulous—"There's a body hanging from a rafter in your neighbor's barn? Is that correct?"—but she soon confirmed the address and promised that assistance was on the way.

I thought about the next call I would make for most of a minute. I pulled Kirsten's card from my pocket and dialed her number. She wasn't home. I tried her mobile.

"Kirsten?"

"Alan," she said. She'd recognized my voice. Maybe she'd seen my name on caller ID but I thought she'd recognized my voice.

How to begin? "I need your help. I just discovered a patient, a dead patient, in my next-door neighbor's barn and—"

"One of your patients?"

"Yes. As bad as that is, it's far . . . more complicated than it sounds."

"You said dead?"

"Hanging. Suicide."

"Who is with you? Right now?"

"No one. I'm outside, sitting on the front porch—you know, where we found the note this morning." *Was that this morning?*

"The body?"

"Still in the barn. I didn't touch it. I'm sure it's all connected somehow. The note, the suicide."

"Where's your neighbor? You said it was in his barn."

"Her barn. She's out of the country with her son."

"How do you . . . How did you—"

"We're friends. I watch her house when she's away."

"So you have a key?"

My attorney was worrying about breaking and entering. It felt quaint. I said, "Yes. Though I didn't need it. The back door had been propped open."

"Have you called the police?"

"I just called 911. Assistance," I said, mimicking the operator, "is on the way. It was him, Kirsten—Michael McClelland."

"How do you know that?"

"He left me another message. Something I wouldn't misinterpret."

"Don't say a word to the cops," she said. "Nothing. I'm near Golden at a soccer tournament. I'll get Amy a ride home with a teammate and I'll be there as soon as I can." She paused. "Did you hear me?"

"You'll be here soon." Golden wasn't a quick drive. "Maybe thirty minutes."

"Not that part. The not-saying-anything part? Tell

them you found a body. Point out where. Nothing else. Okay?"

"Yes," I said.

Five minutes later the dirt and gravel lane began to look like a freeway on-ramp during rush hour. Lauren and her sheriff's deputy shadow returned first—she must have dropped Grace at Teryl's house only a quarter of a mile away. The first two cars were followed in short order by Sam in his personal Jeep Cherokee, then two more marked units from the Boulder County Sheriff's Department. One of the sheriff's vehicles was a cruiser, one was an SUV. They were both running with lights, but no siren. The last spot in the caravan belonged to a rescue truck with a couple of paramedics in the cab. The blue-and-red beacons were lit on it, too. The shape of the boxy rescue van was almost swallowed in the dust already billowing above the lane.

I was no physician but I knew that Kol didn't require emergency medical assistance.

The vehicles pulled to a stop in a haphazard pattern on the wide area between our house and Adrienne's. I took a few steps away from the porch. I glanced at Sam stepping out of his Cherokee and then I looked at the barn. I blinked, and blinked again. My lower lip curled below my upper teeth in order to make an *f* sound. I looked at my feet, blinked a couple of more times, and returned my gaze to the barn.

Damn. I felt the ground shift below me. Instinctively, I spread my feet to maintain my balance. All the confusion I'd been feeling about Kol's death and McClelland's involvement transformed instantly into despair. All my unnatural serenity evaporated. *I am,* I thought, *such a frigging fool.*

The last thing I felt before I heard Lauren calling my name as she ran toward me was just the slightest hint of admiration for the guy. To no one I muttered, "Fuck me."

Lauren heard that. I think she had been about to hug me. Instead she stopped two steps away. "What's wrong?" she said. "What's going on?"

You mean other than the dead guy in the barn? Other than the fact that someone that wants to kill both of us is close by, playing with us? Besides that?

"It's gone," I mumbled. I had enough of my wits about me to know she wouldn't have a clue what I was talking about.

"What? What's gone?"

"He took it." I swiveled my head to look around for McClelland. I scanned the barren hills, then over at Adrienne's house, at her rooftop, and over toward the scenic overlook. I didn't find him but I knew that somewhere close by he was watching my reaction to what he'd just done, and he was laughing.

Lauren moved beside me and touched my face. She must have thought I was upset about what I'd told her I'd found in the barn. "He took what?" Lauren asked. "What's gone?"

I shook my head and said, "Nothing." I gestured at the barn. "Thanks for taking care of Gracie. There's been a . . . Someone's body is . . ." I couldn't find the right words. "A body is hanging inside Peter's studio. It looks like a suicide."

She said, "Oh . . . my . . . God."

I was aware at some level that I had just misled my wife. I'd said "someone," not "one of my patients." I rationalized that I had no choice; I didn't have permission to reveal my therapeutic relationship with Kol. I told myself that I would have admitted the truth to my wife, but I wouldn't admit it to a deputy DA. Lauren happened to be both.

I looked toward Peter's shop one more time. Nothing had changed.

Okay, one important thing had changed. The fuck-me part.

The bandanna was gone from the front doors of the barn.

TWENTY-THREE

KOL'S SUICIDE was one of those emergencies that starts off hot. A cadre of well-intentioned public-safety professionals moved in with determination and alacrity. Every member of the team was primed to do his or her job, prepared to make a difference.

The first thing I did after they'd begun to assemble on the lane was provide a brief explanation of what I'd discovered in the barn. I included the fact that Emily had sniffed out the sleeping bag and air mattress beneath Peter's long workbench. Sam Purdy and one of the sheriff's deputies were first into the building. They used the same door that Emily and I had used.

They came back out after about a couple of minutes. The deputy asked the two paramedics to glove-up and follow him back inside. Sam handed the threesome shoe protectors from a stash he kept in his Cherokee. In explanation he said, "Humor me. Suspicious death."

The younger of the two EMTs, a woman, said,

"Check." Her partner rolled his eyes. At his inexperienced partner, or at Sam, I couldn't tell.

Everyone but Kol was outside the barn again a few minutes later.

The EMT who had earlier said "Check" said "Deceased" to her colleagues. She said it as though it was professional jargon or private code, as though it meant something more than simply dead.

A different deputy added, "It's secure in there." Translation? The quick sweep of the barn had identified no one else inside, certainly no one who was a threat or in imminent danger. "Investigators are on the way." At that moment he recognized Lauren. "You the RP, ma'am? You found the body?"

"No," she said. "The reporting party would be my husband. He found the body." She introduced me to the deputy as though we'd all run into each other in the beer cooler at Liquor Mart during a marital dispute about whether to get a six of Bohemia or a six of Odell's Levity to go with that night's grilled chicken. I thought her voice had a chill to it.

"You live here? The building is yours, ma'am?"

"No," I interjected. "The barn belongs to our neighbor." I pointed at Adrienne's house. "She's in Israel."

After a couple of minutes of awkward silence the deputy who had pronounced the scene secure asked me if I knew the victim.

I said I did. He then asked if I knew the victim's name.

I said I did.

He waited a polite moment for me to reveal that name, pen poised over his notepad. Once he'd recognized my constipation, he said, "What is the victim's name?"

I'd said I was sorry but I couldn't say.

Lauren witnessed the odd little interview from a few steps away. She was apparently on hold with her call downtown; she lowered her phone from her ear and stepped forward to translate. She said, "He just told you in his own way that the victim is one of his patients. Because of doctor/patient privilege he won't reveal the name." She sighed. I thought her explanation sounded less than compassionate.

I said, "There may be some ID on the body. I didn't look." I was trying to be helpful. The truth was that I hadn't even tried to reach Kol's pocket. It had been suspended far above my head.

"Do we need a warrant to go in?" the deputy asked Lauren.

"This won't be my case," she said. She looked at me. "It is, literally and figuratively, too close to home." She looked back at the deputy. "I'll make a call."

"We wait," the deputy said.

I wondered if they'd noticed the fresh food in the barn refrigerator. Or if Sam had spotted something my untrained eyes had missed. *Probably.*

TWENTY-FOUR

LAUREN CLOSED her phone. She said, "Elliot Bell-haven"—Elliot was the chief deputy to the DA—"says we wait for a warrant. Patience. By the book. I assume everyone's been called."

Everyone meant investigators, forensics, the coroner, the DA's office, and a judge to issue the warrant.

The swell of adrenaline at the scene had drained away. The reservoir of testosterone, however, remained. It hung in the air the way the stench of a dead seal lingers at the beach.

The deputies began to mark off a big perimeter with crime-scene tape. The rest of the gang, accustomed to being in situations that require them to kill long periods of time, began to kill some time. They all knew from experience that the process of gaining permission to enter a crime scene could be laborious, especially on a weekend. The EMTs opened the doors to their truck, tuned the radio to KBCO, and upped the volume to help fill the void.

The first music we heard blaring from the speakers was the last few bars of "Mr. Tambourine Man" by the Byrds. After it concluded, a second or two of dead air transitioned into some of the same second Neko Case album that had recently caused Lauren such discomfort on her iPod.

I watched my wife's face as the dead air was annihilated by Case's powerful voice. Lauren marched over and whispered something to the older of the two paramedics. He looked up at her—I think to judge whether or not she was serious—and asked a question. She replied with a nod and a single word. I think the word was "off." He seemed to wait for her to continue, to offer him some explanation. When she didn't, he leaned inside the cab and flicked off the radio.

I'm sure that the assembled personnel thought my wife was being a prude about the boys playing music on the rig radio while a vic hung dead in the nearby building.

I knew differently. Lauren might have thought that the music was disrespectful, even callous. But out here in the country, outside the public view, she would have swallowed her judgment, bit her tongue, and allowed the paramedics and the cops to have their tunes until the work resumed. Lauren had asked them to turn off the radio because the sounds were hurting her brain.

She needed to be thinking clearly. She was concerned she couldn't think clearly while coping with whatever it was that would be playing on KBCO.

*   *   *

I went inside the house and started some coffee. While the coffee dripped I put together a cooler full of soft drinks and bottled water and filled it with ice.

While I found a place in the shade for the cooler I overheard a newly arrived sheriff's investigator making a loud case to Lauren that I had the legal right to grant law enforcement access to the barn since I was the owner's proxy while she was away.

"It's a gray area," she said. "There's no need to rush any of this. Elliot's position is clear. If we can't get Adrienne—she's the homeowner; it's her barn—on the phone for permission, we wait for a warrant. Nobody wants to risk any of this. Let's do it right."

I went back into the house to retrieve the coffee. I recognized that if I wanted some privacy to talk with Adrienne, calling her from inside my own home while Lauren was occupied outside felt like the best option. The time difference between Boulder and Tel Aviv or Jerusalem was nine or ten hours. Simple arithmetic told me that although it was late, it wasn't the middle of the night in Israel. I had Adrienne's travel itinerary someplace in the house and figured I could track her down at her hotel before she went to bed, but I decided to take the path of least resistance and speed-dialed her first on her mobile phone. It was a shot in the dark—I didn't know if she was carrying a phone that would work in Israel.

Half a world away Adrienne answered after two rings. Her greeting, "I just stepped away from a lovely dinner so you'd better not be calling to say hi. Did my damn house burn down? Did it?" From her tone I couldn't tell whether she'd be happier if the answer was "yes" or if the answer was "no." As usual, Adrienne made me smile.

I managed to get her focused on the strange developments in Spanish Hills and from the privacy of my kitchen I explained the situation, including details—like the disappearing bandanna—that I hadn't shared with the police who were assembled outside. A surgeon by training, Adrienne wasn't easily flustered during crises. It was clear from her reaction to my recitation that as long as the body hanging from the rafter in the barn was a stranger to her she wasn't going to lose any holiday sleep over the odd circumstances that were developing half a planet away in Boulder.

She cut right to the chase when I asked her whether she wanted to permit the police access to the barn. "It's your dead patient, so it's your call. If you want to delay them for some reason, that's cool. Put somebody on the phone and I'll tell them I want a warrant. If you want me to give them permission, I'll give them permission. What's it gonna be? Dessert is calling."

Making the cops wait for a warrant wasn't going to gain me any advantage. "I'll put Lauren on. Go ahead and tell her to let them in. You guys having a good time?"

"The best," she said. "Be quick though. I was serious—dessert is on the way. Tell me something—in Boulder, I don't like honey, or raisins, or nuts. Here, I can't get enough of 'em. Dates, too. Dates? Why is that?"

"I don't know, Adrienne. Maybe it's the place."

"Back home I'm not any more of a Jew than you are. I'd get lost if I had to drive to temple. So how come when I'm here I feel like a Jew? How does that work?"

"Is it a good thing, Adrienne?"

She laughed. "Good question, *bubela*. Yes, it's a good thing. A very good thing. We'll need to see if it sticks once I'm home. If it does maybe I'll get bat mitzvahed. Though I'd probably need to find me a very, very, very reformed rabbi."

Adrienne's personal life was sometimes a confused mess. Secret though? Hardly. "Am I invited?"

"You have to ask?"

"I'm walking outside right now to find Lauren so you can give her verbal permission to do the search."

"Before you do," she said, "two things. Call Cozier. That's an order. You're going to need someone to watch your back."

Adrienne and Cozy had been an item a few years back. That was shortly before she and Cozy's ex-wife had become an item. She knew how good a lawyer he was. "Done already. He has my back. What's the second thing?"

"After they're gone? The cops, I mean—open the doors and windows in the barn. Air it out. I don't want to smell the guy when I get home. You understand?"

"He's"— I couldn't think of a better word —"fresh. But you got it. When they let me, I'll air it all out. Be safe. Love to Jonas." I walked outside and spied Lauren across the way peering through the front window of the barn. I strolled over and handed her the phone. I said, "It's Adrienne."

She looked me in the eyes and made a thumbs-up gesture and quickly changed it to a thumbs-down gesture. She wanted to know which it was.

I offered the thumbs-up gesture in reply. My wife mouthed, "Thank you." Into the phone she said, "Hi, Adrienne. Alan told you about our problem?"

She made eye contact with Sam. He was standing a dozen steps away. After ten more seconds she gave him the thumbs-up sign. He nodded to her and then he looked at me. His gaze, I thought, was suspicious.

I could tell he had a dozen questions for me. I knew my friend, and I knew what question would be number one: Why had I gone into the barn?

"McClelland had left a bandanna on the barn door. That's why I went in. A bandanna, just like with Cicero. You remember that, don't you? What he did all those years ago? Don't you remember?"

"Let's say I do. Where is the bandanna from the barn door, Alan?"

"When I came back out and looked again, it was gone."

"It was gone?"

"Yes, I think he took it."

"He took it? Where is he?"

"I don't know."

"Ah," Sam would say.

TWENTY-FIVE

KIRSTEN'S ARRIVAL changed the atmosphere. She pulled me away from any proximity to the law-enforcement types and suggested we talk in her car—she didn't want to risk being overheard at my house. I dangled some keys and suggested Adrienne's home instead. I had to go over there anyway—given what had happened in the barn, I knew prudence dictated that I ensure that no poachers had camped out in Adrienne's place since she'd left for Israel.

I did a quick tour of the house and found nothing worrisome. Kirsten and I settled at the table that Peter had built for his family's kitchen. Emily curled up at Kirsten's feet. I'd already caught her up on what I'd found in the barn, and I was trying to explain the bandanna. "Emily's our second Bouvier," I explained to Kirsten. "The first one was Cicero. Shortly after I started seeing Michael McClelland for treatment, and shortly after I'd started dating Lauren, Cicero went missing. It wasn't like her; she just disappeared one day.

I eventually found her tied outside my house with a piece of twine. Someone had shaved her hair in a one-inch band around her neck and put a bandanna in place over her collar. Other than that, she was fine. It was a message to me—a warning—from McClelland about what had been going on. That's why what he did today is important."

"This morning, after the bike ride, that's what you saw on the front doors of the barn? A bandanna?"

"Not right away. After you left I went downtown and tried to find the guy—"

"What guy?"

"Well, the dead guy. The guy who is hanging in the barn. His name is Kol Cruz. He's the same guy you wanted permission to talk to about the bloody nose. The blood-on-my-shoes guy from last week?"

After digesting the implications, she said, "That complicates things."

It wasn't exactly what I was hoping to hear. "It turns out the phone number he had given me a few weeks ago no longer works, so I went to his loft to ask him if he'd agree to talk to you and maybe to the police. I thought if he could explain how I got the blood on my shoe it would make life easier for me with Lauren and Sam."

"I assume he wasn't home."

I thought she was being sardonic but I wasn't sure. "He'd apparently given me a fake address. The loft where he said he lives has never been occupied. It's not his."

"You wonder . . . why he might do that?"

"People lie to their therapists all the time." Kirsten looked surprised. "What? They don't lie to their lawyers?"

Her delay in answering was pregnant. "Yes, they do. People lie to their lawyers all the time." She raised her eyebrows a few millimeters. "Then you came back home and you saw the bandanna on the barn. And immediately it felt like . . . a private message?"

"Because of the history with McClelland—the bandanna around Cicero's neck? Yeah, it felt like a private message. At first I ran inside and checked on the dogs. After I saw they were okay I decided that the bandanna was telling me to go inside the barn."

She raised her eyebrows. "It was that clear to you?"

"What else could it have meant?"

She ignored my question. "You expected to . . . find what?"

"McClelland. Or something related to him. Something like the note we found this morning. Another taunt. The next step in his provocation. That's his nature. That's what he did last time. He escalates."

"You often check the barn when Adrienne is out of town?"

"I can't remember the last time I was in there. Years, probably. Adrienne doesn't use it."

"And Lauren knows that you don't usually go in there?"

"Yes," I said. I knew that Kirsten's question wasn't whether my wife knew that I didn't go in the barn, it was whether the deputy DA knew that I didn't go in the barn.

"Okay. You went into a building that you admit you never visit. Inside you found a patient of yours—a patient you had just made a special trip downtown to find—hanging dead from a rafter?"

The scenario sounded worse coming from Kirsten's lips than it did banging around in my head. "You should know something else," I said. "The whole thing with Michael McClelland started with the suicide of one of my patients, too."

"Go on."

"The first time it was Michael's sister who died. She was my patient. He had raped her."

Kirsten sat back on her chair. She said, "Is any of this going to be in the old police record? Will I be able to corroborate what you're telling me?"

Why, I wondered, *do you need to corroborate it?* "The suicide will, obviously. What McClelland did to her? No. The bandanna? Cicero wasn't really hurt. It was just a taunt, like the note today. But Lauren suggested I give the bandanna to Sam. And I think I did."

"You think?"

"I think. It was a long time ago."

"But you were sure it was McClelland who took your dog?"

"Yes. I've always been sure it was him."

"And you feel the same way today? McClelland left the bandanna?"

"Absolutely. I can't figure out the connection between Kol and McClelland. Why would Kol kill himself in a barn next door to my house? Why would McClelland announce Kol's suicide by putting a bandanna on the door?"

"Yes?" Kirsten said.

"It makes no sense," I said. "But there has to be a link between them."

It wasn't what she was hoping to hear. "Do either Sam or Lauren know that this guy in the barn is the same patient who was covered with blood in your waiting room?"

"I told Sam that one of my patients had been bleeding in the waiting room. And he's already guessed that the suicide victim is one of my patients. He doesn't know they're the same guy, yet. He'll put it together, though. Sam's good."

"Which means that Sam—who has already tied his missing grand jury witness's purse to your office—is now going to tie this suicide victim to your office. Which gives him a nexus between the grand jury witness and the suicide in the barn."

"How? I don't follow you."

"The blood on your shoe, remember? Purse at your office? Blood in your office? Dead patient in the barn? If it turns out there's the same blood everywhere, Sam will connect those dots."

She was right. "I didn't tell the police about the bandanna, Kirsten."

"Or Lauren?"

"Or Lauren."

She shrugged. "Because there is no bandanna, right?"

"There was."

"I suspect you're going to have a hard time convincing anybody of that now. It's going to sound contrived." Her voice grew soft, almost tender as she added, "They're going to think you made it up."

"I should have told them right away."

"It wouldn't have made any difference. They still would have thought it was contrived."

"I had no reason to think the bandanna would disappear. I intentionally didn't touch it."

"I know," she said. I felt more relieved by that than I should have—the fact that my lawyer believed me wasn't really much of a victory.

"It's hard to describe what I felt when I looked back over there and the bandanna was gone. After the shock, and then after the anger and frustration were gone, I had this feeling of . . . almost admiration. Michael McClelland is setting this up beautifully."

"Yes," she said. "Alan?"

"Yeah?"

"Just what is it he's setting up?"

I thought about it for a moment before I said, "I don't know. Something ugly."

My lawyer shivered as though she had a sudden chill.

TWENTY-SIX

MY CELL rang. I checked the screen. Sam. He knew I was inside Adrienne's house talking with my lawyer. We'd walked right past him as we crossed the lane.

To Kirsten I said, "This will take just a second." Into the phone, I said, "Yes."

"I'm at the door. I need to ask you something."

Dangerous ground. *Did my friend want to ask me something, or did the police detective want a free shot at me?* I could think of only one way to find out.

I covered the microphone and said, "It's Sam." Then I lifted my thumb and said, "My attorney's sitting right beside me, Sam. She can hear what you want to ask."

"I got no problem with that."

I nodded for Kirsten's benefit before I said, "The door's unlocked. Come on in."

"He has a question," I said to Kirsten. "He's fine asking it in front of you."

"As though he has a choice," she said without any apparent attitude. She leaned toward me and lowered her voice.

"I'm allowing him in because I want to hear his question, not because I want him to hear your answer. Do you understand the difference?"

I nodded. I was listening for the sound of Sam opening the door. It hadn't happened.

Kirsten said, "This death is the sheriff's, not Sam's. It's county, not city. He's here as a courtesy, probably fishing for more evidence that ties this back to your office and that damn purse."

The door opened. Emily leapt up and raced toward the front of the house. She wasn't barking—she knew it was Sam.

Kirsten reached up and touched my face, turning my chin toward her. She waited until I was looking in her eyes. "When I say that's it, that's it. You shut up. Yes?"

"Yes," I said.

After Sam was done greeting Emily at the front door, he found us in the kitchen. He had his notebook in one hand, a pen in the other. "Counselor," he said to Kirsten.

She flattened her mouth into a replica of a smile. "Detective," she said. "You realize that this ends when I say it ends. We're on the same page?"

Sam put the pen and the notebook into his left hand and rubbed his right eye with the knuckles on the back of his right hand. I'd seen him do it many times before and it always seemed he did it with enough force to cause pain. "Yeah," he said. Then he yawned. I thought that the yawn was editorial until he contorted his face trying to stifle it. When he recognized that his effort to kill the yawn was futile, he just went ahead and leaned into it. After it was over, he looked up at the ceiling before he looked at me.

"As far as the work I'm doing is concerned our friendship has become toxic." He paused to let the final word sink in. "The purse in the yard, the forensics from your office, this guy hanging dead in your neighbor's barn. It's all too much for the DA to ignore. She knows you and I are friends, and she's ordered me to stand down temporarily so that our friendship doesn't compromise the . . . investigation. I got permission to come in here to tell you that myself. That's why I'm here."

"I appreciate that. Thank you." I wasn't surprised that Sam was being sent to the bench. I was surprised that he was telling me about it in person.

Sam lowered his voice. "Now that I'm here, there's something else I want to say."

I glanced at Kirsten in time to watch her raise her eyebrows.

"The rafter the vic is hanging from?" Sam said. "It is eighteen feet, six and three-sixteenths inches—give or take—above the floor of the barn."

"If you say so," I said.

Kirsten touched my arm. It was a caution.

"You didn't happen to move anything when you were in there?" Sam asked.

I opened my mouth. Kirsten squeezed my wrist. Her fingernails found flesh. "Don't even think about answering that," she said. "Move on, Detective. You know better. I'm not predisposed to let this continue."

Sam bit his lower lip. I knew him well enough to know that he'd done it to keep a grin from erupting. Kirsten might not be predisposed to let him continue, but she hadn't stopped him. In his mind he was up one goal. In Sam's brand of hockey that's a good lead.

"I apologize," he said.

"Go on," my lawyer said.

Sam closed his eyes for a couple of seconds while he shook his head in slow motion. I could tell he was trying hard to be nice and that being nice to a defense attorney in the current circumstance was requiring a monumental effort. I also knew he was taking a risk with me right then, and I was more inclined to feel grateful than suspicious.

Kirsten's sharp nails were telling me that she didn't share that bias.

"Okay, I'll try again. This is shaky ground. It is, Ms. Lord, isn't it?"

Kirsten didn't respond. Where this kind of adversarial waltz was concerned she was an experienced dancer and saw the moves Sam was planning before he made them. He was going to have to try harder to get her to misstep.

"Assuming, Alan, that you didn't move anything when you were in there, like"—at that point he suddenly sped up his cadence, rushing to finish his thought before Kirsten could voice an objection—"let's say, a very long ladder that's currently hanging on a couple of big hooks just below the windows on the wall. Assuming you—"

"Detective Purdy, I—"

"Assuming you didn't do something like that—then how in the hell did the vic get up to that rafter in the first place to tie off the rope before he jumped?"

I looked at Kirsten. She was torn on how to counsel me. She kept her eyes on Sam as she thought it through, but eventually she said to me, "Don't answer that one either."

I think she chose it because it was the default option.

Sam stared at my befuddled face. Kirsten turned toward me too. It didn't take a genius to know that I didn't actually have a ready answer to Sam's question.

He nodded at me with satisfaction in his eyes. He had either just learned exactly what he had hoped to learn by intruding on my meeting with my attorney, or he'd received an unexpected bonus.

Sam's question was something I hadn't considered, and it was much more intriguing to me than the duel I was witnessing between him and Kirsten. *So how the hell,* I was wondering, *did Kol get up there?*

"If there's something you're not telling me, Alan, now would be a good time. A very good time," Sam said.

My lawyer stood up from her chair as though she were popping up from behind the defense table to announce a particularly strenuous objection. She took a step forward, placing herself physically between me and my best friend. "This interview, or whatever it is, is over," she said. She compressed an impressive amount of authority into her voice.

Sam put his pen and pad back into his shirt pocket. He hadn't written a single word during our meeting, had probably never intended to. The implements were props.

He ignored Kirsten's admonition about the end of the meeting, as I assumed he would. Good cops, like good shrinks, and good lawyers, run stop signs. "Thing is? Without a ladder somebody who wanted to hang himself would have had to climb up one of those original old barn posts like a telephone lineman, and then shimmy across toward the middle of the gable on one of those big ol' angled beams—I think they're oak; you think they're oak? Whatever, nice old wood—while he was hanging upside down up there like some kind of big monkey. I don't see it coming down that way. Was your patient a circus acrobat or something like that?"

He didn't wait for a reply from me, or for a fresh admonition from Kirsten. He tipped an imaginary cap to her and said, "I'm sorry for the intrusion."

I waited until the front door had closed before I said, "He didn't come over here to tell me he was off the case. He knew Lauren would tell me that later. He didn't come over here to ask me what I did in the barn. He came over here to tell me something else."

"That's what you're thinking?"

It was apparent that Kirsten didn't share my assessment of what had just happened. I pressed my case. "Sam isn't buying the suicide," I said.

"I got that. But that wasn't Sam's purpose with this little show."

"What was?"

"He was trying to see what bait you were going to snap at."

"I didn't say a thing."

"You didn't have to. You should have seen your face when he asked you about the ladder. I've been in the prosecutor's shoes, Alan. I know how it's done. At this stage of the game, a suspect doesn't have to speak in order to answer. He wasn't looking for anything he could use in court; he was looking for a hint on where to look next."

"He's off the investigation."

"I barely know the man, Alan, and I know that whether or not he's officially assigned to this case any longer, he's not off this investigation."

She was right. I said, "I was that obvious?" I knew I had been. With another cop, I would've been better able to keep a therapist's visage. Not with Sam. With Sam, the doors and windows were usually open.

"When we're all done with this," Kirsten said, "I have some girlfriends who would love to play a little high-stakes poker with you. For now please, please forget that Sam's your friend. He's a cop. You're a suspect in the investigation of a suspicious death. There are lots of ways for cops to play a suspect. You just witnessed one of them. You said it yourself—Sam Purdy is good. I don't disagree."

"A suspect?" I'd been struggling with the personal responsibility I was feeling that one of my patients had committed suicide. I had been worried about the effect of Kol's death on the viability of my clinical practice. I'd started worrying about financial liability and the long-term impact on my family.

Kirsten said, "A person of interest, if you're a fan of euphemisms."

I hadn't been worrying about criminal responsibility.

"Read between the lines," she said. "If Sam's not buying suicide, he's talking homicide. I think we can agree to rule out accident unless you have some great news you've been keeping from me about your patient and high-stakes sexual asphyxia."

I had actually been allowing myself the luxury of believing that Kol's murder—if Sam was right—would absolve me of responsibility for failing to anticipate his suicide. Kirsten was insisting I attend to a much more sinister scenario.

"Sam knows I wouldn't kill anyone." After a second I added, "Like that."

Her eyes grew wide. I saw the frailty in my argument instantly.

"Why would I kill Kol?" I asked.

She leaned forward. "They know you knew the victim, right? Sam's already guessed he was your patient. Your wife knows that the body was discovered in a building you had no good reason to enter. Sam may or may not know that this guy is the same patient who had the volcanic nosebleed in your waiting room. He will soon."

"Yes," I said. "That means—"

She held up a hand and shook her head. "I'll tell you what it means: When homicide is a consideration, the police keep an eye out for perpetrators. Killers. Suspects. Persons of interest. You knew the victim. You found the body. You were here alone around the likely time of death. You had access to the crime scene. Like it or not, Alan, you're on their radar. Currently, the brightest green blip."

I opened my mouth to argue. I was going to argue motive.

The cops might have been able to hang me with means, and maybe with opportunity. But what reason could I possibly have for killing my own patient?

I paused, my mouth open, as Kol's voice in my head—unbidden—provided me with more reason to be cautious. *"I mean it's not like what happened with . : . your dad."*

I had a motive. A motive I didn't want to discuss with Kirsten, or with anybody else.

She rescued me from the impasse in my internal dialogue. She said, "Remember, I know what it's like to be a target." She allowed that thought to pool on the surface and begin to penetrate my porous shell before she continued. "It's like recognizing that someone you love has died. The first stage is denial."

TWENTY-SEVEN

LAUREN AND I entered the twilight of the day under the jointly constructed pretense that the latest series of marital earthquakes hadn't done any structural damage.

Neither of us was inclined to cook but our decision to have a pizza delivered wasn't well considered. We hadn't bothered to warn the sheriff's deputy parked outside to expect a visitor from Abo's. When the delivery guy drove his big Ford pickup down the lane as though he were trying to lock in the best time in the quarter-mile at Bandimere, he blew right past the deputy's SUV. Neither Lauren nor I saw what happened next, but when the knock came at our door, the deputy was standing a few steps behind the pizza delivery guy with his hand hovering close to his holstered handgun.

The pizza guy's eyes had that red-lights-in-the-rearview-mirror look.

The cop suggested that the next time we were expecting someone we should—maybe—let him know in advance.

After dinner—we'd ordered enough for the deputy, too—Lauren took Grace away for a bath and twenty minutes later handed me a warm, pink, sweet-smelling little girl in fresh pajamas. Her flannel pj's were covered with puppies jumping over rainbows on their way to distant planets. As I cradled my sleepy daughter against my chest on the amble down the hall to her room, I watched Lauren retreat to the master bedroom. She was walking slowly, staying close to the wall—she didn't want to limp or lose her balance in front of Grace.

We liked to think we fooled our daughter. We knew we didn't.

Gracie and I laughed and cuddled. She helped me read the night's stories before I tucked her into bed. I consoled myself that we may have succeeded in insulating her from evil for one more day.

The day had been warm, and the evening was too. From the bedroom door I could see that Lauren was enjoying the light breeze on one of the two narrow chaises on the small deck outside our bedroom. Her shoulders were covered in a chenille throw I'd given her for Christmas the previous December. The throw was the color of the *crema* that forms on top of a well-crafted cup of espresso. That night, in the muted light on the deck, her black hair was the coffee.

Before joining her outside I found the shoe box with her bong on the high shelf in the closet. I carried the bong to the kitchen and added water and a few fresh flutes of lemon peel to the reservoir. I splashed a little Zinfandel port—Lauren had recently discovered she had a taste for it—into a glass and carried everything back to the bedroom. I also retrieved her tiny stash of dried buds from a locked drawer in her dressing table, and grabbed a disposable lighter.

I placed everything on a table between the two chaises before I handed her the port. She took a small sip. After a slow minute I lifted the bong and offered it to her.

"No," she said. I thought she'd spoken sharply but allowed that it may have been hypersensitivity on my part. It had been the type of day that could have left me prone to that vulnerability. Two beats passed before she added, "Thank you. I know you're trying to help. But I think I've explained that I don't think it's something I should do anymore. It's not something I'm *going* to do anymore. Respect that, okay? Please."

She had explained. But she hadn't disposed of the bong, or flushed her stash down the toilet. To me, that indicated ambivalence. I could have argued that point with her, but I wasn't that stupid. Or at least not quite that stupid.

"Gracie's in dreamland," I said. "Playing with Teryl all day wiped her out. She's sound asleep. She'll never know." I touched her on the arm. "Even if she does figure it out we can find a way to explain it to her. It's obvious you're in pain. Nothing else seems to help as much as the dope does."

Lauren shook her head, her eyes focused on the shallow moonlight above the Divide, not on me. She sighed with frustration before she continued. "I have it . . . under control right now. Do I look like I'm in pain?"

Like "Does this dress make me look fat?" it was not a question that begged an answer in the affirmative. "You did earlier," I said, straddling the fence she seemed intent on erecting between us.

"Maybe I was, but I'm managing okay right now. Nice night," she said.

"Better than the day that preceded it," I said. I was trying to be sardonic, and I was also trying to goad us to confront the mastodon that had edged its way into our relationship that afternoon.

She sipped some port and wetted her lips with her tongue before she said, "We're in difficult places. Professionally. Both of us. Until we know better what's what with all this, we probably shouldn't talk about it."

Professionally? Did Lauren really think this was just a professional problem?

Her words were relatively benign, her argument somewhat reasonable. But I felt the fissure between us quake into a chasm. My concern about her and me was much more personal than professional.

I considered the possibility that I was catastrophizing and that the day had jaded my perspective. "We've always been able to find ways to talk about things without . . . being too specific," I said. "We can do that same dance. We can do it right now. We're good at it. I think it's important. Essential even."

"This time is different," she replied with no hint of fresh contemplation. "This thing today, it involves both of us. Professionally, I mean. Your patient, my case. Usually it's just one of us that has to do the confidentiality two-step. Right now, it's both of us. That makes it trickier."

"Your case? You won't be involved with what happened here today—not for something that took place right next door. And certainly not if it's even tangentially related to your husband. As—I admit—it appears to be. If it actually turns out there was a crime involved, somebody else in the office will handle this."

I waited for her to say, "Of course." She didn't. That's when I knew that the case she was referring to wasn't just Kol. Kirsten had identified the blood on my shoe as the nexus. Apparently, she'd been right. I asked, "Lauren, does the man who died in the barn have something to do with the other case, the one with Sam?"

I meant the grand jury case, of course, but I couldn't say it. Lauren wouldn't acknowledge the grand jury case. If I wanted to talk about the grand jury, I had to couch my words in code.

"You know I can't talk about things that I can't . . . talk about," she said. She took a long draw from the port, leaving only an opaque puddle in the bottom of the glass. Her purple eyes were the color of the port stain. The color of the night sky.

She reached over and took my hand. "I'm sorry about your patient. It has to be hard."

Her words felt like a cold compress. The late-day gravel-and-honey timbre that the hour and her fatigue had allowed into her voice was something that I always associated with intimacy. I sensed some welcome lift beneath my wings.

"It is hard," I acknowledged. "Thanks."

Lauren shifted her weight, bent a leg, straightened it. Did it all again. It was an effort to interfere with spasticity in her calf or her quad or her hamstrings. I knew what she was doing with her leg was merely a gesture; it wouldn't help. She did many useless things to try to temper the whims of multiple sclerosis. Futile calisthenics was only one of them. Ironically, smoking dope from a lemon-scented bong on our deck facing the Front Range had been one of the few useful ones.

When she spoke again her voice was lower. And less certain. "Were you kidding a minute ago? About what you said?" she asked.

"What I said about what?"

"About the man who died in the barn."

"Jesus, no. I was hoping you'd tell me if he was somehow related to what you've been doing with Sam. I'm trying to figure out all the ways this is complicated. If it came across as a joke, I apologize."

She glanced over at me, disbelief painted on her brow like a tattoo. "You could tell me how you knew the person in the barn if that person wasn't one of your patients, right?"

"Yes."

She swung her legs over the edge of the chaise. She put her left hand on my knee. "Okay then. Will you tell me how you knew that person?"

Lauren was asking me to tell her a story by refusing to tell her a story. Where the grand jury was concerned I had asked her to do the same. I played along. I said, "I'm sorry, I can't . . . tell you."

With that denial I had just informed my wife that Kol was my patient. I considered it no big deal; within moments of getting back home after dropping Grace off at Teryl's house, Lauren had figured out that the dead guy in the barn was my patient. I had done nothing since to dissuade her. Given that she had already guessed, I was wondering why she wanted me to make the indirect admission aloud. I couldn't figure it out. I said, "I wish I could tell you more."

She stood suddenly, leaving her glass on the table. Then she turned her back to me, cocked out one hip, and rested her elbows on the deck railing. "I don't know what's going on, Alan, but I don't like it. I don't know why you're being this way with me. But with everything that's happened—that's happening—it makes me uneasy about . . . whatever else you might not be telling me."

I stood, too. I was suspecting that she'd begun alluding to Michael McClelland's escape from custody and the note he'd left on our door, but I wasn't sure. *And what way was I being with her?* I didn't know the answer to that. I knew I felt an immediate need to close the gap between us, so I stepped closer and put my arms around her from behind.

She didn't return my embrace. She kept her arms by her sides, her elbows bent, her hands up near her neck. All in all, it was a fine posture for a woman concerned she was about to be garroted.

"They'll catch him," I said. I was fishing and I knew it.

She pulled away and looked back over her shoulder. "You think I'm worried about Michael right now, don't you? The note? That that's what I'm talking about?" Her eyes tightened into a squint. "You . . . really don't know about this . . . person today?"

Her face told me that I wasn't the only one who was baffled. I shook my head. I was feeling as off-balance and uninformed as I'd ever felt in my life. "No, I guess maybe I don't," I said. I didn't even know what I didn't know. I was pretty confident I wasn't going to enjoy discovering it, whatever it was.

"The person hanging in the barn today? The one you've been implying was your patient?"

She seemed to want a response. I said, "He was my patient."

"That wasn't a man, sweets. It was a woman."

"No, it wasn't," I said, blurting the words, yet knowing in my marrow that my protest was futile. *A woman? Kol?*

In a soft I'm-so-sorry-but-there-is-no–Santa Claus voice, Lauren said, "Breasts, vagina. All the usual signs. She was all woman, Alan."

TWENTY-EIGHT

I STARED past Lauren toward the mountains, certain that she could spot the confusion persisting in my eyes. Any cushion was gone from her tone when she added, "If you don't believe me, go ahead and ask Scott."

Scott Truscott was the assistant medical examiner. An old boss of mine. A competent, straight-shooting guy. He was among the second wave of responders to the scene. Most likely he would have been the first to open or remove any of Kol's clothing. Scott didn't miss much. He certainly wouldn't have made an error on Kol's sex.

Then I thought, *What difference does it make? Other than making me look more incompetent, what difference does it make?* So Kol had disguised his, or her, gender with me. It didn't change anything. Boy or girl, dead was dead.

I stammered, "His name was—" I stopped myself. Technically, I couldn't reveal my patient's name to Lauren.

Lauren felt no such constraint. She said, "*Her* name

was Nicole Cruz, sweetie. She may not have been the most feminine thing on the planet, but she was a girl."

My wife was waiting for me to react. I tried to keep my face impassive, my eyes in therapeutic neutral.

Lauren said, "You knew your patient's name, didn't you?"

I didn't reply at first. Hinting at what I knew would inevitably open the door to what I didn't know. That path didn't seem likely to ameliorate my disadvantage. "You would think so," I said, finally.

What happened next left me reeling.

Lauren emptied the water from the bong over the deck railing. I followed her inside as she returned the bag of dope to her dressing table. She dug into her purse—the one she carried most days to work—and pulled out a small pump-bottle similar to the one we used for temporary anesthesia when Grace had a sore throat.

She held it up for me to read the label. I didn't recognize the bottle. "Sativex," it read.

"I've been using this," she said. "For the pain in my legs. It works."

This wasn't an oh-by-the-way moment. I recognized that she was making an admission of some kind—moving something with some serious specific gravity from the category of "secret" back to the category of "private." I didn't know if it was an admission of trust on her part, an acknowledgment of a prior mistrust, or—worst of all—a declaration that the issue of trust between us no longer mattered.

That last thought was the one that left me reeling.

"What is it?" I asked, trying to sound nonchalant. "Something new?"

She extended her arm. I took the small container from her hand. My eyes found tiny type on the label that read "delta-9-tetrahydrocannabinol." I recognized the "c-a-n-n-a-b-i" part of the chemical name. The rest was gibberish.

Cannabinol? *Cannabis*? I asked, "Is this that stuff from Canada? The pharmaceutical marijuana spray?"

Months before Lauren and I had discussed the fact that the Canadian government had approved the use of cannabis spray for treatment of neuropathic pain in people with MS while the U.S. government, with the same scientific evidence, had not. Lauren's pain was neuropathic—her legs weren't damaged, but their nerves were conspiring with her central nervous system to read pain signals when none were being sent.

"Yes," she said.

"How did you get it?" I asked.

"Teresa has a friend in Vancouver with MS." Teresa, Lauren's little sister, lived in Seattle. She had plenty of friends in British Columbia and spent a lot of time in Vancouver. That one of her friends had MS was no big surprise—it's not a small club. "Her friend tried it—the Sativex—but it didn't work for her. Teresa asked her friend if I could try whatever she had left. T gave it to me when I visited her in Seattle last month. It worked.

I've been using it now for a little over a month. I sent her friend some money to keep the prescription . . . active; she's been extremely kind about it."

I looked at the little container again. The question in my head was "Why didn't you tell me sooner?" I shoved it into a cage and bolted the gate shut. Instead I asked, "How do you use it?"

"I spray it below my tongue, or inside my cheeks. Two sprays are usually good. Sometimes three."

"And it works?"

She nodded. "It's been great. Remarkable."

The other question blew out the lock and escaped the cage. "Why didn't you tell me before now?"

"I'm not sure," she said. "I wasn't sure it would work, and I'm a little ashamed about doing it, I guess. I didn't want to draw you into it. By having it in the house I'm actually committing . . ."

A federal felony? I handed the small bottle back to her. "This is a lot riskier than taking a couple of hits on your bong."

"I know," she said. She crinkled up her nose and smiled. "It works, Alan. It *works.* And I'm able to work. Think about that. Think about what that means for me."

"That's great," I said. But I felt as much anger and confusion as joy. I was angry that she hadn't trusted me. And I was angry that she'd made a decision that could put our family's future in jeopardy. And that she'd done it without even consulting me.

Had she asked me, what would I have said? I would have said, "If you think it will help, go for it." I should have had that vote. She hadn't concurred, obviously.

She started to walk away. It was probably best that one of us leave before I said something I would regret. But she stopped after a solitary step. She looked my way for a split second. "The grand jury is on hold," she said.

"I'm sorry. I know how much it's meant to you to be part of that."

"Even when it gets going again I probably won't be involved. The DA may have to give the whole thing over to a special prosecutor from another jurisdiction. The conflict of interest is too great."

"Sam told me today that he's been sidelined, too. Is it all because of me?" I said. The clarification wasn't necessary. I was filling the air with words. And a small prayer.

"Yes," she said. The prayer had been that she would say, "No, because of us. McClelland is 'us.'" But she wasn't interested in putting any sugar in the medicine for my benefit. For now she felt her latest travails were because of me.

"I'm sorry," I said again.

She took another step. Again, she stopped. She should have come closer to me then, but she didn't. She had moved farther away. I thought, *She's putting some distance between us.*

"Are you scared?" she asked.

I silently ticked through the long litany of my current

fears before I said, "About? My dead patient? The damn purse? McClelland?"

"Him. Michael."

I didn't like that she called him "Michael." "Yes, yes. I'm . . . scared. He's devious . . . He's dangerous. I worry about you and Grace. What he might do. Everything."

"Me too," she said. She was examining the label on the Sativex as she continued. "Since I'm not going to be working anymore—at least for a while—I've been thinking about taking Gracie someplace, you know . . . someplace safe, until it's clear exactly what . . . he's up to."

It turned out that I had been right: Lauren had been creating distance. The realization, along with her announcement that she was thinking about leaving Boulder with Grace, made me feel as though my heart was being deprived of blood.

I reminded myself I'd been considering the same thing. My voice under control, I asked, "Because of McClelland?"

"Michael's so unpredictable," she said. "You said so yourself. We have to be prudent, Alan. As parents."

"Yes," I said. *Prudent. Parents.*

"I couldn't live with myself if he . . ." She allowed the unspeakable fear to spill onto the floor and puddle between us.

I said, "He probably knows where everyone in your family lives." Why I said that, I don't know. Was it argument? Hardly. Plea? Partly. More words in the air? Probably. But it was no small prayer. The last one had been ignored. Whatever deity was supposed to be taking notes on my need for divine intervention was apparently on a latte break.

"I was thinking of taking her to . . . the beach someplace. To decompress. I'm sure she's picking up our . . . tension. Concern, whatever. I could use that, too. Since I'm not working . . ."

"The beach?" *The fucking beach?*

"Maybe Bimini."

Bimini? Have you ever spoken the word "Bimini" to me? No, she hadn't. *The Bahamas? Maybe,* I thought. *Maybe.* But then again, maybe not. Hawaii, yes. The Caribbean, Mexico—yes. Other islands, other beaches. But certainly not Bimini.

"You think that's necessary, Lauren?"

"You don't?" she fired back. The ammo was softened by framing the issue as Grace's welfare, but there was more explosive power than she'd intended in the shot. The effect was a marshmallow fired from a howitzer. I felt it bruise my bones.

I knew that with my "You think that's necessary?" query I'd invited my wife's retort. But I recognized hers as one of those questions without a correct answer. If I agreed that it was necessary to take my daughter to a faraway island for her safety, I was granting Lauren license. If I disagreed? I was the imprudent parent.

"Bimini?" I said.

"The season's ending. I could probably find someplace cheap."

So this is about money? I thought. I was momentarily proud of myself for not saying it aloud. Then I felt a secondary impact from the blow she'd launched a moment or two before. I hadn't seen it circling above me—it struck hard and suddenly, like a boomerang that arrived from beyond my field of vision.

She wasn't asking me to go to Bimini with them. I said, "And I'll . . . what? Take care of the dogs, and the house?" *Keep an eye out for the bad guy?*

"You have your work still," she said. "I don't. I assumed you wouldn't be able to leave."

I was the losing contestant on the game show. The glamorous hostess was pointing out my consolation prize.

My work? Once news of my latest patient suicide hit the papers, I wasn't sure how much of my work I would have. I said, "And then, later on, once . . . it's clear what's going on . . . you'll come back home?"

How long is hesitation?

Hesitation is just long enough. That's how long she waited before she said, "Sure." Just long enough that I knew she'd hesitated.

That was the moment when I understood that I no longer understood.

TWENTY-NINE

BY TWENTY minutes after nine Lauren was asleep, Anvil curled at her knees. Emily stayed in the great room to keep me company as I drank room-temperature vodka and pondered how I could have possibly missed so much in the past month.

My wife was using pharmaceutical cannabis.

No problem. I could get my arms around that just fine. The small matter of importing illegal drugs across an international border? Federal policy on Sativex was inane. But she should have told me.

She was thinking of taking my daughter to Bimini. Hell, she wasn't just thinking about it. She was planning it.

I had believed that the patient of mine who had just killed himself in Adrienne's barn was a man. But he wasn't. Or she wasn't. I tried to recall if Kol—*Cole? Nicole?*—ever *said* that she was a man, or if it had been a misguided assumption on my part. I'd already replayed everything

I could remember about each of the psychotherapy sessions. She'd never said she was a man. She never intentionally misled me. Her maleness was an assumption on my part. My patient was slight. Effeminate? No, not really, but he wasn't notably masculine either.

I had considered the issue of sexual orientation during the brief treatment, and had entertained the possibility that it might still be in a fluid state. I would not have been surprised to hear that Kol had acted out more than a solitary preference during his journey toward sexual identity.

But what I wasn't actively questioning during the brief psychotherapy was Kol's gender. Kol had presented himself as a young male—"anthracite, man"—and the Kol-is-a-man assignment I'd made had been a reflexive, though admittedly not reflective, assumption on my part. It hadn't been a determination about which I recalled feeling any ambivalence. He dressed like a man. He wore no makeup. He had no obvious female sexual characteristics. The patient information form I ask patients to fill out prior to treatment doesn't even have a M/F option. I never thought I'd be in a circumstance where I couldn't tell. On the first day I saw him in my office—maybe even the first day I'd spoken with him on the phone—I'd assigned Kol a y chromosome and never felt any imperative to replace it with another x.

Funny how that works. One of my enduring guiding principles as a therapist has always been: don't assume. Well, I'd apparently run through the light at that corner as it shined bright red. How surprised could I really be that after I violated that principle, I ended up in a catastrophic wreck in the intersection?

Nights when I was up much later than my family I kept the portable close by so that the sound of the ringing phone wouldn't wake Grace or disturb Lauren. They both needed their sleep, Lauren often more desperately than Grace.

I was thinking about the change of seasons, albeit the wrong seasons, as the phone chirped. I was also thinking of getting more vodka. I'd had enough that the additional vodka seemed like a good idea. I hadn't quite had enough that I was completely unaware that it was actually a bad idea.

Seasons? In quasi-temperate zones that enjoy four—like Colorado—the heralds that announce the transitions from one season to the next differ depending on the time of year. There are constants among the changes. Temperature always varies—cool-to-warm, hot-to-cool, whatever. That's an immutable marker. The length of day is another fixed sign—it reliably stretches or contracts as the sun alters its position in the sky. The dramatic changes that occur with the approach of winter and the approach of summer are mostly about those two universal seasonal harbingers, temperature and light.

But the shoulder seasons, spring and fall, are different. They are almost always more subtle. Spring, for me, announces with color. Even before the chill of winter tempers, tender shoots emerge among the taupe grasses and the fresh butter and ripe lemon of the first crocuses peek through the snow. Above the ground the lime-flesh green of the first buds poke out on the early leafing trees and on the not-yet-fragrant lilacs.

The bare cusp of autumn isn't about color—the tarnished hues come later—it's about aroma. One unpredictable morning in early to mid-September, a morning before the aspen leaves have begun their golden transformation, I will walk outside before dawn with the dogs and smell the first floating molecules carrying the musk of decay. It's a whispered warning that one phase of life is in the process of disintegrating so that another might begin.

I was aware the night that Kol died that I was out of seasonal sync; I was thinking autumn thoughts during April, not seeing shades of green, but instead smelling the sour harbinger of decay.

A glance at the caller ID screen revealed two words: PAY PHONE. Had I been home alone I would have ignored the call and let voice mail do its thing. But the repeated ringing would wake my family and I picked up after half a ring, expecting bad news. No particular bad news. It was late and it had been a bad-news kind of day. A not-autumn day when the aroma was of decay.

"This'll be quick, so if anyone asks later on you can say that the call you received was a wrong number. I will deny this ever happened." The distinctive voice was Sam Purdy's. The volume wasn't as robust as usual, but it

wasn't quite a whisper either. When Sam was tired the in-
fluence to his accent from his years on Minnesota's Iron
Range tended to grow more pronounced. Sam was tired.
Know became a multisyllable word—the vowel sound at
the end just went on and on in that inimitable Minnesota
way. "You got it?" he asked.

"Yes," I said, already wary. *God, what next?*

"If the last thing you said to me this morning on the
trail is true, you have to consider the possibility that . . .
someone is setting you up," Sam said.

I didn't know how to reply. Or if I should reply. Sam
was taking a big risk by calling me. Cozy and Kirsten
would be livid that Sam had called. Almost as livid as they
would be that I hadn't hung up on him.

I had been considering the possibility that McClelland was setting me up since the moment the bandanna
disappeared from the handles on the barn doors. That
my best friend was considering the same possibility was
heartwarming.

"Did you hear me?" Sam asked.

"I did," I said. "There's more about today—things
you don't know."

Phone lines are never actually silent. Sam and I both listened to the sounds that were accompanying our breathing. "Yeah?" he said. "You gonna tell me or what?"

I didn't think he'd believe me about the bandanna. I
opened my mouth, but I didn't speak. I needed to tell him
about the bandanna, but all I was thinking about was the
Sativex, and about Bimini, and about Kol being Nicole.

He hung up. I whispered a profanity. At myself, not at him.

I carried the phone with me as I went out onto the deck off the great room. The night had turned cool. Appropriate to the season. Spring, not fall. Sam thought I was being set up and he didn't even know about the missing bandanna.

Michael McClelland. *If he's setting me up,* I thought, *the guy is good.*

THIRTY

FIVE MINUTES later the phone rang again. It was Diane. She'd heard, of course, about the events of the day. Her domestic intelligence put the NSA to shame.

She wanted to know how I was. She also wanted to know if she knew the suicide victim from crossing paths in the waiting room. She described a number of my patients who wore their depression like some Muslim women wear *burkas*. I told her no, it was none of those. She didn't come close to describing Kol. Diane was sweet and supportive and she even managed to briefly make me laugh. But Diane was fragile. She didn't try to inject herself into my crisis, something she would have done in the past. I didn't consider inviting her to join the fray. She remained much too raw.

The phone rang yet again seconds after I hung up. This time the caller ID read OUT OF AREA. I guessed Sam had something else to say. "Good," I said aloud, allowing myself a pumped fist of triumph without any recognition that the gesture was fueled by alcohol. I picked up the phone and said, "Hello."

"Dr. Gregory? Dr. Alan Gregory?"

I didn't know the voice. But it definitely wasn't that of an Iron Ranger.

"Yes," I said. "This is he." The vodka had a little trouble with the *s*'s in "this" and "is." The one in "yes" hadn't been so much of a problem. I was inebriated enough to find that interesting.

"My name is Tharon Thibodeaux. I'm a psychiatrist at IFP. I apologize for calling so late; I hope I'm not intruding. Your phone's been busy for much of the evening. I assumed that meant you were awake. I thought it was important that we talk."

My reaction? I loved his name. I loved the way he spoke his name. Thibodeaux, while a common enough surname in the South, was one of those rare American monikers that immediately identifies a person not only with a heritage, but also with a region and with a particular city. Dr. Tharon Thibodeaux had roots near New Orleans, Louisiana.

But because my conversation was taking place with Dr. Thibodeaux and not with Sam, as I'd been expecting, I felt as though I had to switch the language I was speaking. Thibodeaux's soft melodic accent helped cushion the shock, but I had to goad my brain to make the transition. I wasn't going to be hearing caution or comfort, or insults, from a northern plains friend. Instead, I needed to prepare to speak with a southern gulf mental-health colleague using the peculiar vernacular we employ with each other in professional circumstances.

Why is this guy calling? I wondered, finally. "Hello, Dr. Thibodeaux," I said. "I'm not familiar with IFP."

"Institute for Forensic Psychiatry. It's the inpatient treatment facility at the Colorado Mental Health Institute that deals with offenders with psychiatric illnesses."

Meant nothing. Then I realized that the Colorado Mental Health Institute was the recently sanitized official name of the old Colorado State Hospital. I didn't know anyone in the field who referred to the facility down south as anything other than the "state hospital" or simply "Pueblo." I wasn't sure I'd ever heard anyone say the "Colorado Mental Health Institute" before. I blamed the vodka for the delay I'd suffered in making the translation.

My solitary connection to the Colorado State Hospital was Michael McClelland. He was most definitely an offender with a psychiatric illness. Or two.

Thibodeaux was calling about McClelland. "It's not too late, not at all," I said.

Thibodeaux must have known Michael McClelland, must have learned about his escape from custody, and knew enough about McClelland's criminal and psychological history to track me down. But why track me down? I didn't know that. Good news? Bad news?

My gut said bad news. Late at night on a weekend? Bad news.

From his brief introduction I thought Dr. Thibodeaux sounded young. Maybe it was the Cajun/Creole/Bayou undertones that sang in his voice. But I also allowed for the possibility that my assessment was just a reflection of the fact that at that moment I was feeling old.

We had lapsed into silence. By training, we were both people accustomed to waiting for other people to talk. "I shouldn't be doing this," he said, finally.

Don't go soft on me now, Tharon. You picked up the phone—now talk.

I began to smell decay again. What was decaying was my hope. Whatever reservations Thibodeaux was having about whatever he was doing and shouldn't be doing, he would have to confront on his own. I wasn't going to help him resolve his dilemma. I had too many of my own to contend with.

He said, "I don't have a release to share any clinical information with you. That should come as no surprise."

Figured that. *Don't think I'm going to help you corral any deviant impulses. I want whatever you're willing to give. Tell me all about McClelland, Dr. Thibodeaux. Tell me what I need to know to find him. To protect my family. To keep them from the sands of Bimini.*

Tharon Thibodeaux was driving north to Denver the next day to attend a basketball game. He was meeting friends to see the Nuggets play the Hornets and asked me to join him before tipoff at a coffeehouse on Evans near the University of Denver.

Two hours and an additional inch of vodka later I found restless sleep while I was formulating the lie I would offer Lauren the next morning.

*   *   *

On my way to Denver I stopped at a pay phone on Federal near the turnpike and called Sam's cell. He didn't pick up. I had decided to tell him about the bandanna.

I didn't leave a voice message. Messages could be subpoenaed. I called Kirsten's home and left her a voice mail with the bad news that I hadn't even known the sex of the patient who had killed herself the previous day. Voice messages to lawyers couldn't be subpoenaed.

Traffic was no problem. I got to Denver around twenty-five minutes later and stopped at another pay phone in a strip center just off I-25 and University near DU. Sam answered after a couple of rings.

The signal was crappy. Even his "Yeah?" broke up.

"It's me," I said.

"You at a pay phone?" he asked. I heard only about half the syllables. That's what I guessed he asked.

"I am. Where are you? You're breaking up."

"Someplace I'm not supposed to be. At the moment, I'm just hoping I'm upwind from some damn dogs. This is the first signal I've had up here."

"You working?" I asked.

"What do you want, Alan?"

"It's about yesterday."

"Am I going to regret hearing it?" Sam asked.

"Maybe."

"Go ahead," he said. That's when the mobile-phone lottery decided to kill the call.

I tried twice more to reach him without success. Whatever cell tower his phone had been kissing was no longer in the mood.

I parked on the street near the place that Thibodeaux had chosen for our rendezvous. I was familiar with the neighborhood from previous visits to the University of Denver, mostly for professional meetings. I didn't know the coffeehouse he had picked, but it was immediately apparent that it was not a close relative of the Starbucks across the street. In the careless ambience department, Kaladi put even the most determinedly déclassé Boulder java roost to shame. The walls were painted the color of the flesh of a blood orange and the red oak on the floor was scratched beyond its years. The place was thrown together as though someone had accumulated enough battered tables and chairs to crowd the back room at a small family-run coffee roaster in Brooklyn or San Francisco's North Beach in the late 1960s.

None of the patrons—mostly hungover DU students and neighborhood types—fit my preconception for a state-hospital psychiatrist. I ordered a drink from the counter and felt fortunate to snare a table. The coffee tasted like mid-morning at a stand-up coffee bar in Siena.

A stained copy of that morning's *Rocky Mountain News* offered a parsed account of what had happened in Peter's barn the day before. I learned the interesting fact that Nicole Cruz had been employed as a maintenance worker at one of Boulder's cemeteries.

I read between the lines: my patient had been a grave-digger. *Great.* I appreciated the irony, even though the tally of my ignorance about her was beginning to reach a sum that in any other circumstance I might have regis-tered as tragic.

My pizza-box-size table was stuck at the bottom of a man-made cliff of sixty-nine-kilo burlap sacks of raw organic coffee beans. The bags were piled high on roll-ing carts stacked double on a steel frame. Once I'd fin-ished turning the pages of Denver's tabloid I'd spent a few moments reading the labels on the burlap and doing the arithmetic necessary to try to decipher why the bags weighed sixty-nine kilos, and not sixty-five or seventy, and what sixty-nine kilos equaled in pounds. It took me longer than it should have to compute the answer—151.8.

The sixty-nine-kilo mystery consumed me until Thibodeaux walked up a few minutes later. Although Thibodeaux was younger than I, he wasn't much youn-ger, nor was he as young as I expected. When I looked up in response to his greeting—"Dr. Gregory?"—my initial guess was that he'd been out of his residency just shy of ten years. I'd been expecting someone only a few years out of training. That he wasn't young meant—if he pos-sessed any skill whatsoever—he had enough experience to know what he was doing clinically and was coming perilously close to having had enough experience to have grown a little jaded while doing it.

If he had appeared to be a few years younger I would

have had an easier time answering one particular question that kept running through my mind: Why the hell would an established, presumably reasonably competent psychiatrist be providing clinical services in the chronically underfunded frontier outpost that was the Colorado State Hospital in Pueblo, or whatever its current name was?

Once I rejected all the benevolent explanations—research opportunities, fascination with serious mental illness, dedication to public service, pathologic affection for dying high-desert mill towns—I was left with the likelihood that at some point in the recent past Dr. Tharon Thibodeaux had fucked up professionally almost as badly as I just had.

My clinical future passed in front of me: when the lawsuits were over and my humiliation was complete, I would end up doing psychometrics and running group-therapy sessions in a state institution—excuse me, "institute"—in some town like Pueblo.

"Dr. Gregory?" he said pleasantly a second time.

I stood up. "Alan, please."

"Tharon," he said.

I slid his name into the mental file where I stored baby names for the second child I hoped to have with Lauren. *Tharon Gregory. Yeah.*

He placed his café au lait on the table and we shook hands. Once we sat, he looked me in the eyes in a way that's peculiar to mental-health types. I stifled a sigh; I consider the eye-lock thing to be a ritualistic pissing contest intended to determine professional advantage—the mental-health practitioner version of the touching of swords by opposing fencers, the tapping of gloves by boxers.

It's basically an eye-contact challenge. Can you match my intensity, my ability to *connect*? I despised the little game and whenever I lost I considered it childish. I lost much more often than I won—which probably said something about my clinical *cojones* that I wasn't eager to admit.

I was in no mood for a new-age joust with some psychiatrist from the state hospital who considered me an elitist clinical psychologist from elitist Boulder. I had just enough ego-observation skills remaining to recognize that given the likelihood that I'd just lost a patient to an absolutely unanticipated suicide, the idea of anyone considering me an elite therapist was as ironic as it was ridiculous.

I held Tharon's magnetic gaze for only a couple of seconds before I looked away, my hope for the meeting evaporating along with my abdication of the eye-lock duel. I'd thrown in the figurative towel. The most attractive option in front of me was also the pettiest—gulping down my coffee and walking away. But if I did that, I knew I would never hear what this guy wanted to tell me about Michael McClelland.

And there was my personal anti-pettiness campaign—which was in some disarray—to consider.

He said, "You're wondering why you're here?"

"Yes."

"You agreed to meet me without many questions. You must have some idea."

I was too drunk to ask them, I thought. I said, "Some." The advantage was all Thibodeaux's.

I was growing more and more accustomed to that posture.

He sat back, supporting his big cup with outstretched fingers the way the prongs of a setting support a diamond. "I grew up in New Orleans," he said. "All my family is still there. Kaladi"—he smiled—"is no Café du Monde, but I like it here. I come whenever I'm in town."

I felt the change in tone viscerally. The wrangle was over. I exhaled, and nodded.

THIRTY-ONE

THIBODEAUX MAY or may not have recognized that my nod contained all the assumptions he'd corrected a hundred times, and all the questions he'd heard a hundred times, or a thousand times, since the storms. Maybe he thought it was easier just to get the story out of the way whenever he met someone new. Regardless, he was ready.

"We had water only a foot deep on the first floor of my parents' house on the edge of the Garden District. Not much wind damage. They were fine; they had evacuated early on. Looters came but only took things that could be replaced. Had to rip up the floors, clean out mold. House is almost the same. City isn't."

He was talking about the destructo-twins, Katrina and Rita. In his voice I heard the kind of stoicism that accompanies the salty crust of dried tears. Katrina had left New Orleans an amputee. The city was alive, but she was missing limbs. The eventual rebuilding of the annihilated neighborhoods would be like fitting New Orleans for prostheses. The city of New Orleans might be able to walk again but Tharon's jury was out as to whether she would ever strut the way she once had.

I thought he might stop his tale right there, but Tharon wasn't done.

"My mama's mother lived in Creole. That's in Cameron Parish. She survived Katrina. But Rita? People forget about Rita, but Rita was hard on the folks to the west. My grandmother died a week to the day after Rita passed. She broke her leg evacuating before the storm, but she died of a broken heart. After the funeral we found a piece of her house—the same house where my mama grew up, the same house where we all used to gather on holidays—we found her parlor where it had floated inland almost a half mile. The table where we sat for family feasts and celebrations, that big mahogany table was still inside the crushed parlor."

I felt the discomfort I feel when I'm in the presence of someone who has suffered a senseless tragedy. Had a child killed by a drunk driver. Had a sister or daughter victimized by a rapist. I didn't know what to say.

He rescued me. He said, "That's the postscript to my story. Here's the Pueblo connection: I went to college and medical school in Florida, made my way back to New Orleans for my residency," he said. "Matched at Charity. That's where I met my wife. As fate would have it, she was from Rocky Ford." For my benefit, he added, "That's east of Pueblo." I already knew—in Colorado if you like sweet melons you know where Rocky Ford is. "She had followed a boyfriend to New Orleans after she finished nursing school up in Greeley. Didn't take long for the boyfriend to become an ex. He was a bit too fond of some of the seamier aspects of the Quarter." He mimed an injection into his forearm.

Tharon's family history was his way of explaining how he'd ended up in the clinical and geographic backwater represented by Colorado's primary psychiatric inpatient facility.

"We had two kids right away. Boy and a girl. I had a good practice. My wife—Willis—asked me to move to Colorado when her mother got ill three years ago. She reminded me a hundred times that she'd agreed to live in Slidell—against her wishes—when I was setting up my first office." He looked up. "Slidell's not that bad, but Willis . . . " He left the thought unfinished.

"That's where we were during the storms—Slidell. Our house survived. But it was the last straw for Willis. I gave in. We rented our house to my brother and his wife. Katrina had taken theirs. I agreed to try Colorado for a year. That's where my grandmother's dining-room table is now, by the way. In Rocky Ford." He smiled ironically. "Dry air here is murder on old mahogany. I think the desert's going to end up proving harder on it than Rita ever was."

I nodded. I agreed with him about the effect of Colorado's dry air on fine furniture, but I nodded to keep him talking.

"I admit that I came here thinking Willis's mother

would die soon enough and we'd head back to Louisiana, or maybe Florida. I hated it here from day one. Staying was never the plan."

I hadn't made the drive down the turnpike to argue with the man about the relative value of cities. If Denver, let alone Pueblo or Rocky Ford, had to go toe-to-toe with New Orleans on cuisine or atmosphere, the fight would be a first-round knockout.

"Five months after we got here my wife's mother died. Complications of emphysema. Three weeks later Willis filed for divorce. She filed"—from his lips the word "filed" rhymed comfortably with "wild"—"in Pueblo County."

"You're stuck," I said. I'd done enough work with divorcing parents to understand the ramifications of custody and visitation prerogatives on parental freedom. If Tharon wanted to see his kids frequently and regularly he would have to find a job in Pueblo County. Or, if he didn't mind a numbing Front Range commute, he could choose to live up the interstate in Colorado Springs.

Colorado Springs was the reddest of cities in this purple-pink state. If his political leanings shaded toward the blue, and I was suspecting that Tharon's did, the Springs would not feel like a welcoming political bosom. Complicating things even more was the fact that Thibodeaux was a psychiatrist. If he desired to practice his specialty in Pueblo, his options were limited to the state hospital. Few small towns close to Pueblo have the population base and the help-seeking culture necessary to support a solo practitioner in psychiatry. There are no large towns close to Pueblo.

"I am stuck," he said. "I adore my children."

I sat back and I waited. Truth was, I was feeling pretty stuck myself. But I suspected that Thibodeaux knew that already.

Often in my career I'd been in the position of trying to find a way to twist reality so that I could share clinical information with someone I thought needed to hear it but to whom I had no right to tell it. My own experiences wrestling with that dilemma had convinced me that prodding Thibodeaux to overcome whatever ethical constraints he was feeling wasn't likely to be salutary. He needed to hurdle the moral and ethical barricades on his own. I thought he could do it.

He had tracked me down, after all, and we were sitting more than a hundred miles away from his reluctant home, beneath an eight-foot levee of 151.8-pound burlap sacks of green free-trade organic coffee beans. Those facts convinced me that Dr. Thibodeaux had arrived in Denver with the momentum to clear the obstacles.

"We have a patient in common," he said, finally.

"I wondered about that," I said, relieved to have finally reached the starting line. "Not one of my proudest clinical moments." I added the qualifier hoping that my contrition would add a little grease to the ethical skids on which Thibodeaux was—I was praying—beginning to slip. And I added it because it was true. If Thibodeaux had bothered to look at any of the early court records that accompanied McClelland's admission to the state hospital, he would have noted my silence regarding the misguided recommendations to the court from so many years before.

He would know that Michael McClelland was a clinical ghost from my early career, and he could probably guess McClelland's ghost was one that I was desperately seeking a chance to banish. He might not have known that I was in Denver figuratively on my knees praying that Thibodeaux was willing to be my exorcist.

My fantasy was that Tharon was about to tell me he knew all about his patient's fixation on blue bandannas. And all about his plans for retribution on my wife. And on me. On my family.

"When you get access to the hospital records, and you will—fortunately or unfortunately—you'll get everything I'm about to tell you," he said. "So although I'm jumping the gun a little, I'm not really breaking the rules. That's my rationalization."

Why will I get access to Michael's hospital records? I wondered. I couldn't think of a single reason that I would be in a position to ever see them, but I wasn't going to tell Tharon that. *Rationalize away*, I thought. *Go for it*.

"I've been in your shoes," he said. I noted with some clinical envy that his voice, like Bill Clinton's, conveyed empathy the way a wheelbarrow transports dirt. "That's part of it, too. The reason I decided to talk with you."

"My shoes?" I asked.

"With a patient, I mean. During my residency at Charity. I don't want anyone else to have to go through what I did."

"I appreciate that," I said. I was curious about what had happened during Tharon's residency. But I didn't ask—the story sounded like a digression waiting to happen.

He went on. "If it helps any with your feelings, or with the legal side of things for that matter, she was always gamey about her meds. From day one. It's all documented in the chart. Not just by me. Nursing notes, too. Not occasionally gamey. Always gamey. I don't think we ever kept her at adequate levels. Diagnostically I always thought we were dealing with a pure unipolar, but that was a minority opinion. The staff thought she was bipolar and that the manic episodes were infrequent."

Thibodeaux had spoken a paragraph packed with clinical jargon. But I'd only heard two three-letter words. I had to go back and replay the sequence of sentences in my head to process anything more than the pair of words that kept floating in front of my eyes like holograms.

She. He'd said "she." *Her*. He'd said "her."

Son of a bitch. I felt the blood pour out of my face all at once like it was bathwater falling over the edge of a tub.

Thibodeaux wasn't in Denver to spill the beans about his work with Michael McClelland. Thibodeaux was in town to talk with me about Nicole Cruz.

Kol Cruz, not Michael McClelland, was the patient

we'd shared. Which meant that Kol—Nicole—had been an inpatient in the forensic unit at the state hospital.

That fact told me two troubling things. First, since mentally healthy people don't tend to spend much time on the wards at facilities like the one in Pueblo, Kol Cruz had apparently been much sicker than I'd recognized. And second, Kol had been at the state hospital at the same time as Michael McClelland.

What did that mean? A lot, I was sure. What exactly? I didn't know.

Tharon watched my stunned reaction to what I'm sure he thought were benign revelations about his patient's reluctance to take her meds and about the esoteric diagnostic dilemma she had presented to the clinical staff. I could tell by the look of concern on his face that he was about to inquire about my cataplexy.

I blurted out a question. "Did Nicole know Michael McClelland?"

My question wasn't one that Thibodeaux expected to hear. I watched the blood leave his face. Same way that it had happened to me a few seconds earlier—all at once, over the dam spillway.

He regained his composure quickly. He lifted his cup, cradled it in both hands, sat back, and said, "How do you know . . . Michael McClelland?"

Holy shit, I was thinking. *What the hell is going on?*

THIRTY-TWO

KIRSTEN LORD lived in a small stone cottage off 4th Street in the warren of lanes of old Boulder that is crammed into the rise of land just north and west of downtown. The neighborhood is charming and convenient. Close to shopping. Close to dining. Close to hiking trails. Close to parks. The Rockies loom only a few blocks away, proximate enough to cast their shadows over the neighborhood by mid-afternoon in the winter months.

Most parcels are small on the narrow lanes and some of the houses tiny by contemporary standards. Although a few of its siblings had been remodeled and rebuilt to reflect McMansion sensibilities, Boulder style, Kirsten's was one of the remaining Lilliputian homes. If she had been willing to give up those other perks—view, convenience, ambience—she could have quintupled the size of her cramped home by moving to one of the dozens of faux-Victorian or suburban chic developments recently constructed a few miles to the east or north of town.

*   *   *

"Amy went to a friend's house," she said when she opened the front door.

I'd called Kirsten from my car a half mile before I'd reached the exit that I normally would have used to turn off to my house in Spanish Hills. I was on my way into Boulder from Kaladi and my meeting with Thibodeaux. I asked her if I could visit briefly to discuss some new information I'd learned regarding the person who'd killed herself in Peter's barn. Kirsten had hesitated for a second before she agreed, finally adding on an inhale, "Amy's home, and this place is pretty small, if you know what I mean."

I guessed that she meant that she didn't want her Sunday interrupted. Although I was still reeling from what I'd learned during my discussion with Thibodeaux, I knew that I could wait until the next day to discuss the news with my lawyers. My situation wasn't an emergency. Not in any legal sense.

"That's all right," I said. I've always felt that natural impediments are a great way to resolve ambivalence. Shall I take the elevator or the stairs? If the elevator is out of service, ambivalence tends to dissipate.

"Don't be silly," she said. "Come on by. We may need to walk over to the office, or maybe we can grab something to eat on the Mall. You like the Kitchen? I'm a regular. It's quiet in the afternoon. We could get a glass of wine upstairs."

I said it didn't matter to me where we met. She gave me her address.

Kirsten's cottage had a new copper-roofed porch over the north-facing entrance. The metal had just begun its evolution toward verdigris. That's where I was standing when she offered the "Amy went to a friend's house" information.

I said, "I appreciate you letting me interrupt your weekend."

She was wearing faded blue jeans and a thin sweater that was the muted gold of the sky just before the sun cracks the dawn horizon. Her hair was in a ponytail, her hands in the back pockets of her jeans. Despite the cool spring day her feet were bare.

She'd painted her toenails the red of Valentine hearts. I didn't miss the fact that I had noticed that her feet were bare. It meant that my eyes were down. I forced myself to bring my gaze up to meet hers. I thought she looked pretty, and soft, and much younger than she did in her going-to-court clothes. I hoped I didn't look as pitiful as I was feeling, but I suspected that I did.

She pulled the door open wide. "Don't be silly. Since Amy's gone we don't have to go out. We can talk here," she said. "Come in, come in."

The cottage was recently renovated. Years before, Kirsten had entered the Witness Security Program with abundant financial assets from her marriage. She had apparently invested a serious chunk of those assets in the purchase and reconstruction of this little house. I felt as though I'd just crossed the threshold into the front room of an overpriced suite at a mountain resort.

The colors in the room were from gemstones thrown in rich soil. Most of the plebian artifacts of the home's humble origins had been replaced by modern flourishes and expensive finishes. The floor was bamboo, the furniture covered with down cushions in soft chenilles. The effect was charming.

Kirsten's home was a cocoon, a place for retreating, not for transitioning. It was the antithesis of my new waiting room, but I thought Diane would approve.

"Nice," I said, taking in the single large room that was visible from the entryway.

"Thank you," she said. "It was a lot of work. The place hadn't been touched in seventy years when I bought it. We took down walls. The original floor was still in the kitchen. Layers and layers of wallpaper everywhere. Eight layers in the bedroom, if you can believe it. And the bathroom? It was cold enough to age meat in there in January. I put in a new boiler and radiant heat. I even heated the floors. Can you feel them? Take off your shoes." She crossed her arms, gripping her biceps. "I get cold in the mountains. Remember, I'm a Southern girl."

I kicked off my shoes. She led me to a loveseat and we sat side by side facing a small fire that was burning in the river-rock fireplace. Horses or donkeys had probably carted the round stones up the hill from nearby Boulder Creek a century before.

"I made tea," she said. "Green? Is that okay?" She had also put out some iced cookies that shared a small platter with an array of dried apples and apricots.

I took the tea from her and cradled it. After my sojourn at Kaladi I didn't need any more caffeine, but the weight and the warmth of the mug felt good in my hands.

"It's cozy here," I said. "Thanks."

The tea tray was resting on a table fashioned from an old wooden hibachi. She put her bare feet up on the edge. A few inches from her painted toes sat a clear glass bowl brimming with Dum Dums. The little lollipops brought back memories. During her time in my care Kirsten had been addicted.

"My mother used to say that cozy is Southern for 'small,' " she said.

I kept my stockinged feet on the warm floor. "It's lovely. Small can be good."

Her feet were slender. I noticed that I'd noticed. I also noted that it was not because I'd been looking down.

She took a deep breath, exhaled slowly, and said, "It's enough for Amy and me. We each have our own rooms and . . . bathrooms." She smiled. "That's important for girls. The contractor removed dump trucks full of rocks and dirt from below the house so I could have a tiny base-ment with an office. I can walk to work in minutes. I ride my bike to Ideal for groceries. I can be on the Mount Sani-tas trail like that." She snapped her fingers. "There are lots of restaurants. Bookstores. The library. I love all of it."

The psychologist in me heard the distortion in the sounds as the faint echoes of her words bounced around the room. I recognized that this darling West Boulder cot-tage wasn't merely a comforting cocoon for my ex-patient and current lawyer, it was also a bit of an emotional abdication, or at least an acknowledgment of circumstances that felt immutable. By renovating this sturdy, intimate house, Kirsten was admitting to herself—in a form as concrete as the mortar between the heavy rocks in the walls—that she no longer had overt hopes that her small family would be getting any larger.

"Amy's getting older," she said. "Growing up. You'll know soon enough what that means."

"What?" I could guess, but making assumptions had been proving dangerous.

"She's gone more than she's here. Friends. School things, sports things. She plays club soccer. You know about club soccer?"

Lauren and I had some friends with kids who played club ball. All I knew is that they traveled a lot on weekends to towns most Coloradans don't visit. Some parents were happier about it than others. "Amy's a keeper, right?" I said.

I could tell that Kirsten was pleased that I remembered her daughter played goal. "You will soon. If it's not soccer it'll be something else. The activities take so much of the kids' time. And then there're her friends, and the phone, and IM. She used to be my best buddy. Sometimes I feel as though I'm getting a taste of what it will be like when . . ." She didn't finish the sentence.

. . . she goes to college? . . . gets married?

I was digesting how different Kirsten felt to me from the woman who had been figuratively—and occasionally

literally—standing toe-to-toe with Sam Purdy on my behalf over the recent past. And how different she felt from
the woman who had stepped into my office so full of
grief and terror after the murder of her husband.

I was disarmed by it all, and realized that I was having a rare opportunity to recognize that what a therapist
sees about a patient in his office has scant correlation
with that person's life the other twenty-three hours and
fifteen minutes of any given day.

I'd sought Kirsten out that afternoon for the comfort
she could provide. I was under orders not to speak with
Lauren or with Sam, and both were under orders not
to speak with me about anything to do with Kol. Diane
would have been willing to hear me out, but she was still
recovering from her own traumas and I didn't entertain
burdening her with mine. Adrienne was in Israel.

The list of people I could turn to for comfort should
maybe have been longer, but it wasn't. My instincts told
me that legal comfort was better than no comfort at all.
But Kirsten was vulnerable, too. Not as acutely as me, but
in her own way perhaps nearly to the same degree. The
awareness shouldn't have surprised me—I'd been her
psychotherapist, after all—but it did. My self-protective
radar failed to recognize that the fact her vulnerability
didn't trouble me enough to back away might signify I
was suffering a problem with my judgment.

"Cozy will be back tonight," she said.

Was she making conversation? Or was she suggesting
that I wait and share my fresh news about Cole's suicide—

I'd decided on the drive back to Boulder to try to goad myself to mentally replace the *K* with a *C* and to add the *e*—with Cozy instead of her? I wasn't sure.

She added, "I think he made an offer on that place in La Jolla."

"I hope he loans it out to clients," I said. "I could use a month at the beach."

She laughed. "And associates," she said. "Though I wish he were buying in Sanibel, or on the Outer Banks somewhere." She crinkled her nose. "In the South."

She had no way of knowing I was being ironic with my comment about the beach.

Bimini was what I'd been thinking.

Boulder sits at about 5,400 feet above sea level. The Continental Divide—up to another 9,000 feet higher yet—vaults skyward only twenty miles to the west. Geometry and astronomy dictate that the imposing Divide casts an especially early shadow on homes that sit closest to the foothills. I was visiting Kirsten during the time of day when sunset's angles prevail and the afternoon's rays leave long shadows in their wake.

Where I lived far across the valley, I could watch the shadows' tides. I could watch each night's dark steal away the light and then see the reflection on the Flatirons as dawn's glow burst and reclaimed the day.

At Kirsten's home, like at my office blocks away, I could *feel* the day ending.

The difference was important.

* * *

"You want a drink?" she asked after a long interlude when the only sounds were the muted explosions of gases escaping tiny caverns in the logs in the fireplace, and a dog barking somewhere in the neighborhood. "A real drink? A glass of wine?"

Her question felt more complicated than it should have. I wasn't sure why at first, but I didn't have a quick reply ready. She filled the void—she stood up, stepped in the direction of the kitchen and said, "Well, I do."

I touched her hand as she moved past me. I stood too.

The fingers of my right hand snaked up into her hair. My left hand pressed on her back, just above her ass. I felt her breath on my neck.

There are moments in life when good and bad collide. A heroin addict described it to me. Just as the needle enters the vein, just before the plunger starts to descend on the syringe. I was there. I knew that moment.

Stopping time—literally—might have allowed me the chance to sort out what I should do next. But stopping time was the province of gods and if I were any god at that moment I would have been the deity the Greeks called Chaos.

THIRTY-THREE

KIRSTEN DID get herself some wine, though I declined to join her.

Going home with alcohol on my breath would have added a level of complication to my already complicated afternoon. I was unwilling to contemplate the house of cards of lies it would take to explain it all to Lauren.

I did not grab Kirsten's hand as she stood to get the wine. Nor did I pull her into an embrace. I didn't bury my fingers in her hair. Or feel her breath on the flesh of my neck. I didn't do any of what would naturally have come next.

I wasn't even on the couch when she returned from the kitchen with the wine. I was standing in front of the fire, looking out a western window at the first pastel stripes on the stratified clouds above the foothills.

She set the bottle of wine and two glasses on the hibachi. She busied herself popping the cork before she stepped over and joined me by the fire. She said, "Hi."

The word felt like a novella.

She put her arms around me—I could feel her hands spread, her fingers curling onto my shoulder blades—and she gave me a firm hug, the side of her face against my chest. I inhaled a soft scent from her, an olfactory whisper, like yesterday's perfume.

"That wasn't very lawyerly," she said when she'd pulled away from me. "But I thought you needed it. You haven't had a very good week."

I had needed it, so much so that I allowed myself the discomfiting awareness that the embrace had ended before I was ready.

The moment she pulled away from me is when the what-happened-next fantasy played out in my head—unbidden, I would argue; undeterred, I would admit. I remained near the fire gazing out the window as I allowed the fantasy to run to credits. Even as the inherent peril caused my pulse to soar I found the prurient daydream oddly comforting.

When I joined her again on the loveseat I poured three inches of wine for her and turned sideways, handing her the glass. She had one leg curled beneath her and her left arm around a cushion that she was hugging to her breasts.

I left my glass unfilled. She noticed. "This must be hard for you," she said.

"It is," I said. "I assume you mean being a suspect in the suspicious death of one of my patients?" It was an awkward attempt to be glib.

"That's part of it," she said with a kind grin. "But simply losing your patient to suicide. The way you did, finding the body? The hostility of her killing herself the way she did, and where she did? At your *home*. At your home, Alan. I mean—oh my God—Grace could have found the body. Plus being cut off from all your usual supports. Lauren. Your best friend. Not being able to talk about this. It must be like being on an island."

"Yes," I said. "It is." *Bimini.*

"I'm glad if I can help," she said. "Even a little. And I'm glad you called," she said, averting her eyes.

"Me too." I felt like a sixteen-year-old. Or somebody else as a sixteen-year-old. I'd totally forgotten what my life had been like at sixteen. Psychologically speaking the correct word was "suppressed." Not "forgotten." My actual sixteenth year, along with the couple before and the couple after, had disappeared into a cave. I hadn't been spelunking in those climes since.

Kirsten said, "I know that part. The island part. I've lived it. But the part I know best is how it feels to have a madman after you and your family. There's nothing worse."

She had given my situation a lot of thought. My breath was growing shallow. Partly because her compassion was disarming me. Partly because she was stumbling closer and closer to the truth.

Kirsten said, "Lauren isn't well, is she?"

What? How did she know that?

"I don't mean generally," she said. "I mean lately."

"How can you tell?"

She shrugged. "Coping is exhausting. She seems . . . especially exhausted. I've seen her . . . during better times. We were close, remember?"

I did remember. "She's not doing . . . great," I admitted. "Things come, things go. It's that kind of disease." It was one or two degrees away from being a platitude. I didn't like to say much about my wife's health to others. Lauren didn't want me to say much about her health to others.

"That must be a major trial for you. Having a wife who is ill. You have to cope too."

"Harder for her," I said. It didn't feel right to talk about what it was like for me.

"My husband's parents were sick. It tore him up. Sometimes," she said, "it's harder to take care of the sick person than it is to be the sick person. Much harder. That's what I think, anyway."

I couldn't acknowledge that truth. *She's going to Bimini*, I thought. *She's taking Grace. It's prudent*. I couldn't acknowledge that, either. Not aloud. Not with Kirsten.

Her eyes softened. I feared it was an indication that she was going to try to entice me to cross the bridge she was erecting across the divide between us. She sipped some wine. Looked away before she looked back toward me. "Did I ever really thank you for what you did? To save us, me and Amy? That night, at your house?"

"You did." I didn't remember if she did or if she didn't. I had been in shock after the night I demolished the front of my house with Adrienne's car, and I stayed that way for longer than I wanted to admit. Appropriately, Kirsten had never come back to see me for therapy.

I'd been relieved at her decision. She had moved on. Had she come back to see me I would have had to use my shovel to dig, rather than to fill. And selfishly, what happened that night was a hole I needed to fill as fast as I could.

For a short while Kirsten and Lauren had become close friends. The bond quickly cooled, though I'd seen her in passing a couple of times in the next year or two. She would pick Lauren up to go shopping or to go to a play.

I ran into them once while they were having lunch at an outside table at Tom's near the Mall. I saw her and Amy in the parking lot at King Soopers on 30th. Kirsten was an ex-patient in a small town. I had a lot of ex-patients in Boulder. I had tried to let her become just one of them—someone I ran into around town. My feelings about her? She was there that night. I was there that night. If seeing her caused me to have to deal with any details about what had happened, then she was worth avoiding.

Occasionally I was unable to stop myself from remembering more. That would happen in the dark in the dead hours when the lucky were asleep.

I didn't like the nights that I remembered more.

Remembering Kirsten meant remembering Carl Luppo. Remembering Kirsten and Carl meant recalling being within arm's reach of an assassin in the wreckage of the front of my house. Steps away my wife was at risk, my unborn daughter was at risk.

I had a gun in my hand. A . . . gun.

Emily barking and barking and barking.

The man's hand around my ankle.

In recent months, at night when everyone else was sleeping, when I would have preferred to be dreaming uninterpretable dreams, I'd awaken because I felt the pressure of his fingers closing like a vise around my leg. I would sit up startled in the night, trying to yank my leg free. I would look up to see Emily's orange eyes staring at me.

Just like that night.

In a blink I would be back in the rubble with the damn gun in my hand. For three seconds, or four, I would feel the terror I felt that night. Part of me would recognize the pull from the past and I would try to make everything stop. Failing that I would try to get reality to rewind. It never worked. I was never able to do any of it.

Emily's eyes would glow with fire, her jaws snapping open and closed as she barked. I don't remember hearing her barks that night. I do remember closing my eyes.

I always pulled the trigger right after I closed my eyes.

Always. That night in the rubble. And every night that I replayed it.

I always closed my eyes. I always pulled the trigger.
Shoot.

*   *   *

During the replays Emily would sense the adrenaline seeping from my pores and she would stare at me in the bedroom or great-room darkness, unblinking. Eventually my pulse would slow and her instincts would tell her that any danger had passed. She'd lie down, sigh, close her eyes, and go back to sleep. Emily wasn't haunted.

Not me. I wouldn't sleep again until daylight filtered into the room. Once the cycle of darkness had been poisoned by those memories it couldn't be safe for me. If I was lucky I'd get an hour of sleep after dawn but before the alarm went off or before Grace called out her insistence that we all start the day.

The shot I fired that night with my eyes closed echoed for months that soon stacked up and became years. It echoed because I hadn't been able to find a way to stop the echoing. God knows I had tried. I'd compartmentalized everything else. The Kirsten part. The Carl Luppo part. The unbelievable danger to my family part.

But I'd failed to compartmentalize the shooting part. That part was the echo I kept hearing. I felt grateful that the intrusions became less frequent over time. The years had begun to scar over what I couldn't heal on my own.

Then I watched my patient's death on national TV.

A man with a secret. A bullet from a gun.

The very night he died I woke to find myself in the dark again. The hand on my ankle. The gun in my hand. Emily's orange eyes. Her silent barks.

Everything came back.

Was it—I didn't know—*about the secret, or the gun?*

"I don't think so," Kirsten said. "I've never thanked you properly."

"What I did that night? Instinct," I said. "Not courage. It was something that had to be done. I did it because not doing it would have been worse. That's all."

What had I done that night?

I'd shot a man intent on killing not only my wife and unborn daughter, but also Kirsten and her daughter. I'd shot him before he shot me for no other reason than because he knew I was in his way.

I'd shot him with a silenced .22 at close range.

I'd shot him once in the head. With my eyes closed. The one shot had killed him.

"I'm no hero," I said.

"You saved us," she said.

Her argument was that since I had saved their lives I was a hero. *Ha.* I'd been down that road before. Just around the bend there was a fork. Each tine of the fork led to a fresh tragedy. She might not be able to see it. I knew the route. I could.

"I closed my eyes when I pulled the trigger," I said. "How heroic is that?"

I'd never told anyone that fact before. The eyes-closed part. Not Lauren, not Sam.

Kirsten shrugged. "You were scared. I was crying.

Lauren was crying. We were all terrified. Doesn't change anything. What you did was . . . heroic."

The word left me nauseous. I tasted vomit in my throat. "It wasn't just fear," I said. "It was . . . more than that."

"What?" she asked.

Anyone would have asked—I'd created the opening—but I wasn't prepared to answer. "It's over. I don't talk about it. I don't think about it."

I do lie about it. If you keep asking, I'll keep lying.

"It's not that simple," she said. "It's one of those things that has to be difficult for you still. For anyone. Killing a man? My God. I don't care about the circumstances. It doesn't just go away."

No, it doesn't. Not soon. Not ever. Eventually I will succeed in pretending that it's gone away. That might be the best that I can hope for.

I didn't want to talk about me, especially about me killing a man. Defensively, I flipped the mirror, pointing it at her. "What about for you?" I asked. "You know about this too. Has that day at Galatoire's gone away?"

Kirsten's husband, Robert, died in her arms outside the famed restaurant in the French Quarter. In front of her eyes an anonymous hitman had put a single slug into his brain. She recoiled from my question and took a quick breath, as though she were recovering from a blow to her gut. Then she shook her head. She said, "Never. Ever."

"Some things are hard, too hard. The load is too heavy,"

I said. "We do our best. We move on. Not always beyond. Just on."

We were quiet for a moment. The neighborhood dog had stopped barking.

"I worry about Amy," she said. Her voice dropped to a whisper with the pronouncement, as though she was concerned that she didn't have a right to be concerned about her daughter.

Of course, I thought. This was about Amy, not about Kirsten. And not about me. I felt a shower of relief. I hadn't seen the change in direction coming. I should have. I'd been outflanked by an amateur. At the mention of her daughter's vulnerability I reached over a few inches and took Kirsten's hand.

Her focus was on her daughter but her eyes were on the fire. She asked, "Should I? Worry about Amy? What she saw? What she heard? What she felt?"

What she felt? I thought. *Who knows?* I knew what I was feeling—I was feeling the cloud resume its rush forward like it was being pushed by a gale. I was exhausted enough that I sniffed for the wolves.

"You want me to comfort you?" I asked in a tone I tried to make as soothing as a father's caress. "Is that . . . where you're going with this?"

I could offer comfort. That was easy. I could hold her in my arms. Whisper soft words into her hair. I could be reassuring. I could talk about hope.

Or I could offer a therapist's comfort. Understanding.

Compassion. Wisdom. If she was lucky and I was having a good day, I could be a dim light in a dark room.

Or, I could lie.

"It is," she said. She looked away from the fire. At me. She then leaned into me, resting her head on my shoulder. "But is comfort what I need?"

I thought about her question. There was so much trust residing in it. Was she asking me as doctor, or as experienced victim? Or simply as a man? I didn't know. I was sure that it would have been easier for me to offer comfort than the alternative. The alternative was empathy. Empathy would have required excavating the piece of me that I had buried.

"We can all . . . use solace. It's not easy to find. I advise taking it where you can get it," I said. I feared that my words were banal. I kept going, trying to find some traction to pull me from the muddy ground to the dry. "But the truth is that you need to be worried about Amy. What happened with those men—in New Orleans, in Slaughter, and in Boulder—changed her. It just did. You can be certain of . . . that."

I watched tears form in both of Kirsten's eyes and knew that I was out of the mud. Her tears formed all at once, as though my words had caused them to spring from surface wells. Within seconds the drops were sliding down the slopes of her cheekbones.

It had been a cheap clinical diversion on my part. Every word I'd said was true. But she had been asking for comfort, not for truth. I'd run from the comfort because what was comforting to her was too dangerous for me.

"How? How has it changed her? What will it do?" she asked.

She wanted relief from her dread. I swallowed. "I don't know. You don't know. For now, she doesn't know."

Well, that's helpful, Doctor.

She squeezed my hand. "I want you to tell me she can leave it all behind. That's what I want. I want to bleach that day for her, to disinfect those memories. I don't want those monsters to have changed her."

I knew the truth would cut like broken glass. "Her father was murdered," I said. "A man chased her down in Slaughter when you were hiding. A hired killer fired a shot into her teddy bear here in Boulder—while she held it in her arms. The man was there to kill you. She saw all that. She knew all that. She felt . . . all that."

Kirsten's muscles tightened involuntarily, as though she was preparing to absorb a punch. But it was too late. My blows had landed. She cried. She didn't sob; her body didn't convulse. She cried with composure. The individual tears melded into streams on her cheeks. Her tongue darted from her mouth to catch the salty drops tumbling on the left side. The ones she missed slid into the thin air before disappearing into the weave of my sweater.

"What's going to happen to her?" she asked.

Like the smart kid in class with his hand in the air, I knew that one. The clinical word is "sublimate." *If she's lucky,* I thought, *Amy will sublimate.* To Freud it was an unconscious defense mechanism that involved rerouting potentially destructive psychological urges into impulses that are neutral or even positive.

For Amy it would mean that she would discover strength that lingers like unspent blessings in ego-restoring reservoirs that are mystifying in their bounty, and she would use that strength to transform the impact of the horrific events that were themselves so transformative and she would end up doing something acceptable, even beneficial, to society.

She will sublimate.

Diane had sublimated her captivity in Las Vegas and we had ended up with a waiting room that was more oasis than parlor.

I had sublimated my failure to change my history to my liking and had become a clinical psychologist, determined to change the history of others.

How would Amy sublimate? I didn't know. But she would. I knew she would.

A clinical supervisor who'd edged too close to understanding my truth pointed out that the chemical meaning of the word "sublimate" is not too different from the psychological one. To chemists, sublimation is the process by which matter changes from a solid state into a vapor without first melting.

The supervisor could tell from watching my face that chemistry wasn't one of my things.

"Think dry ice," she'd said.

In the intervening years I had learned that the tricky

part about sublimation—whether psychological or chemical—was in that qualifying phrase at the end. The tricky part was in making the change without first melting.

The capacity of the human animal to survive hardship and trauma has never ceased to generate my awe. Take ten people and let doom and cruelty—violence, incest, loss, trauma, terror—design an episode or two of horror in their childhoods.

Four or five will refuse to be defined by the assaults and somehow will turn out fine. A couple of others will be damaged. For the fortunate the damage will prove benign, like a dented bumper on an automobile, or manageable, like the impaired vision from a smashed headlight.

Two more—give or take—of the ten will emerge from the swamp of personal history and beyond all odds make a positive difference in the world.

A small minority will become lifelong victims.

One will suffer damage beyond repair.

One in ten to the tenth will transform tragedy into fuel and do something remarkable.

And one in ten to the tenth will become Michael McClelland.

All will have been transformed by their trauma. No one gets away unscathed.

Most will sublimate.

I am a point in fact. *Am I any less scarred than Michael McClelland?* No, I'm not.

Did I become a vapor without first melting? I didn't

know. I didn't even know how to know. But I'd spent the day demonstrating the current status of my personal sublimation and I didn't think that I had melted since breakfast.

Small steps. For many years I'd been taking small steps.

If I was lucky I'd take another one when that day ended and the next one began.

Amy would too.

THIRTY-FOUR

I EXPLAINED sublimation to Kirsten. She rested her head on my shoulder while I spoke. Both her hands were gripping the one of mine that I'd offered in comfort. She was holding on to me as though she were on the verge of drowning.

She heard my words as a cause for hope for her daughter. Maybe for herself, too. The hope was a breeze that washed over her and dried her tears.

I heard Kol speak just then. The sound was so real I almost looked around Kirsten's living room for him. In my imagination he remained a man. Kol's voice—mocking—said, *"I mean it's not like what happened with . . . your dad."*

The next words I spoke came out of a part of me that I'd been confident was so deeply buried that a psychological deep-drilling rig would be necessary to tap the cisterns that stored the toxins excreted by the memories.

I said, "The first time was worse."

Time stopped in the room. I looked at the fireplace to see if the flames were frozen in place.

The flames danced on. I found that oddly reassuring. Oxygen and carbon were doing their things. Chemistry was still chemistry. Chemistry and physics still trumped psychology.

I listened to the room for any evidence that the universe had altered in fundamental ways. It hadn't. My words weren't echoing unnaturally. The neighborhood dog had resumed barking.

Kirsten sensed the change. She lifted her head from my shoulder and lowered her voice into a range that was somewhere between shocked and sultry. She said, "What?"

My eyes went wide. Her simple question almost floored me. I realized that I had just opened the door.

Did I say that the first time was worse? I did. I cracked open the damn door.

My instinct? *Close it. Close it! Slam the thing shut.* Immediately the argument began—*Kick the damn thing open, Alan. Let the beast out. Let it run.*

"Nothing," I said to Kirsten. *That was close.*

She had turned to face me. When? I didn't remember her moving. I thought I smelled her perfume again. Maybe she really wasn't wearing any; maybe it was an illusion or the olfactory equivalent of an echo. The aroma, real or imagined, made me dizzy, as though it wasn't merely alluring, but sedating.

The dried tears had left herringbone trails across the

high ridges on her cheekbones. She asked, "What first time, Alan? What did you mean?" She wiped at her face, obliterating the zigzag lines.

I made no conscious decision to answer. But answer I did. I said, "In the rubble that night? He wasn't the first man I shot. The first was . . . worse."

There had been another time, too, with yet another gun. Another shooting. But that was an accident, absent my volition. I'd never added it to my roster of secrets.

My acknowledgment to Kirsten was, I knew, a reluctant confession. But she couldn't know that. No one would tell. I wouldn't tell. We were good at secrets.

Great at secrets.

That was our thing. It's in the genes.

I was not ready to be absolved. Nor was I eager to be punished.

I heard my words again, saw myself say them. My mind's little hard drive replayed the scene. *He wasn't the first man I shot. The first was worse.* I knew I was the one who had spoken the words, but during the replay I experienced the sounds as listener, not as speaker.

"That night?" Kirsten asked, either confused or, more likely, concerned that I was. "At your house? I think there was only the one man. He shot Carl, remember? He was coming after . . . us."

"No. Yes," I said. Both words were true. I wasn't confused. But I wanted to run. I had to force myself to stay seated. I convinced myself that I'd said enough.

She would be satiated. She would ask no more questions.

She touched me then. A light touch, her fingertips on the side of my face, her index finger on the lobe of my ear. "You're freezing," she said.

Her touch was a caress. My defenses, under assault for years, withering for days, cracked and swayed and collapsed into a heap. *Just like the garage,* I thought, *that Sam tugged down.* The barricade I'd been supporting for so long was gone. As the dust was rising from the ruins the words rushed out of my mouth like Emily taking off after a squirrel. "I shot someone else," I said.

Four words. One sentence.

Subject, predicate, object, adjective.

They hung diagrammed in front of my eyes, translucent like a hologram.

I had only once ever said anything like them aloud before. The most surprising thing was that I thought they sounded all right.

When I looked back up I was engulfed by the cloud.

Damn.

Kirsten was a smart woman. She immediately saw the implications of my confession. An attorney again, she said, "Whoever wrote that note that we found on your front door knows what you just told me."

The intimacy between us fractured. I was relieved.

Michael McClelland. "Yes," I said. *Kol knew, or McClelland knows. Maybe both.*

"Who have you told? Anyone?"

"One person," I said.

"Lauren?"

"She doesn't know."

Kirsten digested that. Or she tried. "Who then?" she asked.

"It doesn't matter," I said.

Of course it mattered. I had told Adrienne my secret in the months after her husband's death, when she was drowning in her grief and in the despair she felt from learning things he had kept from her. She had asked me if I had any secrets as serious as the one Peter had hidden. I admitted I did.

Adrienne physically recoiled from me. She told me she could no longer be my friend if I was keeping an important secret from her.

"It happened a long, long time ago," I said to Kirsten.

"The secret, or the telling?"

"A few years for one. Many years for the other."

"How hard would it be for someone to find out?" she asked.

She was thinking about the note on my porch.

"The court records were sealed," I said.

"Court records? A crime?"

I didn't reply. I didn't know the answer.

She said, "What about newspapers?"

"My name isn't in them." That was what I'd been told. I'd never checked.

I could tell Kirsten was editing some other questions

before she asked, "Then how does he know what he wrote in the note? This guy, McClelland."

I shook my head.

She asked, "Does your family know?"

"What's left of it, yes."

"What does that mean, Alan?"

"My parents were both only children. Three of my four grandparents are dead. The other one has dementia."

Kirsten folded her arms across her chest and grabbed the opposing biceps. I could tell that my acknowledgment worried her. That concern caused her to miss the obvious. A good interviewer would not have run past the opening I'd just offered.

"You don't ever talk about it?" she said.

"Once I did. Not before. Not since."

"Why?"

Her question wasn't a challenge. She was genuinely curious. As a friend, and maybe as a lawyer. "I didn't want what happened . . . to define who I am for the rest of my life. I didn't want to be . . . that person. The person who had . . . shot . . . someone. I didn't want everything I did afterward to be viewed through that lens. Not for one day, not for the rest of my life. How do you ever get away from something that . . . big?" I caught her puzzled gaze. "I'm serious. How? Does Amy ever talk about what happened?"

"No. Never." Her tone became hushed.

"Do you? When you meet some new guy? Someone asks you out. Do you tell him about the night at Galatoire's? Or the night at my house? About your buddy, Carl?"

"Of course not. But later maybe, I will, after there's . . . some trust."

Her voice was so quiet I had to strain to hear her. "Has that happened, Kirsten? In real life? Has it?"

She was making honesty sound easy. It wasn't. I knew it wasn't.

She shook her head. "Love . . . has been difficult for me since Robert died. He was a . . . special man. I've had a high standard . . . for that kind of intimacy. For romance."

"And no one's reached that bar?" My question was intended to reflect my cynicism about her resistance. Therapists called it confrontation. I could be good at it.

I could also use it to deflect attention from me.

She heard my words more literally than I'd intended. She said, "One man did." Her face softened at some memory. "Maybe he spoiled me . . . that probably made everything that's come since harder, though, not easier."

I felt the cloud retreat, relieved that we were no longer talking about me. "What happened?" I asked. *Carl Luppo*, I guessed.

She put her hands on each side of my face, leaned forward, and touched her lips to mine for two seconds that felt like an hour. She moved back only an inch before she said, "I fell in love with my therapist. His honesty. His kindness. You must know how that goes."

THIRTY-FIVE

THARON THIBODEAUX knew Michael McClelland but hadn't been directly involved in his inpatient treatment in Pueblo.

When I'd been sitting in Kaladi with the transplanted Louisiana psychiatrist, I'd had to shake off the distraction I was feeling as a result of the shock of learning that the purpose of the meeting had turned out to be different from the one I'd anticipated. One of the blind alleys I had wandered down was a futile attempt to try to understand the complexities of the clinic and unit structure that Tharon was describing in the inpatient forensic institute, and why the security and clinical architecture meant that he knew Nicole Cruz better than he knew Michael McClelland. I gave up, accepting the alternative proposition that the psychiatrist had some clinical insight into Michael McClelland, but nowhere nearly as much as he had about his own patient, Nicole Cruz.

From his revelations I began to understand the scope of what I had missed during my few sessions with Nicole.

If the simple fact that she had spent seven months at the state hospital—the last four of those under the care of Dr. Thibodeaux—was any indication of her true mental state, my clinical errors of omission and commission were multiple and serious.

At my patient's urging I'd willingly mistaken her hypomania for ADHD and residual autism. I'd been almost totally blinded to her underlying depression, certainly to its severity. And I'd fallen hook, line, and sinker for her captivating malingering about her family's oil wealth in Mexico.

My list of transgressions included all the things I had missed by failing to pause long enough to take a formal health history, let alone even a cursory mental-health history. Those omissions meant that I had ended up failing to discover Nicole's adolescent preoccupation with cutting, her infatuation with crystal meth, and her five previous known instances of overt suicidal behavior— including three serious attempts and two gestures. I also had managed to stay oblivious to the fact that she had made ER visits too frequent to enumerate, and had a history of at least seven—count 'em, seven—acute psychiatric hospitalizations at various Colorado facilities prior to her ultimate admission to the state hospital in Pueblo.

I had never learned that the most common reason for her to lose privileges on the unit while hospitalized in Pueblo was her propensity to turn any length of cord or string she found into a noose.

I'd also missed the teensy-weensy tidbit that Nicole

had a rap sheet with fourteen assorted entries—mostly minor-league infractions having to do with possessing meth or the ingredients to make it, or for stealing to get the money to buy it—and that the litany of legal transgressions included the use of numerous AKAs, including "Cruise," "Crews," "Crus," "Cole," "Kol," "Coal," "Col," and just for a change of pace, "Nicki."

With an *i*.

The good news? It turned out that I wasn't the first mental-health, medical, or law enforcement professional to make the mistake of assuming that Nicole's gender was male. Nicole had used her androgyny to her advantage whenever she thought the system would let her get away with it, which was apparently frequently.

My shame over my piss-poor clinical-practice skills wasn't pacified by the discovery that I wasn't alone in misjudging Kol's gender. I had enough professional pride left, barely, to recognize that if the sole good tidings generated by my ten minutes listening to Dr. Thibodeaux talk about my recently deceased patient was that I had plentiful professional company in mistaking her for a man, I was in a whole peck of trouble.

Tharon and I paused from our discussion long enough to get refills from the woman running the big espresso machine. We returned to the table below the burlap sacks of unroasted beans and moved our discussion on to Michael McClelland.

I already knew that McClelland was in the Colorado

State Hospital with at least one treatment goal that had been mandated by the judicial branch of the state of Colorado: his state caregivers had been mandated by the trial judge to provide care to help Michael attain a particular legal threshold—competence to proceed within the criminal justice system. They were to notify the court when they had determined that Michael had reached that ambiguous, but attainable threshold of mental health.

A conviction on any of the serious pending charges would undoubtedly have forced Michael to change his mailing address from the quasi-urban Pueblo hospital to someplace decidedly more rural and slightly farther north and west—the much less hospitable environs of the maximum security wing of the Colorado State Penitentiary, New Max, outside Cañon City.

Michael, despite his many character flaws, was a bright guy. Sometime in the summer of 2002 he had apparently recognized that his crazy act was getting worn around the edges and had determined that his physicians were getting perilously close to declaring him competent to proceed to trial for his earlier crimes in Pitkin County. Even if he escaped justice for those, Boulder County was waiting its prosecutorial turn. He had, not surprisingly, responded to the threat by tossing impediments in the state's path.

The golden sabot? Michael stopped talking to hospital staff.

According to Tharon, in the month or two just prior to going dumb, Michael elucidated and embellished to his therapists a series of paranoid delusions involving his father, his sister, and some colorful characters from the *Harry Potter* saga, a number of whom he had concluded were remarkably similar in appearance and behavior to staff at the forensic facility in Pueblo.

His psychiatrist responded to his patient's apparent increase in psychotic thinking by upping his antipsychotic meds. Michael responded by refusing to talk to professional staff. He told his fellow patients enough about what was going on in his head that the staff soon learned that he was convinced that some of his *Potter* antagonists had infiltrated the clinical ranks of the hospital.

"To the best of my knowledge he hasn't spoken to a member of the clinical staff since the summer of 2002," Tharon said.

"But he talks to other patients?" I asked.

"Specific people. Patients. Some people in housekeeping, too. He can act pretty crazy."

"Act?"

He shrugged. "Act. It's been a topic of some vocal disagreements among the clinical staff. Some think he's malingering."

"You?"

"Never knew him well enough to have an opinion."

"People you respect?"

"Thought he was playing us. Some of the best clinicians in the forensics institute thought he should be the poster child for what's wrong with 16-8-112."

"Excuse me?"

"That's the statute that addresses the question of offenders who are judged incompetent to proceed within the criminal justice system. If a gifted sociopath gets a foot inside the door and can seduce a professional ally or two, he can play the system like Hendrix played the guitar. Some people on staff think that where that statute is concerned, Michael McClelland is Hendrix. Others think his paranoia is real."

"The patients he did talk with? They included Nicole Cruz?"

"See, that's what's interesting. I don't think Michael ever had much contact, if any, with Nicole. Not directly anyway." Tharon began to rehash his description of the unit demarcations at the state hospital.

I stopped him. "Why is that interesting, Tharon?" I asked. "That he didn't have much contact with Nicole?"

"One of Michael's confidantes among the patients was a woman who became a friend of Nicole's prior to her discharge."

"You can't tell me her name, can you?"

"No, I can't." He wasn't apologetic about it. I hadn't given him any reason to be.

"Is she still there? Has that woman been discharged?"

"Nicole was discharged in January of this year. We wanted to watch her through the holidays. You know how that goes." I did. I nodded. "Her friend had been discharged a while before. Four months? Five? I'd have to go back and check."

"But this woman—Nicole's friend—had also been a confidante of Michael McClelland's? You're sure?"

"The security requirements of their respective units prohibited a lot of contact. But their relationship—even at a distance—created some clinical and community issues. The two of them were complementary colors. Yin and yang."

"What issues?"

"Nicole's friend is a psychologist. Made things complicated clinically in the institute. And in the community at large."

"I can only imagine."

"Unless you've treated a colleague, especially a violent colleague, in an inpatient environment, I really doubt that you can imagine how complex it is."

"What was her diagnosis? Why was she in the forensic institute?" I asked.

He thought about my question for a moment. "Sorry," he said. "I really shouldn't."

My meeting with Tharon made many things clear for me, one of which was why he had called me.

After I discovered Nicole's body in Peter's barn, the authorities had obviously quickly tracked her identity—even if she didn't have ID on her person, her fingerprints were on file all over the Colorado criminal justice system—and had quickly been able to confirm her recent prolonged stay at the state hospital. Someone from Boulder's law enforcement community, probably one of the sheriff's investigators, had then called Dr. Thibodeaux to ask some questions about his ex-patient. The name of her current therapist—me—had come up during the conversation, and Thibodeaux had tracked down my home number and called me as an act of rather dubious, but much-appreciated, professional courtesy.

When Tharon said that it was time for him to leave to meet his friends for the basketball game, I asked him if he would answer one more question.

"Depends on the question," he said, glancing at his watch.

"That's fair. Earlier, you said you'd been in my shoes during your residency, that you didn't want what happened to you to happen to anyone else. What did happen during your residency?"

He didn't hesitate. "I had a borderline guy I'd been treating for a while. The transference was . . . let's say, labile. Constant splitting. He was a cutter, among other things. Very manipulative. Multiple suicidal gestures." He forced a small smile. "It wasn't my best clinical work."

He reached for his jacket.

"Borderlines can do that," I said. "I'm not good with them. Never have been. I think it takes a certain type of therapist."

"Yeah, well." He shook his head, shooing away some memory. "You want to know what happened?"

"Yes." And I thought he wanted to tell me.

He folded the coat across his lap. "Okay. We were having a department Christmas party. Second year of my residency. The party was at an attending's new apartment in a building near the Quarter. Somehow my patient found out where the party was being held. One of the other residents was on call that night. She was at the party, too."

"The on-call resident was an optimist?" I said.

"Marlene was an optimist. My borderline guy calls the psychiatric clinic, says it's an emergency, and gets his call returned by Marlene. She just went into one of the bedrooms of the apartment and called him. My guy is no virgin at badgering on-call residents—he immediately says he's in treatment with me and in his own overwrought diva way conveys that he's in crisis. Marlene begins to do her intervention. He stops her and says he wants to talk with me, no one but me. She begins to dig deeper into her clinical bag of tricks—Marlene was good—but he stops her again. He demands to talk to me. She begins to explain the call system and tries to get him to understand why that's not possible. He stops her again. He's getting more agitated. When she persists, he tells her he's on top of a building, and he is going to jump if I won't talk to him right then."

"Wow. On a manipulative scale, that's a ten," I said.

Tharon made a what-are-you-going-to-do face. "Marlene goes into one final song-and-dance about how the emergency call system works and tries to convince him that I'm unavailable and tells him he will need to talk with her. She's sure she can help. I'm sure you know the script. My patient says he knows all about the call system and that he also knows I'm standing close enough to her at that moment that she could hand me the phone."

"What?" I asked. "How did—"

"Marlene's quick. She asks what building roof he is on. He says, 'The one where your party is. The one you're in this very minute. The one that Dr. Thibodeaux is in this very minute. In fact, when I jump, I should pass right by the living room window on my way down.' The building was six stories tall."

"Holy . . ." I said.

"The party was on the fourth floor."

"Crap," I said.

"After a couple more minutes trying to get any connection with the guy, Marlene hands me a note explaining what's going on. My first reaction is I think he's bluffing—he's manipulative and self-destructive, but I never saw him as suicidal. Not intentionally, anyway. But just to be safe I borrow a phone and call 911 to report a possible jumper. Marlene scribbles me another note telling me she's sure she can handle him.

"The rescue truck shows up a few minutes later with siren and lights. Couple of cop cars, too. By then, the whole psychiatry department—all the attendings, all the other residents, everybody's dates and significant others—knows exactly what's coming down on the roof. Half the party is at the window watching, wondering what's going to happen. One of the other residents is actually joking about where my patient will land."

"Hostile," I said. "Your patient, and your colleague."

Tharon shrugged. "Actually, 'hostile' was just beginning. Hostile was a few minutes later when he did exactly what he was threatening to do. He jumped. True to his word, he did indeed pass right in front of the living room window. For me, it was a blur. He was there; he was gone. He landed on top of a car. He died on impact ten feet from the rescue truck."

"I'm so sorry," I said. "I can't imagine."

"Old wound, old story," he said. "Before we had coffee today I thought that what Nicole did to you was something similar. Killing herself so close to your house. Suicide as weapon. Hostility. Humiliation. Anyway, I thought I might be able to cushion the blow a little bit by giving you some of her history."

"Do you still think that? That Nicole's death is the same kind of thing your guy did to you?"

He shook his head. "Maybe not."

"It's not the same, is it?" I said. "I'm not convinced that what Nicole did was part of a crazy transference. I don't think it was even a medication failure. I may have made some diagnostic mistakes, but she wasn't a character disorder out of control. And she wasn't that depressed."

Tharon shrugged. "From a distance that's what I thought it was. But if Michael M.'s involved—and especially if his friend is—you may have a whole different problem on your hands."

I thanked him. We shook hands. We exchanged business cards. He left.

THIRTY-SIX

KIRSTEN SAT back and retrieved her wine from the hibachi.

I could taste her on my lips.

"God," she exclaimed. "What a relief that was. I didn't realize how badly I needed to say that." She looked at my bewildered face. "Oh . . . I didn't say it to put you on the spot. I said it for me." She spread both hands on her chest. Her face broke into a wide smile. "Now maybe I can let it go. We can both let it go. Pretend I didn't say it."

It had been a secret.

"I didn't know," I said. I had felt transferential breezes of affection blowing from her during the brief interval she was my patient. That wasn't unusual. But the admission she'd just made did not feel like an unresolved transference from Kirsten's therapy.

It did not.

"Men are dense." She laughed. The trill was a lovely note that hung in the air. "Dear God, I feel better," she said. "Oh . . . but I bet you don't. I'm sorry."

"You bet right."

"Will you tell me about it?" she asked. It was her turn to change the subject. "What happened back then?"

She was inviting me to spill my secret as she had spilled hers. I recited the familiar relationship equation in my head: disclosure plus vulnerability equals intimacy.

Did I want that? Could I handle that? I wouldn't go near the first question, but knew the answer to the second. I could not handle it. I shook my head. My therapist rationalization machinery kicked in—*It's unresolved transference she's feeling. That's all it is. She didn't really love me. Doesn't. She loved what I represented.*

"I'd be honored," she said. "If you would tell me."

"I don't think I can, Kirsten."

Maybe she loved me. Maybe she still does. God.

"Did you do something . . . terrible?" she asked.

Yes. "I don't think I'm capable of making that judgment."

"Was it so bad the last time you talked about it?"

Bad? Adrienne held me in her arms for about a minute after I told her. Then she said, "Pretty good secret, meshuggah. Top ten. Better than Peter's fire story. And definitely better than him shagging the nanny."

Telling Adrienne had been fine. In life she was the exception. Not the rule.

"I think you might have to tell me," Kirsten said.

Was that the lawyer talking? Or the woman who had loved me?

"How old were you?" she asked.

"Young."

"How young?"

"How old is Amy?" I asked.

"Dear Jesus," she said.

THIRTY-SEVEN

ALTHOUGH I'D intended to tell Kirsten about my meeting with Tharon Thibodeaux, she and I never got around to talking about it in detail. That afternoon visit at her West Boulder cottage proved to be about other things.

All she heard about Kaladi were the headlines.

I returned home from my visit to her house just before dusk. Lauren had spent most of the day working while Grace had been off with friends. When I walked in the door Lauren asked me where I'd been. I told her I'd been meeting with my lawyers about Nicole Cruz.

"Go well?" she asked.

"Okay," I said.

That ended the conversation.

As Lauren was getting ready for bed I asked, "You still thinking Bimini is a good idea?"

"I am," she said. "I think we'll go. I couldn't live with myself if anything happened to Grace."

Her back was turned when she spoke. I was grateful she couldn't see me attempt to process her words. I continued to feel paralyzed by her plans. That my vote on the matter had been rendered superfluous no longer surprised me.

Lauren climbed onto the bed and flicked off the lights.

I said, "Good night."

In the dark she said, "Are you seeing someone? Another woman?"

I moved toward the bed. "Lauren, what are—"

"No," she said. "Just answer me. I don't want a speech. I don't want a thousand questions. Just tell me, dammit. You're so different lately, the last few months. So distant. So . . . just tell me. Are you having an affair?"

"No," I said.

"Then good night," she said.

"Can we talk about this?" I asked.

"I'm too tired," she said. "Please."

I stood in the dark for a few seconds before I accepted the reality that she didn't want me there. Emily followed me out to the living room. I finished what was left of the vodka. I knew before I started drinking it that the couple of slogs in the bottle weren't going to be sufficient.

The dog snoozed. I remembered seeing a big bank of parking lot lights near the Foothills Parkway south of Arapahoe flick off right on schedule at two-fifteen. I had been thinking about Michael McClelland conducting an orchestra that was playing my requiem march. Sometime after that, I found sleep.

The next morning came quickly. I was up and out of the house to see an early patient before Lauren and Grace were out of bed.

"I'd like to think I can leave you alone for a weekend without the world falling apart," Cozy said to me a few minutes before noon. From Cozy, that constituted a greeting.

He was back from San Diego.

I had seen only two patients that morning. One other had canceled. Another was a no-show. The inevitable attrition to my caseload as a result of my public connection to a patient's suicide had begun. I expected that my patient roster would be diminished by half in another week. If the controversy didn't resolve soon, and my name continued to be plastered ignominiously on the inside pages of the local paper, the remaining half would be diminished by half within the next fortnight.

I'd used the extra time from the last cancellation of the morning to stroll east on Pearl to get something to eat before my meeting with Cozy. I stopped at Allison for a pick-me-up shot of espresso while I weighed my options. Sal's or Snarf's? Snarf's or Sal's? Snarf's won. As I absorbed Cozy's quasi-insulting overture I still felt the warm buzz from my sandwich. I suspected it would be the most enduring pleasure of my day.

The tone of Cozy's comments wasn't only an awkward jab at humor, it was also that of a father expressing his disappointment to a teenager who had demolished the trust his parents had placed in him while they were out of town. Most days I would have parried with some move in the same key. Or I would have allowed Cozy his interpersonal imperialism, knowing that in the near future he would be using the honed skill not at my expense, but in my defense.

Not that day. I wasn't even looking at him when I said, "Stop, Cozy. Save it for somebody else. I'm not in the mood." I looked at my watch. "I'm going to work all day to make enough money to pay for half of this little chat. I have thirty-five minutes until my next appointment. Let's get something done before I have to leave."

Cozy liked to sit behind his big desk so clients were forced to take him in as part of the grandeur of the scenery. The wall of windows behind him on the top floor of the Colorado Building in downtown Boulder had a billion-dollar bird's-eye view of historic Boulder, the foothills, the Flatirons, and a wide-angle slice of the Rocky Mountains, including a hundred-mile chunk of the Continental Divide.

As gorgeous as the view was—and it was world-class—that's how ugly a stain the building where Cozy worked left on the Boulder downtown landscape. If architects could be shot for malpractice, the one who designed the monstrosity would have long before taken a bullet into his or her soul. The Colorado Building had been erected as though someone with unrefined modernist sensibilities had determined that a late-nineteenth-century Colorado Victorian frontier town needed nothing more than it needed a horrendously out-of-scale, eighty-foot-tall, red brick and reflective glass cereal box to cleave the very soul of downtown into two roughly equal halves. When I got worked up about it, something I did just about every time I was confronted by the thing, I tried to remind myself that the architect shared the responsibility for the travesty with myriad owners, developers, and city planners. Most days the reminder failed to modulate my criticism, or diminish the fact that I wanted the architect's throat.

"Don't you feel . . . unclean working in this building, Cozy? It's the architectural equivalent of driving a Hummer."

He manufactured a smile. He glanced out the window. He said, "No."

From our present perch it was hard to argue with him. Despite its lack of aesthetic virtue—with its most recent fenestration the building looked like a gingham glass gate hung between two brick walls—the views to the west from its upper floors were so stunning that it was easy to forget that I was standing inside a monument to architectural pornography.

"You wanted to move on. Anything else you would like to criticize first?" he asked. I shook my head. "Okay, Alan. The dead . . . person . . . hanging in your neighbor's barn was your patient? I have that right?"

I thought I was ready to follow him, but I wasn't. "Ever go to Snarf's, Cozy? Best thing to happen to that end of Pearl since Don's."

"What," he asked, "is Snarf's?"

Snarf's wasn't Cozy's kind of place. "It's a dive of a sandwich shop at 21st and Pearl. The old A&W? You really should try it, but promise me you'll be nice to the girls at the counter." I was about to add a caution that the girls at the counter might not always be nice to him until I noted that he was staring at me as though he had just realized I was mentally challenged. I pressed on, unfazed. "What about Salvaggio's, Cozy? You go there, right? Hell, there's one at the damn corner. The capicolla? Come on. Tell me you do."

"Your dead patient, Alan? If I may divert your attention from . . . cold cuts."

I was ready to follow him. "You can call her Nicole. You can call her a woman. You can call me a fuckup. None of it's germane to what happened on Saturday."

He sighed. He'd been hoping for a little less attitude. No longer expecting it, but still, hoping. After muttering, "But Snarf's is?" under his breath, he said, "You didn't know she was suicidal?"

"She wasn't."

"O-kay. We'll just set aside the"—he spread the fingers of both hands, and palms up, seemed to be trying to capture something as it floated past him—"fact . . . that the evidence seems to indicate that she hung herself a few yards from the front door of your home. Some might consider that prima facie evidence that she was suicidal, at least . . . momentarily. But why quibble? My next question: You didn't know she was depressed?"

I clenched my jaw tightly enough that I could feel the enamel surface of my teeth grinding and could hear the squeal from the friction. "You're not asking the right questions, Cozy. If you don't ask me the right questions, you're playing into their hands."

He leaned back, laced his fingers behind his head, and put his gargantuan feet up on his desk. I suspected he was about to train a spotlight on my paranoia and ask exactly whose hands I was talking about him playing into. Instead he asked, "How about I sit here and you answer the right questions. We'll both pretend that I asked them."

That was fine with me. "Kol—Nicole—didn't demonstrate any depression during the few weeks I was treating her. She mentioned depression, but denied any currently. Note the time frame in that qualifier: I treated her for only a few weeks. Three sessions to be precise. I will acknowledge that it does turn out that she was depressed by history, and I will admit that I did not know the details of that history until yesterday's meeting with her psychiatrist from the state hospital. My clinical failure wasn't a failure of diagnosis, however—in psychotherapy diagnosis is a process, not an event. My failure—and, yes, there was one—entailed not reviewing pertinent history with her at the beginning of her treatment. I screwed that up. Mea culpa. Next?"

"Your clinical failure would also include some failure to intervene . . . in a timely manner?"

"My clinical judgment was that no dramatic clinical intervention was indicated."

"Then perhaps there's some failure evidenced by your . . . gullibility? Is that a good word for the fact that you didn't apply any skepticism to her narrative?"

I stared at him.

"It did," he added, "prove false. Her narrative."

Cozy apparently wanted me to whelp additional mea culpas. I didn't feel much like complying. Given the mood I was in, I was more likely to scream profanities than squeal apologies.

"You bought her story," my lawyer said, proving his determination to get me to capitulate to having committed some additional sin. "Despite the fact that it was all lies, right? Am I missing something?"

"Facts aren't always relevant," I said.

"Please try convincing a jury of that," he muttered under his breath before I could add the qualifier *in psychotherapy*. He went on, "Oh, I forgot, you don't have to worry about such mundanities. That's my job."

"What do you want from me today?"

"Some cooperation with your defense would be nice," he said. "You made an errant assumption about her gender, and you didn't take even a cursory mental-health history. You failed to recognize her underlying depression. Those statements are correct?"

"Yes. Want more, Cozy? I didn't know until I read it in the paper that Kol had a job at the cemetery. I thought he was a trust-fund baby. I still don't know where he was living. He'd given me a false address."

"She," Cozy corrected.

I was tempted to bite back but I had no enthusiasm for a jostle. If Cozy were the lawyer who would end up defending me on the malpractice suit that was certain to follow Nicole Cruz's death, I might have bothered to explain how my failure to take a formal history from my patient didn't really diverge that much from generally accepted standards of practice. But that defense, even if true, was lame. I didn't feel like rehearsing its recitation with Cozy.

The fact that my fatal mistakes were largely the result of an act of omission—not taking a formal history—that was committed by psychotherapists every day didn't excuse my failings or mitigate their gravity. Those lapses wouldn't exonerate me as much as they would indict my colleagues along with me.

The fact that Kol would likely have lied had I gone ahead and asked about mental-health history wasn't relevant either. The fact was that I hadn't asked the right questions. Whether or not I might have learned something crucial if I had, I would never know.

In a civil proceeding it would all come back to the uncontestable reality that I didn't ask.

The current, pertinent truth was that Cozy was a criminal defense attorney and not the lawyer who would defend me against malpractice claims. My failure to ponder aloud with Nicole Cruz whether she'd ever been in a jail, on psychotropic medication, in a psychiatric hospital, or whether she had ever tried to kill herself wasn't likely to be particularly relevant if the charges Cozy ended up defending me against were charges not that I negligently failed to anticipate my patient's suicide, but rather that I had participated in her murder.

If I somehow managed to avoid the charge of homicide that Kirsten feared the authorities were contemplating, the recitation of my defense on malpractice, however futile, would occur with some lawyer other than Cozy, an attorney who handled civil, not criminal, defense. It was to that lawyer that I'd have to admit that I'd made a clinical judgment by choosing to spend those early weeks of treatment ruling out Kol's self-diagnosis of residual autism and ADHD, and not asking for her hospitalization history or assessing her suicidal risk.

Before I'd decided which of Cozy's unasked questions I would address next, the intercom on his desk came alive. His receptionist was a black man from Kenya named Nigel. Nigel's English was accented, formal, and impeccable. In contrast to most of Boulder, he always dressed like he was expecting *GQ* to show up for a photo shoot at any minute. Cozy had told me that Nigel had originally visited Boulder while running with the elite field in the Bolder Boulder, had fallen in love with our town, and moved. He was supporting his family so that his wife could continue her studies at the university. When she was done, he would get his turn at graduate school.

From my limited observation, Nigel seemed to take no shit from Cozy, which endeared him to me. Nigel wanted to be an architect. He despised the aesthetics and placement of the building in which he worked as much as I did. That endeared him to me. His architectural dream was to design and build inexpensive modular green housing that could be mass produced in his native Kenya. That endeared him to me, too.

Nigel's voice on the intercom: "Ms. Lord instructed me to interrupt you."

Cozy raised his not insignificant eyebrows, punched a button, and picked up the phone. "Hello, Kirsten," he said.

I didn't know how much Kirsten had told her boss about my visit to her home the previous afternoon, but I felt it was prudent to assume that she'd already told him everything that I'd told her, but probably not everything she had told me. The point of this particular call to her boss? I'd have to try to discern it from Cozy's end of the conversation. But Cozy's end turned out to be mostly silence. Kirsten was doing most of the talking.

I stood and soaked in the view until Cozy got off the phone. He walked over next to me, put an arm around my shoulders, and said, "I'll continue to prod you until you recognize the extent of your jeopardy. We have a lot of work to do, Alan. What's going on is serious. This isn't going to go away because you believe you didn't do anything wrong."

"I understand that."

"You're not acting like you do. Fighting me is a waste of energy. The civil-liability issues might end your career. The criminal-liability issues could have much more serious consequences. We have to get focused. Not next week. Now. I'll be in touch."

I turned toward the door.

He said, "Just for the record? I'm a regular at Sal's. Pastrami."

He was smiling.

THIRTY-EIGHT

THE MEETING with Cozy didn't improve my mood. I doubted that it improved my legal prospects. It certainly hadn't improved my financial condition.

I suspected that Kirsten's call had been bad news. When I'd asked Cozy about it before I left his office, he denied the call had been about my case. I don't think he really expected me to believe him.

I didn't.

I was looking forward to the walk back up the Mall toward my office. The odd intersection of lives that collided on Boulder's most egalitarian public thoroughfare was almost always distracting to me, usually in a positive way. On most days the stroll west toward the looming panorama of the foothills with the midday sun over my left shoulder would soften any ill mood. The riot of color in the brick planters should have been an added bonus—the regiments of tulips that the Mall's groomer, Paul, nursed every year were in prime springtime explosion.

That day nothing seemed to help.

My phone vibrated in my pocket. The screen read PAY PHONE. I thought *Sam*. I was right. "You tell anyone we talked yesterday while I was . . . away from Boulder?" he asked in lieu of a greeting.

I could tell he didn't want it to be true—he didn't want me to have talked to anyone. I didn't hesitate to inform him that I hadn't. "No."

"You didn't tell anyone where I said I was?"

"I don't think you said where you were. Something about some dogs."

"You were at a pay phone when you called?"

"I was. Down in Denver, by DU."

He was silent for a moment. I wondered if he was trying to decide if he believed me. Or if he was trying to figure out why I'd made the long drive to south Denver.

"You're sure?"

"I haven't told anyone we talked, Sam. I still don't know where you were when we did. Hell, I don't know where you are now. What's going on?" I asked.

"Somebody is saying they saw me someplace I wasn't supposed to be."

"Were you where they thought they saw you?"

"I was. But there's no way anybody saw me."

I picked some mental dominos out of the pile and lined them up in formation like Paul's tulip army on the Mall: The missing grand jury witness. Sam had been ordered off the case. He'd ignored the order. And someone had spied him ignoring the order.

Sam was wary that the first domino was about to tumble.

"Who saw you?" I asked.

"I don't know. I got an e-mail from some bogus Yahoo account. Says someone saw me yesterday where I was. I'm thinking if they tell my bosses I should just deny everything." He was thinking out loud with me, something he rarely did. "What are they going to do? Believe some civilian or believe me?"

"Who do you think it was?" I asked again.

"This thing breaks wrong and I may have just lost my job," he said. "Listen, here's a freebie for you: The prints under the workbench, and on the side of the fridge?"

My amble west on the Mall was interrupted by the light at Broadway. I somehow ended up standing between two baby strollers. One of the strollers was a double that was about the size of my first car. The women who were pushing the large-wheeled behemoths continued the conversation they'd been having as though I wasn't there. It was something about sun and hair mixed in with something about flying to Frankfurt on Lufthansa. I assumed I'd missed an important transition in their discussion.

"We're talking about Peter's shop now?" I said to Sam.

"Yeah, we are. The latents weren't McClelland's. No hit in AFIS."

The light changed. I stayed put. The mothers took off behind their strollers.

I had been certain that Michael had been camping out in the barn prior to Kol's suicide. It was the only way to begin to make sense of what I knew.

Now what?

"Were the prints Kol's? I mean, Nicole's?"

"No. We don't know whose they are. The lab needs a complete set of exemplars from Adrienne and Jonas to rule them out. And anybody who's worked for them in the past, you know, while."

"Could they be Peter's?"

"Unlikely, but it's possible." He paused. "Could they be yours?"

Shit. "The way my luck's been running? Could be."

"Wouldn't be good."

"Adrienne and Jonas are still in Israel," I said.

"Yeah," Sam said. "Complicates things."

"I appreciate the information."

He hesitated before he said, "This may feel like a series of ambushes to you. Or more benignly, like the pieces of a puzzle. It isn't. It's one big web. From where I stand, it's being constructed to snare you."

"What do you mean?"

"The purse? The blood on your shoe? The note on your door? The body? The forensics that we're getting? If you're not guilty of something, then somebody's going to great lengths to make it look like you are."

I watched the electronic scoreboard that let pedestrians know how long they had to get across Broadway count down from sixteen to fifteen to fourteen to thirteen.

"Sam, I know things you don't know. You know things that I don't know. Together we might know enough. Help me. I'll help you."

Eleven, ten, nine. "I can't help you, Alan. You know that."

"I shouldn't help you, Sam. You know that. But I will."

He hung up.

I rushed across Broadway as the light changed. The strollers rolled ahead of me, hub to hub.

I finished the day's work with the efficiency of a robot. And probably with about the same amount of clinical skill.

I picked up Grace at school and we came home to an empty house.

Since Kol's death in the barn Emily and I had developed a new end-of-the-day routine. As soon as I got home and got Grace settled, the big dog and I searched our house, inside and out, checking for bad guys, unlocked windows, forced doors. After we did the house we did the garage and then we did the perimeter of the barn and the perimeter of Adrienne's house.

Emily had the DNA of a herding dog but she had a reasonable nose for trouble and could be as intimidating to strangers as a grizzly mom protecting her cubs. I always felt better when she gave me the all clear.

Grace retreated to her room while I fed the dogs and started dinner. Getting ready to cook that night's meal was mostly prep. I partially boiled some wide noodles, cleaned some spinach and arugula, took some sliced ham out of the refrigerator, and rested a few eggs and a stick of sweet butter on the counter to bring everything to room temperature. The final steps would take only minutes; I wouldn't throw the ingredients together on a plate until everyone was at the table.

The only tricky part of the meal I had planned was the brown butter. Making brown butter isn't culinary jujitsu, but experience had taught me that brown butter is one of those things that should be made by an attentive cook.

When six-thirty came and went and Lauren didn't get home, I started to worry. Fifteen minutes later, I was using most of my mental energy to try to keep from panicking.

I tried Lauren's cell. No answer. I tried her office. No answer.

I checked on Grace. She was fine.

Seven o'clock came. Two minutes later the phone rang. Caller ID read PRIVATE CALLER. I answered with an anxious "Where are you? Are you okay?"

"I'm fine. Alan? What's going on?"

It wasn't Lauren on the line. It was Kirsten.

I looked out the window. Lauren was driving down the lane, her security escort right behind her car. She was okay. Grace was okay.

"Can I call you back?" I asked.

"Soon? Tonight? It's important."

"What kind of important?"

"We know what the grand jury is investigating."

"Soon," I said. I hung up before Lauren made it in the door.

The meal was a simple toss of inch-wide noodles, wilted greens, and sliced ham. The heat from the brown butter and cooked noodles warmed the ham and softened the greens. I arranged the savory mix on a plate and topped it all with an egg that I fried sunny-side up in more brown butter. For Lauren, the concoction screamed comfort food. The meal was an undisguised entreaty from me—intended as a kindness and invitation. Nothing romantic. Just my acknowledgment that we desperately needed to talk.

She had another agenda. Lauren chose that supper to tell Grace that they were going to someplace called Bimini for a vacation. Daddy had to work; he was going to stay home and take care of the dogs. Gracie ran from the table and got her globe. It was clear that she loved the way the word "Bimini" felt rolling off her innocent lips. "Can we look for a *book* about Bimini?" she asked.

"Of course," Lauren said, smiling. "We can go online and try to find one."

"Can I *Google* it?"

"If one of us is with you."

"What about school?" Gracie asked after her mother had helped her find the Bahamas on the globe.

"I'll work that out," Lauren told her. "Don't worry. But one thing?"

"What?" my daughter asked.

"This has to be our secret? Okay? You and me." A second later Lauren added, "And Daddy."

Lauren was at the sink cleaning the brown butter from the egg pan.

Grace was back in her room singing a song she was making up about Bimini and the Bahamas. The rhymes were proving a challenge. I finished clearing the table and asked Lauren if we could talk.

"Maybe when we get back, Alan. Not now. Let it rest for a while, okay? There's too much going on."

"I don't like that you're leaving feeling . . . the way you're feeling," I said.

"What way am I feeling?" she said. "You think you know? Grace and I won't be gone long. They'll find Michael soon enough. When it's safe, we'll be back. When we're back, we can talk."

I was hurt and angry. I would counsel someone else that it was time to let the passion I felt for her fuel me enough to fight. I tried to swallow both my hurt and my anger. The passion? At that moment it barely felt combustible. I said, "That's it?"

"For now," she said. "Yes, that's it."

"When will you leave?"

"I need to go to the office tomorrow to tie up a few things. As soon as I can finish making travel arrangements, we'll go. If I can get it together we could fly to Miami as early as tomorrow night, or maybe the next day. We have to spend one night in Miami to get a connection to Bimini."

I started to leave the kitchen, my tail between my legs.

She said, "For what it's worth, I always thought that if it ever happened to us that you would be the one leaving me."

Without turning around, I said, "Is that what this is? You leaving me?"

"No," she said, after a heartbeat passed. "But you've been leaving me for months. You just never packed your things."

I held my breath. I was concerned that I couldn't inhale without making a noise that sounded like a gasp.

In a whisper that was so low it approached silence, I thought she said, "Coward."

But it could have been my imagination.

THIRTY-NINE

I SPENT some time with Grace and finally got her to bed forty-five minutes past her bedtime. She asked lots of questions. I noted with some sadness that a scant majority of her sentences placed emphasis on a specific word. I did my best to share her enthusiasm about the upcoming adventure to Bimini. Given her excitement I wanted to see some serious yawning before I tucked her in that night.

The master bedroom was dark and the door closed when I turned off Grace's light. I retreated to the kitchen, opened the pantry, and spotted an empty spot on the top shelf.

I'd forgotten to buy more vodka. I said, "Shit."

I returned Kirsten's call from the deck off the great room. "It's Alan," I said.

"I called hours ago. You call this 'soon'?"

She was being playful. I said, "It's been a difficult night."

She ditched the jovial tone. "Anything I can do?"

"No. Thanks for asking."

"We have news."

"Good news?"

"News. Are you someplace Lauren can overhear you? I don't want her to know we know this."

"She can't hear me," I said. The multiple meanings didn't escape me.

"You know Amanda Ross?" Kirsten asked.

"Of course." Ross was a rookie Boulder cop who'd been seriously hurt in a hit-and-run late the previous summer after she'd stopped her cruiser to examine an abandoned car near Eben Fine Park at the entrance to Boulder Canyon. Like almost everyone else in town I'd stopped paying attention to her tragedy at some point. Last I'd heard Ross was in a rehab facility.

The accident was one of those senseless tragedies that captivates a community for a while. But only for a while. The community heals. Amanda Ross, however, didn't. Her injuries had been severe. She would apparently never be the same.

The investigation of the incident had been vigorous and thorough. My impression was that it had also been fruitless. Sam had mentioned it to me a few times, mostly to vent his frustration that the perpetrator was still out there. It hadn't been his case, but its impact on him was clear. "What if it were me?" he asked me once. "What would happen to Simon if I couldn't work? You think disability is enough?"

I didn't have an answer for him.

Kirsten said, "That's what the grand jury is investigating."

"That explains a lot," I said. The secrecy. Sam's tenaciousness about the purse. The over-the-top forensic response at my office. If a guy almost kills a cop he can expect the cops to use their best game to track him down.

"Yes," Kirsten agreed. "The grand jury witness who disappeared? The one whose purse was in your yard? She apparently saw some or all of what happened right after the hit-and-run. She came forward late—I don't know how late—gave a partial statement to the police and then refused to cooperate any further. The police think someone got to her—that she was threatened."

I filled in the blanks. "And the grand jury was the method the DA chose to compel her testimony, despite the threat?" One of the rare reasons that Colorado District Attorneys utilize a grand jury is to force testimony from recalcitrant witnesses. Although cops have plenty of ways to encourage witnesses to talk, they have no legal means to force a witness to cooperate prior to trial. Grand juries do.

"Yes," Kirsten said. "We heard that she was offered protection. She declined."

"Without her they have no case? Safe assumption?"

"Basically."

I waited a few seconds. I said, "You and I need to talk, Kirsten."

She hesitated before she said, "Maybe . . . but maybe not. I didn't mean to put you in an awkward place the other day. I'm sorry if I did. I was . . . smitten with you, Alan. I admit it."

"Was?"

"Please, don't . . ."

"I think it's—"

"No, no—stop," she said softly. "You touched something in me. I will be forever grateful to you. You'll always have a special place in my heart."

I was summoned back to Cozy's office at eleven o'clock the next morning to discuss the ramifications of the news about Amanda Ross. When we were done I planned to go to Salvaggio's for the sandwich I'd passed on the previous day. I was thinking of going with the spicy capicolla. It was the kind of hot that could take my mind off things.

Kirsten was late for the meeting. I wondered if it was an intentional ploy to avoid having any time with me. It was probably a good thing.

My phone vibrated in my pocket. Had Cozy not just taken a call of his own—in a replay of my last visit Nigel's voice on the intercom identified the caller as Ms. Lord— I probably would have ignored the intrusion. Instead I pulled the cell from my coat and looked at the screen.

Lauren on her mobile. My attention was divided; I was anxious to eavesdrop on Cozy's conversation with Kirsten. I let the call roll over to voice mail. I figured Lauren was going to tell me what time she and Grace were leaving for Miami. I rationalized that it was the kind of detail better recorded by voice mail or text.

Fifteen seconds later my phone vibrated again. Lauren, again.

I stood up and walked as far from Cozy's desk as I could. I went to the southern end of the wall of windows and let my eyes follow the wide lanes of Canyon Boulevard to the west. From my high perch I had no difficulty seeing the long horizontal wall of concrete-framed windows that included Lauren's office at the Justice Center ten blocks away.

I hit the button to return her call. While the connection was going through, I pondered the unpleasant reality that, in its own squat, horizontal, prestressed concrete kind of way, the original wing of the Boulder County Justice Center where my wife worked was almost as much of an architectural blight on the entrance to Boulder Canyon as the Colorado Building was on downtown.

Neither effort was ever going to be part of a retrospective on the golden age of Boulder architecture.

"Hi," I said when Lauren answered. I didn't know what to expect. We hadn't had a meaningful conversation since she shared her impression that I'd been in the process of leaving her for months.

Her greeting wasn't a hello—it was the kind of noise someone makes when they try to speak during the rushed inhale between sobs.

"Lauren?"

She continued to attempt to talk in between gasps. "He's . . . sitting in my office. In my . . . desk . . . chair. Right now. The police are . . ."

"Where are you?"

"I'm in . . . the DA's office."

"You're okay?"

She sobbed, "Yes."

When people around me get frantic, I tend to adopt a false calm. It's not a skill I was born with—overreaction to crisis was once as natural to me as bleeding from a wound. Maybe the faux composure was a skill I'd acquired during my training as a therapist. Regardless, it had become reflexive for me, like opening an umbrella in a deluge.

My voice lower and softer, the volume reduced, I asked, "Sweetie, who is it that's sitting in your office?"

Lauren said, "Michael"—swallow—"McClelland."

FORTY

MICHAEL HAD used nylon chains inserted into rein-
forced rubber hoses to affix one leg to Lauren's desk and
one wrist to her chair. Otherwise he would undoubtedly have been taken into custody and transported to the
public safety building or the county jail before I arrived
at the Justice Center.

I had strolled the few blocks to Cozy's office from mine.
Cozy and Kirsten both walked to work as a matter of
routine, so I couldn't beg a ride from either of them.
Likewise, Nigel did me no good; his wife dropped him
off at work each morning. Boulder is not the kind of
town where a pedestrian can stand on a busy corner and
flag down a passing taxi. The wait could be five minutes, or five hours. The bus? Going west on Canyon?
Not likely.

My wife was terrified. My nemesis—Jesus, I had a
nemesis—was blocks away, terrorizing her. And maybe
worse. My only way to cover the distance between us—

nine or ten blocks, depending how I counted—was on foot. I did consider the wisdom of adding to my accumulating roster of alleged felonies by committing a poorly planned carjacking, but rejected it.

I jogged to Lauren's rescue. Along the way I speed-dialed her office number and her cell number a half-dozen times. No one picked up her office phone. Her mobile went straight to voice mail each time. I tried Sam, too, but he didn't answer any of his numbers. Along the way I actually passed within a half-block of my office, and my car, but by then I figured I could cover the remaining distance more quickly on foot.

Completely out of breath from the exertion and the spent adrenaline, I somehow managed to clear security before I was stopped at the entrance to the ground floor staircase in the Justice Center by a uniformed deputy. That was the bad news.

The good news was that she didn't seem to recognize me.

She was a stout woman with some kind of dermatological condition on the part of her neck that was visible above her collar. Her arms were folded across her chest and her feet were set well over a foot apart. Even had she been without a weapon—she wasn't—she would have presented an imposing obstacle. As I walked closer she seemed to be treating my approach like a minor annoyance, a fly buzzing near her head. She didn't even bother to look me in the eyes when she swatted me away with, "No one is allowed upstairs right now. Move on, away from the stairs."

No "Sir." No "I'm sorry."

In a less frantic moment I might have deliberated about how to play the situation. But I wasn't feeling deliberative. Naïvely, I thought I'd try the truth. I said, "My wife—"

Before I could finish making my plea the courtroom doors to Division Six, about ten yards behind me, burst open and some guy in a corduroy suit and sneakers started running toward the main entrance to the building, well over a hundred feet away. A cacophony of shouts from inside the courtroom informed both the deputy and me that the guy who was running away shouldn't be, and should be stopped.

That was the deputy's job.

"Stay right here," she said to me with a sigh that let me know she had chased felons down this corridor before, and that it wasn't a favorite part of her job. She took off in a dead run. The man's corduroy trousers squeaked with every one of his stubby strides. A blind cop could have tracked his getaway. The deputy, stout though she was, was blessed with fine form and surprising speed. The race was going to be no contest.

I muttered, "Thank you," to the escaping idiot and pulled open the door to the staircase. I hopped the stairs three at a time and sprinted the short distance toward my wife.

The DA's office suite usually hummed with a quiet foreboding efficiency. I knew almost all of the players who worked there and considered some of them friends.

From my occasional visits I was also accustomed to the prevailing attitude toward the public inside the suite. The attitude was, yes, we are aware that we're public servants but no, do not take that fact too personally. We may work for you, but we don't work for *you*.

That morning, the professional and support staff were clustered together in the public anteroom where a solitary receptionist greeted visitors near the door that led to the offices. Through the interior windows that flanked the connecting door it was apparent that the offices beyond the reception area had been taken over by uniformed law enforcement from both the sheriff and the police.

I picked Elliot Bellhaven, the new senior deputy to the DA, from the group in the reception area. Elliot and I were friends, though not buddies. If Elliot had been evacuated from the offices, almost everybody had been evacuated.

I didn't say hi. I said, "Where's Lauren, Elliot?"

"Alan?" he said. Then he paused. Elliot could be counted on to be three things: impeccably well dressed, polite in social situations, and deliberative in adversarial ones. He didn't use the pause to straighten his tie. He used it to decide what to say to me. That meant that in his eyes our encounter was an adversarial situation. "What are you doing here? How did—"

I'd been hoping for compassion. I didn't get it. It stung. I shook it off.

I could've told him about the idiot in the corduroy suit and the sneakers and the conscientious and swift deputy, but at that moment I wasn't interested in answering his questions about why I happened to be visiting or how I'd bypassed security. "Where is Lauren, Elliot? Is she okay?"

"She's in the DA's office surrounded by cops. She's fine. A little shook up." He paused again. "Somebody she prosecuted once—"

Somebody she prosecuted once? Come on, Elliot, you can do better than that. How about "Somebody who tried to kill her once"?

My patience was not exemplary. A little too tersely I said, "Where is McClelland?"

Although he'd been fresh out of Harvard Law at the time, Elliot was one of the few people in the DA's office who had been around when Michael McClelland began to assemble his roster of felonies in Boulder and Aspen. I didn't have to explain my interest in McClelland to Elliot. He knew the history. Not as well as I did, but he knew it.

He deliberated some more in reaction to my question about McClelland's whereabouts. It was apparent from his consternated expression that he didn't like the fact that I already had some idea of what was going on. "The police can handle this. Your wife is safe. Go home, go back to your office. I promise that I'll call you when—"

"Please don't patronize me, Elliot."

With that I offended him. A slight man, he reacted to the offense by squaring his shoulders, straightening his spine, and raising his chin an inch. Then he said, "Okay,

try this: Given . . . everything—everything—you really
shouldn't be here at all."

His caviling was disappointing. Even worse, it felt unkind. "Elliot, thanks for your help. I'll remember it."

One of the reasons I'd entered the New Year determined to control my pettiness was that it was becoming
a more frequent occurrence.

"Alan," he said. He was imploring me to be reasonable. All I felt was his judgment that I was being unrea-
sonable. I blew past him. He called after me. "Go. It's
better for everyone. Especially Lauren."

I took two steps closer to the door to try to see what
was going on in the offices. People parted in front of me
as though I were a drunk panhandler in need of a shower.
I could have interpreted the gesture as a sign of respect
or compassion because of Lauren's circumstances. But
Elliot's reaction to my presence in the DA's office was
enough to convince me that I shouldn't allow myself the
luxury of perceiving generosity in the staff's behavior.
In my heart I knew Lauren's colleagues were giving me
room because I was radioactive and no one wanted to be
in my orbit.

What I didn't know was how radioactive I was. Or precisely why.

From my fresh vantage at the front of the throng I could
see down the hall into Lauren's office. At least five cops
were crowded into the small space near the door. They
blocked my view of her desk.

Behind me someone with a pleasant tenor and an appealingly warped sense of humor started humming the score of the battle scene in *Star Wars*. The cavalry was coming. I looked down the hall. A big cop was striding down the corridor from stage right carrying a set of bolt cutters big enough to slice off a man's arm in one thwack.

Despite the commotion and despite the glass partition separating me from the corridor I could hear him call out to his colleagues, "Coming through." The cops who were crammed into Lauren's office backed off to clear a path for him.

That's when I saw Michael McClelland's face for the first time in years.

He was sitting at my wife's desk. In her *chair*. His hands—his wrists now cuffed together by the cops—rested on the desktop. Michael hadn't aged as much as I thought he should have. He hadn't lost any of the baby fat in his jowls, his hair hadn't lost any of its color. I saw no anxiety in his clear eyes, no skin sagging from the gravity of despair.

Behind him I spotted a familiar framed photograph of Grace. In the picture my daughter was hugging Emily. Anvil was standing in his always-odd tough-guy pose at her knees. I loved that picture. I hated that it was over Michael's shoulder.

I felt still. For five or six seconds I watched McClelland's impassive face. I watched his eyes follow the action of the cops who were moving around him. I watched the acknowledgment wash over his expression as he spotted the bolt cutters and realized that the next act of the play he was directing was about to begin.

He looked up. The second his eyes found mine, I stopped feeling still.

McClelland smiled when he spotted me. He lifted his hands from the desktop. He did it slowly, probably so that he wouldn't startle his captors. With his left hand he pointed at me using his index finger. With his right hand he formed his fingers into a position with the middle three fingers curled to his palm, his pinky and thumb extended. I initially mistook it for a University of Texas "Hook 'em, 'Horns" cheer—but realized he was extending his thumb instead of his index finger. I next mistook the gesture as the laid-back *shaka* sign that native Hawaiians use to spread a little nonverbal aloha. It was neither.

He lowered his head and raised the hand toward his face with the end of his thumb up toward his right ear, the end of his pinky near his lips. The woman beside me translated. She said, "I think he wants to talk to you." There was surprise in her voice.

I said, "I think you're right." I wasn't at all ambushed by the fact that Michael McClelland wanted to talk with me. I was already considering other things. *Why had he chosen this place? This drama? This audience?*

The cops in Lauren's office saw his gesture, too, and they followed his gaze out the door. A couple of the cops turned and spotted me at the glass, staring right back at their prisoner. Without hesitation they closed ranks so that their thick torsos again blocked me from seeing Mc-Clelland. And him from seeing me.

Elliot Bellhaven used his voice well, forming crisp consonants and resonant vowels. His vocal skills made him a formidable courtroom orator. When I heard someone behind me begin to address the room, I knew that it was Elliot.

"We're going to clear this office," he said in a louder than necessary voice. "Everyone move downstairs to the first floor, please. Calmly. No need to rush. No need to go to your desks."

I neither turned to watch him nor moved to obey him. My eyes stayed focused on the doorway to Lauren's office.

The people beside me did turn. Elliot was their boss. He wasn't mine.

Elliot waited a few seconds before he repeated, "Everyone."

With that I figured he was talking directly to me. Ten seconds later I heard his voice again. He had moved so that he was right behind me.

"Come on, Alan," he said, just a trace of conciliation in his tone. "She's fine. You'll meet up with her downstairs after she's debriefed."

"Why is he here, Elliot? Why did he turn himself in?"

He had a ready reply. "Cons get comfortable inside. They want to go back. Happens all the time."

"Not McClelland. He could be in Mexico by now. Or on his way to Peru. Why give up?"

"He's crazy. Right?" Elliot shrugged. He wasn't interested in why.

"People with mental illnesses don't have judgment? That's your explanation?"

He snorted. "What's yours, Doctor? You were so good at understanding him last time around."

Although I would have preferred to hit him, I answered him. "For most of us freedom is an overriding motivation. For some of us it's not. We need to know what's more important to this guy than his freedom."

"He'll be interviewed."

"He wants to talk with me."

"You and I both know that's not going to happen."

"Why not?" I asked, fighting to keep my exasperation under wraps.

"He won't be rewarded for this stunt. McClelland's not calling the shots here. He's a fugitive. He'll be treated like a fugitive."

"You're not curious?" I asked in a conversational tone that I was pleased remained in my repertoire. "What he might want? What he's been up to for the past few days? Why he chained himself to her desk instead of running for his life?"

"He wanted to taste freedom. Found it overwhelming. How complicated is that?"

Whatever conciliation had occurred between us was fleeting; I tasted a fresh undertone of condescension. It bit at my palate, like too much salt in the soup.

"He's not going to talk to you," I said.

"How can you be so sure of that?" he asked. He thought I was challenging him. Perhaps I was.

I turned and faced him. "Because I know him."

"That's all you got? You know him?"

Elliot had given up any pretense of disguising his condescension. I said, "He's not going to talk to anyone from your office or to any cops. He hasn't spoken to a single member of the hospital clinical staff in Pueblo in years, Elliot. Not a syllable. He's been playing the system like a virtuoso." I was tempted to use Thibodeaux's Hendrix analogy, but I resisted.

"How do you know . . . that?"

I was pleased again. Elliot didn't know that McClelland had gone electively mute in Pueblo. I liked the advantage his ignorance gave me. Not because it would mean anything beyond the moment. I liked it because it allowed me a temporary petty perch just a little bit above him. In reply to his question I simply sighed. Telling Elliot how I knew about Michael's treatment progress in Pueblo, or lack thereof, wouldn't help my cause and it would be a betrayal of Tharon Thibodeaux's generosity.

"He's not done, Elliot. He didn't walk away from the state hospital so he could have a holiday at the Boulderado or spend a weekend enjoying the pleasures of the Pearl Street Mall. He had something he wanted to accomplish, and he's not done."

"What?" he asked.

I tasted derision, not curiosity, in Elliot's question. Condescension was one thing; derision was something else entirely. I was being viewed through a translucent screen of contempt. Things were worse than I had imagined. I wondered what they had on me.

I swallowed an impulsive, juvenile *"Fuck you."* Instead I said, "I don't know. What? You think it was an accident that he was camped out in a building fifty feet from my family's front door?"

"You don't know that was him."

I recalled Sam's caution about the forensic evidence collected in Peter's barn, and decided not to press that point. "You think it's a coincidence that he chained himself to Lauren's desk?"

"Go home, Alan. Your family is safe. Enjoy the good news. We got the bad guy. He's back in custody."

"*You* got the bad guy? Maybe I'm missing something, but I think the bad guy turned himself in. And I guarantee you it wasn't an act of capitulation on his part. McClelland has just gained some advantage. What? I don't know yet. But don't be naïve, Elliot. My family isn't safe. All that's happened is that McClelland knocked on your door so that you guys will make the mistake of thinking that's he's completed his sabbatical."

Elliot sighed. The drama of his sigh put mine to shame. "Tell you what, Alan—I'll try not to be naïve if you'll try not to be so damn demeaning. How's that?"

He was right; my condescension was coloring our interaction. If in no other way, my anti-pettiness campaign was paying off in self-awareness. That was something.

Elliot's condescension and derision were invisible to

him—denial means that zits and gray hair are unlikely to appear in the mirror. Contempt? Not a chance.

I allowed myself the pleasant spray of a small victory. Although it was true that I hadn't exhibited anything resembling composure since I had made it up the stairs at the Justice Center, I had just managed to get the relentlessly charming Chief Deputy of the DA's office to lose any semblance of his. "I'll consider it," I said in response to his earlier offer about killing both his naïveté and my condescension with the same arrow.

He stuffed his hands in his pockets and said, "Go home right now or I swear I'll get somebody to take you there whether you like it or not."

With absolutely no condescension in my voice I said, "I'll leave after I talk to my wife."

He scoffed, "You think you have that kind of leverage? Any leverage?"

"I need leverage to talk with my wife?"

He said, "I've been with her. She hasn't asked to talk to you."

My own biased assessment was that he hadn't been as successful as I had been in getting all the contempt out of his delivery. I didn't want to discuss the state of my marriage with Elliot, so I made a quick decision to change the subject to something more pertinent to my well-being than how long I would get to stay in the reception area of the DA's office. "I'm curious about something. Are you thinking of arresting me?"

I knocked him off balance with the question. Just a little.

It had been my intent to thwart the advantage he'd gained with his quip about Lauren not wanting to talk to me. He raised a finger to scratch at his eyebrow. The move was misdirection. Elliot was deliberating. If there was a way to play my query to his advantage, Elliot would find it.

"For this? I just want you out of our way. We have work to do. Go home."

"I'm not talking about this," I said.

He touched his ear lobe, gave it a gentle squeeze. Raised his chin a centimeter. He reminded me of a third-base coach trying to set up a suicide squeeze. "You know that you and I can't talk about . . . any of the things that happened over the weekend. Certainly not without your attorney present."

A voice emerged from behind us. "His attorney is present, Mr. Bellhaven. But thank you so much for extending the constitutional courtesy. An often neglected gesture, but always appreciated."

Elliot turned to the voice. He found himself eye-to-eye with Kirsten Lord. She was in modest heels.

Elliot, modest wingtips.

"Kirsten Lord," she said, holding out her hand. "I don't think we've had the pleasure. I'm an associate of Cozier Maitlin. We represent Dr. Gregory."

"Ms. Lord," he said. "I had heard that Cozy took on an associate. Don't know whether to offer my congratulations or my condolences. Regardless, it's a pleasure to meet you." In most circumstances Elliot did courtesy like cornstarch did silky.

He stepped forward and shook her hand. He then re-treated to the neutral territory halfway between me and my lawyer.

Kirsten smiled pleasantly as though she had all the time in the world. Her Southern manners were a natural match for Elliot's patrician ones. She said, "As far as I'm concerned, you may go right ahead and answer Dr. Gregory's question. There is no longer any need to use my absence as an excuse not to reply. And I'm as anxious as my client is to hear what you have to say."

Elliot scratched that itchy eyebrow again. Then he straightened his perfectly straight eyeglasses. "Now isn't the appropriate time," he said. "Will you please persuade your client to clear this office? The alternative is something . . . I would prefer to avoid."

She looked at me then. Her glance was exceedingly brief, just long enough to allow her to make a determination about my disposition. Then she turned back to Elliot. "If you'll excuse us for just a few moments, Dr. Gregory and I will talk. I've always preferred to do my persuading in private."

FORTY-ONE

"YOU'RE NOT going to win this one, Alan. Let's get out of here," Kirsten said. "We live to fight another day."

I was back at the glass partition. Elliot had gone through the door into the interior corridor—if for no other reason than to demonstrate to me that he could and that I couldn't. It was apparent that the bolt cutter had worked on Michael's nylon chains. The cops were standing him up from Lauren's desk.

"Just a second, Kirsten. I want to watch this." I knew he'd look for me again. I wanted to see what was in his eyes when he spotted me.

McClelland had a bare grin on his face when he looked my way. It wasn't glee, and it wasn't the expression of someone who had just surrendered after a lost battle. It was the face of someone who had sacrificed a pawn to set up an opponent's rook, the face of the guy who had marched his squadron of soldiers into the belly of the Trojan horse.

The cops pushed him and shoved him toward the door. He lowered his head as though he was on a perp-walk trying to shield his face from the camera. At the very last moment he raised his head again, looked up directly at me, and smiled a full-toothed smile. His expression was triumphant.

Like he'd just hit a three-pointer at the buzzer. From half-court.

Two seconds later he was gone, whisked down the hall. Next stop? Probably the county jail. Soon enough he'd be back in Pueblo. It was possible because of the escape he'd be moved someplace more secure. I'd learn that soon enough.

I said, "This stunt was a warning to Lauren and me that it's not over."

"What's not over?" Kirsten asked.

I didn't have an easy answer. Plenty of candidates to choose from. But no answer that wouldn't require a retelling of my therapy with McClelland all those years before. I thought of saying the single word that was bouncing around in my head: *retribution*. Although it sounded melodramatic it had always been the defining psychological motivation in Michael's pathetic life. I had been his therapist. I knew that he carried enough vengeance within him to fuel a lifetime of psychological terrorism.

Kirsten put her hand on my back, between my shoulder blades. She was close enough that I could smell her. Her perfume softened me. I let it. A slap of reactive guilt diminished in an instant.

"He's back in custody, Alan. It should be over now."

It's not. But I didn't argue. I said, "I'm done here. Let's go."

As we stepped into the elevator my cell phone vibrated in my pocket. I checked the screen.

It read, ALARMS INC.

The doors closed. I flipped open my phone and put it to my ear. Nothing. The west side of Boulder's cell-phone lottery had eaten another one of my calls.

I was thinking, *Alarms Inc. shouldn't be calling me. I don't need this.*

Alarms Incorporated was the local company that monitored the intrusion and fire-alarm systems at our home. When they received a signal indicating a potential problem they initiated a series of calls. My mobile phone was the first number on the list.

Since I don't answer my phone when I'm in session with a patient, I'd instructed them to call Sam Purdy immediately, too. If neither of us responded Adrienne's home phone was the third option. If nothing else worked Alarms Inc. was supposed to call the sheriff or the fire department to investigate.

By the time I managed to get a clear cell signal and return the call, the dispatcher informed me they had reached Mr. Purdy. He had assured them he was on his way to my home to investigate the breach, which involved the sensor on the door that led from our basement below the two decks on the west side of the house.

"That sounded ominous. What is it?" Kirsten said after I was done with the call. We were outside standing on the edge of the parking lot adjacent to the Justice Center.

"An alarm at my house, probably nothing. It's a sensor on a door that's given us trouble before."

She put her hand on my back again. "Probably nothing? That's not the way your luck has been running."

"Sam's on his way there. I'll wait to hear from him. Right now I need to find Lauren."

"Yes, you do."

"We still need to talk. You and I."

She held my gaze. "If you want me off the case, I understand. Say the word and I'll speak to Cozy about it. But right now? You do need to find your wife."

All I was able to learn in the next ten minutes at the Justice Center was that Lauren was "detained" by something that had to do with the Michael McClelland fiasco in her office. She sent word through Melissa—the young deputy DA who had been so pleasant during the meeting at our house the day the grand jury witness disappeared—that I should go on home. She would be in touch.

I was five minutes from the house when Sam called my cell. "You talked to the alarm company?" he asked.

"I did."

"I just got to your place. I don't see any problems," he said.

"Thanks, I'll be there in a few minutes. I'm crossing under Foothills right now."

He was leaning against his Cherokee when I pulled up to the house, his legs crossed at the ankles, his arms crossed over his chest. I hopped out of my car. "I'm sorry you had to do this, Sam."

"No big deal. It's not like I have much of a caseload right now. Gives me an excuse to talk to you face-to-face."

"The alarm company said the signal came from the west basement door."

"That's what they told me, too. I checked. If somebody went in that way, they used a key. It's all locked up. No sign of forced entry."

"Did you check Adrienne's house and the barn?"

He nodded. "I'm quick. No bodies hanging anywhere."

"Funny." My keys were in my hand. I dangled them. "Check inside?"

The April day was lovely. Lauren had been last to leave the house in the morning; she'd put the dogs in the fenced run for the day. I greeted them and set them free. I thought they seemed squirrelly, especially Emily, which raised my anxiety a notch.

I held the dogs back as Sam walked ahead of us down the front hall. "No sign of trouble here," he called from the direction of the kitchen and great room. "You want to check the bedrooms or should I?"

I thought of Lauren's bong. "I'll be right there," I said.

The dogs beat me to him. He was standing near the

kitchen island. He surprised me with his next question. "Does it feel to you like anyone's been here?"

I weighed his words for nuance. Sam wasn't a touchy-feely kind of cop. He didn't often ask for affective impressions of events. I decided to answer as though he were sincere, and hope that I didn't regret it. "The dogs are different. Mostly Emily. Could be they're excited about seeing you, but they're edgy about something."

"That's it?"

"Could have been a fox getting close to their run. A stray dog on the lane."

"Or a stranger wandering around their house, eh? Basement or bedrooms first? You choose."

I gestured toward the stairs. Sam went down first. Emily passed him on the way to the basement. She wasn't about to let anyone get down ahead of her. That wasn't unusual behavior; that was her nature. She had as much alpha in her as any female I'd ever met.

Our basement consisted of a dark guest bedroom, a cramped bathroom with cranberry tile and pink fixtures that had been on its knees begging for renovation since the first time I'd seen it, a small sitting room that Lauren and I had set up as a makeshift home office by sticking an old partner's desk in the middle, and some laundry and utility space. The best part of the basement was that it was a walk-out. A solitary exterior door opened to the downhill slope on the west side of the house beneath the great room deck. Lauren and I had plans for a big patio down there. Flagstone, with a hot tub and a fire pit.

We'd had the plans for years.

The iPod was sitting in its dock adjacent to the spot on the partner's desk where Lauren kept her laptop. I pointed at it. "A thief would've grabbed that first, right?"

"If it was a thief," Sam said.

I didn't know what that meant. One of the only things that had been keeping me calm about the alarm signal was my absolute assurance that the intruder hadn't been Michael McClelland. He had been otherwise occupied. "Nothing looks amiss," I said.

Sam was examining the interior of the doorjamb and the moldings, and checking the integrity of the lockset. He was wearing green latex gloves. I hadn't seen him put them on. "Amiss? That's a good one. I'll put that in the report I'm not going to write: 'Homeowner saw nothing amiss.'"

"Do you see something?"

"No." He inhaled and exhaled in a rhythm that was at once unnatural and familiar—in his nose, out his mouth through pursed lips. *Yoga?* Maybe. *Sam?*

He asked, "What about now—does it feel right down here?"

Everything feels right but the nature of your questions and the fact that you're breathing like the Sultan of Iyengar, I thought. But I nodded. "Yeah. It's okay."

We did a quick perusal of the other downstairs rooms and climbed back up to the main floor. Emily raced to be the first to join Anvil on the landing. Anvil hadn't bothered to make the initial descent. He was getting old. His hips could do the stairs in an emergency if he had to. This trip hadn't been an imperative for him.

"Bedrooms?" Sam said. He was deferring to me.

I went down the hall first. I started with the master. Our bed wasn't made, but that had nothing to do with the linens being tossed by an intruder. The clutter on each side of the bed seemed more severe than I recalled, but I knew it wasn't. Lauren and I were both capable of being serious slobs. The territory surrounding our bedside tables and the limited countertops in the master bathroom tended to display that tendency more radically than other surfaces in the house.

I spotted Sam standing near the door. "This is how it usually looks," I said in explanation. I probably sounded a little defensive.

"Mine too. It's odd having somebody in your bedroom, isn't it? I think it is. Maybe that's just me. Living room? Kitchen? It's cool. But my bedroom, that's . . ."

I let my eyes cover the room. I walked over and opened the drawer in the dressing table where Lauren kept her nicer jewelry. She wasn't big on bling. I didn't do an inventory, but what I expected to be there—a little gold, a little silver, a gaudy platinum ring from an aunt—was there along with costume pieces that made up most of her collection.

Sam said, "Sherry used to have this neat-freak devil that she let out of a cage once in a while, but since she split, this is how things look in my room. Stuff doesn't ever get put away. Sometimes I think what's the point; other times I think I'm just a lazy fart."

"If you weren't here I wouldn't give the mess a second thought," I said.

"Nothing catches your eye as being out of place? Missing? Just . . . odd?"

"Nothing, Sam," I said.

"Smells? Any aroma that doesn't fit?"

"What?"

"People smell, Alan. They leave scents behind after they've been in a room. B.O., perfume, deodorant, whatever."

I sniffed the air. It smelled like our bedroom. "Nothing." Emily still wouldn't settle. She was definitely thinking something was amiss. "Emily's not herself. That's for sure. Ask her about aroma."

He scratched the dog's neck. "I have something to show you," he said. "Can I come in?"

I remembered the innocuous question that had led to the standoff about the purse in my office. I almost laughed. I said, "Sure."

He walked across the room until he was standing beside me. He reached into the inside pocket of his coat and handed me a couple of four-by-six photos. Grainy. Bad focus. Low light.

"That's my bedroom," Sam said.

"You keep these with you for moments like this?"

"Don't be an asshole."

I was having trouble figuring out what I was supposed to be seeing in the images. A rectangular flash of brilliance centered near the top of each snapshot was apparently a window. "Okay," I said. "I'll try."

He reached over my shoulder and pointed at a silhouette slightly off center on the left side. Not much resolution. The outline of the person was dark on darker. He said, "That's me."

I felt as though I were interpreting a Gestalt puzzle, sorting out what was figure and what was ground. It took me a couple of seconds to make sense of the profile of Sam's body in the photo. He was sitting on a bed facing in the direction of the camera, but not quite at it. One foot was on the floor, the other leg bent at the knee, up on the bed. It was a queen bed, I thought. The sheets were stripes in light colors. Since the bed was unmade, the stripes went every which way.

"I see." *Whoa. I see something else.* I saw a second silhouette.

"My shirt's open," he said. He didn't want me to notice that on my own.

"Yeah, I can tell. And, the woman?" I asked. "Who's she?"

FORTY-TWO

THE WOMAN was completely in profile. She was facing Sam. Her shirt wasn't open; it was off. She was sitting with her right leg crossed over the left, her arms extended toward him. Her hands were lost in the dark pigment that seemed to obliterate his torso but I thought that they may have been locked behind his neck.

In contrast to the variegated shadows that obscured her face the crisp whiteness of the side view of her bra caused a distracting delta image in the center of the shot.

Light from the windows reflected off her blond hair.

Blond hair meant the woman wasn't Carmen, Sam's California girlfriend. And although Sam's ex had gone through intermittent blond phases during their relationship, the woman in the photograph was way too slender to be Sherry, which meant this wasn't some old snapshot from their distant marriage.

"Nothing happened. We kissed. Made out, whatever. I stopped it." Sam was embarrassed. "Her bra stayed on. Right where you see it there, exactly."

"Okay." His defensiveness made the moment more awkward than it already was.

"You can't really tell in the picture, but her pants are on, too."

I looked at the photo again. He was right; I couldn't really tell if the woman's pants were on. If this were the only angle for an instant replay, the officials wouldn't have changed the call. Insufficient visual evidence.

I glanced at him. "Sam, you're single. You're allowed."

"She's married. Currie, the woman. Separated, you know, but still married. Technically. She's the nutritionist I've been seeing. I mentioned her, I think."

Sam seeing a nutritionist took on a fresh connotation for me. "Currie?" I said. "You met at Rallysport?"

"At the juice bar. She didn't like what I ordered. Her first name is Curran. It's a family thing. Currie. She's from Virginia."

"Okay." I nodded as though I understood why any of the details—the juice bar, Currie's name, her marital status, her profession, the fact that she was originally from Virginia—mattered to this moment. I decided they probably did not—that Sam was chattering because of his discomfort. "You did tell me about her. That you were seeing a nutritionist, I mean. I thought for . . . nutrition . . . advice."

A secret, I was thinking. This photo was about Sam sharing a secret. I was instinctively aware that I was seeing the secret simultaneously in two of its evolutionary forms, not only as pupa but also as butterfly. The pupa was the lingering shame Sam felt even while the knowledge had remained private. The butterfly? Butterflies always fly unpredictably—Sam was demonstrating his unease that the secret was no longer under lock and key.

"That's all it was," he said. "At first."

"Don't worry. I'm good at secrets." *I'm great at secrets. When it becomes an Olympic event, I will take the gold.* "Who took these pictures?" I asked.

"That's the thing. I don't know. Somebody stuffed them in my mailbox last night. No note, no message. Just the photos in a plain white envelope. Unsealed."

"That makes no sense. Colorado's a no-fault state. Currie's husband doesn't need to prove adultery. What's his advantage? Is he picking a fight with you?" Sam was a physically imposing guy, but it was possible that Currie's husband hadn't done his homework. "He might be in for a surprise if he takes you on."

"They weren't delivered to Currie. I called her and asked her if she got any unexpected packages. She didn't. But she got all excited. Now I think she's waiting for me to send her flowers or something. Jeez." He rubbed his hand across his face. "Shit."

"I'm not following."

"The pictures were delivered to *me*," Sam said.

"Again, why? What's your vulnerability?" I held the photos out to him. He didn't take them from me. "You had a woman in your bedroom? What's the big deal? If you hadn't told me I wouldn't have known it was you in the photo."

Sam ran his fingers through the short hair on his head, but stopped when his big right palm reached the crown of his skull. With theatrical understatement, he said, "Carmen wouldn't be thrilled, that's for sure. But I'm not showing these to you because I'm so worried about the *why* of all this. I'm showing these to you because I'm worried about the *how*. How the hell did somebody get these photographs, Alan? My bedroom is about the size of your closet." He finally pulled his hand down from on top of his head.

I took his word for the relative size of his bedroom. I couldn't recall ever being in there. His house in North Boulder was tiny, though; I'd grant him that.

I looked at the pictures again. They had been taken only seconds apart. The two images were almost identical. The brilliant window dominated both of them.

"Through the window? Is there a mirror on the opposite wall? Is that possible?"

"I thought of that, but it doesn't work. There's a cheap mirror from McGuckins on the closet door, but the angles are wrong. Someone had to set up a camera in my bedroom. Remote, or a timer, something. It's the only way."

"What about someone . . . in your closet?"

"I can't even get another pair of shoes in my closet. It's an old house. The closets are tiny. Nobody could hide in there. Door won't even close all the way. Anyway, I checked inside. All I found in there that wasn't mine was an old prescription for Sherry for Elavil. What is that? Elavil?"

Sam knew what it was. I confirmed it. "It's an antidepressant. An old one."

"Date on it was a couple of months before she left me." He nodded, slid his lower jaw side to side. "Makes sense, I guess."

More secrets. "Why would someone take the pictures?"

I thought he was getting exasperated with my questions. "The point was to show me that they took them. And that's why I'm showing them to you."

"I don't get it."

He responded by looking around my bedroom, rotating a full 360 degrees. Then he shrugged and sighed. The sigh was disappointment that he had to connect the dots for me. "Just because nothing's missing doesn't mean no one has been here. If somebody got hold of a key—and they were careful—they could be in and out of your house in minutes."

"The dogs were outside today," I said. "They're not out every day, Sam. Sometimes they're in."

"That would make it even easier for someone to pay a visit."

"Adrienne's house is empty."

"Ditto. Nobody to keep an eye on things. Maybe they got lucky. Or maybe somebody was waiting. Picking the right time. Watching."

"How would someone get a key?"

"You leave a spare outside?"

"It's pretty well hidden."

"Bet you ten bucks I can find it in two minutes. A hundred bucks I can find it in twenty."

I granted him the point. "You heard about McClelland? What happened at the Justice Center today?" I said.

"We are not going to talk about him. At all. But go ahead and presume I'm up to speed. I'll pretend for a moment you're not changing the subject."

"The alarm went off here after he was in custody at the Justice Center," I said. "He didn't do this."

Sam nodded. What I was saying wasn't news. He was trying to goad me to leap forward and catch up with him. I wasn't able to see where he was going. As I'd felt from the moment I saw the card stuck in my front door the previous weekend, my mind didn't seem to be able to handle the variables. I felt like I did as an undergraduate when I'd still been toying with going to medical school. I'd signed up for an advanced math class freshman year and within days knew that I was out of my league. Concepts that my classmates seemed to recognize immediately eluded me. Comprehension floated just out of my reach and I couldn't reel it in.

I had dropped that class. I wasn't going to be allowed to drop this one.

"Cameras can be tiny," Sam said.

"I can't get too worked up about that possibility, Sam. There's nothing to see."

"There're people who would love to have a video of this conversation."

He was right. I said, "I'm more worried about who

it is that's helping McClelland, Sam. He has to have an accomplice."

Sam smiled. "Now we're on the same page. Ideas?"

"I've been working under the assumption that Kol was involved. They were at the state hospital at the same time." I watched his eyes. "You must know that."

"Yeah, I know that. The question is how do you know that?" he asked. "No, don't tell me how you know. What's your theory? McClelland gets Kol to kill himself in the barn to . . . what? Make you look bad?"

"As plans go it seems to have worked out pretty well. My practice is disintegrating. Because of the way it was all set up, my lawyers hear that the sheriff's looking at the possibility of homicide, not suicide. If that happens, it would indeed make me look bad. Life-sentence bad."

Sam countered, "Nicole Cruz is dead. We can say with a reasonable degree of medical certainty that she didn't break into your house today."

"Which means there's an additional accomplice," I said. "Any candidates come to mind?"

"If I had anywhere to look I'd be looking. I wouldn't be here risking my career talking to you."

I sat down on the edge of the mattress on Lauren's side of the bed. I could smell her scent on the sheets. It reminded me that my current problems didn't start, or stop, with McClelland. I walked myself through the recent events, trying to figure out who might be helping him. It was like looking for an unfamiliar trailhead in the fog.

"You think this is a message? Like those pictures from your bedroom?"

"Go on."

"The timing is impeccable. Minutes—literally minutes—after Michael McClelland is taken into custody somebody breaches my home-security system."

Sam took over. "The message being that whatever is going on isn't over because McClelland's back in custody." Sam yawned. "You got any coffee, or a Coke? I need some caffeine."

My associations skipped along from his yawn to the coffee to the caffeine to Kaladi. Without any sense of "eureka" I said, "I have a thought about the accomplice."

Sam looked skeptical. "Yeah?"

"It's a long shot. And it isn't going to be easy to get the confirmation I'll need."

"Why?"

"Goddamn doctor-patient privilege," I said.

"I take it you're not the constipated doctor in question?"

"I'm not."

Sam laughed. "Sometimes life is very unfair," he said. "And sometimes it seems like the most just place imaginable."

FORTY-THREE

SAM GRABBED a Pepsi from the kitchen before we searched the rest of the bedroom. We couldn't find a camera. We couldn't find a microphone. I couldn't identify a single thing that might be missing from the master bedroom.

"Not finding anything doesn't mean shit," Sam said. "Could just mean that somebody is better at hiding than we are at seeking. I could get a forensics team back out here but . . ."

"No," I said. I knew Sam could be correct—it was possible someone had left something in my house. But I wasn't convinced there was any margin in bugging my bedroom. I was much more concerned about my continuing vulnerability regarding the missing grand jury witness—if someone had left something in the house, I thought it would be incriminating evidence, not a camera.

We finished up. Sam reminded me not to forget to check Grace's room. As I preceded him down the short hallway to her door his cell phone rang. He usually kept his phone on vibrate; I was surprised to hear it chirp. He glanced at the screen and walked away from me, toward the western windows of the great room.

He wanted to take his call in private. I wondered if it was Currie. Or Carmen. I opened Grace's door.

Her bedroom looked like it had been attacked with a chain saw.

I felt Sam move into the space right behind me. At my feet was the torso of Grace's favorite stuffed bear, the one that spent each day reclining on the pillow of her bed, each night snuggled in the crook of her arm.

I couldn't see the head anywhere in the cluttered mess that had been my daughter's private haven. Grace's things were tossed all over the room, but the most obscene part of the destruction was the amount of cutting and ripping that had been done. Bedding, mattress, curtains, toys, books. All shredded.

Straight edges on many of the cuts.

As though someone had used a machete, I thought. I shuddered.

I said, "I need to call Lauren. Tell her not to bring Grace home to this."

My reaction to the profanity of this assault? It surprised me.

Fight or flight? I found comfort that at that moment I didn't feel much like running.

*   *   *

Sam's strong hands clenched hard on the bicep of each of my arms. He was holding me back from entering Grace's room. "Can't go in there. You know that."

"Grace can't see this," I said. "Ever. There're some things a kid should never see. She'd never forget this."

I'll never forget this. He pulled me back from the door. I said, "Let go of me."

He stepped around me so that he was standing between me and the entrance to Grace's bedroom. "Come with me. I can't leave you here. God knows what you'll do. And God knows that I don't want to have to stop you."

I followed him to the great room, pretending to have control of my impulses.

"We have to decide how to play this," he said, forcing calm into his manner.

"What does that mean?"

"Grace's room. Me being here with you. Those are problems. For both of us. We shouldn't be together."

I thought about it, decided I didn't share his level of concern. "The alarm company called you. They'd already called me. It was a predetermined thing. We ended up here at the same time. Events were out of our control."

Sam considered my argument. "Okay, all right. Then you should call 911. I'll wait outside for the sheriff to get here. I'll let the deputy see me sitting outside, tell him what happened, and then I'll leave before they come in to look around." He was thinking out loud.

"The sheriff's not coming in here," I said. "And I'm

not calling 911. You should just leave now, Sam. Forget what you saw in Grace's room. It never happened."

"You have to call."

"Why? Nothing important is missing from the house. The alarm company has two previous false alarms from that door sensor. You've already convinced me that the most likely reason for the break-in was to leave something here, not to take something from here. Why would I want to invite the sheriff back inside my house to look for whatever was left behind? How well did that work out for me last time, Sam? At my office? Inviting you in?"

For a moment he thought I was taking a shot at him. The flame of that flare burned out quickly, though, and his eyes soon belied some empathy for my position. But he wasn't convinced. "Grace's room, Alan? It's been . . ."

"Violated," I said. "Obscenely violated. The pertinent question remains why?"

"To terrorize you."

"Done. It worked. Why else?"

Sam was ready. "For the same reason they took the pictures in my bedroom. To show that they can."

"Agreed. I'm vulnerable. There's a news flash. Again, done. Why else? Why plunder my daughter's room?"

He looked frustrated for a moment and then he exhaled loudly. "So that you would have no choice but to call the sheriff to investigate."

I almost said, "Bingo." I didn't. I said, "Yes. Whoever was in here today wants the sheriff to have an excuse to come into my house."

I felt neurons firing. Little sparks were flying. In micro-time, potassium and sodium imbalances were being set-tled by infinitesimal flashes of brain lightning. My mind was catching up with reality. It felt good.

The cloud fell back, just a little.

"Sam, I need you to do something for me. Get a cruiser to go by Grace's school until Lauren or I can get there to pick her up. I don't want to be misreading this message—what they did to her room—if you know what I mean."

He opened his cell and held down a single button. A few seconds later he said, "Luce? Me. I need a favor. Off the record." He covered the microphone and looked at me. "What's the address of the school?"

I gave him the intersection. He repeated it to Lucy, his partner, and vaguely explained the situation. "No trail on this. Understand? . . . Just a little extra attention would be great. Few extra passes by whatever cruiser is already there. I'll let you know when her parents have her home . . . Right, tell the patrol guys that wide-eyes would be great."

"Wait, Sam."

"Hold on, Lucy. What?"

I said, "They should be looking for a woman."

"How do you know that?" he said. He wasn't merely curious; that could have waited. He was challenging me.

"Because that's McClelland's history. His psycholog-ical advantage is with women. He doesn't have a good record with men. Men have proven to be his downfall."

Sam stared at me as though he was deciding whether to trust my psychological voodoo this time. The last time I'd applied it to McClelland had certainly been a fiasco. Finally, he said, "Luce? Tell them to keep a special eye out for a woman—or women—who doesn't seem to belong . . . Any age, but don't rule out young . . . I know that makes things trickier outside a school. Sorry."

He closed the phone. To me he said, "Done." As he put the phone back in his coat the white edges of the two photographs were briefly visible sticking out of his pocket.

I said, "Call Lucy back, Sam."

He snapped, "Jesus. Why?"

I modulated my voice as much as I could. "Because you need to get some patrols to go by Simon's school, too."

Sam blinked. He retrieved his phone and flipped it open. He covered the necessary territory with Lucy in less than a minute. The moment he killed the call he placed another one, again with speed-dial. He turned and took two steps farther away.

For the new call he found a conciliatory tone that I'd rarely heard come out of his mouth. "Sherry? Me. Sorry to bug you . . . Hey, is this a bad time? . . . Okay, I'll be quick. I've been thinking about this weekend. The trade you wanted to make? I was being a hardass before, and . . . I apologize. If you still want to take Simon to the mountains, you and, uh, Kevin can have him. We'll work out an exchange weekend later on . . . I know, I know . . . No, not a holiday, Sherry. No, I'm not trying

to get the Fourth of July from you. We'll just find an-
other regular weekend . . . I know it's late notice. I said
I was sorry. I'm stubborn sometimes, you know that . . .
Five-thirty's fine. He'll be ready."

Sam turned to me as he shut the phone. "Sherry's boyfriend. Kevin? The root-canal guy? He has a condo in
Avon. There's some endodont-ical gathering up in Vail
this weekend. They wanted to take Simon."

Sam rolled his eyes. "Now the kid has to spend the weekend with a bunch of guys who've been doing root canals all
week long. I bet there'll be a lot of alcohol involved."

I had a less cynical perspective. I said, "Simon should
be safe up there, Sam."

"Yeah."

"Grace is going to Bimini," I said.

"Bimini? Cool," Sam said, knowing it wasn't. He held
his phone up for me to look at. "You still haven't called
Lauren."

"She'll want me to have the cops investigate this.
That's a problem."

"Probably," Sam agreed. "You two are having a rough
patch?"

"Rough patch" sounded quaint. I sighed. "Yes."

"That's what Bimini's about?"

"Partially. That and McClelland."

I picked up the portable, walked out the front door,
and called Lauren's mobile from the porch.

"I was just about to call you," she said in greeting.
"What a day."

"You're all right?"

"I was pretty shook up, but I'm okay. I can't tell you how glad I am that he's back in custody."

"I'm sorry you had to go through it," I said. "Elliot wouldn't let me see you."

"I heard," she said.

I couldn't tell how to interpret that, but I wasn't inclined toward assuming she was grateful. I was about to tell her about the break-in when she took a breath deep enough that I could hear the inhale over the phone. She said, "Alan? Grace and I have a six-forty-five flight to Miami. Tonight. I was going to tell you this afternoon, but . . . well. Things are going to be tight. Could you bring Gracie here? And feed her something first? I'm not going to be able to get home before we go to the airport. I've totally run out of time."

"What about your things?"

She hesitated. The hesitation left me feeling like I was sucking bus exhaust. Finally, she said, "We're all packed."

Oh. "Where are . . . the bags?" *Please, tell me Grace's things were not in her room.*

"In the trunk of my car."

More bus exhaust filled my lungs. My relief that the suitcases weren't in Grace's room was overwhelmed by the hollowness I felt that my wife had packed and prepared to leave.

"Yes, I'll bring her over. You want something to eat, too?"

FORTY-FOUR

THE HOUSE was quiet.

I monitored the six-forty-five flight from Denver to Miami on the Web. It took off eighteen minutes late from DIA and was due into Miami International fourteen minutes early. I realized I didn't know what flight, or even what airline, my family would be taking to the Bahamas the next morning.

I felt as empty as a fallow field.

I took a credit card from my wallet and poured a tumbler of whiskey—it was either that or gin, and I couldn't do gin. I carried the provisions to the basement and set the card and the drink on my side of the old partner's desk. Lauren had her laptop with her, so I booted my aging desktop. What I planned—or hoped—to do on the Internet wasn't complicated. Although I would have preferred the speed and reliability of Lauren's computer, I didn't think the task should be too much for my old machine. My main concern was that I maintained my computer almost as well as I maintained my car, which wasn't well, and I suspected it was infested with more bugs than a picnic in the tropics.

I followed a few false Google leads before I found the path I was looking for. The credit card proved an essential tool for buying my way into databases and archives that contained the specific information I was seeking. The whole process took me less than an hour. By the time I had what I wanted, it was clear to me that if I were a more skilled Internet researcher and had known what I was doing, I could have done the job in ten minutes. I comforted myself with the realization that back in my graduate-school days when research involved walking into actual brick and stone libraries, flipping through card catalogs, wandering through stacks, doing interlibrary loan, and reading musty newsprint—or juggling endless rolls of microfiche—the search would've taken me a week, easy.

The lesson? Secrets are much more difficult to bury than they once were. A determined idiot like me, with a crappy old computer and a credit card with room left on its credit limit, could dig up a well-buried doozy in no time.

In the end I'd had to print out only about a dozen pages.

I'd finished all the whiskey. If I wanted to sleep for a few hours, though, I would need some more alcohol.

Secrets, I was thinking as Emily and I climbed the stairs. *If you keep one, it chases you relentlessly. Ironic how easy it has become to sneak up on someone else's from behind.*

Anvil was curled up in a ball close to the heat vent in the great room. I woke him and took both dogs out to pee. The night was clear. In the springtime along the Front Range of the Rockies, clear usually meant cold.

Tharon Thibodeaux had distorted a few pertinent details in the story he'd told me at Kaladi. The behavior of the patient who had jumped off the roof during the psychiatry department Christmas party when Thibodeaux was a resident wasn't quite as unpredictable as Tharon had made it seem.

The original incident had been reported dispassionately on an inner page in the metro news section in the New Orleans *Times-Picayune* the morning after the man's suicide. N.O. MAN JUMPS TO DEATH was the headline. The patient's name was Carson Leopold. The story was probably filed close to deadline; other details about the incident were sparse. Friends who were interviewed for a follow-up story in the next day's edition called Mr. Leopold "Cars." He'd been born in Philadelphia and had been living in New Orleans for a "couple of years." He worked as a cashier in some kind of porn/sex-toy shop on the fringe of the Quarter.

The reporter on the story was a woman named Joanna Eusto. I assumed that since she was chasing suicide stories for the metro pages in the week just prior to the holidays, she was a novice. From the tone of her reporting of the initial story and especially in that first follow-up, I could also surmise that she hadn't been around long enough to become jaded. I could taste outrage in her measured words.

Maybe the story of Carson Leopold's death got traction because it was the holidays, or maybe not much else of note was happening in New Orleans that week, or maybe Eusto's enthusiasm for digging at the edges of what looked like a garden-variety suicide grabbed her editor's attention, but Leopold's death earned five long follow-up pieces before the story permanently disappeared from the pages of the *Times-Picayune* just before New Year's.

The part about Cars jumping from the roof in view of the assembled clinicians of the psychiatry department turned out to be true. But Cars hadn't actually been on the roof of the apartment building where the party was being held—according to Eusto he had been on the roof of the building across the street. At first reading I didn't grasp the significance of that simple fact, but soon realized that as word spread at the party that a patient of Tharon's was threatening to jump from the roof, all his colleagues would have actually been in a perfect position to watch the man's manipulative antics on the ledge of the rooftop across the street.

Leopold would not have been invisible to the partygoers, as Tharon had suggested to me. He wouldn't have been invisible to Marlene, the resident who he said had been on-call for emergencies that night. He certainly wouldn't have been invisible to Tharon Thibodeaux, who would've been watching in horror as his patient dove from the rooftop of the building across the street.

A skillful photographer for the *Times-Picayune* had managed to gain access to the flat directly above the one where the Christmas party had taken place. He used the access to frame a photograph that accompanied Eusto's third piece on Carson Leopold's suicide, the one in which she revealed that Carson had apparently chosen the time and place for his leap to maximize the audience for his death among the various doctors of the psychiatry department. The photo demonstrated—using perfect framing and spot-on depth-of-field—the view that the assembled psychiatrists would have had of Cars as he made his threats via mobile phone, and later, as he jumped to his death.

They would have seen him leave the roof, and a second or two later they would have seen him crash into the top of the car below. And die.

Cars Leopold was one of those patients whose story would sound familiar to anyone who had ever worked in the outpatient clinic of an urban psychiatric training facility. He was one of those difficult-to-treat, unrewarding patients who gets handed from psychology intern to social-work trainee to psychiatry resident as each clinician in turn completes his or her outpatient rotation and moves on to some new training opportunity in another setting. Carson might, or might not, have looked or felt better for a short time during each clinician's window of care before he undoubtedly deteriorated again during each artificial transition from one training therapist to the next.

The system was set up to maximize learning opportunities for young clinicians, not to maximize quality of care for the difficult-to-treat patients who predominated in the sliding-scale environment of the training clinic. A side effect of the training-first bias was that the system also maximized the opportunities for patients like Carson Leopold to repeatedly experience the disruption of the loss of a therapist.

I had discovered no reason to doubt that Carson was, as Tharon had maintained, burdened with borderline personality disorder. Carrying that unenviable and difficult-to-treat diagnosis into an outpatient training clinic, he would have found himself at the bottom of the roster of patients that the young clinicians would be likely to select to continue to follow after they'd moved on to a new rotation. Psychopathologically speaking, Carson was the scrawny, unathletic kid with thick glasses who got chosen last, if at all, when sports teams were chosen at school. No therapist was likely to pick Carson as one of the few patients he or she would choose for their ongoing outpatient caseload after the clinic rotation was complete.

Eusto had reported in her second *Times-Picayune* article that Leopold had already been through three therapists in a little over a year when he killed himself. Tharon had told me that the suicidal patient had been handed off to him the July before the suicide, just as Tharon began his outpatient clinic rotation. One of Leopold's friends told the reporter that Cars's last session with his current therapist was scheduled for the second week in January the following year.

Would that be because Carson was better? No, it would be because Tharon's rotation was ending.

The second fact about which Tharon had been disingenuous to me was his contention that Carson Leopold had no prior history of suicidal behavior.

During the course of her investigation of his death, Joanna Eusto had interviewed Carson's boss at the porn shop. She'd talked with five people who identified themselves as Cars's friends, and she spoke by phone with his sister in Philadelphia. She noted that she had been unable to interview any spokesperson from the outpatient clinic where Carson Leopold was being treated.

Eusto had learned that Leopold had been hospitalized twice in the previous twelve months. Both hospitalizations had been brief, and both had been precipitated by suicidal behavior. The first was a threat to kill himself with a gun. The police who burst into his rented room found the gun, but no ammunition. The second admission was for treatment of an overdose of various medicines that he had stolen from friends' homes. The lethality risk of the attempt had been judged low. Both suicidal gestures had taken place during windows of time when Leopold was being transferred from one clinician to another at the outpatient clinic.

*   *   *

The last of the distortions in Thibodeaux's retelling of what happened to Carson Leopold was the most damning.

Joanna Eusto didn't uncover the revealing facts until she was approached by a psychiatric nurse employed at the clinic. Eusto's subsequent article, the fourth piece on the saga for the *Times-Picayune*, was headlined: SEVENTEEN PSYCHIATRISTS WATCHED MAN JUMP.

The story wasn't about the failures of a healthcare discipline. It was about the failure of a system. If Cars Leopold's therapist had been a clinical psych intern, and not a psychiatric resident, the headline could just as easily have read: SEVENTEEN PSYCHOLOGISTS WATCHED MAN JUMP.

In her article, Eusto named names.

Marlene Martinez wasn't the on-call psychiatrist that night. She, not Tharon Thibodeaux, was Carson Leopold's outpatient therapist in the clinic. Dr. Martinez had been present at the party, Eusto reported. She had been drinking. Her clinical supervisor—a senior faculty member very familiar with Leopold's case—had been at the party, too. He, too, had been drinking.

Eusto described the emergency on-call system that the clinic employed for after-hours emergencies. The nurse who had volunteered to talk to Eusto suggested that the on-call resident had mishandled the crisis that had transpired during the department Christmas party. She identified the psychiatrist taking the first call that night as Dr. Tharon Thibodeaux.

The nurse also told the reporter that Thibodeaux, too,

had been drinking while at the party. She disclosed the detail that Tharon liked single-malt Scotch.

It was Thibodeaux who returned the first emergency call to Carson. It was Thibodeaux who was convinced he could manage the crisis. It was Thibodeaux who was too full of pride, or hubris, to turn the phone call over to Marlene Martinez, Carson's doctor. It was Thibodeaux who was determined to demonstrate his clinical acumen in front of the assembled faculty of the psychiatry department.

And it was Thibodeaux holding the phone as Carson Leopold jumped.

I didn't learn from the articles if Tharon Thibodeaux had ever been professionally disciplined for his involvement in the death of Cars Leopold. I assumed he had been. But I also assumed that given the reality that during the entire crisis he was within spitting distance of his immediate clinical supervisor, the director of his clinical training program, and the department chair, not to mention the patient's own therapist and her supervising psychiatrist, any discipline was handed out gingerly, and privately.

In the intervening years the incident had become Tharon's secret, though. That much was clear.

Tharon's business card was still in my wallet, where I'd stashed it after leaving Kaladi. I e-mailed him at the state hospital. I attached a link to the fourth of Joanna Eusto's articles in the *Times-Picayune*. The subject line on the message read, "You can have your secret. I want her name." I tagged on a list of all my phone numbers.

Tharon had been kind to me. I felt a pang about black-mailing him. I walked back upstairs and stood in the doorway to my daughter's room. The guilt disappeared in about two seconds.

The final thing I did before I climbed into bed was to return to the flight-tracking Web site and confirm that the plane with my family was safely on the ground in Florida.

FORTY-FIVE

I WOKE with a headache early the next morning, aware that I was alone in the house with the dogs. I'd left my cell charging in the kitchen. One glance at it and I knew I'd received a call overnight. It was from a pay phone. The voice mail message was simple. "Wynne—I think it's w-y-n-n-e—Brown—b-r-o-w-n."

Tharon had decided that my price for protecting his secret was something he was willing to pay.

Now what? I thought. *I have a name. Now what?*

During our meeting in Denver Tharon had volunteered that Michael's friend at the state hospital was a psychologist. He had also implied, though never said directly, that she was a clinician.

I started digging through old membership rosters from professional associations that I had belonged to over my years in practice: American Psychological Association, Colorado Psychological Association, the National Register of Health Service Providers in Psychology. I couldn't find Wynne Brown listed anywhere.

I tried a Google search. "Your search did not match any documents," was the instantaneous reply.

I went back through everything I had, looking through the voluminous lists of Browns for alternative spellings of female first names that might leave the diminutive of "Wynne." Assuming that Tharon might have gotten the spelling wrong, I included "Wyn," "Wynn," and "Win."

Winifred? Winston? Winfred? Wynonna?

Nothing.

I finally spotted a candidate the third time through a five-year-old directory of members of the Colorado Psychological Association: J. Winter Brown, Ph.D.

Wynne Brown.

The *J.* had thrown me, of course.

The phone rang. Not my cell—the landline in the house. Caller ID was no help. It read OUT OF AREA.

"Hello," I said.

The voice was Lauren's. It was as tight as my hamstrings after a tough mountain climb, as cold as Gunnison in mid-January. She said, "I hope you didn't have anything to do with this."

I could have asked *"With what?"* but that appeared to be a trap waiting to be sprung. I looked at the digital clock in the corner of the computer screen. Seven-ten a.m. That meant it was nine-ten in Florida. I said, "You guys are still in Miami?"

"We're in Denver, Alan."

It was a simple declarative sentence, but it was also an accusation. She knew it, and I knew it. The sentence didn't include a whole lot of information. I couldn't guess what I had done.

"Why? What happened?" I asked.

"You don't know? That's what you're telling me?"

"I don't know. That's exactly what I'm telling you. I tracked your flight last night. It landed in Miami. What's wrong? What happened?"

"TSA pulled me aside for a search as I was going through security with Grace. They found the Sativex in my purse. We weren't allowed to fly to Miami. I had to turn over our passports."

"Where are you?"

"One of those bed-in-a-box hotels by DIA." Lauren wasn't a big fan of the franchising of hotels and motels. The bed-in-a-box moniker was one of her kinder diminutives for them.

"Grace is okay?"

"You know Grace—it's all lemons and lemonade for her. She's having a great time. She's counting takeoffs and landings." Lauren's voice changed completely as she asked our daughter, "How many now, honey?"

I heard Gracie call out, "Ninety-six."

I smiled.

"You didn't tell anyone, Alan?"

"About your drugs? Of course not." I knew from the tone of her question that she wasn't predisposed to believe my denial. "What's going to happen? Were you arrested?"

"No. Detained for a while. I'm waiting for a call from the U.S. Attorney's office. It's a mess." She changed her voice to a whisper. "This is a federal felony they're discussing, Alan."

"God."

"No one knew but you. No one."

I fought my impulse to argue. I said, "Maybe it was incidental to the search. Maybe they found it when they were looking for . . . whatever the hell it is that TSA is searching for lately."

She was completely prepared for me to launch that argument—she took aim at it as though she'd been shooting skeet and my argument was the clay pigeon she was most determined to obliterate. "And how many TSA agents do you think could identify a bottle of Sativex even if the damn thing was hanging from a chain under their noses? It looks completely benign. I had other medicines in my purse. Narcotics. Injectable interferon. They barely looked at them. Why would they focus on the Sativex? Why? There's no good reason. They were looking for it. They opened my purse and went right for it."

I chose silence. In her current state of mind Lauren's focus on the topic of how the TSA employee found the Sativex had no margin for me. Finally in a voice as kind as I could manage I said, "Why would you think I would tell anyone?"

"Please, Alan. Don't, dammit. Don't get all offended on me. Can you focus on *my* problem for a second?"

I almost snapped back. Almost. "Forget the hurt, Lauren. What about the logic? What possible advantage would it give me to have you arrested at the airport in front of our daughter?"

She was quiet for a few seconds. Then she said, "My cell is vibrating—I have to go. I'll call you back when I know something."

Was her phone really vibrating? I had my doubts.

I made some more coffee. In my mind I was staring at the puzzle. The pieces were floating. I moved them around. I was trying to find the right place for the confusing contours of the newest piece—what had happened to my wife in the security line at DIA.

I came up with no good place to stick that news. *Coincidence?* Maybe. But probably not. *What?*

I went back to the computer. Two reasons: One, my task with J. Winter wasn't done. And two, it gave me something to do.

Another Google search confirmed J. Winter Brown's gender. The information was contained in the most innocuous of data: She had run in a 5K charity race in Vail in 1998. Her results were listed among the women participants. J. Winter wasn't an elite runner, but she wasn't bad. At that altitude I could not have kept up with her.

I kept waiting for the phone to ring with news from Lauren. It didn't.

Another hour of diligent searching filled out J. Winter's professional background for me. B.A., University of Michigan, Ph.D., UCLA. She'd worked professionally—doing forensic evaluations, among other things—in Arizona, Nevada, and Oregon before setting up a private practice in Greeley, Colorado, in 1996. I could find no professional mention of her after 2002.

I went into the kitchen and ate some yogurt—even though the container warned me that it had expired around the time that Nicole Cruz had been hanging in the barn—and some applesauce while standing at the counter. The snack was like going to a gas station to fill my car. Fuel.

Then I went back to J. Winter Brown. I struck researching gold in an online edition of a January 1999 issue of an alumni bulletin published by the University of Northern Colorado in Greeley. In it was a photograph of four local psychologists who were generously donating their time as volunteer faculty in the psychology department. The third of the four, second from the right, was identified as Dr. Wynne Brown.

No *J. Winter*.

I immediately recognized her. *Son of a bitch*, I thought.

Some of my colleagues considered me crazy to do it, but the intake policy I employed for my practice gave potential patients a free session to decide if I was the right therapist for them. If the patient decided I was a good match and chose to continue to see me for treatment I would charge them for the initial visit. But if they never came back I didn't bill them for the trial session.

J. Winter Brown was one of those patients who never came back.

I'd seen her once—my appointment calendar said it was the previous fall, about ten days after I'd watched that other patient shot on the evening news. I probably wasn't at the top of my clinical game during that appointment; my patient's public, violent death had shaken me up. Brown had used her real name with me right from the start; my records showed that I had set a time for the intake late on a Tuesday afternoon with a woman named Justine Brown.

Although I recalled seeing her, the session wasn't particularly memorable. She had admitted from the start that she was therapist-shopping—not an unusual form of mental-health recreation in Boulder, where more psychotherapists labor within five blocks of my office than live in all of Wyoming—and she'd spent much of the forty-five minutes we were together asking me questions about my practice, my experience, and my background, both professional and personal. I'd answered some of her questions, deflected others.

I'd suggested, as I routinely did during sessions that developed like that one did, that interviewing me was perhaps not the best way to get a sense of how I worked, or what it would be like to be in treatment with me. The subtle confrontation had deflected off Justine Brown like a hailstone off a pitched metal roof.

I was certain that she had not mentioned the fact that she was a psychologist. I would have remembered that. At the end of that first session I'd offered her the opportunity to schedule a second. She demurred; she would think about it and call if she was interested in continuing. I didn't think I would hear from her again.

She'd never called back. In that sense, I'd been right.

But I had heard from her again. I no longer had doubts about that.

The brainstorm about where she fit came in the shower. I had a towel around my waist but I was still wet when I reached Sam on his cell. We spoke at the exact same instant.

He said, "You idiot—you're at home. This can't happen. You dialed by mistake. Got it? Jesus." Or something to that effect.

I said, "I'm sending an attachment to Lucy's e-mail."

We both hung up as though it had been a race to see who could disconnect first.

I put on the same clothes I'd taken off the night before and forwarded the photo from the University of Northern Colorado to Lucy's computer in an e-mail.

I'd expected to get confirmation of my suspicion from Sam immediately. I didn't. After the first ten minutes passed I began thinking that I might have been wrong about my conclusion regarding J. Winter Brown.

Sam didn't get back to me for almost half an hour. The call came in on the landline. Caller ID read PAY PHONE. "How did you get this?" he asked.

I was relieved to hear his confirmation. "Online. I think I have most of it."

"I can't frigging believe this. Jesus. We have to talk—now."

"I have one more thing to nail down. Call me again in an hour. Then we'll find a way to meet."

"Wait, Alan. You shouldn't—"

I hung up. Immediately I had second thoughts. It might be prudent to meet with Sam first and wait to do the additional research. Then I thought about Lauren stewing in the DIA airport hotel, eager to learn how she'd been snared by TSA.

Sam undoubtedly had a list of things he didn't want me to do. Just in case what I planned to do next was on that list, I decided I would wait to hear his admonitions.

He called back right away, as I suspected he would. I let voice mail take over. I knew he couldn't leave me a message; a digital record would provide enduring evidence that he had phoned. If someone looked later on that wouldn't look good. All he did on the voice message was growl.

Lauren's little sister's e-mail address was in my computer's address book.

I lost twenty minutes downloading some free software that would help me crop the photo of J. Winter Brown.

I was a novice; taking care of the digital family photo album was Lauren's job, not mine.

I lost twenty more minutes trying to figure out how to use the new software. The process looked like it should be easy. And because it looked like it should be idiot-proof, I felt like a complete dolt when it took me so long to crop a solitary photograph. Once I had eliminated Brown's colleagues from the picture, I enlarged what was left and attached the photo to an e-mail that I sent to Teresa.

On the subject line I wrote, simply, "Recognize this woman?"

Two minutes later I received an effervescent reply. "Hi!!!! That's Barbara, my friend from Vancouver? Do you know her?!! That's soooo great!!!!"

Teresa used exclamation points as though she'd won a lifetime supply on a game show. She thought she'd never run out. By contrast I lived life as though I'd been granted half a dozen at birth, and was told they had to last me until I took my last breath. I saved most of my allotment for Grace.

Was attitude about punctuation nature or nurture? I promised myself I'd ponder that at some other time.

Some people who knew Teresa only casually considered her to be naïve. It wasn't a fair description. Teresa lived life with an abundance of trust. Most of the time it was an endearing trait.

Occasionally it bit her in the ass. This was one of those

times. This time Teresa's free-trust attitude had also bitten Lauren in the ass.

I picked up the phone to tell Kirsten what I'd learned about the grand jury witness. I got no answer at her home, at the office, or on her mobile.

Rehearsing the words made my discovery seem much less consequential than it had when it had been bouncing around silently in my brain. So I knew the grand jury witness had an alias? Sam and Lauren may have known that all along. How was that going to help me?

A fleeting dulcet tone indicated that another e-mail had arrived at my computer. I clicked the message open. It was from Lucy, Sam's partner. Or from Sam, using his partner's account.

The message was curt. "You know about L.?"

I clicked "Reply," typed "Yes," and clicked "Send."

My enthusiasm about what I'd accomplished by discovering the photo of J. Winter Brown continued to fade.

I reminded myself that I had learned something significant and that Lauren needed to know that she'd been set up with the Sativex—and that it hadn't been by me. I also weighed how urgent it was to let Sam in on the fact that J. Winter was involved in Lauren's pharmaceutical entrapment. I decided that could wait until I'd told Lauren what was going on—I had to allow for the possibility that she might want me to guard the information and not share it with Sam.

Another e-mail arrived. Teresa. Nothing in the subject line.

The message: "Lauren just texted me. OMG!!! OMG!!!"

Oh my God, indeed. I replied, "shhhh, keep it to yourself" and hit "Enter."

I called my wife's mobile from my mobile. The call went right to voice mail. I figured it meant Lauren was using her phone. Maybe she was talking with the U.S. Attorney.

I knew that since Lauren was trapped in a bed-in-a-box motel room near DIA, her laptop would be open on the faux wood desktop and the machine would be hooked up to whatever kind of broadband connection was available in the room.

I sent her an e-mail. In the subject line, I typed, "News." In the body of the message I wrote, "T's friend in BC is a friend of M."

I waited ten minutes for a reply. Nothing came back. I tried Lauren's cell twice more. Each time I was routed directly to her voice mail. I didn't leave messages.

Another call came in on the landline. PAY PHONE was my clue. Sam.

"Yeah," I said.

"Go up the Royal Arch Trail from Chautauqua. He'll find you on the other side of the Bluebell Shelter, past the creek on the ridge."

"Lucy?" I thought the voice on the line had been Sam's partner, but I wasn't a hundred-percent sure.

She'd already hung up. I e-mailed Lauren again. "I'll be on my cell for a while. Call me."

"Emily?" I said to my sleeping Bouvier. "Want to go for a hike?" For a small child Emily didn't have a large receptive vocabulary, but for a middle-aged dog I thought she was an eighty-pound Einstein. "Want," "go," and "hike" were three of her favorite words. She went nuts. That meant yes.

I changed my shoes, threw on a fleece vest, deliberately chose a few things to toss into a shoulder pack, ran back inside to get a second bottle of water—the first had been for Emily—and shuttled the big dog into my car.

FORTY-SIX

HOW MANY times had I done the Royal Arch Trail? Twenty? Fifty? For a short roundtrip hike from an urban center like Boulder a day hiker couldn't ask for much more reward from a short investment. Heading in, the view toward the hills—Emily and I entered via the worn Mesa Trail from Chautauqua—provided a picture-window close-up of all three Flatirons against a deepwater blue sky. After cutting off onto the Royal Arch—the route starts in the shadows as a short climb along a causeway-like ridge—the trail follows some uphill cutbacks until it descends for a short stretch. From there a steep approach carries hikers toward the rock arch and the reward of an unusual angle view of all three Flatirons, an eagle's perspective on Boulder and, on a clear day, Denver glistening like some dirty quartz spilled on the threshold of the Great Plains.

It was a clear day. The prize at the end of the climb promised to be breathtaking, but I doubted I'd get that far. According to the message Sam wanted to meet along the trail's first ridge past the Bluebell Shelter. No way would the Royal Arch Trail be deserted on a fine spring day—the first section, the Mesa Trail traverse across the greenbelt above Chautauqua, was the closest thing in Boulder to a hiking Main Street—but I figured that was part of Sam's strategy. He'd purposefully picked a well-traveled path, the kind of place in Boulder that people unexpectedly run into friends. With any luck he and I could find a place to talk that provided privacy and maybe the bonus of a peekaboo view of the Third Flatiron.

Even though we jogged all the way to the creek I had to hold Emily back on her retractable lead. She was in one of her moods that left me incapable of moving fast enough to keep up with the pace that she had determined was reasonable. Shortly after we passed the ranger station she dropped her snout to the packed earth and locked onto the scent of some critter that didn't meet her olfactory criteria for friendliness. At first I thought she might have picked up evidence that Sam had ascended right in front of us but Emily's behavior wasn't the excited, playful dance she uses to respond to a friendly scent; it was the businesslike march of wariness with which she approaches a foe.

I wondered whether she was detecting the presence of a dog she'd had a run-in with before, or if maybe she was sensing the recent passing of her local adversary, a red fox. I definitely didn't want her to be on the trail of a mountain lion or brown bear, and I hoped it wasn't a porcupine awaiting us. Those encounters didn't end well. On another day I might have taken her off her lead to see where she might go exploring on her own, but Boulder was constantly changing its enforcement policy about dogs and leashes on the greenbelt and in the mountain parks and I hadn't been paying enough attention to know whether we were in a period of laissez-faire enforcement, or whether it was one of those times when the dog-poop intolerant were mapping canine feces with GPS and posting the hard, and occasionally soft, evidence on the Web. I did know that this was a day I could not risk getting a citation from the dog police, so I kept Emily within the range her lead allowed.

She tugged on the line to communicate what she thought of my caution.

Emily and I had to wait on the ridge for Sam to arrive. We said hello to a few hikers descending from the arch, but no one followed us uphill while we waited. I assumed that the wind—it had begun blowing hard from the south and the gusts were accelerating as they cleaved along the spine of the ridge—was keeping people on the lower trails. I wasn't dressed for a spring gale. Emily was—subarctic was fine with her—but the insistent southern blow was bringing in distant, uninteresting smells and I could feel her frustration as her nose twitched and her head turned and darted with her realization that she'd lost the scent she had been scurrying after up the hill.

Our ten-minute wait was on the verge of becoming fifteen and I'd begun to question the wisdom of the rendezvous. My mobile-phone signal was jumping back and forth between no signal and a solitary bar. I was cold and getting colder. The lovely view had stopped feeling mesmerizing.

Most of all I had started wondering if I had been set up. Was someone other than Sam waiting to meet me up the Royal Arch Trail? Or had someone wanted to get me away from my home? *I should have stopped at Chautauqua at a pay phone and confirmed the plans with Sam.* Once I'd let that regret out of the cage a slew of others stampeded out right after it.

I should have told Lauren what had happened when I was a kid.

I should have left the purse in the backyard.

I should have let my patient pick a different therapist to watch him die on the evening news.

I should have long ago stopped trying to be so damn helpful.

Emily barked. The sound startled me so much I almost yelped back at her.

I was sitting facing back down the trail in order to spot Sam's approach. Emily was beside me looking up the trail toward the nearest crest, her nose in the wind, her long facial hair blown back so she looked like Chewbacca's first cousin. Her initial solitary bark—the one that almost stopped my heart—was followed by a rat-a-tat series of roars that sounded like she was shooting them from a Gatling gun.

I spun around, but saw no one. Not uphill. Not down. "What is it, girl?" I asked.

She jumped 180 degrees and stared down the trail, standing like a statue—the only motion was her wet black nose twitching to catch molecules that were to her as prey-specific as a DNA profile.

She didn't answer me. She twirled again and launched herself past me up the ridge. I almost lost hold of her lead.

Sam had made it to within five feet of us before he said, "Sorry, you weren't here before, and I thought maybe I had time to make it to the arch. I'd forgotten how nice it is up there. You been waiting long? This wind, huh?"

He saw the aggravation on my face. Wisely, he allowed Emily to have most of his attention. "Hey. I said I was sorry. I needed the distraction."

I had no energy to squander on being angry at Sam. I had too many other things to be angry about. He started the conversation in exactly the right key to soften my mood. "You ever feel that your life is about to turn to shit?"

"Yeah," I said. "I do."

"You said you were checking on something else? The other piece you mentioned when you hung up on me?"

"Lauren's problem at the airport? You know the details?" I asked.

Sam nodded. "Broad strokes? Yes. Details? No."

"The woman in the picture I sent you set her up. The 'how' is a little complicated. I'll fill you in on that whenever you want."

"About that picture you sent, I—"

"I know—your witness. I don't know where she fits, but I know her real name. Or her alias, whatever. It's not much, but it's something."

"My what?" he asked. Until then his voice had been floating along on the insistent wind, its volume varying with the gusts. It suddenly pierced through.

"Your witness. The grand jury?" I said.

"What the hell are you talking about? You found her too?"

Too? "The photo I e-mailed. Your witness?" I was beginning to get the sense that Sam and I were reading from different scripts.

He stood up. He twisted his head to look up the ridge, and then down the trail. Satisfied no one was in our vicinity he said, "That wasn't our witness in the picture you sent, Alan. That was Currie."

FORTY-SEVEN

I STOOD up beside him. The wind seemed to pause. Emily's nose twitched and she wandered away the full length of her lead. "Your nutritionist?" I said.

Sam wasn't interested in dealing with my surprise. He said, "I need to know exactly how you found out whatever you found out. And what the hell she has to do with the rest of this mess."

"Your nutritionist?" I said again. The picture in my head wasn't of a woman in a lab coat studying dietary records, but rather of the woman with blond hair captured in profiled silhouette in Sam's bedroom. The white crescent of the cup of her bra figured prominently in the image I was blinking from my consciousness.

"Yeah, my frigging nutritionist. Now tell me where she fits."

What? I was distracted with the piece of the puzzle that I thought I had solved but that had been suddenly cast into the still-elusive category: If J. Winter Brown wasn't the missing grand jury witness, who was? Why had she set Lauren up with the Sativex? And what role did either woman play in Michael McClelland's scheme?

"The woman in the photograph was a patient in the Colorado State Hospital with McClelland. They were friends. Confidants. Much closer than the professional staff was comfortable with." "Confidants" had been one of Tharon's words. "I thought she was the grand jury witness, Sam. I didn't know she was . . ."

The woman seducing you in your bedroom.

"Shit," Sam said. "I had a whole list of bad answers I was afraid I was going to hear from you. That one wasn't even on my list. Goddammit. God . . . dammit."

I stared at the board. There were Parcheesi pieces on the Monopoly board. I meekly accepted the fact that with my assumptions proven errant, I was lost. I said, "He's had a lot of years to plan this."

Sam was silent for almost a minute while he digested the new information. "How did you find out that she was at the state hospital?"

"I blackmailed someone in a position to know both of them."

He raised his eyebrows. "A doctor?"

I nodded.

"Bravo," he said.

"She got out last year. She's been planning this—whatever her part of this is—for a while. She came in to see me as a patient late last fall. One session. She never came back. I thought she was therapist-shopping. Obviously, she was checking me out . . . for something else."

I didn't realize until I'd completed the disclosure that I'd just cavalierly massacred J. Winter's confidentiality. It didn't bother me a bit.

"She saw you for therapy? So we can tie her directly to you?"

"Yes."

"And you're sure about her ties to Lauren?"

"No doubt. She posed as a friend of Teresa—you remember Lauren's sister? Teresa confirmed that the same woman is the one who got the drug that's causing so much trouble for Lauren at the airport. That part's complicated. Impressive from a planning point of view."

"And now she got me," he said.

"Yes. And now you." *She made it all the way into your bed,* I thought.

"She's good," Sam said. "I didn't even consider the possibility that she took those pictures, Alan. It didn't even cross my mind." He shook his head. "Jesus."

"McClelland's the maestro."

He was ignoring me. I stepped away to give him some room and to allow Emily enough play on her lead to explore the nearby woods she was dying to get into.

My phone vibrated. I pulled it from my pocket and glanced at the screen. The source of the call was Lauren's cell. I had one bar. Just one. I flicked the phone open.

"Hey," I said. "You okay?"

Lauren told me I was breaking up. Anyway, that's what I thought she told me. Reflexively I stood on my toes, as though that would make me a better target for cell signals. *Idiot.* I raised my voice as though talking louder would compensate for the signal weakness and said, "I'll get a better signal and call you back in a few minutes."

The call died. Another glance at the screen confirmed that the solitary bar was gone and had been replaced by an *X*. "I need to head down the hill to call Lauren, Sam. I can't get a signal up here. She doesn't know the details about this woman yet. She doesn't know how she was set up."

He checked his phone's screen. "I don't have a signal either. I should have thought about that when I picked this place. I was just trying to find someplace we wouldn't be spotted." Sam was already thinking about other things. "We need to stay in touch. You're thinking this Brown woman was involved with the purse?"

"Yes. Which means she had something to do with the disappearance of your grand jury witness. And I also think she had something to do with the . . . hanging in the barn. How? What? I don't know."

Sam narrowed his eyes. "What makes you think she's involved in what happened in the barn?"

He wasn't challenging me. He wanted to hear my theory. "She was close to Nicole Cruz when they were in the state hospital, Sam. They—McClelland, Nicole Cruz, and J. Winter—were all patients in Pueblo at the same time. Nicole Cruz didn't know Michael McClelland in Pueblo, or knew him very little, but she knew J. Winter. They were close."

"Who's J. Winter?"

"Currie," I said. "Her real name is J. Winter Brown, like in the caption of the picture. The J. is for Justine. Professionally, she went by J. Winter."

"Professionally?"

"She's a psychologist."

"Shit. Figures," Sam said. "I need to get Lucy to run her."

"I have to get down the hill and get a cell signal."

He said, "I'll give you a few minutes' head start so nobody sees us walking out of here together."

I struggled to keep my feet as Emily yanked me down the trail. Near the bottom of the ridge she pulled me toward the woods with the determination of a tugboat moving a barge against the current on the Mississippi.

I resisted for a moment—long enough to check my cell. Still no bars. "Two minutes," I said to the dog, pretending to be her master. I trailed her by the length of her lead as she motored nose-down into the woods parallel to the ridge. We were climbing again. The southern wind had resumed blowing hard and we were heading straight into it. I was cold.

The noise in the woods from the air knifing through the trees was spooky and I was anxious. I was anxious to figure out what was going on. I was anxious about the time I was wasting. And I was anxious that Emily was leading me into an unwelcome confrontation with some unfriendly critter that wasn't going to be thrilled that we'd invaded his or her habitat. I was about to pretend to assert my authority when suddenly Emily stilled.

Bouviers aren't pointers, but when they're not herding they have some hunting instincts. Many times in the past I'd watched Emily mark and then slowly approach squirrels and prairie dogs in the fields near the house, so I knew the signs she exhibited when she thought she had spotted prey. I also knew that her confidence was often misplaced. She never caught anything.

It was definitely hunting behavior that she was exhibiting. She raised her head, lowered her haunches an inch or two, and moved her legs into a stalking position. If I drew lines connecting her paws they would have formed a parallelogram.

What do you see, girl? Following her eyes, I didn't see a thing.

Her nose was up. From the back end of the long lead I could see it twitching. Her ears were up, too. Their musculature allowed them to scan around her like radar antennae. I let my eyes wander into the trees and onto some nearby outcroppings of rocks. *Big cat,* I was thinking. I'd only seen a couple in my life. I wasn't looking forward to seeing the third.

I whispered, "Settle." The caution was for me as much as my dog. We had edged all the way back up the hill near the spot where we'd left Sam. Was she picking up his scent? Was that what this was about? Emily's tenacity was spooking me. I tugged on her lead and whispered, "Let's go. Come on, heel."

The wind ate my words. The big dog didn't budge. Her nose was locked onto something like a leech on flesh. She took a hunting step. A quiet, slow-dancing, I'm-sneaking-up-on-you-now step. But her motion wasn't in a straight line. It was forty-five degrees to her left.

She had something pegged. My eyes made a path through the trees in that direction. Nothing at first. Then, *there*. Forty yards ahead.

No cat. No bear. "Holy shit."

I don't need this, I thought.

The angle of the body was so awkward that I thought the person was dead.

Someone, man, woman—I no longer considered myself a reliable judge of gender—was wedged into a cut in the top of a rock outcropping. In distant geological times the ten-foot thrust of stone had probably been part of the spine of the ridge where Sam and I were talking a few minutes earlier. The fracture in the top of the formation wasn't wide enough for the person to lie prone, so he—was it a he?—had wedged himself into the crack on his left side, his arms extended in front of him, away from me.

I saw what appeared to be a readjusting motion—a quick bend of the knee, a flex of the right leg, and an extension and rotation of the right shoulder. That was it. Not much. But it was enough to let me know the person was alive. And it was enough to reveal that the person was holding something silver and black in his right hand.

The hand was encased in a tight glove, like a liner.

Shit. Sam.

My options? I could release Emily. The problem was that Emily wouldn't attack. I knew my dog well. She'd charge, ferocity in her eyes, and then she'd stop and try to bark the person into submission. Five feet away from him, ten feet away from him—she'd stop. She'd bare her fangs and bring the fear of God into the equation. But that was it. Then in all likelihood she would get shot.

After that, I might get shot.

Or I could scream to warn Sam. Would he hear me through the wind? I couldn't be sure. But if Sam heard me, so would the person with the gun. He would turn.

Emily might get shot. I might get shot.

The third option was so natural I found myself choosing it without any further deliberation. I took two steps to my right until I was behind the narrow trunk of a beetle-kill pine. I rotated my day pack to one side, reached into the zippered front section, and removed Lauren's Glock.

When she wasn't carrying it—she had a permit for the 9 mm; the airport was one of the few locations where she didn't have it with her—Lauren stored her loaded pistol in a locked cabinet in our closet at home. I had assumed that it was loaded when I'd grabbed it an hour before and stuck it in my rucksack. It certainly had a magazine in it, but I was intentionally so ignorant about guns that I didn't know how to determine if the magazine had bullets in it. Nor did I know how to put ammunition into the magazine if it didn't.

I'd probably held Lauren's gun three times before that day. Pulling the trigger? I'd performed that act on handguns exactly three times in my life—only two of those intentionally—but neither time with the Glock.

I spread my feet, leaned back against the tree, extended my arm, supported my right wrist with my left hand, and tried to line up the sights on the gun on the person in front of me.

What am I doing? I was doing things I'd seen actors do in the movies. *How sorry is this?*

Sam. That's what I was doing.

I adjusted my aim about two feet. One foot higher, one foot to the right.

My eyes were open. Wide open.

I squeezed the trigger.

Nothing happened.

The Glock doesn't have a conventional safety, but Lauren had once insisted on demonstrating for me how to work the manual lock on the back of the grip. Just in case.

I exhaled. Found the cylindrical lock. Released it. And then I started the process of aiming all over again. *Sam.*

The branch I was leaning on snapped. The crack sounded as loud as a shot.

I watched my target react by lifting himself up from the crevice—he or she was wearing a stocking cap the same gray-brown as the rocks—and then rotate back toward the noise, and me. I squeezed the trigger, firing a round. By then Emily had started barking. The man made a wise decision—he moved forward and crouched to leap down from the outcropping toward the Royal Arch Trail below.

I thought he was going after Sam.

Shoot! Shoot!

The person jumped. I fired two more rounds into the rocks where he'd been perched. My eyes were still open.

I knew I shot three times because I pulled the trigger three times and I felt the kick of the Glock three times. The sound? I heard the first crack from the broken branch. That was it. I don't recall hearing any of the explosions from the handgun.

Still thinking *Sam, Sam, Sam,* I moved two steps closer to the outcropping, ratcheting Emily's lead shorter with each step, bringing her nearer to me. Then I did it all again.

I wasn't thrilled to see the lack of blood on the rocks. Nor was I disappointed. The ambivalence paralyzed me for a moment. "Sam!" I yelled. "Sam!"

Emily's retractable lead was locked down at about two yards. She literally pulled me off my feet when she lurched toward the downhill side of the outcropping. I managed to hang on to the big red trigger grip of her lead as I fell.

I was gratified that I also managed to keep hold of the Glock without shooting myself or my dog.

FORTY-EIGHT

SAM FOUND Emily and me tangled up in her lead. He helped me to my feet. Emily popped up by herself.

"I was pretty sure you were dead," he said.

"I was thinking the same thing about you."

He saw the Glock in my hand. I saw his service pistol in his.

"That was you?" he said. "Those shots?"

"Yes."

"All of them?"

"How many were there?" I asked.

"Three."

"Yes. All of them were me."

His eyes communicated alarm and something else. He raised an eyebrow to let me know what the something else was: amazement. "You're pretty trigger happy all of a sudden."

"Someone was on that outcropping—right there— waiting to ambush you. I tried to stop him. Or her. I couldn't tell."

Odds were even whether he was going to thank me, or chastise me.

"That's Lauren's?" he said. He meant the Glock. His voice was calm, almost soothing. I think he was afraid of what I might do next.

"Yes."

"And you shot it . . . Why?"

"The person had a gun. He started to come at me. Then . . . at you."

Sam's eyes were still wide. My recklessness had unnerved him. "Want to see what he was trying to ambush me with?" Sam pulled a compact 35 mm SLR from his jacket pocket. "This. You almost shot a photographer, Alan." He held out his other hand. "Give me the Glock. Half the valley heard those shots. A ranger's going to be up here any minute. You do not want to be carrying a gun that's just been fired."

"You do?"

"I'll show them my shield and my service weapon. It hasn't been fired. Let's get out of here."

I handed Sam the weapon. He checked the gun, set the manual lock like he did it every day, and stuffed the weapon into his waistband at the small of his back where it was covered by his jacket. I then handed him Emily's lead and scrambled back up the slope into the woods. I was on my knees for a good minute before I found what I wanted. I jogged back to Sam and dropped the three spent shells from the Glock into his palm.

"You watch too much TV," he said.

What I had done hit me. *Shoot! Shoot!*

I barely had time to turn my head to the side before I puked at Sam's feet.

We ran into a ranger near the creek. She ordered us to stop. Sam was ready—he had his shield wallet hanging on his belt. He pointed at it and explained he heard the shots, too, but that he couldn't tell where they came from, and hadn't seen anything between the creek and the ridge below the Royal Arch. The ranger, a comely woman around thirty who had to put some effort into making her pleasant face taciturn, asked Sam if he was carrying his service weapon. Sam provided it to her. She checked the gun and handed it back. I gave her my driver's license. She asked a half-dozen more questions about the gunfire, where we were, what we heard.

Sam answered honestly, within the limits of his lie. I kept my mouth shut—I figured my breath smelled like vomit—except to offer my agreement in as few syllables as possible.

She wrote some notes and continued up the trail.

As soon as the ranger was out of earshot, Sam said, "Whoever you fired at didn't report anything. If he had, her response would be much different."

"Which means—"

"I know what it means."

Down in the parking lot at Chautauqua Sam climbed into the passenger seat of my wagon. I rinsed the vomit out of my mouth and poured some water into a bowl in the back for Emily before I joined him up front. He slid Lauren's Glock into the glove box and tossed the spent shells into the ashtray. He had the camera on his lap.

I spotted the digital screen on the back. "Let me see that," I said, grabbing the camera. I powered it up and hit a few buttons—I was much more proficient with digital cameras than I was with iPods, or guns. I scrolled back two shots. "Look."

I held the screen up for Sam. It was a shot of us talking on the ridge. He took the camera back and scrolled through a half-dozen more photos of us before the selection changed from the trail to some close-ups of horses.

He said, "Either there's a tap on your phone—which is possible—or one of us was followed up here."

"You," I said. I explained about Emily's wariness on the trail on the way up. "She picked up a scent of somebody she already knew and already didn't like. That's why we were in the woods. She tugged me up there—she was insisting we track whoever it was."

"Why does that mean I was the one who was followed? Emily likes me." Sam didn't want to be the one who had been followed.

"Because Emily picked up the person's scent on the way up. You were the first one up the trail. The person she didn't like was following you. Ergo . . ."

"Currie," he said. "Damn. Has to be. Emily knew her scent from your house. Didn't you say it was a guy on that outcropping of rock?"

I rolled my eyes. "I didn't see a face. The person was

wearing a hat—could have been either. Given my recent track record, it might have been a chimp wearing a people suit. It could have been Currie, Sam. Or your grand jury witness. Or someone we don't even know about. If it was Currie, has she done anything that would allow you guys to pick her up?"

He looked frustrated. "I can't think of anything. But she has stuff on us. We have to be careful."

"The only legal vulnerability I can think of is what she did with Lauren's sister. That's not going to be easy to prove. And it's not going to be of any interest to the Boulder police," I said. "But I don't know everything you know about the missing grand jury witness. Is there any way to tie Currie to her?"

Sam narrowed his eyes. "Do you know anything about that witness or her purse that you're not telling me?"

My mouth was dry. I finished the water in the bottle that I'd opened for the dog. "I know what the grand jury is investigating. The hit-and-run on that cop."

He mouthed a profanity. "Any point in asking how you know?"

"Lauren didn't tell me. Leave it at that."

He twisted on his seat to face me as much as the confined space would allow. "I'm going to ask once: Do you know anything at all about that hit-and-run? Don't fuck with me on this, Alan."

"Not a thing I didn't learn from reading the *Camera* or looking in that damn purse," I said. "I assume the purse-lady is still missing?"

"Yes," Sam said.

"Can you tie Currie to her? That would get the police department's attention."

"The accident was late last summer."

"The witness didn't come forward until . . . ?"

His eyes got wide. I watched his hands round into fists the size of cantaloupes. "You're implying—"

"I don't know anything about what happened, but it seems to me that it'd be pretty easy to pretend to be a solitary witness to a traffic accident that had already been described publicly down to the last detail. How would you guys know whether or not she was fabricating what she was telling you?"

Sam said, "Especially since she got cold feet before she gave us anything we could use."

"There you go."

I checked my phone. Three bars. Two missed calls from my wife. "I need to get back to Lauren."

He climbed out of the car. "I'll be in touch," he said before he closed the door. "Amanda Ross will never be the same. That asshole crushed her leg. She was a triathlete. She was training for that hundred-mile run up in Leadville."

He walked toward his Jeep. He stopped halfway there, retraced his steps and opened the door to my car. "Thanks," he said. "For what you did up there. It was stupid . . . and it was absolutely reckless." He grinned. "But I appreciate that you had my back."

He closed the door. I hit the speed-dial for Lauren's mobile.

"Hey," I said. "Sorry about the signal problem earlier." I'd already decided not to worry her with what had happened on the trail. At some point before she came home I'd get Sam to show me how to reload the magazine of her Glock. "You got my e-mail about your sister?"

I expected anger from her that I'd been out of touch. I didn't get any. She said, "I just got off the phone with her. She told me about the picture you sent. This is all Michael's doing?"

"Appears to be. He has some pretty good help."

Her voice was hollow. "It won't change anything with the U.S. Attorney. The federal prosecutors won't care that I was entrapped. I was in possession of a controlled substance. I conspired to bring it across an international border. I'm screwed."

"I figured that. I'm sorry. Did you talk to him today? The U.S. Attorney?"

"Briefly. We agreed I need a lawyer. I'm going to see a guy in the morning here in Denver. He's supposed to be good. How did you put this together?" she asked.

"I'll walk you through it later. Basically, I got a break tracking down Michael's accomplice. I assumed there would be a state-hospital connection. There was. Once I found out that Nicole Cruz had been a patient there, and was—"

"So what happened in the barn—you were set up, too?"

"I was set up too. I'm in the same position you are, though. My patient died. Won't matter to anybody that she knew McClelland in Pueblo."

"God."

"Nicole Cruz led me indirectly to a woman named J. Winter Brown. She was another patient in the forensic unit in Pueblo. A friend of McCelland's. She's the one who befriended Teresa in Washington, and fed her the drugs for you."

"It just goes on," she said.

"Sam's been pulled into it too."

"How?"

"Long story. McClelland's getting even with all of us, Lauren."

"He's back in custody."

Her voice was hollow. She knew that McClelland being back in custody wasn't much of a victory for our side. "Doesn't matter. The woman is still out there and she's as dangerous as McClelland. You can't come home until we know what she's up to."

"I can't go to Bimini."

"Pick someplace else. If you need to stay in the state, do it. But take Grace someplace, please. Don't tell me until you get there. And start using pay phones."

We agreed to talk again soon. I spoke to Gracie for a few minutes. When we hung up I drove across the parking lot and found a public phone near the Dining Hall.

"Sam?"

"Yeah."

"It's possible that Currie may not know we're on to her. That could be an advantage."

He was silent for a moment. "I didn't consider that.

I'm almost to her apartment right now. Maybe I'll send her those flowers instead."

I got back in the car and looked at the spent shells.

I'd fired the gun with my eyes open. I wondered if that was progress.

The cloud was no closer than it had been before. There were no wolves in the vicinity. That was good.

FORTY-NINE

I WAS sorting the detritus of the desecration of my daughter's bedroom into two piles—salvageable, and not—when I got a call from Cozy. "You've had an interesting couple of days," he said.

You don't know the half of it, I thought. "Kirsten filled you in on what happened at the Justice Center?"

"She did. During a crisis when you could have been a sympathetic figure you managed to offend the very people who will ultimately decide whether to prosecute you. A curious tactic. Someday I hope you will explain it."

I couldn't think of a noninflammatory reply, so I stayed silent. I chalked it up as a small victory in my anti-pettiness campaign.

Cozy went on. "I thought you would want to know that I just got a call from Elliot Bellhaven. He proclaimed it a courtesy, which concerns me no end. The news is that McClelland's on his way to New Max in Cañon City. He'll be reevaluated there—from a security point of view and a psychiatric one—to see if he can or should be returned to the forensic facility in Pueblo. The state may petition the court to have him stay in the penitentiary while his competency status is reevaluated."

"Thanks for that news," I said. I wasn't surprised.

"The DA's office is in some disarray right now—getting a special prosecutor in place to take over that grand jury is awkward for them—but I don't think you should become complacent about the death in your neighbor's barn. When the rest of the forensics and the labs come back you could find yourself in fresh jeopardy. Certainly civil, possibly criminal."

That wasn't news, either. I said, "Complacence isn't something you need to be concerned with." I thought about telling Cozy all the things I knew that he didn't know. None of it was urgent and I would prefer to have that conversation with Kirsten. I would be admitting some things that wouldn't present me in the best possible light and Cozy's bedside manner needed some work.

Assuming my family was safely out of town, my biggest remaining personal jeopardy had to be something that would make me appear criminally liable for Kol's death, or something that would tie me to the missing grand jury witness. For Michael McClelland to do any more damage than he'd done, he would have to reveal some evidence that aggravated one or both of those vulnerabilities.

I hoped there were no witnesses to my recklessness with Lauren's Glock.

As I cleaned up my daughter's room and made a list of

all the things I needed to replace, I wondered what time bomb McClelland or his minions might have planted in my house during the break-in that would stain me with the taint of the first two problems, and when it was scheduled to explode.

Just before dusk Sam called from a pay phone. The man had a huge stash of quarters. No greeting. His voice was icy, with just a hint of the warmth of irony at the edges. "Justine Winter Brown—aka Currie the nutritionist— has one solitary prior. Assault with a deadly weapon. The victim? Her boyfriend. The weapon? A ball-peen hammer. Gives you the shivers, don't it? Her defense? PTSD from chronic domestic abuse. Jury bought her story, or her lawyer's story; I don't actually know whose story it was. But that's why she was in Pueblo. Not guilty by reason of insanity. She was there getting . . . well. According to her jacket, she was planning to live somewhere near Ft. Morgan after her discharge. Want to hear the psychobabble?"

"Of course," I said. "It's the best part." I was thinking about all the psychological excuses I'd devised for Michael McClelland after his crime spree.

"Beyond post-traumatic stress disorder, the buzz-words are 'hostile-dependent,' 'passive aggressive,' and 'cunning.'"

"Not too imaginative. Anything there that doesn't fit?"

"I'm not done. Her boyfriend? No, not me—the one

she hit with a hammer while he was sleeping—was a retired cop from Cheyenne. She hit him in the eye, by the way. One blow. He was never charged with abusing her. Insufficient evidence. She saw it otherwise, of course. Apparently now she has . . . issues with cops. Prior to busting out his eyeball with the hammer, she'd had a couple of documented ER visits with suspicious bruising, another with a broken bone in her wrist. She had some statements from girlfriends about what an asshole he was. She thinks he got off because he was wrapped in a blue blanket."

I said, "She hooked up with another abuser in Pueblo."

Sam wasn't interested. "Last September twenty-eighth her boyfriend—eye patch and all—came home with a first date to his house in Cheyenne. His date was a juvenile court judge. They walked into his living room to find the wall area above his fireplace filled with child porn. Elegantly framed child porn. The juvy judge ran for the Tetons. Cops showed up within the hour along with a warrant to search his house and his computer. Turned out he was dirty up to his . . . well, eyeball.

"Three o'clock the next morning he died in a head-on with an eighteen-wheeler on I-80 just west of Laramie. Manner of death was suicide. Report says he'd been drinking."

"I assume J. Winter didn't leave any fingerprints in Wyoming. Literally or figuratively."

"None there's any record of."

"These people are good."

"They are."

"Why is she helping McClelland?"

"I figure they're helping each other," Sam said. "He helped her set her boyfriend up. She's helping him set us up."

"How would McClelland have done it? Set up her old boyfriend from Pueblo?"

"Cons run computer scams from inside all the time. Walls just aren't walls anymore. They get a proxy outside to do the Internet shit they can't get away with inside. The guy has had a lot of free time to get skilled on the Internet. Plan shit."

"He could have been setting us up for years."

"Everybody needs a hobby."

A question that I suspected might prove irrelevant came to mind. "Did anyone ever determine whether the porn was the boyfriend's and she just displayed it in his house? Or did she plant it?"

Sam paused a moment to frame his answer. "Officially she's not tied to this, Alan. She was interviewed during the investigation. That's all. There's a contact note in her jacket; that's the only way I found out about it. No witnesses put her on the scene. No forensics place her in his house. What are you asking?"

I was thinking about the photos taken in Sam's bedroom, and about TSA's suspicious focus on Lauren's bottle of Sativex at the airport. "I'm wondering whether she sets people up—like she did with you and those photos, and with Lauren and her drug, like she was trying to do with us earlier on the trail—or whether she sometimes just discovers people have existing vulnerabilities and exploits them? Reveals their secrets?"

"Is that a difference that makes a difference?" he asked.

It does to me. An ancient concept from the psychology of perception that I'd learned, and forgotten, from graduate school came buzzing into my skull like a mosquito taking advantage of a rip in a screen door. The JND—the just-noticeable-difference. If humans can't perceive the difference between one measurement and another, does the difference really matter, psychologically speaking? Only when delta crosses the threshold of human perception—the JND—does the difference prove meaningful from the perspective of human behavior. Of psychology.

"Tell me this," I said. "If the kiddie porn didn't belong to the ex-cop in Cheyenne, why did he kill himself?"

"So maybe it was his," Sam said. "Point?"

"It makes a difference, Sam." *A just-noticeable difference.* "This woman is a different adversary if she has two weapons. With Lauren and with you she created new vulnerabilities. With her old boyfriend and the porn, we don't know. He could have had an existing vulnerability and she and McClelland exploited it. Or she could have created it from whole cloth."

Sam said, "You're giving me a headache. I just don't see how it makes any difference."

That's because your secret has already been revealed, I thought. *Mine hasn't.*

I let it go, and filled him in on the situation with Lauren. Told him I'd begun sorting the damage in Grace's room, making an inventory of essentials and favorite things I'd need to replace.

"Find any kiddie porn in there?" he asked.

"Not funny."

"You're right. It's not. But my point is—"

"I get your point. I don't think you're getting mine. From what I could see in those two grainy photographs you showed me, she was enticing you—or trying to entice you—into having sex with her, Sam. In my mind that makes it different than if you were seducing her."

He sighed. "Sorry," he said. "I don't see it. I did what I did. I"—he emphasized the pronoun—"allowed her into my bedroom. I"—he did it again—"didn't walk out when she took off her shirt. That was all me, all my doing. So she enticed me. It takes more willpower not to eat chocolate cake when you're standing inside a bakery. Don't care. Responsibility is responsibility."

I knew it wasn't that simple. Not for me.

I spent the evening trying to determine my personal vulnerability to J. Winter Brown. My efforts took two distinct directions. The first was concrete: I reexamined the house with as fine a comb as I could muster, searching for anything she might have left behind during her intrusion the day before.

That search came up empty. I wasn't reassured; I assumed that my filter had been too coarse.

The second search was virtual. Armed with my aging Pentium and my credit card—and with more clues than Michael McClelland or J. Winter could have had when they started a similar search—I began to do the kind of reexamination of my own life's most tragic day using the same strategies that I'd used to uncover the truth about Tharon Thibodeaux's fateful Christmas party in the French Quarter.

After an hour on the Internet I had found a couple of old newspaper articles that referenced the events that had taken place in my family's home in Thousand Oaks, California, when I was thirteen, but my name wasn't in either article. My parents were identified. I was not. At no point was there a suggestion that what happened had been anything more than a domestic disturbance gone very badly.

I had known where to look, though. I knew about Thousand Oaks. I knew the year, the month, and the day. I knew the key words that would allow the Web's search engines to filter through the googols of bytes of archived data to zero in on that hour on that day in that place.

After I succeeded in finding the articles using what I knew, I tried to find them pretending that I didn't know where to look. Without the benefit of my inside knowledge I couldn't get there. I couldn't get back to Thousand Oaks. I couldn't get back to that kitchen.

I couldn't get back to that indelible day.

If I couldn't get there I tried to convince myself that neither Michael McClelland nor J. Winter Brown could get there. The only reasonable conclusion: my secret was safe.

It didn't feel safe.

Lauren called just before eight. She and Grace were in a "nice enough" hotel with a pool in Grand Junction, on the other side of the state. "It's close to the airport," she explained. "We can get out quickly." We talked about her meeting with the attorney in Denver, whether charges were likely—the short answer was "yes"—and we talked about Grace. I let her know that Michael McClelland was being assessed at the state penitentiary, but she'd already heard that news through her office.

The last time the phone rang that evening was the most surprising. It was Sam again. Pay phone again. He started the conversation by saying, "Don't interrupt me. I don't want to be telling you this. You understand?"

"Yes," I said. Sam sounded exhausted. Totally spent.

"This has to do with whether Currie was in the uncovering-secrets business, or the creating-secrets business."

"Okay." I hoped Sam didn't consider my word an interruption.

"Amanda Ross's parents live out in Gunbarrel. She's been recuperating there since she was discharged from the rehab hospital."

Sam was telling me that the rookie cop who'd been clipped and hurt during the hit-and-run the grand jury was investigating was likely a Boulder native, and that she was living in town with her parents. He was also implying that her injuries continued to interfere with her ability to live independently. I resisted my temptation to ask a clarifying question or two.

"I visited her tonight." He hesitated. "That part is . . . not new. My visiting." He paused again. He was, I thought, allowing some time for what he'd just admitted to sink in, or allowing himself some time to recover from the disclosure. Maybe both. "I showed her the photo of J. Winter Brown that you sent me. Ready to be surprised?" His monotone made a sudden turn down Sardonic Lane. "Turns out Amanda knows her. Knows her . . . well."

No. I hadn't been prepared for how sharp the turn was going to be.

The monotone came back. "Amanda said that Justine—that's what she calls her—goes to the same church Amanda's parents do. She was part of a group of people who offered to help out the family after the accident."

Oh shit. Oh shit.

"Amanda says she's been an angel. They've become friends."

I'm so sorry, Sam.

The connection was close to silent for a long interlude. His breathing, my breathing, digital clicks and pops. No words. Ten seconds or ten times ten seconds passed. I lost track. Finally he said, "You know what they call it? People Amanda's age? What I was before she got hurt?"

I thought I remembered from news reports that

Amanda's age when she was injured was twenty-six, maybe twenty-seven. I also thought I knew the answer to Sam's question. I was hoping I was wrong.

I said, "No, I don't."

" 'Fuck buddy,' " he said. "I was Amanda's fuck buddy."

I hadn't been wrong. *Jesus.*

"Now I'm her fucked buddy. Your question is answered," Sam said. Then he hung up.

FIFTY

I AWAKENED the next morning to discover that someone had called a time-out.

The frantic events and the stunning sequence of disclosures had all stopped.

I did my part to contribute to the lull. I canceled my few remaining patients for the week and holed up at the house with the dogs. I hadn't shopped for a while and quickly ran out of fresh food. My appetite was almost nonexistent, so I had no trouble sustaining myself out of the freezer and the cupboard.

I made a halfhearted vow not to drink the alcohol that remained in the house. All that was left to tempt me was half a bottle of Dewar's, a dusty, almost-full fifth of Beefeater, some old Amontillado that we used for cooking, Lauren's Zin port, and a few nice wines that we were saving for a special day.

I made only one trip away from home and didn't include a stop at a liquor store. I drove to Westminster—the risk of running into someone I knew in Boulder or at

Flatiron Crossing seemed too great—to replace as many of the desecrated books and toys from Grace's room as I could. I bought new bedding and pillows and curtains and drove home with a mattress sticking out from the back of the wagon.

I got busy reconstructing Grace's room. Nigel interrupted me a couple of times with some specific timeline questions about Kol's treatment. I e-mailed him the details he wanted.

Neither Kirsten nor Cozy tried to contact me. Diane did check in. Once I answered the phone when I saw her name on caller ID; the other times I didn't. She left a message promising never to play Enya in the waiting room if I came back to work.

I didn't read the papers, didn't watch the news.

Sam ceased his frequent forays to pay phones.

Adrienne called from Israel. "It's your Jewish friend," she said in greeting. "Calling from the homeland." She wanted to know how things were with the barn. I assured her she'd never be able to tell that anyone had been hanging from the rafters. She thought that was funny. Mostly she was calling to share her excitement about being in Israel, and about her newly discovered satisfaction that she and her son were Jews.

I tried to share her joy. I didn't tell her about the mess Lauren and I were in. That could wait until she got back to Spanish Hills.

Lauren and I talked. We were polite. Grace was good. During one call I heard my daughter singing along to

Simon & Garfunkel in the background. I allowed myself
to perceive it as a good sign—perhaps Lauren's aversion
to music was declining.

Michael McClelland and J. Winter Brown had maneu-
vered each of us—Lauren, Sam, and me—to the edge of
our own personal cliffs.

McClelland was behind the most secure walls the state
of Colorado had to offer.

J. Winter Brown was nowhere to be found.

Lauren, I figured, was about to be indicted on federal
drug charges.

Sam's relationship with Amanda Ross was likely soon
to be revealed. The fact that he had failed to alert the
DA about the sexual nature of that relationship prior to
taking the job as the DA's investigator on the grand jury
investigating her hit-and-run could prove to be a career-
ending decision for him.

I assumed that he was suffering other consequences
from the choices he'd made, specifically that he and Carmen were a romantic footnote. I didn't know how he felt
about that. Knowing Sam, certainly some guilt. Knowing
Carmen a little, probably some loss.

I thought I was on the verge of the next shoe dropping
in my own jeopardy. What would it be? Something awful
about the missing grand jury witness? Something awful
about my responsibility for Kol's death? A witness to my
target practice near the Flatirons?

Although I continued to fear the disclosure of my longest-held secret, I wasn't convinced that those concerns were anything more than paranoia.

A knock on my door startled me a few minutes after eight o'clock the next morning. Emily, as she usually did, took the sharp rap to be a clarion of an imminent assault on the castle, and she went into the kind of tommy-gun barking she'd last exhibited when we'd been up on the Royal Arch Trail.

I was hungover. I definitely didn't need the percussion.

Vodka wasn't the culprit. It was long gone. The bourbon bottle, too, had already spent a couple of nights in the Eco-Cycle bin. Historically I couldn't swallow Scotch to save my life, and gin left me with regrettable hangovers. Late the night before I'd spotted a bottle of Lanson on the top shelf of the refrigerator, hiding behind a box of moldy strawberries. Lauren and I had been given the champagne at a holiday gathering at our house. We had promised each other we'd drink it like table wine— no waiting for a celebration.

We hadn't gotten around to it.

My drinking decision the night before had been a choice among the Lanson, the Amontillado, or Lauren's Zin port.

It was in the table-wine spirit that I had opened the champagne. I drank it while I sat on the sofa and sewed the head back onto my daughter's favorite stuffed bear, performing the delicate surgery three times before I was content with my efforts.

Experience had taught me that I could drink half a bottle of champagne without rude consequences. The knock on the door the next morning taught me that apparently the same immunity didn't apply to a full bottle. My tolerance for bubbly was dose specific. I would have to remember that.

"Emily, please," I muttered. I was begging her to stop barking. She didn't stop barking. I opened the door.

"Elliot," I said. I could hardly have been more surprised. The Chief Deputy DA was at my door in full going-to-court attire. A dark suit. A shirt starched stiffly enough to keep a wave from crashing. An orange necktie that made me think of Indonesia. Those wingtips.

"I tried to call yesterday," he said. "You weren't home. Or you wouldn't answer. The machine was . . . off."

Caller ID had indeed read BOULDER COUNTY a few times the previous afternoon as the phone rang. Elliot was correct; I'd ignored those calls. I couldn't think of anyone I wanted to speak with who worked for the county. I said, "Sounds about right."

Emily had stopped barking. I released her collar. I didn't recall grabbing it.

"May I come in?"

Here we go again, I thought. "As an officer of the fucking court, Elliot?"

He raised his chin a smidge to deflect my profanity. "No," he said. "As a visitor . . . to your home."

"Do my attorneys know you're here?"

"No. This doesn't concern any possible legal . . . jeopardy. It's another matter, entirely. If you feel uncomfortable you may call them. By all means. I'll wait out here."

I stepped back and swept my left arm toward the family room. In for a dime . . . "There's coffee in the kitchen. Help yourself."

I wandered away from him to collect my wits. I strolled onto the deck just long enough to learn how cold it was outside. Some weather was rolling in. I hadn't been aware a front was approaching but I could feel the leading edge and could see a tsunami of white fluff spilling over the distant Divide. I went back inside the house. Elliot was leaning against the kitchen island holding a mug of coffee.

Emily wasn't sure she liked Elliot. Consistent with his nature, Anvil was less suspicious. Emily had always been the better judge of character.

"We need a favor, Alan."

I laughed. It wasn't a judicious move on my part, but in my defense I didn't deliberate before chuckling. I just chuckled. "Yes?" I said as an afterthought. I then had an afterthought to the afterthought. "Who is 'we,' Elliot?"

"The state of Colorado."

I lifted both eyebrows. "We talking your little chunk of it here in Boulder County? Or the whole thing, the part the governor usually runs?"

He tensed his jaw before he replied. "Alan, I'm sorry about your situation. I truly am. Will you hear me out?"

My situation, baby. As the bastardized snippet of the

Who's legendary anthem ran uninvited through my brain, I placed my mug on the coffee table and used both hands to tug my sweatpants higher on my hips and to retie the drawstring.

I felt eminently more presentable. "Of course," I said. Ever the gracious host.

"The Colorado Department of Corrections, the Department of Human Services—more specifically the Mental Health Institute in Pueblo—and the Boulder County District Attorney's Office would like your assistance."

For some reason my brain—insistent on reconstructing the old song by the Who—wandered to the lyric about *f-fad*-ing away.

"How?" I asked, determined to keep any more of the song out of my head.

"As you predicted . . . Michael McClelland hasn't spoken a word to law enforcement since we removed him from Lauren's office and returned him to custody. He told another inmate that he would speak only to you. He also asked that inmate to relay an offer to give you permission to speak with us after the two of you talked. We are wondering if you would be willing to have such a meeting on our behalf."

Another matter entirely? Ha.

I turned away from Elliot. Although I was pleased my internal dialogue had moved away from "My Generation" lyrics, I was way too hungover to manage to mount a workable facsimile of my therapist-facade and I was afraid that if I tried I would instead end up looking like some devilish Pixar villain after a bender. My back to him, I said, "Did McClelland say anything to the other inmate about *Harry Potter* by any chance? Voldemort maybe?"

Elliot was momentarily speechless. He recovered with, "Yes. He did. How do you know that?"

I ignored him. "Where's this rendezvous supposed to take place?"

"In Cañon City."

Cañon City meant the state penitentiary. New Max. I turned. "When?"

"As soon as possible. Later today, if we can arrange it."

Elliot was gazing across the room at the empty champagne bottle. If he was having trouble counting the number of glasses on the table he needed to use only the middle finger of one hand.

I was prepared to volunteer one of mine.

My anti-pettiness campaign was in tatters.

"I'll think about it," I said.

Elliot blinked twice. He hadn't expected reticence. He said, "That's it? I thought you would jump at the opportunity."

The inside of my mouth felt as though someone had slathered it overnight with Elmer's Glue and covered the glue with grass clippings. I ran my tongue into the area between my front teeth and whatever it was that had replaced my gums. "I can see how you would think that," I said. "I'll be in touch in the next couple of hours. How's that? I need a shower, in case you hadn't noticed." I raised my arm and smelled my left pit. As an act of disrespect I thought it was quite, well, pithy.

Elliot didn't bite. I would have been disappointed if he had. "I was hoping for an answer before I left," he said.

"Do you have a few extra minutes, Elliot? If you do, please have a seat—I'll give you a list of all the things that I've been hoping for lately. We can do a comparison, see how much good hope is doing each of us these days."

FIFTY-ONE

I SANG the hell out of "My Generation" in the shower until Townshend's and Daltrey's rebellion swirled down the drain.

Kirsten cut a deal with Elliot. I stayed out of it.

She insisted on driving me south to Cañon City. Part of the arrangement was that Cozy's law firm's fees for Kirsten's journey would be paid for by one of the state agencies so eager for my appearance at New Max.

I put on some decent corduroys and a cotton sweater for the trip. I had chosen not to wear a tie, assuming that would be on the prohibited clothing list. The sweater I was wearing would disguise the fact that I wasn't wearing a belt for the same reason. I folded my favorite black sport jacket over the back of a bar stool in the kitchen. I hoped the relative formality of the blazer might distract attention from my bloodshot eyes.

Kirsten called me from South Boulder Road. "Two-minute warning," she said and hung up. I'd already taken the dogs out in preparation for their long after-noon alone. I reached for my coat. A splash of color caught my eye.

The top half of a bright red diamond.

I stepped back. I stepped forward. I leaned over. A playing card—specifically the six of diamonds—had been tucked into the outer lapel pocket of my sport jacket.

I hadn't put it there. It was a pocket I never use.

Without touching the card I could see that someone with a neat feminine hand had written on it with a felt-tip pen. By leaning way over I was able to read the message. It said, "Dr. G—you were a great help, xxxox, D."

D? I wasn't so mentally impaired that I failed to rec-ognize the implication: the missing grand jury witness's first name was Donna. It was on the prescription bottle for Valtrex that I'd found in her purse.

The phone rang. Emily started sprinting toward the front of the house. Kirsten must have pulled up outside. I grabbed the phone and said, "Couple more minutes."

I leaned over and stared at the playing card.

Bingo, I thought.

It took longer than the promised two minutes for me to get out to Kirsten's car. I wasted most of that interval standing catatonic in the great room.

Her dashboard clock said it was lunchtime. My stom-ach wasn't sure it agreed. I was still quaking from the discovery of the six of diamonds and I was repeatedly cautioning myself to act cool—for the rest of the day I knew I needed to manage a reasonable masquerade of a Boulder psychologist.

Telling Kirsten about the playing card was tempting but it would have meant telling her about a lot of other things that I wasn't ready to divulge. The list included the ransacking of Grace's room, the gunplay on the Royal Arch Trail, Sam and Currie, and my fears about J. Winter B.

A second consequence of the previous night's champagne indulgence—the hangover was the first—was that J. Winter Brown's name had morphed in my consciousness into the more symmetric "J. Winter B." and had apparently stuck there, which had, in turn, caused me to recall Diane's caution about the dangers of too much symmetry. At the time she had been talking about the placement of the purple rug in the waiting room. But did the lesson generalize? Shit, I didn't know.

Although the shower had helped burn off some fog, the "My Generation" episode had convinced me that my brain chemistry wasn't sufficiently recovered from the hangover to deal with any abstract dangers presented by a sudden predilection toward symmetry. I decided to postpone giving Kirsten the latest updates until I was much more clearheaded about the potential ramifications.

She turned right onto South Boulder Road toward Louisville. When we approached the nearest convenience store I asked her to stop. There was a pay phone inside. I'd used it recently.

"I'll be right back," I said. Kirsten waited in the car.

I called Sam from the store phone. "It's me," I said when he answered. I was distracted watching a teenager in a black business suit turn his back to the register and stick a bag of sunflower seeds down his pants.

"Okay," he said. "I'm kind of busy."

"There was a deck of cards in the grand jury witness's purse. Wound with a rubber band. I need to know—was it a full deck, or were any cards missing?" He didn't respond right away. I added, "Time is kind of tight."

"I don't know," he said. "I think it was a full deck."

"It's, um, important. Can you check and call me on my cell?"

"You found something," he said. It wasn't a question.

I bought two bottles of water and walked back to the car.

Most of the way out Highway 36 from Boulder Kirsten and I spoke like colleagues who were catching up after not seeing each other for a while. We pretended I hadn't once been her therapist and that she hadn't once fallen in love with me. The pretense was weird, but in my life weird was the new black. I tried to make like Grace and roll with it.

As we crossed over Federal Boulevard she fumbled in her satchel and pulled out an envelope. Inside were two copies of a three-page agreement. "Elliot has requested that you sign this prior to seeing Michael McClelland."

I flipped through the document. The letterhead was from the Boulder County DA's office. "What does it say?"

"It says you'll tell the . . . interested parties about your conversation with McClelland. It specifically denies you the right to claim doctor-patient privilege."

"That's not my privilege to renounce. The privilege belongs to the patient."

She audibly swallowed a sigh. Kirsten knew to whom the privilege belonged and had been hoping to avoid an argument with me about the document. "In the agreement you acknowledge he is not a current patient. That's all."

"You think I should sign it?" I asked. I didn't want to read the damn thing.

"The agreement includes a release of all liability should you be injured. You should think about that. Informally, Cozy and I were able to negotiate . . . certain considerations. If you want to talk to McClelland, yes, I think you should sign it."

I took a pen from my inside coat pocket and scribbled a signature on the last page of each copy. I refolded them and returned them to the envelope. I rested the envelope on top of her satchel.

"You want to know what the considerations are?" she asked.

"Not really," I said. "I would have driven all night in a blizzard and talked to McClelland for nothing. Elliot knows that."

"That's why you have attorneys," she said.

"That, and keeping me out of jail."

She found that amusing. I didn't. I was too distracted

wondering why Michael McClelland and J. Winter B. had chosen the six of diamonds.

We were quiet until we'd crossed the T-REX–improved Denver metro grid into Douglas County. Traffic used to cramp up near Denver's borders and then thin out to the south. No longer. Taxpayers had spent a fortune to shove the congestion five miles away. The billions hadn't bought a solution—they'd merely rented one. What a bargain.

We pushed down I-25 through Douglas County at the pace of a fast-food drive-through. A few flurries were falling along the Palmer Divide. Wet flakes. Nothing unusual, nothing serious. Springtime in the Rockies.

Kirsten said, "Snow."

I said, "Yeah."

The skies were gray on the back side of Monument Hill but the storm stayed confined to the ridgeline. Traffic had thinned.

We were approaching the Air Force Academy north of the Springs when I said, "I don't want you in the room, Kirsten."

"With Elliot? That's a mistake."

"With McClelland. That needs to be just me and him. No recording devices. No witnesses. I'd like you to make sure that there isn't any one-way glass, or any cameras into the room. Just McClelland and me."

"That's my understanding of how it's arranged, Alan. But later, when you speak with Elliot and whoever is there representing the Department of Corrections and the Institute for Forensic Psychiatry, I think I should be in the room."

My phone vibrated. "That's fine," I said to Kirsten. The screen read PAY PHONE.

I flipped it open. "Yeah."

"Can you talk?" Sam asked. He'd apparently heard the tentativeness in my "Yeah."

"Not really."

"Deck doesn't have jokers. Does that change anything?"

"Nope. I appreciate the irony though."

He said, "Hearts, diamonds, clubs, spades. A, B, C, or D?"

"B," I said.

"Shit. I'm going to count. Tell me when to stop. Ace . . . two . . . three . . . four . . . five . . . six—"

"There you go."

"Shit," Sam said. "We didn't catch there was a missing card in the deck. We should've caught it."

"Some things are hard to notice," I said.

"Where is it now? The card?"

"Can't say."

"Call me later? There's some stuff cooking here, too."

"Count on it." I folded the phone. Traffic in Colorado Springs was almost as coagulated as it had been in Denver's suburbs. "You don't mind if I sleep the rest of the way down, Kirsten? I'm kind of . . . tired."

"No, go right ahead," she said.

I eased the seat back and closed my eyes. I said, "Sam's the one who's been feeding all the information from the investigation to you and Cozy, isn't he?"

Kirsten didn't answer right away. For some reason Sam wanted his generosity to me to remain a secret.

"The lab info? The other evidence?" I asked. "You know what I mean."

She said, "I don't want to lie to you."

"And if I press this you might have to?"

"Something like that." Kirsten softened her tone from the attorney range into the friend range and added, "You know you might feel better if you tell me what happened." She paused. "When you were a child."

She emphasized "child."

"Want to bet?" I said. I immediately regretted it. "I'm sorry, Kirsten. That wasn't kind. Maybe later."

Then again, maybe not.

She woke me just outside Cañon City with a hand above my knee. "You ever been here before, Alan?"

I opened my eyes to the sign for the huge correctional complex. "No," I said. "You?"

"In Louisiana and Florida? Plenty of times. Here, no. This is a first."

I began to get anxious. I wasn't accustomed to homicidal impulses. But as we drove into the small parking lot outside New Max, I felt them. I could imagine beating Michael Mc-Clelland to death. I could imagine strangling him. I could imagine stabbing him. I could imagine shooting him.

All with my eyes wide open.

Kirsten sensed something. "You're not going to do anything stupid, are you?" she asked.

"Here?" I said. The modern complex looked less like my fantasy of a penitentiary than like some supersecret industrial facility with plenty of safeguards to keep visitors out. The most visible barriers were the redundant lines of concertina wire-topped fences, miles of them, it seemed.

"Good," she said. "I don't want to make the drive back by myself."

FIFTY-TWO

GETTING THROUGH security was laborious. Kirsten warned me to leave any sharps and metal—pens, keys, coins, whatever—in her car, but even stripped of anything resembling contraband the searches and scans that we endured to get inside the prison were much more thorough than anything I was accustomed to at the airport.

Elliot Bellhaven was waiting on the other side of security with two people I didn't know. One was an attractive fortyish woman with an uncomplicated smile who was representing the interests of the Department of Corrections; the other was a tall, balding man with small eyes who introduced himself as "Smith." He was an assistant warden for New Max, the facility we were in. He had no soft edges. Not physically, not in manner, not in his voice. My immediate appraisal: *I would hate to be an adolescent boy dating his daughter.*

The assistant warden led us to a conference room that was appropriately institutional. A minute or two after Kirsten and I chose seats at the table, Tharon Thibodeaux joined the gathering as the representative of the Department of Human Services and the IFP in Pueblo. I was neither pleased nor displeased by his presence.

I took my cues from him as he introduced himself to Elliot and to the assistant warden. It was apparent from the kiss she got on the cheek that he already knew the woman from the Department of Corrections. Kirsten stood and shook Tharon's hand; I thought she seemed pleased that another Southerner was present. He seemed delighted that an attractive Southern woman with a naked ring finger was present. When she turned to sit down he looked at her ass.

To me he said, "Nice to meet you, Dr. Gregory."

We shook hands. I said, "Likewise, Dr. Thibodeaux."

Elliot and Tharon got right to work, talking ground rules and goals for "the interview"—that's what everyone was calling my upcoming tête-à-tête with Michael McClelland. Kirsten seemed rapt by the minutiae of the process. In contrast, the woman from the Department of Corrections appeared to be there mostly as an observer. She was covering some superior's butt.

I zoned out. Whatever agenda was on the table wasn't mine.

The assistant warden brought me back to the present a few moments later. He spoke my name with an authority that was the homo-sapien equivalent of one of Emily's "attention" barks. In reality all he said was, "Dr. Gregory?"

"Yes?" I said, my pulse accelerating.

"The room you will be in is intended for confidential discussions. No security will be present. We will neither be able to observe you nor overhear normal conversation. If you scream loudly enough we might be able to hear you. Per agreement, the inmate will not—I repeat, not—be shackled. The table in the room is fixed to the floor. The chairs—there will be two—are not. An emergency call button—it's bright red; you're unlikely to miss it—is beside the door that is approximately six feet behind your chair. The inmate will have already been seated when you enter the room. He will have been thoroughly searched. Any questions thus far?"

"No," I said.

"Upon conclusion of your interview a simple knock on the door will alert the correctional officer outside that you are ready to exit. I suggest you ask the inmate to remain seated while you do that. After you knock there may be a brief delay to make sure adequate security is in place before the door is opened. Is all that clear?"

"Yes."

"Ms. Lord?" Elliot said. "The agreement? Has Dr. Gregory signed it?"

"Of course, Mr. Bellhaven," she said. She withdrew the envelope from her satchel and handed one of the two signed copies to Elliot. He shuffled through the pages quickly, and pocketed the document inside his jacket. He was wearing the same suit he'd had on when he'd visited me earlier that day. The damn shirt hadn't wrinkled a bit.

I had no idea how people did that.

The assistant warden stood. He said, "We're set then. Dr. Gregory, right this way. Everyone else, please remain in this room."

I followed him down a corridor, through a locked steel door, and down another corridor. We turned left. We turned left again. When we passed through yet another security door it was apparent to me that we had crossed an important line. The final security barricade we cleared was electronic and more substantial than the ones before, and the architecture on the other side revealed we had left a transitional wing and entered a correctional one. We stopped thirty seconds later outside a nondescript room with a heavy steel door. A correctional officer stood sentry.

The assistant warden said, "The inmate is waiting inside."

"Okay," I replied.

"You frightened?" he asked me on an inhale.

I said, "More nervous than frightened, but yeah, I'm scared."

"You should be. I read his jacket. Guys like him? They're like old munitions. Designed to be dangerous, kind of unstable. They can go off at any time."

"Old bombs don't hold grudges," I said. "He does."

He flattened his mouth into a wry smile. "Don't be a hero in there, Doctor."

"Not in my repertoire," I said.

"If that was the case you wouldn't be here," he said.

You don't know why I'm here. You have no idea, I thought. He wanted me to reply, to reveal something.

"Good luck," he said.

A decent bullshit detector would be a prerequisite for a job like his, and he seemed to have one. I hoped that he had been the only one at the conference table who was questioning my motives for being in Pueblo to see McClelland.

He said, "I'll be present later at the debriefing. See you then." He nodded at the officer. The officer unlocked the door.

Bingo, I thought.

FIFTY-THREE

"I KNEW you'd come."

Michael McClelland was in prison garb. The clothes made him look a little pudgier than I recalled from my brief glances at him in Lauren's office. He didn't appear villainous. I saw no lingering signs of the wounds he'd suffered during his arrest years before. All the institutional food he'd been eating over the years at the state's expense had helped him put on a few pounds. My overall impression was of a State Farm agent whose office had been stuck for a decade between a Wendy's and a KFC.

After locating the bright red panic button, I sat down across from him with my back to the door. Three feet of brushed-steel tabletop separated us.

On my side of the table someone had scratched, "My mother made me a queer." Below it, a different hand had etched out a retort: "Will she make me one too?"

"Nervous?" McClelland asked.

I hadn't yet spoken a word. My first was not going to be a reply to that question.

I waited. It's what I do.

"I thought I was the one who was supposed to be mute," he said, elevating his eyebrows.

"This is your meeting," I said. "If I'm not convinced within the next five minutes why you wanted me here, I'll knock on that door and leave. I won't come back."

He made a *tsking* sound with his tongue on the roof of his mouth.

I had an impulse to stand up and do a side-kick into his Adam's apple. I wondered if a clean hit would snap his neck. Although I had no martial-arts skills—attempting the maneuver was more likely to rip my groin than break his neck—the fantasy soothed me. I felt my breathing slow. My blood pressure descended from the stratosphere.

I waited. After a reasonable interval—I'd left my watch in the car, so I was guessing—I said, "Four minutes."

I silently counted to sixty. I said, "Three."

I did it again. I said, "Two." The room was quiet. I could hear the *pop-swish* of my pulse as blood rushed close to my ears.

He said, "You won't leave."

I counted to fifty. I said, "One more minute."

At my internal count of forty-five, I stood up, pushed my chair back into place and stepped toward the door.

"I know what happened in Thousand Oaks, you hypocritical asshole."

I looked over my shoulder at him. I was trying to look blasé. I'd been preparing myself for that one. Didn't really believe it would happen. Still . . .

You do know. Wow.

I said, "That's all you got?"

I watched his reaction for about five seconds. I thought he was a little taken aback by my lack of response, but I wasn't sure. He had a pretty good poker face.

I knocked on the door. The steel absorbed the sound as though I'd pounded on foam rubber. I hoped the officer outside had heard my knock. I eyed the emergency button.

McClelland pushed his chair back from the table. I didn't have to turn around to know what he was doing. The sound was distinctive.

How long did the assistant warden say this interval was going to be? Between knocking and the door opening?

I knocked again. I used the side of my fist.

"My escape from Pueblo wasn't planned and I'm in a position I didn't anticipate. I have a deal for you."

An officer opened the door. He was a tall black man with shoulders that could make a yardstick disappear. "Sit," he barked at McClelland. I flinched at the sharp crack of his voice. Behind him, I could see another officer—a woman—holding two sets of steel shackles. Another male officer was behind her.

I turned my head and saw McClelland sit.

"Are we permitted some water, sir?" I asked the correctional officer with the meter of shoulders.

He looked into my eyes for a few seconds, gauging my sincerity. Apparently satisfied, he nodded and then closed the door. I stayed where I was. The door reopened in about a minute. After staring McClelland into ten seconds of paralysis, he handed me two foam cups of water. I said, "Thank you."

I placed the water on the table. I sat back down. To McClelland I said, "Why didn't you just run? When you walked away from the clinic?"

"And spare you this? By 'you' I mean Lauren and Purdy too, of course. I had too much invested in this plan to run."

"Vengeance is more satisfying than freedom?"

"For the first hour or so I was out, I was tempted to head for Mexico. But I hadn't planned it out. I didn't have money. Hadn't done any research. I'm a planner by character, not an improviser. I knew there was a chance I might make it to freedom, but I thought the odds were greater I'd get caught first and that I'd just end up having to stand trial. Then? All the work I'd put into fucking up your life would have been for naught." He smiled. "Getting even with you personally was an acceptable alternative."

I wasn't surprised that vindictiveness was so high on his list of motivations. It always had been. I said, "Tell me what you want."

He drank half the water before he sat back on his chair. "I want to go back to Pueblo. I don't belong here. Needless to say, I don't want to be judged competent. I don't want to stand trial. I want you to . . . help me with that."

Michael didn't want to be in the state penitentiary.

And he wanted me to make a clinical argument that he remained too mentally ill to be declared competent to proceed within the criminal-justice system. He was suffering a contemporary version of Yossarian's catch-22—if you don't want to be in a place like New Max, then you're not too crazy to be there. The irony was sweet.

I said, "What's in it for me?"

"I keep your secret."

I shrugged. "And what? I wait until the next time you feel like pulling it out for a little blackmail?"

He shrugged back. "Maybe you'll have to trust me."

"Trust won't be part of any agreement we reach."

"You're talking about an agreement. We're halfway there." He paused. His next words sounded academic, as though he were a scientist addressing a colleague. "The truth is that you have a weakness for flawed people, Doctor. You've spent a career believing in people who don't deserve your faith. You did it with my sister. You did it with me. With your friend the detective. You even did it with your wife. You'll do it again." He paused. "And again. And again. We both know why. Just us. Let's leave it that way."

His simple assessment of my professional life and my personal vulnerabilities wounded me. I tried not to let him see the blood flowing from the gash he cut.

Believing that the most flawed among us could change and believing that even the most flawed among us deserved a chance to change had been the fuel in the motor that had driven me through college and graduate school.

Before that it had been the argument I'd made to my mother about my father.

And to my father about my mother.

To myself about both of them.

I'd been a thirteen-year-old philosopher/psychologist who knew shit about philosophy or psychology.

What had changed since? I feared not much. I'd read a lot of books. Taken a lot of classes. I'd gotten older. But I continued to find myself ambushed by psychopaths and sociopaths and by lesser versions of evil, too.

I needed to change the subject with McClelland. "Back up," I said. "Walking away from that clinic wasn't planned?"

"Planned? How about stupid? The fool left me unshackled. Five seconds later I was walking out the door. It was so . . . enticing. So much had been set up by then and . . . I had to go and get impulsive. Greedy."

"And now you're here. That wasn't part of the plan either. Yes? The stunt you pulled at the Justice Center? You were trying to show everybody how nuts you were?"

"Pretty much. 'Cunning, but severely psychotic. Extremely paranoid.' That's what the psychiatrist said about me last time. I spend a lot of my time trying to reinforce that impression. I didn't have much choice at the end. A cop almost spotted me in your neighborhood. Then two cops followed me into the Boulder Army Store when I was lifting bandannas. Turned out they were after a different shoplifter." He made an exasperated face. "I didn't have money. No safe place to stay. I was afraid I'd get picked up for some petty crime or that some cop would stumble on me in Boulder and I would lose control of events." He shook his head. Then he smiled. "This was never about getting free. It was about getting even."

"But they brought you here, not to Pueblo. Miscalculation? Yes?"

"I'm here. It wasn't part of the plan. Get them to send me back to Pueblo and all is forgiven. And forgotten. I call off what's pending. Your bride doesn't have to know what you did. Your future is in your hands now."

"Forgiven? You don't have the currency you need to buy that kind of favor."

"Because I'm such a nice guy, I'll even tell you who's been helping me."

That was his sweetener. I was assuming that Michael didn't know that Sam and I knew about J. Winter B. He was either confirming that fact or he was screwing with me. I wasn't sure it mattered which was true. The fact I already knew she was out there and that I knew her identity made me invulnerable to the leverage McClelland was counting on using.

"And why would I care about that? The cops might care. I don't."

"My accomplice helped me set up your wife," he said. "You must have some feelings about that. Aren't you curious how we did it?"

"It's not too hard for me to see how that was done. Your accomplice is resourceful. He probably watched Lauren smoking dope outside our house at night. Somehow he tied Lauren to her sister in Seattle and . . ." I shrugged. "The rest? Inventive, yes."

"Reading her e-mail helped. Did you know the signal from your wireless network makes it out to the barn?" Michael said. "The security settings? Pure bullshit. Your wife really should use passwords. Here's a freebie: call a locksmith. We made a copy of the key you hide under the flagstone."

Note to self: Change locks. Secure network. Get new e-mail accounts. Use passwords.

"Lauren was set up with aplomb, I admit that. Though I'm still not sure how your friend managed to do the thing with the grand jury witness. That was more complicated."

His vanity was showing. I was praying he would keep talking. "I've been waiting—patiently—for a witnessless crime in Boulder that would keep the cops' interest. When we finally got one—the hit-and-run—we created a witness. We tantalized the cops with what the witness might know. We created a threat to the witness. That was all prelude.

"Then we planted the purse at your office. That was the trap."

"The purse was risky, Michael. What if I hadn't spotted it?"

"The purse was *elegant*, Alan. And I always have a plan B. Always."

"The witness was another accomplice? How do you find these people?" I asked as if I didn't care.

"That was paid help, actually. It's somebody my ac- complice recruited in town. We convinced the 'witness' that her role would be simple. She needed a friend, and she needed money—we gave her the first and promised her enough of the second to move back to Alaska. That's where she's from."

He waited for me to react. I didn't.

He went on. "The blood was a nice touch, don't you think? The nosebleed? Nicole said you never suspected it wasn't hers."

Nicole was right.

He sat back. "You thought she was a man, didn't you? She thought you did."

I didn't respond to that provocation. "You couldn't have predicted that the hit-and-run would become a grand jury investigation," I said.

He shook his head. "No, that ambushed us. We ad- justed. I saw it as an opportunity, but I never did figure out a way to use it to our advantage with Lauren. But Sam Purdy? God bless him, he walked right into the fire for us. What a hero that man is. A little undisciplined, but I already knew that, didn't I?"

Damn. You know about Amanda Ross.

"Where is the witness now, Michael?"

"The witness is . . . gone. Alaska? Maybe. Telling you where she is won't help me. I'd rather talk about your wife. I've always liked talking about your wife."

I imagined a shotgun spray of buckshot turning his chest into pink mist. It calmed me like a good massage.

"The problem is—*your* problem is, Michael—that your friend did too good a job of setting up my wife. He set her up in such a way that nothing is going to make her legal problems go away now. Nothing you can say will un-ring that bell. I think you, more than anyone, should know what it feels like to be painted into that kind of corner."

He thought about it for a moment. "You may be right. Obviously doesn't matter to me beyond the current negotiation. The setups we did? Those were our insurance policies. The true vulnerabilities that you have—that all of you have—are the secrets I learned before we started. That was a lesson from my own life—one you helped me learn way back when. True vulnerability is in our secrets. You know damn well that it's the case in your life. But maybe you want to believe it isn't true for your wife's or your friend's? That's naïve, Alan. Everyone has a secret. Or six. With the Net, and a little money to pay some data brokers? Secrets aren't secret. They're just hidden treasures, waiting to be exploited."

FIFTY-FOUR

LAUREN'S MARIJUANA? Sam's affair? I thought. *Is that what he's talking about?*

"I'm not sure what you mean."

"Ever talk to a pickpocket?" Michael asked. "They'll tell you that if you give a mark a few minutes he'll touch his money. He'll put his hand near his wallet or brush his fingers on the pocket where he keeps his billfold, or whatever. With secrets, it's different. It can go either way. People either visit their secrets surreptitiously—like Sam with his little friend. You know about her? Or your wife with her dope at night. Or, people completely avoid their secrets." He paused. "Like you. You really should see your mother more often, Alan. Yes, yes, she's a bit of a martyr, but she's not the most disagreeable old lady on the planet."

He watched me, waiting for a reaction. *J. Winter B. visited my mother.* I was stone.

"Observe people closely and you learn which way they handle their secrets. Sam Purdy? He's a visitor. He can't stay away from his torment. You? You're an avoider. God, are you an avoider. With people like you it takes more effort to uncover what's hidden. We had to read your phone bills for a while before we realized where you never went, who you never called." Michael raised his eyebrows. "Your mother generously pointed us in the right direction."

He wanted me to react. I wouldn't.

"Now, Lauren?" he went on. "Turns out she's both a visitor and an avoider. I didn't predict that. I thought she'd be an avoider like her husband."

"Tell me," I said, trying the universal therapist prompt. I wanted to know what he meant about Lauren. What secret was she avoiding?

He had a different agenda. "Purdy's problems aren't over," McClelland said. "Neither are yours. Help me. They'll go away. You'll be glad you did."

I assumed he was alluding to the fact that Sam's fuck-buddy affair with Amanda Ross wasn't yet public. I had already surmised that J. Winter B. joined the church and befriended Amanda after following Sam to the hospital or to her house one night after the accident. Amanda eventually confided to her new friend about her affair with the detective, giving Michael fresh bullets for his gun. What was breathtaking to me was how effective a strategy he had used to acquire the ammunition for blackmail and disgrace.

I felt a measure of relief that McClelland appeared to be running out of leverage. I savored the sour hint of desperation I'd begun tasting in his words.

I said, "Then you should talk to Purdy. See if he can keep you out of permanent residency in one of the cellblocks down the hall." I was hoping that McClelland didn't have any more rounds in his magazine. "Your act was wearing thin in Pueblo before your latest campaign to ruin my life, Michael. I don't think I'm predisposed to help you out any longer."

"Not so hasty. My friend is still out there. You really want to risk it? I'm owed a favor."

An image floated in front of my face like a hologram. I watched myself stand up and put a knife to Michael's neck. I slid the blade back and forth until he bled. A lot. My fingers felt warm before they felt wet.

The whole time I was as cool as a shaman.

He actually laughed at me then. "Where's your honor? You helped convince these fools once with your silence. Do it again. Loudly, this time. What's the big deal?"

I responded with a provocation, just to see how he'd react. "Tell me something—why don't you belong here, Michael? Rapists, murderers, sociopaths—I think you fit right in."

He smirked. "These guys aren't my peeps. Who knew?" He winked. "Ya think?"

Unbidden, I imagined him with a *y*-incision on an autopsy table. His skin pallid.

I'm fine. Just fine.

"You're frightened," I said. "You know it's not going to work with me this time."

He wouldn't go there. He said, "Don't . . . challenge . . .

me. You will regret it. Save your friend. Save your wife. Save your career. It's almost all you have left."

I realized then that he didn't know that my career was on life support. It had suffocated at the end of the noose that had broken Kol Cruz's neck.

"You've now precipitated the deaths of the only two patients I've ever lost to suicide, Michael. You really think my career is going to survive the second one?" When he didn't reply right away, I asked, "Did you get Nicole to jump?"

"Wasn't supposed to be me, obviously. But since I was out, I volunteered. We had two ropes, two nooses, in the barn. One was on my neck; one was on hers. We had created some . . . serious despair for her. Drugs, lies." He shrugged. "It wasn't hard. The kid was a mess. She was ready to die, desperate for a friend to come along for the ride. She followed me up there willingly. Then all I had to do was . . . encourage her to lose her balance. Nicole was a born follower. She thought the plan was that we were both going to die that day—some grand adventure my accomplice had cooked up to screw up your life, her parents' lives. I counted to three. On three, she leaned forward."

"You pushed her?"

He shrugged. "I prefer 'encouraged.' "

"You used the ladder to get up there?"

He was puzzled at the question. "I'm smart, Alan. But I can't fly."

I remembered the look of surprise that had been frozen on Kol's postmortem face. The shock was that she was alone at the end of a rope.

"Were you the one living in the barn?"

He shook his head. "'Camping' is more accurate. But no. My accomplice needed access to your house. It made all the research more convenient to be close. I stayed a night at Nicole's. Then I moved on. I picked up girls after that. Slept at their places." He winked. "I missed fucking. Who knew?"

I straightened my therapist mask. The thought of J. Winter B. having unfettered access to my home made me livid. I hid my rage behind it.

Michael had gone through life expecting to be forgiven. I'd been one in a long series of his enablers. His father, his sister, the Pitkin County judge, so many others.

I said, "You fucked up, Michael. You believed I wouldn't change. Guess what? I'm immune to your problems. Enjoy your stay in Cañon City. I hope it goes on for a long, long time. You've earned every day of it."

"I'll die here if that happens," he said. "You know that."

His announcement was almost void of affect. I realized that he was counting on me to find the concept of his death a tragedy. What a sap I'd been.

"Fine," I said. "I pray there will be some unpleasant moments for you before that happens." I stood and stepped toward the door.

"I mean soon. I'll die soon."

"That's a threat of some kind?" I said. My back was

to him. There wasn't a gram of compassion in my question.

"Yes," he said. Malevolence covered him the way frosting tops a cake. Thick and rich. "Leave me here and I'll kill myself."

"That's my problem?"

"I'll leave notes that say you were warned."

"And I'll deny it." I turned and waited until he looked me in the eye. "You know what? I almost believe you'd do it. But I really haven't been that lucky lately."

"If you know I'm suicidal you have a professional obligation to act."

Another milliliter of fear oozed from the edges of his facade. "That's your trump card, Michael? You're counting on me to act honorably?"

My words surprised him. I savored the moment.

"You always have," he said.

He made it sound like the vilest of accusations. I had no defense. "I was a fool for not intervening at your competency hearing. I won't repeat the mistake."

His breathing was accelerating. I could hear his exhales across the room. *Good. The advantage is shifting.*

Over the space of two or three seconds, his face morphed from one of surprise and unease into the victorious one I'd witnessed as he was marched out of Lauren's office back into custody. Once again he thought he was about to hit the game-winning shot.

Not this time, I thought. I didn't know what would

come next. Part of me thought he was bluffing. Another part of me was terrified of what he had planned.

"Do you like the new look in your daughter's bedroom?" he asked.

Time stopped.

No—that's trump, I thought. His final card was on the table.

I retraced my steps, walking across the room until I stood about two feet from him.

He smirked. It was a mistake on his part, one for which I'll be forever grateful.

Without any deliberation I swung my left fist into the surprisingly soft flesh just below his solar plexus. It was like punching a top sirloin. He'd had no time to protect himself and he reflexively doubled over in response to the blow. As his head came down my right fist became a missile shooting upward at his descending jaw.

The impact made a sound like a boot stomping on a seashell. Crack, thud. After absorbing the blow to his gut Michael didn't have enough air in his lungs to scream in pain—the sound he made in reaction to my second sucker punch was a dull, throaty gargle of misery and surprise.

I stepped back as he crumpled at my feet. I didn't want to get blood on my shoes again. That hadn't worked out well the first time.

I said, "Come near my daughter and I'll spend whatever life I have left finding ways to torture you for it."

As I stepped backward toward the door I gingerly slid my right hand into the pocket of my trousers.

"You little fuck. You don't know what you just did. You'll be looking over your shoulder until the day you die." Although his words were malicious, McClelland's voice wasn't loud or especially threatening. He sounded like a child playing tough in the mirror while brushing his teeth, the brush dangling from his foaming mouth.

"I've tried that. It's no fun. You've cured me. I'm done with you. My biggest fear is right in front of me. I'll survive it. Yours . . . is down the hall. Will you survive it?"

I pounded on the door with the side of my left hand. I did it again.

Thirty seconds later—it felt like a month—the big metal door swung open.

The officer with the shoulders yelled, "Duck!"

Reflexively, I turned and raised my arm.

Michael's chair was flying at my head.

I'd forgotten an important lesson. When Michael's intellect failed to gain him the advantage he sought, he tended to get impulsively violent.

Especially after he'd been provoked.

I could relate.

FIFTY-FIVE

I'D TAKEN the bulk of the impact of the chair on my left forearm and triceps. I knew it was going to hurt. Maybe in five minutes. Maybe the next morning.

But for that moment the pain in my left arm was so much less significant than the pain in my right hand that I felt a kind of tortuous balance. In all important ways I was fine.

When I walked away from the meeting room Michael had been bleeding from his mouth and nose. The three guards were shackling him. To my untrained eye his jaw looked like a blind man had assembled it from spare parts. Nothing lined up quite right.

Using the bored tone of a traffic cop wondering, "Do you know why I pulled you over?" the assistant warden asked, "What happened?"

"A sudden disagreement," I said.

"He attacked you?"

I thought about the question for a moment. *Sure, why not?* "Yes," I said. "I had to protect myself."

He narrowed his eyes. "Do you need a doctor?"

"No, that's not necessary. But thank you."

That was it. I was in a porous fugue as I followed him back to the conference room—a walking-the-corridors version of highway hypnosis. He opened the door and preceded me into the room. He didn't say a word to the group about the flying chair or the altercation.

I was starting to like the guy.

Elliot Bellhaven said, "Alan, sit. Tell us what happened. What he said."

I despised his eagerness. I despised the fact that he'd taken control of the meeting.

I didn't sit. I stood at the head of the table, near the door. My right hand remained in my pocket. I positioned myself so that I didn't have to look Kirsten in the eye.

I said, "Michael McClelland is faking his mental illness to protect his competency status. He's been faking it for years. His silence is purely strategic. He admitted that. He also said that if for some reason the people in this room don't buy his act and agree to send him back to Pueblo for continued treatment, he's going to become a suicidal risk. That, too, will be theater." I paused. "That's all I got."

Elliot blurted, "You were in there for over half an hour."

"We were negotiating," I said. "The negotiations failed. I've told you what I learned."

"Sit down, Alan," Elliot said in a tone that was so demeaning I knew I would never forgive him for it. In his left hand he was holding the agreement that Kirsten had given me in the car. He waved it. "Tell us what you were negotiating. Tell us how the negotiations broke down. Every step. You agreed to share all details of the conversation you had with him. That was our deal."

"Did I?" I said. I turned to Kirsten. "I'd like to leave now, if that's all right with you."

"Ms. Lord," Elliot said, standing. "Your client signed an agreement to—"

I interrupted. I didn't want Kirsten to appear responsible for what I'd done. "No, Elliot, I didn't sign anything. Check your papers."

He flipped to the last page. His face turned the mottled red and white of the top of an underripe strawberry.

I said, "I figured you wouldn't look. You count on other people to dot your *i*'s."

Kirsten opened her copy and turned to the signature page. She tried, almost successfully, not to grin at what she saw.

I'd signed it, "Carl Luppo."

Elliot said, "Who the hell is Carl Luppo?"

Kirsten stood. Carl Luppo had been her ex-Mafia protector in the Witness Protection Program. "Someone who has a penchant for getting people out of uncomfortable situations, and putting others in them," she said. "I do apologize for the misunderstanding about the document. Like you, Mr. Bellhaven, I was unaware that it hadn't been properly executed. I'll be speaking further with my client about this, and I will get back to you all as soon as . . . I have something to report."

Tharon Thibodeaux winked at me. Michael McClel-land's reign as the poster child for 16-8-112 was over. Tharon was pleased.

The woman from the Department of Corrections had started knitting while I was visiting McClelland. As far as I could tell she didn't drop a single stitch during my performance in the conference room.

I wondered how she'd gotten the knitting needles past security.

"You want to talk?" Kirsten said. We were on the edge of the high plateau above the sprawling Fort Carson army base between Cañon City and Colorado Springs. Traffic was sparse. On that stretch of high-desert plateau every-thing was sparse but dirt and sky.

And felons. Lots and lots of felons.

We'd been silent since leaving the penitentiary.

"I want to apologize. I put you in an untenable posi-tion in there. I regret that I involved you, but I needed to talk to McClelland on my terms. I'm sorry."

"That's not what I meant," she said. "Do you want to talk?" She took her eyes from the road momentarily and glanced at me.

Eliminating what had just happened at New Max—I wasn't prepared to discuss that—I began doing an inven-tory of the possible topics for our talk. I quickly narrowed the list to two. One, my toxic history. Two, Kirsten once loving me. Did I want to talk? Hardly.

My phone vibrated in my pocket. Saved by the bell.

"Just a second," I said to Kirsten. The screen told me the call was from Lauren's mobile. Involuntarily, I tensed. I flipped open the phone and said, "Hello."

"Elliot just called," Lauren said. Her tone was light, playful. "He wants me to talk some sense into you."

"Based on the look in his eyes the last time I saw him I would wager that he would prefer you beat some sense into me," I said.

Lauren laughed. "That too. Michael admitted it was all an act?"

"Basically." I paused. I didn't want Lauren to have to do Elliot's bidding. Putting her in the middle wouldn't help me. It certainly wouldn't help her. "I've told Elliot all I'm going to tell him, Lauren."

"He said Michael attacked you. Are you okay?"

"Fine," I said. In our family "fine" covered a lot of ground.

"His jaw is broken," Lauren said.

Really? Cool. "Let's not . . . go there."

"Okay—that's not why I'm calling. Gracie and I are heading home. We're at the airport; we'll board in a few minutes. You and I have some things to talk about."

I did another inventory. Again, I quickly narrowed the topics down to two. One, my toxic history. Two, the state of our marriage.

This is going to be a fun night.

"Yes, we do," I agreed. McClelland's final threat to go after Grace reverberated in my head. "It may not be safe yet—you know that?" I was painfully aware that J. Winter B. remained unaccounted for.

"I know," she said. She told me that a deputy would pick them up for the ride from DIA to Boulder. "The sheriff promised me a few more days of protection. We can decide . . . together what happens after that."

My wife wasn't asking for me to place my imprimatur on her plans. Continued protest would have been futile. We would have the prudent-parent talk face-to-face.

"That was Lauren," I said to Kirsten after I closed the phone.

Before Kirsten could comment her cell started singing in her satchel. Some classical riff. I thought Brahms. I reached over and took the wheel so she could track down the phone.

She found it, eyed the screen, and said, "My boss."

Cozy. I released the wheel. "Elliot must be calling everyone we know," I said.

Kirsten did more listening than talking during the call. I couldn't discern much from her end of the conversation. She closed the phone after three or four minutes.

"Cozy's not happy," she said. "With you."

"It's a big club," I replied without any compassion for his predicament. I figured his dismay was an act—he couldn't admit it, but I thought he approved of what I did.

"Or me," Kirsten added.

"I'll explain to him that I set you up."

"The police located the missing grand jury witness late this morning," Kirsten said, changing directions.

"Dead?" McClelland's evasiveness had convinced me that the witness was dead.

"Buried below a grave out in that cemetery over by the Diagonal."

I recalled the article I'd read in the *News*. "'Below'? Is that what you said?"

"Sam had his partner—Lucy?—interview Nicole's co-workers at the cemetery. Nicole's supervisor remembered that shortly before she died she worked late one evening by herself doing final preparations on a grave for a morning interment. He knew exactly which grave it was. The 'alone' part concerned Lucy. She got an order to exhume, but the only corpse in the casket was the one that was supposed to be there. They were getting ready to reinter when Sam phoned Lucy and suggested they dig down a little.

"The witness's body was below the casket, buried a few inches deeper in the dirt than the normal grave. They almost missed it."

An effective place to hide a dead body. How did Sam know to look there?

"Cause?" I asked. Of death, I meant. Kirsten knew that.

"There's serious decomposition, but the coroner's assistant told Sam that there were some deep lacerations and that the woman's hyoid was crushed. Post is tomorrow."

"Asphyxiation," I said. Specifically strangulation. The missing witness had been murdered. "Sam put all this together?"

"That's what Cozy said."

"I thought he was off the case."

"Not so much, apparently," Kirsten said. "There's more. You want to hear it?"

"Please."

"They finally found where your patient—Nicole—had been living. She was renting a trailer east of town just off Valmont. Her landlord thought she was a flight attendant, so he didn't give her absence a second thought. The sheriff executed a warrant. The bathroom in the trailer lit up with Luminol and violet light. It had been cleaned but there had been a lot of blood. Sam's take is that the grand jury witness was killed in the bathtub. Cut first, then strangled."

Ah. She probably wouldn't die when she was supposed to. "Kol's nosebleed in my office? That's where the blood was from?"

"Cozy said they're checking to see if it matches the blood from the woman's body they exhumed at the cemetery. And from your shoe. He's hoping it does."

Me too.

The adrenaline rush from the fight with McClelland had worn off and the anesthetic insulation of shock had disappeared by the time we entered Colorado Springs on Highway 115. Kirsten prepared to pull onto I-25 for the shot north to Denver. I said, "Please keep going straight. I think I remember a hospital not too far up ahead. I'm pretty sure my hand is broken."

"What?"

It wasn't a difficult diagnosis. I couldn't move either my pinky or the ring finger of my right hand without an exquisite agony that burned like a molten hammer striking my bones.

"You don't want to know. But I do need to see a doctor. I'm going to lie to him or her—I would be grateful if you don't insist on witnessing that."

We left the emergency room at Penrose Hospital about two hours later. I found it fitting and ironic that the cast on my hand looked like a boxing glove.

I had a dozen Vicodin in my pocket. I left them there. The throbbing seemed important.

About an hour outside of Boulder Kirsten asked, "Would you like to talk now?"

"Yes," I said, "I would. But I need to tell Lauren before I tell anyone else."

"Is it as bad as you make it seem?"

"I don't know anymore," I said. "It feels monumental, but I'm not sure."

"Robert's murder felt like the end of the world, Alan. It wasn't." She paused. "It was close, but it wasn't. But remember . . . I had some help."

Robert was Kirsten's dead husband.

"Thank you," I said.

FIFTY-SIX

IT TOOK a long time to get Grace settled that night. By the time we were all back home I'd done all I could to obscure the profanity of what had happened in my daughter's bedroom, but I could tell that Grace sensed that her space had been violated and that she had suffered some kind of intimate assault.

I ached for her as she tried to process the muted obscenity of it all.

I asked Lauren not to check her e-mail until we had a chance to talk. Why? I suspected that Michael's threat about revealing my secret would take place that way. I wanted the chance to tell her myself first.

Lauren took a long bath after Grace was asleep. I found her later wrapped in her heaviest robe on the chaise on the bedroom deck. The night was crystalline, but not warm. She was toking on her bong, the musty smoke furling out above the high prairie. Her iPod was playing in its speaker dock in the bedroom. The playlist was one

I'd remembered from just before the device had been mothballed. She was listening to a set of Dusty Springfield. The set started and stopped with Lauren's favorite Dusty song, "You Don't Have to Say You Love Me."

I had a Vicodin buzz. With the help of the narcotics the percussion in my broken hand was subdued and almost equivalent to the pain in the places in my left arm that had absorbed the thrust of the chair McClelland had thrown at me. Either ache in isolation would have interfered with my concentration—I appreciated the balance of the stereo agony.

I had no regrets about sucker punching McClelland. None. I assumed his jaw hurt more than my hand did. I wondered how long he would survive at New Max. If the over/under was six weeks, I would have bet the mortgage money on the under.

Wishful thinking.

I settled onto the other chaise.

Lauren and I had covered the easy ground already. We'd done that during the remaining daylight hours.

Her health? Music no longer hurt, but her legs did. Her legal and work situation? Not good. The U.S. Attorney thought he had a case against her. The grand jury investigation that had been so important to Lauren had died along with its star witness. I didn't know how to let her know that the witness had been a fraud. I knew I'd find a way. Other deputies in Lauren's office were assigned to prosecute the witness's murder.

My legal and work situation? Not good. My practice was in tatters. Cozy and Kirsten were doing their best to clean up after me legally. Would they be successful? The jury was out. Even if the criminal problems went away, my civil liability was malignant.

Sam's situation? A mess. He and I had talked briefly. He was on paid leave from the police department, awaiting word what his discipline would be for failing to alert the DA about his romantic relationship with Amanda Ross. The next time Simon was scheduled to stay with his mother, Sam was planning to fly to California to end things with Carmen.

I made sure he understood the continuing threat to our families from McClelland and Currie. Sam volunteered to keep an eye on my family during his leave of absence. I accepted. I liked that he had my back. I hoped it was enough.

The whereabouts of J. Winter B.? Unknown. The apartment near Euclid and 30th Street where Sam thought she was living after separating from her husband had been vacated. The authorities would be of no help; no peace officer in any jurisdiction had tied her to a single crime associated with Michael McClelland.

J. Winter B. remained worrisome to me, and to Sam, to say the least. Michael's final threat hadn't faded from my memory at all. I knew the deputy on the lane wasn't going to be sufficient.

My visit to Pueblo? My tête-à-tête with Michael? I wouldn't tell Lauren any more than that I'd broken my hand while I was there. The circumstances? She was better off not knowing. She accepted that reality like a pro. She said that she was hoping I'd broken my hand on Michael's face. I didn't pop that balloon. If I felt compelled to admit what I did to Michael's face, I would probably end up choosing Kirsten so that I could enjoy the legal shelter of her advocacy. She was prohibited from telling anyone. Lauren wasn't.

Lauren had asked me if I knew what had happened to the three rounds that were missing from her Glock. I told her I knew. She wondered aloud if she should be concerned.

I said I didn't think so. I pondered what else I might have forgotten to do to cover my tracks.

Elliot had informed Lauren that Michael McClelland was on suicide watch in the infirmary at New Max and that he was acting more paranoid than ever. I knew that the heightened scrutiny would diminish over time. That was the nature of institutions. If McClelland wanted to kill himself he would find a way. If he did, I suspected he would goad someone else to do it for him.

I expected to have frequent moments when I fantasized about being that man.

The more difficult conversation I needed to have with Lauren had been waiting around since before that night on the beach in Cabo. Since leaving Cañon City that afternoon I'd been mulling how to start the discussion, but never came up with any magic words.

I took a deeper breath than usual, counted to three, and said, "I've been keeping something big from you."

She looked at me. Slowly, her violet eyes narrowed in resignation. Not alarm. They were asking, "Another woman?"

I shook my head. "It goes back to before we met."

"Your family?" she said.

She knew. "Do you know?"

She shook her head while she shrugged her shoulders. "I never really understood your . . . thing with your mother. You know that. The distance, especially. You've always given me the impression the topic was . . . unwelcome. Except for T., I'm not that close to my family either. Neither of us has ever questioned . . . the other one's old garbage. If I left you alone, I hoped you would leave me alone. You did." She flicked the lighter, toked from the bong, and while trying to trap the smoke in her lungs admitted, "Maybe I didn't really want to know."

Too late for that, I thought as the sweet smoke began to drift my way.

"Can I go first?" she asked.

"What do you mean?" I said. My naïveté was almost innocent. Almost. The reality had much more to do with gullibility than with innocence.

"I have something to tell you too," she said. "A secret, I guess."

The careful choreography I'd been sketching in my head didn't include a solo for Lauren. Only my solitary lament followed by an unrehearsed pas de deux. The last duet would be a tragedy, I feared. "You do?" I said. *Another man?* I must have missed that.

She said, "Here goes. I have already had . . . two children." She watched my eyes for a reaction. All she got was a blink. The "two children" was reproductive calculus that my brain couldn't do.

Grace was . . . well, one child. Lauren and I had each been married previously, but both had been childless unions. There was no "two."

She waited a decent interval for me to reply before she went on. "I got pregnant when I was twenty. During my junior year when I was in Amsterdam. The father is Dutch. I decided not . . . to have an abortion."

Again she paused long enough for me to interject something were I so inclined. I wasn't. Her news was major. But my radar said it wasn't that big a deal. I began to tighten up. I felt a second blow coming.

"I stayed in Holland and gave the . . . child up for adoption. I never saw her again."

Huge. But still not enough. *That's not it,* I thought. *There's more.*

She sighed. *Here it comes.* "After Gracie was born Priscilla told me I couldn't safely carry any more kids . . . because of damage that had occurred with that first delivery."

Priscilla was Lauren's OB/GYN. Instinctively I argued. I said, "Priscilla never said anything to me about—"

"I asked her not to tell you I'd had another child."

Oh. Another secret. "Why?"

She knew I'd ask. She was ready. Her words sounded rehearsed. "When we first met I was expecting you to leave me, so I didn't tell you. I didn't want to be judged. After Grace was born I thought she'd be enough for us, and I wouldn't have to tell you.

"Mostly? I don't like to think about . . . her. My baby. My teenage daughter. It hurts too much. You would want to talk it to death, Alan. It's who you are. I can't . . . do that."

"Grace has a . . ."

"Half-sister."

I nodded. It was mock understanding, at best. "And you can't have any more . . . children?"

Lauren said, "My ovaries are okay, but I can't carry any more, no." She began a soliloquy on the gynecological details.

I stopped her. I said, "I believe you." In my heart I knew this wasn't a new lie—it was the end of an old one. My pulse had slowed to a crawl and I felt as though my blood pressure was insufficient to sustain circulation. The conflicting emotions—sorrow and anger mostly—were canceling each other out and my autonomic nervous system was shutting down. I didn't know what else to say. Silence seemed wise.

Lauren didn't want to be a woman who could give away her child. *I can accept that,* I thought. *I can.* Dissembling with me? Harder to accept. Did it say more about her, or about her vision of me? I didn't know.

That's the thing about secrets. They are never really

dormant. They are termites; unseen, they eat away at foundations.

She said, "You had something to tell me."

Lauren wanted to change the subject. I didn't blame her.

I blinked the blink of someone coming out of a trance. *One, two, three.* "I shot my father when I was thirteen. I killed him."

My wife gasped and shrunk back against the chaise. Her fingertips flew up to cover her lips.

Dusty Springfield sang, *"You don't have to say you love me/Just be close at hand."*

FIFTY-SEVEN

I THINK they loved each other. My parents. They just never figured out how to be together.

By the time I was old enough to make sense of what was going on, I saw a father who was jealous and unsatisfied with his fate. A mother who felt neglected and had never learned to fulfill herself. After keeping her fulfilled had stopped being her father's job, my mother was certain that it had become my father's job. When he accepted that assignment they loved each other like they were a couple in the movies. When he resisted that assignment they fought each other like they were a couple in the movies. There wasn't much in between.

Each was capable of being an enchanting parent. Although circumstances seemed to insist that my memories be more strychnine than honey, the truth is that I had good times with each of them—where nonfamily matters were concerned my father could be a sage, and my mother could be as funny as anyone on *Johnny Carson*. Occasionally the three of us were as sweet as dessert.

By the time I approached adolescence they were coping inelegantly. My father drank and stayed away. My mother had what she called "friends who happen to be men." I was a kid; I didn't understand why they couldn't get along. During periods when they weren't fighting they seemed almost like other kids' parents. I prayed for those interludes.

They separated when I was twelve. Reconciled when I was thirteen. Separated again four months later. The second separation was short—only a couple of weeks. My father promised to stop drinking. My mother promised to "clean up her act." We were living in a small house on a nothing block in a bland subdivision on the outer fringe of Thousand Oaks, California, a bedroom far north of L.A. My father was a loud drunk. They were both loud lovers and they were both loud fighters. I was privy to all his recriminations and all her assignations.

When my parents' friends asked me what I wanted to be when I grew up, I would tell them I wanted to be a referee. Neither my mother nor my father ever spotted the irony.

Their second reconciliation fractured on a Monday night. I was on summer vacation from school. My father came home an hour late, alcohol seeping from his pores like cheap cologne. They fought.

The next night was looking like the second half of a double feature. My father didn't come home from work on time. My mother left his supper on the table. It was pot roast and gravy, boiled potatoes and carrots, and an iceberg-lettuce salad slathered with poor man's Thousand Island—ketchup and mayonnaise pebbled with pickle relish. A short stack of Wonder Bread completed the tableau. After chain-smoking and pacing for three hours with her arms folded across her breasts, she left the house.

"I'm going out," she said to me. "Don't you dare touch that food." She knew that I would have. For her the rotting food was a battle flag being hoisted. I considered it my duty to lower those flags whenever I spotted them.

A few flies had already claimed the meal like squatters moving into a tenement.

He came home first. I was up late listening to Vin Scully call the bottom of the eleventh inning of a Dodgers game. They were playing the Giants at Candlestick. He was drunk. My father, not Vin Scully.

"Is your mother out?" he asked.

I shrugged. I'd learned when it was prudent to be invisible—a good referee needs to know when to swallow the whistle. He left my room. I heard a sequence of noises that let me know he'd grabbed a six-pack and retreated to the patio. If cell phones had existed he would have been harassing my mother on hers. But cells didn't exist, so he drank cheap beer until he could simmer in the broth.

I was asleep when she came home.

His bellowed call of "You slut" woke me up. The clock by my bed read 2:35. I'd heard the yelling before and knew it would last a while. I reached for my pillow to cover my ears.

"Drunk," she screamed back. They were in the kitchen.

I knew his next line.

"Whore," he yelled, proving me correct. As lovers they showed some occasional flair, but they weren't imaginative fighters.

"Your boyfriend give you that?" my father asked in his most condescending tone. He was a better-than-average bowler, and he could fix things around the house. He could be a sensitive father. People said he was good at work. But his most marked skill? He could do derision as though he held the patent for it. Snidely he said, "You're going to shoot me now?"

Shoot? We didn't own a gun.

I climbed out of bed at that improvisation.

"Put that knife down," she warned him. The knife, too, was a new prop.

She'd later tell me he had the knife in his hand when she walked into the kitchen and that she was lucky she had borrowed the gun from a "friend" "just in case." I didn't believe her. They had abused each other plenty. But until that night they had never used weapons any sharper than their tongues. She'd thrown a few things on occasion, but her aim inevitably sucked.

"Drop it!" she screamed, up two octaves at least.

"You drop it!" he yelled, matching her volume.

I began to walk down the short hallway wearing nothing but my white briefs. I hadn't had time to put on my striped shirt or grab my whistle.

I heard more yelling and commotion from the kitchen and then I watched a blue-black revolver with a dark wooden grip—I'd later learn it was a .38—come skittering through the doorway until it stopped inches from my bare feet.

I picked it up.

My mother ran toward me and started screaming, "Give me that! Give me that!"

Giving it to her didn't seem wise. I was as tall as she, and stronger. With one arm I stopped her advance. With the other arm I held the pistol by my side. The damn thing was heavy.

My father stood beside the dinette set six feet away. He did indeed have one of the kitchen knives in his hand. He held it as though he were preparing to chop some onions.

"Don't give the slut the gun," he slurred. "That a boy. Give it here." He took a step toward us. My mother reached across me and forcibly raised my arm until the revolver was pointed in the direction of my father. "Stay there!" she shrieked.

He lunged for the gun. The motion surprised me. His quickness surprised me. She screamed, "Shoot! Shoot!"

The knife was at his side. His outstretched hand was empty. I still see that moment in my mind as though it had been photographed by a professional and put on the cover of *Life* magazine.

"Shoot!" she screamed again.

I closed my eyes. I pulled the trigger.

Gut shot.

He died as the ambulance arrived.

FIFTY-EIGHT

I WAS awake on the sofa when the phone erupted a few minutes before three.

I was sober. The season's first miller moth was flitting above me in the darkness.

Lauren was asleep. The e-mail from Michael McClelland with the newspaper accounts of the shooting had indeed been in her in-box. Some police records that my mother had promised me would never be unsealed were the last things my wife read before she climbed into bed.

Perfect.

Digesting a decade of distrust—mine and hers—kept me awake. The exact same digestive process put her to sleep. We were different in many ways. I'd never considered that a problem and I still didn't.

We didn't react to each other the way my parents had. That had always been enough for me.

My cloud was gone. Its absence provided much less relief than I had hoped. Would it stay away? Would the wolves return when exhaustion slowed me? What would replace the cloud? I didn't know.

I pounced on the call, catching it after half a ring.

Not much good news arrives at three o'clock in the morning. Most celebratory events that occur overnight—births, engagements, Vegas jackpots, whatever—can wait to be announced until after dawn. Three o'clock in the morning is for drunks on mobile phones, wrong numbers, and bad news.

Caller ID read OUT OF AREA. I thought, *Sam. He has bad news about J. Winter B.*

The voice I heard when I answered was foreign and female. "Alan Gregory?" The woman pronounced my name with accents on unfamiliar syllables.

"Yes," I said.

"You are . . . ice? For your . . . For . . . Sorry, sorry. For . . . I don't have . . . Just . . . Uh, one . . . one moment." I heard papers being shuffled. She placed the phone on a hard surface. Picked it back up. "Adrienne? Yes? Her mobile, you are Adrienne's . . . You are ice? Yes? No? A moment please." She moved more papers. I heard loud voices in the background. One of them was hers.

My ears and my brain weren't cooperating. My ears heard "ice." They heard "eyes." Neither made any sense to my brain. But she'd said "Adrienne." Twice. Hearing my friend's name spoken by a Middle Eastern–sounding woman in the middle of the night caused my pulse to accelerate from its torpor like a sprinter exploding from the blocks. Instinctively, I did the math. It was around noon in Israel.

Noon is good, I thought. *Bad things don't happen at noon.*

"Eye, see, eee," she said. "In case of emergency, yes? You? Alan Gregory?"

I-C-E. In case of emergency. Oh dear God. In Adrienne's cell-phone directory she had listed me as her "ICE"—the person whom rescue personnel should contact in case of emergency. I knew I was her ICE. She had shown me the acronym in her cell phone.

Adrienne didn't keep secrets any more than she permitted them.

I tried to leash in the panic that was ripping at my heart. "Yes, yes. This is Alan Gregory. I am Adrienne's ICE. Is she okay? What happened? Is Jonas all right?"

"A moment," she said. Loud voices. Unfamiliar tongues. The woman was doing three things at once. Talking to me was only one of them.

Lauren appeared at the end of the hall, the comforter from the bed covering her nakedness above her thighs. Her closed fists clasped the duvet in a fat knot between her breasts. I watched her mouth fall open. I watched her squint as she tried to make sense of what was happening in the dark room. She was bewildered. Frightened and bewildered.

Emily poked her black nose and one pointed ear out from behind the comforter.

The woman with the accent came back on the line. She began talking quickly. She had a story to tell me and she was in a rush to tell it.

Within a few seconds—"There was a bombing" was all it took—I was crying. I cradled the phone between my ear and my shoulder and I tried to scribble words and numbers with my useless left hand. The woman talked for minutes. Three? Five? I couldn't have said. She provided details that meant nothing.

This town. Near that intersection. A plaza. The entrance to some café. She said the name of the café as though she thought I would recognize it. A checkpoint somewhere. Something about a bus stop.

Lauren covered her mouth with her hand and her dark eyes became as big as egg yolks. Her chin quivered before she too began to sob.

To the woman on the phone I said, "You are sure?"

She was. She said, "Passport. Mobile. And . . . ICE." She asked me if I would be able to come.

"Yes, today," I said. "As soon as I can get a flight."

She gave me addresses and phone numbers. I scribbled southpaw. I repeated the numbers to her.

She told me I had them wrong. Forcing calm into her voice, she asked for my mobile number and my e-mail address. I gave her both. She said she would send me an e-mail or a text with the information. She could tell I was crying and she said she was sorry for my loss. "So many," she said. "So many others." She had to go. Her last words were in Hebrew. They sounded kind.

I thanked her. *Thanked* her.

Tremulous, Lauren said, "What?"

"Adrienne," I said.

FIFTY-NINE

LATER THAT day I flew Air Canada to Toronto from DIA then nonstop to Tel Aviv, arriving in Israel early the next evening. The trip took eighteen hours.

I had no troubles for those eighteen hours, the same way I had no troubles on 9/11, or 9/12 or 9/13, no troubles for weeks after the Indian Ocean tsunami, no troubles for a month after I realized what was really happening in Darfur, and no troubles on the many days after Katrina hit.

Raw tragedy trumps personal drama every time.

Adrienne and her second cousin were dead.

Jonas was in good condition in a local hospital. He had been standing in the shadow of a concrete pillar that shielded his body from the nails imbedded in the explosive device worn by the suicide bomber. The bomber was a woman. The authorities thought she had worn the explosives over her chest in the shape of a vest or camisole. Jonas and his mother and his mother's second cousin were outside a popular café in a resort on the Mediterranean, waiting to go inside for something to eat. Security at the café kept the bomber outside the door. The police thought that the bomber had waited until a bus was arriving at the nearby stop and the crowd on the sidewalk was dense before exploding her device.

Seven people were killed, including the bomber. Thirteen others were injured.

I was Adrienne's ICE. As her ICE I would accompany my friend's body home. I would wrap her son in all the love my heart could muster and I would bring Jonas home too. I would find the strength to do it because I had to. I was Adrienne's ICE.

Cold and hard.

But not dry. If I were dry ice I would have been transformed from my solid state into a vapor long before I accomplished my required tasks. I needed to stay solid.

For Jonas.

I was sitting beside Jonas's hospital bed envying his sleep when I read a text message from Cozy informing me that Adrienne's will named Lauren and me as guardians of her son. It wasn't news; I had already known we were Jonas's guardians. Years before, after her husband Peter was murdered, Adrienne had told me that if she "kicked"—her word—she wanted Lauren and me to be Jonas's "next parents."

Adrienne didn't keep secrets.

Two days later I returned from Israel with my son. We left Tel Aviv near midnight and after eighteen hours in the air and a blurry sojourn in Toronto's airport we were back home in Spanish Hills for dinner.

Lauren had spent the time I was away buying design magazines and sketching out plans for remodeling the basement for Jonas's new room. Her energy and enthusiasm for the project surprised me. She wanted to gut the cranberry and pink bathroom and build something that was right "for our little boy."

I scanned her plans for a water feature. Nada.

Lauren's design was practical. She would move a couple of walls to steal space from our office and to give Jonas a larger room and a built-in desk for a computer. She wanted to frame-in a bigger closet and enlarge the basement window for better light and for better egress during emergencies.

Lauren was making room for our expanded family. She was concerned with safety, and comfort, and light.

I saw sublimation at work.

Hers was going to be a big job. I knew that at least one of the walls she wanted to move was a foundation wall. It bore a lot of load.

For a while Jonas would share a room with his new sister.

SIXTY

I DIDN'T start sleeping any better. For the first couple of weeks that Jonas was in our home I allowed him to stay up with me long after his bedtime. We'd watch TV and play cards, mostly gin, in the great room. Sometimes he'd ask questions about Adrienne and Peter. More often he didn't. I told myself he was healing, even though I knew better.

Even in the brightest sun the worst stains don't bleach.

Reruns of *The Simpsons* made us both laugh, though we laughed at different parts.

One night we wandered the house where he'd lived with his parents. I held his hand as he padded slowly through every room. He was, I think, making sure his mother wasn't really there. I swallowed tears the whole time.

Twice he asked if we could play cards in the barn. Those evenings we sat on stools at Peter's wood-carving bench. He wanted to know what his father's power tools were for. I tried my best to explain the difference between the jointer and the planer. A length of hickory Peter had been turning was still in the lathe. I let Jonas flip it on to watch the wood spin. He wondered if Peter and I had been friends.

"The best," I said.

He cried that night in the barn. It was the first time. He allowed me to hold him while he shook. His body melded to mine like memory foam.

Each of those nights we went out to the barn he ended the visit by peeing in the Good Head.

With Jonas up late to provide company the hours when the house was quiet and dark were shorter each night, but they were just as quiet and just as dark as they had been before the bomb in Israel.

In my grief it was always three a.m.

Seventeen days after Adrienne's death—fifteen days after the simple wooden box containing her body was lowered into the ground at Green Mountain—a woman from New Mexico I didn't know called Adrienne's cell phone while I was driving to get Grace from school. I had chosen to carry Adrienne's phone with me for a while. Every few days I ended up giving some ignorant stranger news about the tragedy in Israel. I hated having to do it but reminded myself that was the point—that was why I was answering her phone.

I was heading north on 28th Street just past Arapahoe when the phone started to buzz. Adrienne's cell didn't ring—it buzzed. I'd found the noise annoying when she was alive. I found it comforting after she died. I made a quick right off 28th into the redevelopment of Crossroads and stopped the car in a loading zone before I answered the call. Experience had taught me that the conversations I had on Adrienne's phone required all the concentration I could muster.

I explained to the woman that I was a friend of Adrienne's and was about to relay the bad news about her death when she informed me that she knew what had happened. She said she was calling to find out if Jonas still wanted the puppy.

"Puppy?" I said.

Adrienne, she explained, had arranged to get Jonas a dog as a birthday gift. A surprise.

I was parked facing away from the mountains with the monster 29th Street redevelopment all around me, and I was lost. The new Crossroads was not quite Boulder, and not quite suburbia. I was in the middle of the town where I'd lived for twenty years and I didn't really know where I was.

"It's a Havanese," she said. "The litter is ready. Adrienne has been waiting over six months for this little darling."

"A Havanese," I repeated. I couldn't have picked a Havanese out of the jumble of dogs at the Dumb Friends League if my life depended on it. *Twenty-ninth Street? Havanese?* So much unfamiliarity. I wondered if I'd descended into a fugue and then watched that question segue into another: Could a person in a fugue wonder if he was in a fugue?

I checked the rearview mirror and spotted the mountains. *It's okay,* I thought. *Boulder is Boulder.*

"It would be my gift to Jonas," the breeder said. "Callie's a wonderful little girl. The only bitch in the litter. She has more spunk than all her brothers combined. She's just what Jonas needs."

I liked that she thought she knew what Jonas needed. I sure didn't.

Jonas and I drove to New Mexico to pick up his Havanese puppy. We talked a lot about names as we headed south. He was still trying to decide what to call me and Lauren—Jonas had called us by our first names since he'd learned to talk, but it was clear that option didn't feel quite right to him anymore. "Mom" and "Dad" weren't on his radar yet.

It was important that his dog's name feel perfect to him.

Much of psychology isn't complicated. It's just stuff grandmothers know.

Our route took us on I-25 through Pueblo. Just before we got there he announced that the name "Callie" was officially out of the running.

Pueblo. I still held out hope that Michael McClelland wouldn't be returning to the nearby Institute for Forensic

Psychiatry. Despite a failed suicide attempt in the infirmary at New Max—Michael had tried to slice an artery in his neck with a blade he'd fashioned from a sliver of a credit card—the state continued the interminable process of evaluating his competency to proceed.

Smith, the assistant warden, had personally called to tell me the news about McClelland's suicide attempt. "You blew that call," he said. "About his suicidal risk."

There had been no recrimination in his tone. "I guess," I'd said. *Bummer.* Referees aren't perfect. I suspected that the assistant warden knew that if I'd blown that particular call, I'd done it with my eyes wide open.

Let's say it was a make-up call.

If there were any justice Michael McClelland would never get to enjoy the modern facility the recalcitrant Colorado legislature had recently approved to replace the ancient dungeon of a structure in Pueblo. Instead, if there were any justice, McClelland would soon get sent back to Pitkin County for trial, he'd finally be convicted—by an Aspen jury, no less—and he'd spend the rest of his life in the sterile, dangerous confines of New Max.

Or he'd kill himself first. That would be fine with me, too.

If there were any justice.

Jonas and I stopped in Pueblo, filled the car with gas, and picked up lunch at a local burger place. I still had half a tank of fuel but I needed an excuse to scrape bug exoskeletons and their splattered innards off the windshield.

Lauren phoned just as we were climbing up the on-ramp onto I-25. She asked where we were. I told her.

Her tone changed. "The sheriff found that woman's body," she said. "I thought you would want to know."

"What woman is that?" I asked pleasantly. *Please,* I thought. *Let it be her. Let this be the end.*

Lauren knew I was in the car with Jonas and that I couldn't ask any revealing questions.

"Justine . . . Brown."

J. Winter B. "Okay." *Yes.*

"She'd been living in a rented cottage on a ranch near Frederick. Looks like suicide, though she was apparently pretty ambivalent about the whole question of method. She had a pile of drugs and a bottle of whiskey on her kitchen table. She had a tub full of water in the bathroom and a fresh razor blade on the sink. But she ended up shooting herself below her chin—it went right through her brain stem. Dead a few days, at least. A guy servicing her propane tank reported the smell."

That's not right.

"What was it on her kitchen table? Specifically?"

"Jack Daniel's and . . . amitriptyline," Lauren said. The unfamiliar word caused her to stumble—she'd put the accent on the wrong syllable and pronounced the final one "line," not "lean." The innocuous mispronunciation yanked me back to the indelible memory of the night I was Adrienne's ICE. I fought reflex tears.

She continued, "A pile of pills. Maybe twenty."

Amitriptyline—the accent goes on the "trip"—is a pre-

Prozac antidepressant. Its most common brand name is Elavil.

Elavil? Damn.

"No bottle?" I asked.

"For the Jack, yes. For the drugs, no."

Holy shit. Holy . . . shit. "Thank you . . . for the news. You and Grace are good?"

"We're fine," Lauren said. "Can I talk to Jonas?"

While Jonas got acquainted with his puppy and her brothers at the breeder's home outside Los Alamos, I walked a quarter of a mile down her rural lane until I was in sight of the town. I had two bars on my cell. Good enough. But not wise. I kept walking until I saw a shuttered structure that was sufficiently antiquated that I would call it a "filling station," not a gas station. I used a Costco calling card to call Sam from a phone booth. The phone was battered. The booth was nothing more than an aluminum lattice. It had no door and no glass.

The PAY PHONE identifier on Sam's caller ID told him all he needed to know about why I was calling. It was about our newest secret.

His greeting was, "I was hoping you'd be smart enough . . . not to want to have this conversation."

"I'm not that smart." Sam knew I wasn't that smart.

"Give me the number of your pay phone. I'll call you right back."

He did, less than five minutes later. It was just enough

time for him to get the few blocks from his house down to Broadway and the closest public phone.

We were talking pay phone to pay phone. Serious subterfuge. "That digital camera?" he said. "The one from the Royal Arch Trail? Had a big memory card in it."

Ah. "You've known this for a while."

He didn't answer. "Go on," I said, but the single clue was all that I needed to guess the broad outlines of what Sam was going to tell me. I was aware that he'd been spending much of his time on suspension in a fruitless search for Currie—J. Winter B. I didn't know exactly what Sam found on her camera's memory card; I'm not that prescient. But I knew his megapixel story was going to speak volumes about Sam's motivation for his protracted search and for what I was thinking he'd done on that ranch near Frederick.

"Out of maybe a hundred and fifty shots there were about a dozen pictures of your kid. About a dozen pictures of mine. Simon at school, at hockey. Grace at school, at soccer." He paused for five seconds, at least. "That's all."

The air in my lungs felt cold, my legs inadequate to support my weight. My tongue felt like it was made of peanut butter. I was able to say, "I think it's enough."

"Took me a while but I found her. One of the pictures was of a horse with a horse trailer in the background. Partial plate, Nebraska. Wasn't easy but I tracked down the trailer, found the guy who owned it, got him to tell me where it was about the time we were on the

Royal Arch Trail. Staked out the ranch. And . . . there she was."

"Frederick?"

"Exactly. We talked. At first she denied everything."

"Then?"

"Remember something, Alan: We had nothing on her. Nothing that I could take to my bosses or to the sheriff."

We did have the digital photographs but my reckless-ness with Lauren's Glock rendered them impractical as leverage. In reality they proved little anyway.

"She gave Teresa the Sativex," I said. "We can prove that." I was groping for magic—a fool trying to change the past. I knew better.

"That might be a crime in Canada. Not here," Sam said. "Didn't help us." I watched a dirty white van pull up to the shuttered gas station, slow to a crawl, and speed away. A dozen heads popped up as it accelerated down the road.

Coyote, I thought.

Sam went on. "I showed her a few of the pictures. She admitted she'd followed me that day that you were in Denver and she'd sent me that e-mail threatening to reveal that I'd been staking out the grand jury witness's house. The witness lived up Coal Creek, if you care."

"Gotcha," I said. I didn't want to interrupt him with the news that I didn't care.

"Currie prepared your patient, Nicole, for her therapy with you. 'Rehearsing her,' she called it. I could tell she enjoyed that part. She told me to ask you if you liked the Angelina Jolie thing. I don't know what that means, but there it is. Currie softened Nicole up for the suicide too, but McClelland was the one who ended up doing it. It was Currie living in the barn. And she was the one who tore up Grace's room later on."

"She's . . . loquacious? Or you were being persuasive?"

"At the beginning, persuasion. Once she realized I had the camera, what I knew already, she got chatty. Nothing had really changed for her, Alan. She was still willing to . . . planning to . . . I made sure of that—110 percent sure—before . . ."

"I understand," I said. I didn't want him to have to say it. Currie had been willing to hurt our kids to hurt us.

"She said they'd made a pact to help each other. Her and . . . The whole time I was with her—I mean before—I missed her cold heart. Totally missed it. Part of their deal was if he was unable, she would . . . tie up loose ends. That's what she called them. 'Loose ends.' I asked her if she'd consider backing out of the deal. She didn't answer, but . . . her eyes told me she wouldn't."

Our kids were the loose ends. "Was she still in touch with him? At New Max?"

"She wouldn't say. I asked. I think she might have been in love with him. People. Go figure."

More than half a century before, Los Alamos had been one of those obscure places where good and evil came together so seamlessly that wise, decent people couldn't tell them apart.

I had known for most of my life what that demarcation looked like just before it disappeared.

Sam knew too—Frederick, Colorado, had become his Los Alamos.

"Thank you," I said. "Are you okay?"

He thought for a while before he replied. "My kid's safe. I'm sleeping fine. Your kids are safe. You should be too."

Shortly after getting back from Israel with Jonas I'd told Sam about Thousand Oaks over a couple of beers on the rooftop deck of the West End Tavern. He let me talk it out, but he didn't try to convince me anything would make it better. As we were heading back to our cars he told me two other things: He was leaving the next day for Laguna Beach to end things with Carmen. And the unidentified prints in the barn had turned out to be Jonas's.

Damn, and damn.

I'd let Diane know about Thousand Oaks, too—over Nebbiolo, *salumi,* and speck at Frasca.

And I kept my promise to tell Kirsten, as we ate #5s—I was over-easy, she was scrambled—at the Village on Folsom.

Sam knew what I was up against when he suggested how I should be sleeping.

"Should be," I said. "Maybe soon."

"I'm not proud of any of this," he said. "But I don't regret it either. Had to be done. I tried to see it work out some other way. Couldn't. Kept thinking about the ball-peen hammer and the framed porn and the eighteen-wheeler near Laramie. Nicole's neck. Grace's room. The pictures of the kids."

Tell me about it, I thought. The connection was especially noisy. I blamed it on the antique phone and my proximity to all that plutonium.

He went on. "What you did on the trail? With Lauren's Glock? That was kind of preemptive, don't you think?"

"What do you mean?" I was afraid Sam was launching some unwelcome, ill-timed political allegory.

"You didn't wait for her to shoot first. You recognized danger. You protected me."

I saw where he was going. "Yeah."

"That's all I did. Preemption. I couldn't wait for her to shoot first." He paused. "Couldn't."

The kids, I thought. I never would have endorsed a death sentence for McClelland for what he had done years before. Never. But I was copacetic about J. Winter B.'s capital end. Didn't add up.

I was looking for right and wrong. They were nowhere to be found.

"If I was the one who found her," I said, "I'm not sure I could have done it."

"Yeah, well. You don't know. Until you're in the room and you see the alternatives . . . Until then, you don't really know." He paused. "Backed into a corner with your kid behind you? I think you'd do whatever's necessary."

"Yeah." He was right. I would. And how would I cope with having done whatever was necessary?

Dry ice.

"I should go," Sam said.

"Can I ask you one more thing? Something I've been wondering?"

"What?"

"How did you know the grand jury witness's body would be buried below that grave in the cemetery? How did you guess to look there?"

For a moment I wasn't sure he planned to answer me. Then he said, "Wasn't a guess. The dead girl—Nicole—was alone that night while she was digging the grave. That's what the supervisor told Lucy. But she was never alone with the casket—it was still at the funeral home. There was no way for her to switch bodies or to stick an extra corpse into the box. Her only option for hiding a body would be to have a funeral before the funeral."

His voice trailed off at the end. Sam wasn't done—I could tell something had gone unsaid. Something important. "What?" I said. "What else?"

Quick inhale, long exhale. "The witness? Donna? She'd been buried wearing jeans and a sweatshirt. No shoes or socks. No ID. No underwear. But your business card was in the front pocket of her jeans."

"Son of a bitch," I said. J. Winter must have picked up one of my cards during her therapist-shopping visit the previous fall. "Elliot didn't tell Cozy about that."

"He may not even have told Lauren. Elliot's willing—not eager—to believe you were framed. But the card doesn't

help you—and it won't go away. Don't be confused—
Elliot's not . . . your ally. In the wrong hands . . . Thought
you should know."

"McClelland and Currie were thorough."

"I'm sleeping okay now, Alan. Let this go. It's our
turn to get lucky."

The walk back up the hill to the breeder's home was almost half a mile. I took the six of diamonds from my wallet. That's where I'd stashed it minutes after I discovered it
in my sport-coat pocket. Over the intervening weeks I had
concluded that had it been chosen out of the deck for any
reason at all, it had been chosen because it was a crappy
card. That's what Michael McClelland and J. Winter B.
had worked so hard to deal me. A crappy card.

I ripped off a tiny piece of the card every fifty yards or
so, scattering the fragments one at a time into the windy
landscape above Los Alamos. The cast on my hand made
the task much more difficult than it should have been.

Los Alamos had proven to be almost as good at keeping
secrets as I had.

I didn't bother to glance behind me as I paced up the
hill. I knew I had a fresh cloud chasing me.

I felt it there, looming. And I smelled the stink of
wolf.

Damn. The list of people I could never tell stretched
out for miles.

SIXTY-ONE

HAVANESE ARE the national dogs of Cuba. To aficionados, like the kind New Mexico breeder, they are every bit the island treasure that is a fine Cohiba, and more. To Jonas, his new puppy was a bundle of verve, an injection of hope, and a talisman granted to him by his dead mother.

The drive north was a riot. The portable kennel was big; the dog was not. The breeder promised us she would eventually top out at ten or twelve pounds. From the looks of her I suspected half of it would be hair. She was a silky soccer ball with legs and a tail that curled up like an apostrophe above her ass. She treated the kennel like she was a platinum rock star and it was a five-star hotel suite she was determined to trash. While Jonas continued to ponder names for the exuberant dog, I silently tagged her Haldol. It would take a healthy dose of the drug to dent her effervescent energy.

She made me laugh. She made Jonas laugh. It was all good.

At uneven intervals between Taos and the state line I dropped the three spent shells from Lauren's Glock out the window along the highway. I'd forgotten I'd left them in the ashtray until Jonas had spotted them there.

During a brief interlude north of Alamosa while both Jonas and the Havanese slept, I ran through a half-dozen scenarios of what had happened in the cottage on the ranch near Frederick between Sam and the woman he knew as Currie.

I settled on one.

Sam wouldn't have taken any pleasure in what he had to do.

I suspected he had used darkness and arrived at her home on foot just before midnight, after her neighbors—if she had any—were in bed. He pulled on gloves before he surprised her. They talked. Within moments he reached a decision about whether he could trust her or not. Once he arrived at "not" he offered her the Elavil that Sherry had left behind when she moved out of their house. Sam didn't give Currie a choice of method. The selection of Jack Daniel's as a chaser was, I think, hers. Sam would have wanted her to drink whatever booze she kept at home. They—a cop and a therapist—would both have known that alcohol increased the lethality of an Elavil overdose.

The bath and the razor blade were probably J. Winter's bargain for an alternative ending. Sam allowed her the option. He would have insisted she leave the door to the bath open while she carved her wrists. I suspect she soaked in the bath for a while but couldn't bring herself to put the vertical slices into her arteries.

It's a notoriously tough cut.

Sam was a thorough cop. He would have checked her home for a weapon. After she climbed out of the bath with her blood vessels intact, she returned to the front room to find Sam resigned to what was coming. He had added a Tyvek jumpsuit, shoe covers, and eye protection to his costume. He was holding a pistol—either one he found during his search or a throw-down he'd brought along. Sam wasn't careless; he wouldn't have trusted her not to turn the weapon on him. Although he'd make certain her hand was on the grip to be sure that investigators would find gunshot residue and metals in all the right places, Sam was the one who put the barrel to her throat below her chin and he was the one who pulled the trigger.

Shoot!

I couldn't begin to guess where between Boulder and Frederick he'd dumped them all, which was just as well.

SIXTY-TWO

LAUREN AND I had our second child.

Neither of us felt certain in our marriage. We were civil with each other, occasionally warm. At unguarded moments I had begun to feel hope for us. What she had done when she was twenty felt inconsequential to us as a couple. What I'd done when I was thirteen had been transformed into toxic history, but it was no longer a secret.

It would never be inconsequential.

We had two kids, just like I'd wanted.

My new son and I had some crucial things in common: We had both watched a parent murdered.

We'd both had indelible days, things we'd been part of that we would go forward in life not wanting to be true. We would each need to find the strength not to be defined by what had happened to us.

And we each had a future that was as difficult to decipher as the way out of a sandstorm.

What it would take for us to survive was clear, at least

to me. We would need to sublimate, to use strength we had no reason to trust to transform the impact of the events that were themselves so transformative. Phoenix-like, we would try to end up doing something acceptable with our lives, even beneficial, despite our traumas.

We would sublimate.

We would both try to change from a solid state into a vapor without first melting.

It was tricky stuff, the not melting.

ACKNOWLEDGMENTS

The people who help me with each book not only spare readers from all manner of my idiocy, they also refresh my faith in the generosity of the human heart.

This time I offer my thanks to Jane Davis for a thousand things done remarkably, to Chuck Lepley for his cogent and thoughtful instruction, to Judy Pomerantz for the early read, to Nancy Hall for the late one, and to Al Silverman and Patricia Limerick for the lift. Elyse Morgan's astute eyes always capture more of my errors and inconsistencies than do anyone else's—and this time her critical perspective, along with her absolute lack of hesitation to point out my failings, proved even more crucial than usual.

Brian Tart, together with Neil Gordon, edited this book with great care and with vision to match. I thank them for their skill, and for all they do during the year to shepherd my work from desk to marketplace. My gratitude goes out to their colleagues at Dutton and NAL, as well—especially Lisa Johnson and Claire Zion.

Special thanks to Robert Barnett for his graciousness and guidance.

My family provides the platform that makes what I do possible. I will never be able to thank them enough.

Read on for an excerpt from
Stephen White's thrilling novel

DEAD TIME

Available in hardcover from Dutton

JACK PULLED his digital camera from his pack and powered it up.

Jules, the woman with the confident voice who'd remembered that the missing woman had curly brown hair and lovely eyes, noticed the stranger eyeing the camera. She said, "That's Jack. It's what he does. Ignore him. He'll stop soon."

Jack said, "Not much light. My last battery's almost dead."

Jules untied a red kerchief from around her neck and walked up to the shirtless man the way a mother with a washcloth approaches a young child with the detritus of breakfast stuck to his chin. Without asking if he minded being groomed by a stranger, she used the kerchief to flick the dried snot from his nose. She then used her fingers to push his hair back so that it didn't completely shadow his eyes.

She said, "That's better. Tell us your friend's name."

The shirtless man crinkled his nose and rubbed at his

nostril. He was baffled as to why the woman had just wiped a bandanna across his face. And why that had made anything better. He had to force himself to refocus in order to ponder her question.

His apparent distraction and his hesitation in replying were not encouraging signs. Finally he said, "Jaana," as though he was pleased to have remembered the woman's name. "Two a's. Or three, I guess."

The shirtless man's demeanor about the woman's absence was so low-key and his concern about her whereabouts so off-key that the larger group was losing interest in his dilemma. Most had returned their attention to packing their equipment and supplies to finish preparations for their imminent ascent of the canyon wall.

"She your girlfriend?" Jules asked.

"We're . . . friends. We hang out. We see each other sometimes. I live in Vegas. She brought me down here."

The group digested the news.

"Coming on this . . . hike, trip . . . was her idea," the shirtless man said. It was as though he was determined to hang any bad-judgment tag on Jaana's back. "I'm not much of an outdoorsman. Kind of sore this morning. You guys have blisters?" He bent his left leg, raising his foot. An angry red orb the size of a quarter was sprouting on his heel.

"I can give you something for that. What time did Jaana get up to pee?" Jules asked. "Do you remember?"

"I was asleep. I don't know."

"About . . . what time? Was it ten o'clock? One o'clock? Four o'clock?"

He shrugged. "I don't know."

"Early? Late?"

"Not too late."

"Lisa?" Jules said to one of the other women. "Were you able to sleep last night? You see anything?"

Lisa was one of the group of singles, the high school friend of Jack's. The heat had been troubling Lisa more than anyone else in the group. She hadn't been able to sleep for more than an hour or two at a stretch since she had reached the canyon floor. She said, "Not much. I was up for a while, like always." She looked away before she said, "Other people were up, too." She quickly scanned the group. "But I didn't see her."

The shirtless man fixated on the news that others were up. "Anybody see her after dark?"

Jules pressed Lisa. "You didn't see this girl? Jaana?"

Lisa hesitated for a moment. "No."

"You're sure?" Jules asked.

"No, Jules. Nothing."

Jules made eye contact with the other four in the group. "You guys?"

Head shakes. Shoulder shrugs.

The shirtless man said, "Okay."

Jules' boyfriend, Eric, paused from a long pull on a water bottle. He made an effort not to sound dismissive as he said, "I'm sure she's around someplace. She has to be. I mean, where the hell would she go?"

On a hot black night on the banks of the mighty Colorado River, at the bottom of the deepest gash on the continental surface of the planet, few people went wandering.

Without a raft, or a kayak, or a riverboard and a lot of safety equipment, where the hell would someone go? The only places to meander on foot were either up one of the trails that herringbone up one side of the canyon or the other, or down one of the convoluted footpaths that hug the river or curve off into its estuaries or dead-end in the infinite variety of water-carved box canyons. In the dark, alone, without the aid of a good flashlight, every one of those hikes is reserved for the reckless, depressed, or self-destructive. Or drunk.

"She wasn't . . . upset, was she?" Jules' boyfriend added when no one responded to his earlier remark.

The shirtless man shook his head while he comported his face into a puzzled expression, as though he didn't really understand the question. He said, "No. She was pretty . . . happy." He smiled at some thought. "We had a good time last night. I did."

A woman who had been standing slightly away from the group, taking it all in, spoke up for the first time. Line the seven of them up—the six friends and the shirtless stranger—and ninety-nine out of a hundred people would select her as the youngest in the bunch. And not just by months, but by a few years. Although she was nineteen, she looked like a high school sophomore.

Or freshman.

She was part of the group of singles, a sophomore at

Oxy. Her name was Carmel, pronounced like the town on the Monterey Peninsula.

She was wearing what the others in the group had come to think of as her Grand Canyon uniform: A tight tank top, shorts that barely covered her crotch—and didn't completely cover her ass—and a canvas hat with a brim the size of a parasol. The narrow backpack she was preparing to lift to her shoulders appeared taller than she was.

Her smile was almost constant. Her uncomplicated manner and natural beauty earned her a lot of attention in life. She was a girl men tried to separate from the pack when she was out at bars or clubs with her girlfriends.

She turned to the shirtless man and spoke, her voice carrying the kind of persistent hope that could be mistaken for innocence. "She's probably someplace waiting to watch the sun rise." She lifted her eyebrows and smiled again. "That's what I did the first night we were here when I couldn't sleep because it was so hot. I walked down to the river and I sat on a rock and I looked east and I waited. For daybreak. It was soooo peaceful. The waiting. The water rushing in the river. The air so still. And at sunrise, the very first light? It is just amazing down here early, just before dawn."

She glanced up toward the rim while she waited for the man to reply. When he didn't, she said, "You'll get to see for yourself in a little while. It's absolutely . . . I don't know. Illuminating." She laughed at herself. "That was dumb. Jeez. But I bet that's where your friend is right now. She's on a rock someplace, looking east, waiting for the first light. Letting the sound from the river clear her head. Cleanse her spirit. She'll be back with you soon, once she's done taking it in." She concluded with a fresh teeth-baring smile aimed directly at the shirtless man. She knew from experience that her big eyes and kind smile were reassuring to people.

Her girlfriends had often warned her that she was guilty of mistaking men's interest for men's *interest*. Her friends' well-intended caution had never done the young woman any good. She'd been shocked by bad intentions more often than a cute blonde in teenage horror movies.

Carmel tugged on the strap hanging at her left hip and turned ninety degrees. "I can never, ever, ever get it right. Is this thing straight, Jack?"

"Hello," replied Kanyn, her female friend from school. Kanyn was a lithe woman who wore her own heavy backpack as comfortably as she would wear a T-shirt to bed. "Jack doesn't know from straight."

Some of the group laughed. Some didn't. Jack laughed.

"Where exactly did . . . Where did you go that morning? To watch the sun rise, I mean," the shirtless man asked Carmel. "I can go look there. For Jaana."

Carmel said, "Down past the beach." She pointed in the direction of the trail that led from the cabins, past the campground, toward the river. "Not the first beach you see on the path, but downstream a little bit. Not too far. Past that first set of rocks. That rise? There's a trail. I know it just looks dark right now, but you'll see it. You know which one I'm talking about?"

The guy nodded. He said, "No, not really."

"You won't miss it—I mean, you can't get lost. It's a canyon, right? Head downstream, stay by the river, and don't climb. I just sat on a flat rock."

Jules chimed in with some questions for the shirtless man. "Your friend's things are still in your camp, right? She isn't someone who would try to climb out during the night? Or go in the river for anything? By herself, I mean . . . She wouldn't . . .?"

Do something that stupid?

The shirtless man said, "Her stuff's here. Everything's there: her pack, her bag. Our water. She's the one who warned me about the river. She told me not to get fooled, that the river water is really cold.

"She has to go back up today. This morning. Like, now. This trip was just a . . . you know. Come down. One . . . night . . . here. And then . . . back up. You know."

Jules said, "And you two were . . . getting along okay?"

"No. Great. Just great."

Jack started making some adjustments to Carmel's pack. He lifted the weight higher on the provocative curve of her hips—the allure of that arc was one to which Jack was completely immune—and pulled at the shoulder straps to encourage the heft to stay where he wanted it to stay. He asked the man, "She works up at the rim? Your friend?"

The shirtless man nodded. "North rim. The cafeteria at the visitors' center? She's a cook. You may have seen her. Up there, I mean."

Eric wanted to get started up the trail. He was the oldest member of the group—a twenty-seven-year-old with a law degree who had just finished doing a fellowship at Stanford's Hoover Institute. If it turned out that a leader needed to emerge for any reason on the march up to the rim, he would be the one the others would look to. He took a long look at his watch, as though he was having difficulty making sense of the numbers, before he gazed up toward the canyon walls.

A buttery aura had just begun to whisper dawn in the eastern sky, painting the ragged edge of the rim like a spill of diluted watercolor.

He said, "We're heading up the North Kaibab in a few minutes. When we get to the rim, we'll let somebody know that your friend may be late for her shift. Okay? It looks like you two are going to get a late start, and it's going to be slow going today. Make sure you take extra water because of the heat. And take care of that blister first." He tapped the crystal of his watch. "Come on, everybody. What do you say we go and deplete some glycogen?"

All the other hikers, with one exception, responded to the call to get moving. The exception was Jules, his girlfriend.

She caught Kanyn's eyes for a split second. Thought she saw something there.